W9-CGW-220

THE
PERICLES
COMMISSION

Also by Gary Corby

The Pericles Commission
The Ionia Sanction
Sacred Games
The Marathon Conspiracy
Death Ex Machina
The Singer from Memphis
Death on Delos

THE
PERICLES
COMMISSION

Gary Corby

Copyright © 2010 by Gary Corby.

All rights reserved.

This is a work of fiction. All of the characters, organizations, and events
portrayed in this novel are either products of the author's imagination
or are used fictitiously.

Originally published in the United States by Minotaur Books.

Published in 2013 by
Soho Press, Inc.
227 W 17th Street
New York, NY 10011

Library of Congress Cataloging-in-Publication Data

Corby, Gary.
The Pericles Commission / Gary Corby.
ISBN 978-1-61695-251-8

1. Private investigators—Fiction. 2. Murder—Investigation—Fiction.
3. Greec—History—Athenian supremacy, 479–431 B.C.—Fiction. 4. Athens
(Greece)—Fiction. 5. Mystery fiction. 6. Historical fiction. I. Title.
PR9619.4.C665P47 2013
823'.92—dc23
2012046444

Interior design by Rich Arnold

Printed in the United States of America

10   9   8   7   6   5

For Helen

ACKNOWLEDGMENTS

This book exists because my wife, Helen, backed me throughout the clearly insane process of writing it. She's also the first line of defense for punctuation: you have Helen to thank for half the commas and all of the semicolons. Our daughters, Catriona and Megan, likewise have coped brilliantly with a Daddy who writes.

Anneke Klein and Bill Kirton read multiple versions of the manuscript and gave valuable criticism. Vicki Skarratt provided an outstanding author photo and Catherine Hammond critiqued an early version of the manuscript.

Professor Margaret Miller very kindly read the manuscript and pointed out a number of errors and improvements. You have Margaret to thank for the characters wearing correct clothing. Any errors that remain are all my fault, and I wish you joy of finding them.

There would be no book were it not for my agent, the inimitable Janet Reid, and the good people at FinePrint Literary Agency. Joanna Volpe, now a successful agent in her own right, edited the manuscript before submission and has been one of my most enthusiastic fans.

Straight after I queried Janet with my manuscript, I very

cleverly shut down my e-mail and Web site. This created the bizarre case of a writer who disappeared from the face of the planet the moment a literary agent became interested; not something you see every day. Janet's loyal blog readers came to the rescue for a spot of real-life sleuthing, in particular Rachael de Vienne, who tracked me down, using her excellent research skills, to an old e-mail address. Thank you all!

Finally, thanks to Kathleen Conn at Minotaur for her editorship and for coping with a debut author.

TIME LINE TO DEMOCRACY

Democratic Athens was 130 years in the making. It was the work of three men: Solon, Cleisthenes, and Ephialtes.

Circa 590 BC
- Solon the Wise writes a constitution for Athens.
- Nine archons run the city, elected from among the wealthy landholders.
- Retired archons join the Council of the Areopagus, which sets the laws.
- The Ecclesia of all the citizens can vote, but the Areopagus has the final say.

508–506 BC
- Cleisthenes reforms the constitution to give the people more power.
- The Ecclesia gains control of domestic laws.
- The Council of the Areopagus can nullify any law, and decides all foreign policy, so Athens remains an oligarchy.
- Candidates for the archonship are selected by lot from among the wealthy.
- Ostracism begins to be practiced. Once a year, the people can vote for whomever they dislike most. The "winner" is exiled for ten years. Nobody is ostracized until 487 BC, and then there's a flurry of high-profile victims.

- The people are demanding ever more control. Full democracy is getting close, but then a major interruption arrives . . .

490 BC
- The Battle of Marathon.
- A Persian expeditionary force lands down the road from Athens. The Athenians drive the Persians into the sea.

480 BC
- The Persians return, this time with a massive army. The Greeks unite for the first time. Incredibly, the Persians lose again.

477–462 BC
- Ephialtes, "a man uncorrupt and upright in political matters," does his best to complete the reforms begun by Cleisthenes fifty years before.
- The arch-conservative military hero Cimon protects the Council of the Areopagus and blocks Ephialtes. While Cimon is there, Ephialtes can make no headway.

461 BC
- Cimon leads an unpopular expedition to aid Sparta during a slave revolt.
- Pericles prosecutes Cimon when the expedition ends badly. It's the first time Pericles is prominent in public affairs.
- Cimon is ostracized.
- The moment Cimon is gone, Ephialtes pushes through his reforms. Athens becomes the world's first total democracy, with the Ecclesia as its parliament.
- Days later, Ephialtes is murdered, and *The Pericles Commission* begins.

THE ACTORS

Characters with an asterisk by their name were real historical people.

Ephialtes* *effy-alt-eez*	A dead man	He doesn't say much.
Nicolaos *nee-co-lay-os* (Nicholas)	Our protagonist	"I am Nicolaos, of the deme Alopece, son of Sophroniscus the sculptor."
Pericles* *perry-cleez*	Radical politician	"I want you to investigate this crime. Find out what really happened."
Xanthippus* *zanth-ee-puss*	Father of Pericles. War hero and member of the ruling oligarchy.	"Did my son hire a simpleton?"
Socrates* *sock-ra-teez*	An irritant	"Nico, I've been thinking . . ."

Diotima* *deo-teema*	A priestess of Artemis	"You fool, Nicolaos, how could you let this happen?"
Lysimachus* *lie-sim-ak-us*	Social connector	"Political destruction is one thing, but to murder a man for his politics is the next best thing to armed insurrection."
Euterpe *you-terpy*	High-priced hooker	"So, what may I do for you, young man?"
Phaenarete* *fain-a-ret-ee*	Mother of Nicolaos	"Don't look so shocked, son. I am a midwife, you know."
Archestratus* *ark-ee-stray-tuss*	A legal eagle	"Terrible as your ordeal was, I don't think you need fear pregnancy."
Achilles *ack-hill-eez*	A slave with sore heels	"Is this in the nature of a jest, sir?"
Pythax *pie-thax*	Chief of the Scythians	"We don't take piss-poor little Mama's boys in this outfit. So if you've run away from home, go find some other place to cry."
Conon* *co-non*	No, he's not a barbarian, he's the city mayor.	"Oh Gods! I can't believe I volunteered for this job."
The Polemarch* *polly-mark*	Government official	"The Government can't spend its time catching criminals, or we'd never get any work done."

Sophroniscus* _soff-ron-isk-us_	Father of Nicolaos	"Do one thing for this old man, Nicolaos: make sure your play is a comedy, not a tragedy."
Brasidas _bras-i-das_	A bowyer	"Look, when I sell a weapon, should I care who buys it?"
Stratonike _strato-ny-kee_	A madwoman	"He's coming back, he's coming back!"
Callias* _kall-ee-us_	The richest man in Athens	"Let's see if you can manage the first rule of the diplomat: separating your personal feelings from business."
Rizon _ree-zon_	A boor. Also something of a pig.	"So you're going to attack me again, are you? You're a violent man, I've warned the magistrates about you."
Lysanias* _lie-san-ee-us_	Former archon, now a member of the ruling oligarchy.	"Ah yes, Pericles' little attack dog. I've heard of you."
Telemenes _tel-em-een-eez_	A dodgy merchant	"My dear Nicolaos. I am a legitimate merchant."
Ephron _eff-ron_	A drunkard	"Do I owe you money?"

The Chorus

Assorted innkeepers, city guards, shopkeepers, bankers, nurses, slaves, thugs, travelers, maddened rioters, and ordinary citizens.

THE
PERICLES
COMMISSION

1

A dead man fell from the sky, landing at my feet with a thud. I stopped and stood there like a fool, astonished to see him lying where I was about to step. He lay facedown in the dirt, arms spread wide, with an arrow protruding out his back. He'd been shot through the heart.

It was obvious he was dead, but I knelt down and touched him anyway, perhaps because I needed to assure myself that he was real. The body was warm to my touch. The blood that stained my fingertips, from where I had touched his wound, was slippery and wet but already beginning to dry in the heat, and the small cloud of dust his fall had raised made my nose itch as it settled.

It doesn't normally rain corpses, so where had this one come from? I looked up. There was a ledge above me, and another to the left. The one directly above was the Rock of the Areopagus, home to the council chambers of our elder statesmen. The other to the left, but much farther away, was the Acropolis. There was no doubt about it; this man had fallen from the political heights.

I was about to rise when I heard the footsteps of someone coming down the road, and my immediate thought was the natural one: this might be the murderer coming to make sure of his victim, or perhaps the killer might lean over the ledge and shoot me too. I stepped backward to take cover at the side of the path, at a place deep in shadow, and waited, with no weapon other than the short dagger any citizen might carry. It wasn't much but it would have to do, so I gripped the hilt in my right hand, and was aware of the stickiness of sweat in my palm.

A man came into sight, walking downhill from what could have been either rock above me. The man stopped and exclaimed when he saw the body lying in full view. He stepped forward and leaned over, much as I had done myself. A glance up the path showed me there was no one behind him. The opportunity was too good to miss, so I stepped out of the shadows, took two quick steps, and placed my dagger at his back.

He flinched and started to turn, but I pressed the blade firmly to dissuade him. I was ready to send it home if I had to.

"Do not move," I said. "Do not stand up."

He remained bowed over the victim, and without turning to look at me he said, "So, you are going to murder me too?"

"Me?" I said, surprised. "Of course not, I didn't kill him."

"There's no point denying it, why else would you have a dagger at my back?" There was no fear in his voice, only contempt.

"Because you killed him."

"Not I. You saw me come down the path."

"That's where he died. He fell from above."

The man looked up and saw the ledge directly above us. "I see. Because I came down the path you think I'm here to make sure my victim is dead, but I give you my word I haven't murdered this man."

"That doesn't count for much."

"You're right, though perhaps the fact I hold no bow helps?"

The same objection had occurred to me, and I had already thought of the simple answer. "You could have thrown it away before descending." If he had, it would not be far.

The man nodded. "Yes, I had a feeling you were going to say that, but it seems to me a murderer is somewhat unlikely to throw away his weapon and then stroll past his victim.

Shouldn't I at least have walked in the opposite direction, knowing what I would find if I came this way?"

His point was very persuasive, and I'm sure he felt my hesitation because I saw the muscles in his shoulders relax a trifle. That irritated me, so without removing my dagger I said, "Let's find out more. Turn him over."

He said carefully, "To do so I will have to stand."

"Go ahead."

The man grabbed the body and heaved. The arrow made it difficult, but the body slowly turned and we saw his face.

I gasped. Lying in the dirt before us was the man who had brought full democracy to Athens.

"Dear Gods, it's Ephialtes!" the man cried.

"B-but . . . why would anyone want to kill *him*?" I stammered. "Everyone loves Ephialtes."

The man shook his head. "The people might have loved him, but think of the men he took the power *from*!" Then he snarled, "Could they be so brazen as to kill him in their own chambers? An undeniable crime?"

I boggled at what he was saying. "You think the Council of the Areopagus murdered Ephialtes?"

"Didn't he just fall from their rock? They killed my friend in revenge for what he did to them."

He ignored my dagger and fell to his knees to examine the body, confirmed Ephialtes had departed for Hades, and wept softly.

I stood with my dagger hanging from my hand, wondering what this meant for me. With Ephialtes' death the Council of the Areopagus might resume their traditional rule, and if that happened then it would matter once again what family you came from, who your father was. If the democracy failed, I would have no chance of rising in society, and I would be doomed never to be more than apprentice to my father. It was a personal disaster that I couldn't bear to contemplate.

The man still wept over the body, which was enough to convince me it was safe to turn my back on him. There was something I had to do, and quickly. I ran up the path to the fork in the road, took the turn to the right, and stopped at the edge of the Areopagus, where I peered about. If anyone stepped out from cover to take a shot I would be down the path and back to the Agora before he could put arrow to string. But no one did; the killer was gone.

I returned down the path up which I'd run, and inspected the bushes alongside, being careful to keep an eye at all times on the ledge above us. The man bent over Ephialtes was done weeping but continued to kneel as he watched me.

"What were you doing?" he asked.

"Looking for a bow."

He sputtered, "You still suspect me?"

"No, not anymore. There's no bow here, and you haven't had time to lose it farther."

He nodded. "Who are you, young man?"

"I am Nicolaos, of the deme Alopece, son of Sophroniscus the sculptor."

He hadn't anything to say to that. I hesitated, expecting his name in return, and not getting it. He'd called Ephialtes "my friend." He looked down at the corpse and I followed his gaze, thinking as I did that it was astonishing how quickly a man can be reduced from greatness to nothing. The death of this man had the power to change Athens forever.

"And who are you, sir?" I asked, unable to contain my curiosity.

"I am Pericles, of the deme Cholargos, son of Xanthippus."

I hesitated. "Would that be the Xanthippus who—"

"Is a member of the Council of the Areopagus, which has just murdered my friend Ephialtes. Yes, that Xanthippus." Pericles spoke grimly.

My mouth hung open. This was a man with problems.

"It might not be as you think," I said warily. If a whole

Council of men had been atop the Areopagus murdering Ephialtes, they had managed to disappear with astonishing alacrity.

"What do you mean?" he demanded.

I waved my hand at the arrow. "It's not a close-range weapon. If someone pointed a bow and arrow at you, what would you do?"

"Duck, swerve, charge my attacker, run away?" he suggested. "I certainly wouldn't stand still."

"And an arrow square in the chest? Is that the position for a man who knows he's a target?"

Pericles nodded. "Ephialtes did not see death coming, and the Rock of the Areopagus is small. Therefore the killer was not on the Areopagus, or perhaps he was hidden. Let's see if there's anyone there to tell us more."

Since I was a young man of no consequence I was happy for Pericles to lead the way. Besides which, if I was wrong and the killer remained hidden up there, Pericles would be the one used for target practice.

I had walked up the Panathenaic Way from the Agora to the Acropolis many times in my life, but not once had I stepped onto the Areopagus. I looked about with interest. The council met upon rock that had been chiseled to create a flat base, and about it stone had been cut away and smoothed to form seats. Elsewhere the Rock of the Areopagus was as rough as any outcrop. There were a few bushes, several thick enough to hide a man. I walked over to the spot where Ephialtes must have been standing. It commanded a fine view of the Agora to the north, where I could see tiny figures going about their business, setting up their stalls for the day, placing their wares, all of them unaware that their world had just changed. The wide, paved Panathenaic Way snaked southwards and upwards from the Agora to where the body of Ephialtes lay. I couldn't see anyone walking up the road, but with morning well advanced on such a fine day, that wouldn't last. To my right the Acropolis loomed high above me, a great solid fortress of almost unclimbable stone. A saddle of land separated the Areopagus from the Acropolis. I looked down into the valley to see Ephialtes' body below. Yes, this was the spot. The force of the blow must have pushed him over the edge; I could see a splash of blood on an outcrop where he bounced off the rock face on the way down, pushing him still farther away. I turned around and scanned the rest of the Rock. It was clear to me that whoever had fired the arrow had either hidden among the seating of the council, or popped out from behind a bush, or perhaps was someone Ephialtes knew and did not fear.

There was no one there but a couple of slaves, old men tidying the place. It was early morning, when the Councilors would be about their own business.

"You two there!" Pericles barked. The slaves dropped their brooms and came to him. "What happened here?"

They looked blank. "We're cleaning, sir," one said.

"A man has just been murdered on this rock. Tell me what you saw."

The slaves quaked.

This was no way to handle it. It is the law that slaves must be tortured when they testify in court; the greater the crime, the greater the pain.

"We saw nothing, sir," the first said.

"And we didn't hear nothing either," the second added for good measure. They would have been fools to say anything else.

I said smoothly, "I'm sure these men aren't witnesses, Pericles. They would have raised the alarm if they'd seen anything, wouldn't you, men?"

Both nodded vigorously.

"But perhaps you can tell us, does anyone come here in the mornings?"

"Sometimes there'll be a Councilor, sir, and someone will come to talk to him, official-like."

"What happens then?"

"Don't know, sir! We disappear until it's over. Orders."

"And this morning?"

"Don't know, sir! We only just returned."

"Returned?"

"Yes, sir! The Councilor ordered us to clear off."

"Who! Who was it?" Pericles demanded.

The man shrank back, looking at Pericles in fear.

"But, sir, isn't that why you're here? Didn't you say he died this morning?"

"What are you talking about?" Pericles asked.

The slave looked perplexed. "Why, sir, your father, Xanthippus," he said. "That's why we didn't see anything. He ordered us away."

I found myself at the home of Pericles, in his private office, where for half the morning he had paced to and fro, tearing out his hair. The performance had given me ample opportunity to study the man. I was struck by how almost perfectly proportioned he was, so much so that he could have worked as an artist's model for my father, but for his head. The head of Pericles was his only aberration from classical beauty, strangely elongated at the top, as if someone had placed a blunt cone there. He was graceful in his movements, with the same sort of economy of action as a tragic actor, or a great athlete; even in his distress he held his head high, never looking at the ground.

He was dressed in the same simple chiton that any man would wear, though I could see the material of his was superior, and he wore a fashionable short beard and hair that was well barbered. A himation of finest, pure white Milesian wool was draped across his shoulders as a cloak which hung in large, flowing folds down his back and over his left arm. The clothing marked him as one of the wealthy elite who did not have to work for a living.

His voice was remarkable, the most astonishing thing about him; it rang with a beautiful, rich timbre. I could have listened to him speak all day, and at the rate we were going, I probably would.

"It can't be true, Nicolaos. I refuse to believe it!"

"Then perhaps you should ask your father what happened."

That stopped him dead. "I don't dare," he whispered. He resumed his pacing.

I sat upright upon a couch, not quite daring to lean back in the manner of a normal visitor, a cup of wine beside me. The cup was silver, which did nothing to relax me; in my father's home it would have been clay. Even the table on which my wine stood was imposing; it was a circular top, patterned around the edge, its three legs carved to resemble the legs of horses, ending in finely wrought hooves.

As Pericles paced, my head swung left and right, left and right, as if I were watching a ball thrown by two boys.

"Ephialtes was my friend. More than that, he has been my mentor ever since I entered politics. He has a clearer vision of where to take Athens than any man alive."

"You mean had," I reminded him.

Pericles stopped pacing and glared at me with a sour expression. "Yes, I do mean had. He knew we had to take the final steps to democracy."

Pericles resumed his to-and-fro march. "That meant removing from power the last ruling institution still controlled by the unelected elite: the Council of the Areopagus."

I said, "Because the Areopagus is not elected by the people?"

"Because the Areopagus obstructs the people. For generations now, ever since the reforms of Solon the Wise, we have had the Ecclesia—the People's Assembly to which all citizens belong— and in theory the people had sovereignty. But the Ecclesia had no power to set foreign policy; that was reserved for the old men of the Areopagus, and even when the Ecclesia voted on domestic affairs, the Areopagus might overturn any decision it didn't like. The whole thing was a sham.

"A month ago Ephialtes persuaded the Ecclesia to vote away from the Areopagus almost all their powers, and the Areopagus had no choice but to accept it. All those powers are now divided between the Ecclesia and the courts."

"Then what was the Areopagus left with?"

"The power to hear cases of murder and heresy. That's all."

"So they went from being the most powerful men in Athens to a court of law?"

"Correct. The Areopagus members resent it bitterly, they loathe the democratic movement, and, above all, they hated Ephialtes."

"Has the Areopagus tried to harm Ephialtes before this?"

"Not that I know of, only abused him verbally, which they did often and with malice."

"Did they threaten his life?"

"Not in public. He wasn't the type of man to admit it if he received private threats."

"So the Areopagus hated Ephialtes, but did they hate him enough to murder him? It seems hard to believe."

"The guilt of the Areopagus is obvious, whether my father had a hand in it or not. All that's lacking is the proof." He stopped his pacing once more, this time by the window, and looked down into his courtyard. He was silhouetted by the light streaming in.

I said, "Then the answer is for someone to find out who killed Ephialtes."

"I think you must be right."

"But keep in mind, the answer might not be as certain as you think, Pericles."

Pericles waved his hand in dismissal. "I'm not worried about that. Now, be silent for a moment, I must think about this."

Pericles remained silent for such a long time that I became uncomfortable. I'd begun to wonder if I should take my leave when he turned to me and said, "You seem a remarkably logical man, Nicolaos, especially for one so young. How old are you?"

"Twenty. I've just finished ephebe training." Every young man, when he reaches eighteen, is required to spend two years in a training unit in the army. After that, he is expected to volunteer for service whenever the state needs him.

Something in my tone must have alerted Pericles, because he laughed humorlessly. "Ah, and did you enjoy it?"

"I did well enough." I was careful to keep my voice and face expressionless.

In fact, I was relieved to be done with it, but it would never do to complain. I hadn't minded too much the rough lifestyle, the deliberate starvation, and the punishments—the sergeants do that to toughen us—but I found having to be part of a squad claustrophobic. I preferred to rely only on myself.

Pericles studied me critically. "Yes, you have that starved, weathered look. Don't worry, everyone's like that when they finish training."

Two years in the army had left me thin, and my normal light olive skin was dark where the armor didn't cover me, especially my face and arms. I'd already been well muscled when I'd joined—working with my father from an early age had seen to that—but the army had taught me combat, with only a few small scars to show for my pains. I'd decided to follow the latest fashion among the young men and shaved my beard. I'd thought it would enhance my looks, but instead, where the beard had been, my skin was noticeably lighter than the rest. Now I was spending a lot of time out of doors to even the color.

"What are your plans now?" Pericles asked.

I was as free as any citizen. Free to be a young man in Athens, and free also to consider my future. I knew what I wanted, but had no idea how to achieve it. I wondered what Pericles would say if I told him I wanted his position.

"I have no particular plans."

Pericles nodded approval. "I noticed back at the Rock of the Areopagus you didn't panic and you didn't run away. Instead you stayed calm, kept your head about you, and dealt with the situation as you thought best. That would be remarkable in a man twice your age. For one as young as you, it's astonishing. I like that. I want you to investigate this crime. Find out what really happened."

"Me?" I couldn't believe he meant it.

"You. Athens is poised between the powerful old oligarchs, led by the Areopagus, and the Ecclesia, led by Ephialtes until this day. If you can prove he was struck down by the Areopagus, then they'll be finished as a political force and the democracy will be safe."

"But . . . when I said someone should find the killer, I wasn't talking about *myself*!"

"I will reward you greatly if you succeed."

Pericles was the son of an aristocratic family, and therefore wealthy. He could afford whatever sum he had in mind, and I could certainly use the money and, more to the point, I *needed* the democracy as much as he did. Did I want to investigate this murder? I knew immediately that I did; I was burning with curiosity to know what had happened.

But Pericles had something I wanted more than wealth, only it was something he probably wouldn't care to give me. Should I ask? I decided not. Why court failure, when already before me was a fine offer he might easily retract? I began to say yes, then stopped, realizing I was being a fool. Here was an opportunity that would never come again. It was up to me whether I grabbed it with both hands, or let it pass by for fear of rejection. I took a deep breath.

"You offer great reward, sir, so I will ask for two things," I said.

"The first?" Pericles didn't blink. He'd been expecting me to bargain!

"Sufficient wealth to establish a modest home and a small, steady income."

Pericles grunted. "No wish to follow in your father's foot-steps, eh?"

"None whatsoever."

"I accept. The second?"

"You will teach me politics."

Pericles pulled up short. His eyes widened, and he stood still for the briefest of moments.

"You're right, Pericles. I don't want to follow in my father's footsteps. I want to follow in yours."

"You surprise me. Are you sure about this? No one can simply become a successful politician, like putting on a hat. It's the same as any craft, it takes years to learn."

"Yes, I know."

"Am I correct in thinking you support the democracy?"

"I'm not going to rise any other way. My father's a sculptor, he isn't wealthy like yours."

"Good, because I'm hardly going to agree to train an opponent. Let me think."

Pericles folded his arms, and considered me as if I were some horse he might buy. It was lucky I'd chosen to wear my best clothes that morning: a chitoniskos—a little chiton, of the same style as Pericles', but stopping at the thighs rather than full length—and a small chlamys cloak pinned about my neck. My chitoniskos was new and therefore still white, with a fancy red key pattern about every edge. Pericles probably thought I was of a higher station than I was.

He held his pose for what felt an interminable time, during which I could feel my heart thudding. I looked back at him, attempting to keep my expression neutral and, I have no doubt, failing miserably.

Pericles frowned. "You must learn rhetoric. With your logical mind that should be easy." He paused. "Your voice. There's nothing we can do about your voice."

I clutched my throat. "What's wrong with my voice?" I asked, alarmed.

"But perhaps it can be trained a little, to remove the roughest edges."

I relaxed.

"You're young, of course. The bumptious manner will wear off with time, I hope. You'll have to learn to fake being calm and confident. Acting is a large part of the skill, but you must learn it without ever being seen on a stage. That would be shameful. No one in their right mind would vote for an actor."

"I'm willing to learn."

"You realize I can teach you the basic skills, to whatever degree you can learn them, but in a democracy it's the will of the people that decides who leads? I cannot guarantee your success as the second price."

"Of course. I accept your commission."

We heard commotion from the front of the house, slaves exclaiming, and running feet. Four men burst through the doorway.

"Pericles, Archestratus is saying Ephialtes is dead!" They were so agitated they were almost jumping on the spot.

Pericles waited until they had relaxed a little, then said, "It's true. I have seen the body." Before, in speaking to me, there'd been fear and worry in his voice. Now it was pure calm, which I knew for a pose.

"And is it true too, then, what Archestratus is saying, that he was murdered?"

"Yes," Pericles said quietly.

One man wailed, what would become of the democracy with Ephialtes gone, another shouted revenge against the Areopagus, and the third demanded the men of Athens take arms immediately to defend the democracy. The fourth man thought for a moment, then asked who would lead the democrats now.

"Pericles," answered the first man, calming down.

"Archestratus has a claim to leadership too," said the second.

"What we need now is an experienced commander of war to lead us against the aristocrats," said the third. "I would be the right man for that."

"You're talking civil war!" the fourth man protested.

"Yes. The Areopagus has started it, and we'll finish it for them."

They shouted at one another all at once.

Pericles looked at me, and I at him.

"And so it begins. Don't fail me in this, Nicolaos. I will do my best to limit the political damage, but I can only do so much without your answer. This pot will boil, and it is a mere matter of time before it explodes."

2

I walked straight to the place I love best in all the world: the Agora of Athens, the heart and soul of our city. It isn't merely the marketplace; it's also where men gather to talk, argue, and exchange opinions. In Athens, if it isn't said in the Agora, then it may as well not be said at all. I wanted to observe the reaction of the people to Ephialtes' death. Besides, it was lunchtime, no one would agree to see me during the meal, and my stomach needed attention.

I pushed my way through the crowd, picking up a fish cake from one stall and watered wine in a wooden cup from another. I nibbled at the fish cake in my left hand while I sipped the wine in my right. When the cup was empty I put it back on the stall and wandered about listening to the babble.

The open space in the middle was covered in a jumble of stalls, each little more than a rough plank resting upon a barrel at each end, with perhaps an awning to keep the vendors and their goods in the shade. I walked past the many stalls selling produce from the farms. These stalls were covered with jars and baskets of olives, olive oil, figs and grapes, corn, goat's cheese, and, rarely, smoked goat meat. Behind every stall stood a farmer, his skin leathery and dark from years working in the sun, his hands calloused, wearing rough clothes and a floppy sheep-skin hat, shouting his products or dealing with a customer.

These weren't men to care much of politics; it was all they could do to scratch a living from the stony soil. Barely visible, fenced off from the chaos, was the Altar of the Twelve Gods. The altar was the very center of Athens, the point from which all distances were measured. It was the only place in Athens dedicated to all twelve Gods, and so especially sacred: a place of sanctuary for anyone who could make it inside the fence before their pursuers reached them. The altar stone was made of marble, flat on top and somewhat weathered, though it had been set in place only sixty years before.

The people at the stalls were too intent on trading to talk politics; haggling was in full swing all about me. When a price was agreed on, the customer would reach into his mouth and pull out the coins he had put there before he left home. Only the rich had so many coins that they needed a purse, and no man would be so foolish as to display a money bag in the Agora. The thieves would have it cut away before he took two steps, and if he was lucky that would be all they cut.

A number of women were moving between the vegetable stalls, each with a man or boy to carry for her. Since the women were barefoot and buying, I knew them to be slaves. I recognized some of the young women since I look out for them; most households have a regular slave who does the shopping each morning, and their faces are a pleasant fixture in the Agora. I always smiled at the pretty ones but never approached; it doesn't do to interfere with someone else's property—at least, not in public.

To one side of the farmers were the fishmongers who had hauled their catch up in carts from the port of Piraeus before dawn. Anything they hadn't sold yet would be unfit to eat before long. They would mark down their prices after lunch and the poor would arrive to buy it. This was the one place where most of the vendors were women. The fishwives would sell the catch while the men saw to their boats, mended the nets, and went to bed in preparation for their early rise next day. A fish-wife might have plenty to say, and whatever she said would be in language strong enough to make a soldier blush, but no woman knew anything about politics. The aroma here was strong and I passed them by quickly.

Next to the fishmongers came the bronze ware, and the famous pottery of Athens, which could also be bought at its source in the deme—the suburb—of Ceramicus. Most of the pottery was newly made, painted in fashionable red figures on a black background: kraters for mixing wine, hydriai for water, pyxides for cosmetics and jewelry, pelikai for storing olive oil in the kitchen, ordinary cups and bowls. There were still second-hand dealers selling cracked or chipped examples of the older style black figure on red, but only the poor, the tasteless, or the hopelessly traditional would touch them. There were five or six middle-aged women—respectable married women—inspecting the goods at the better stalls, each accompanied by several slaves. They talked to one another, picked up the pieces, no doubt to complain about them, and put them back down. Not one was smiling. I pitied the vendors who had to deal with them.

I looked about, but there were no respectable maidens to be seen. In any case, no girl would be allowed in public without slaves and a chaperone, and any man who approached would be asking for trouble from her guard.

All the other people jostling one another in the crowded lanes were men. How many were slaves and how many citizens I couldn't say, because in Athens the slave of a rich man might be better dressed than a poor but free laborer. Even the resident aliens, called metics, adopted Athenian dress, and more often than not the local accent too.

The haggling was less intense here. The people were mutter-ing to one another, asking if anyone had heard any news about what had happened.

"He was set upon by ten men," I heard one man say.

"I heard it was twenty, and they beat Ephialtes with clubs."

"He put up a fight, though. I heard he killed two of them."

"You're all wrong! What I heard, he was speaking to the Council of the Areopagus, and when he angered them with his words they rushed upon him all together and beat him with their fists."

"No, it was clubs."

I realized with a shock that I knew what had happened, and the people of Athens did not. I felt a thrill of power and excitement, and I had to bite my lip to stay silent and not contribute to the rumors. Contrary to the general opinion, I knew for sure that the rock had not been awash with homicidal statesmen. It would have been the most fun of my life to hold court among the men as the only one present with any sure knowledge, but I knew instinctively that calling attention to myself would destroy any chance of succeeding in my mission. I told myself firmly I was there to gauge the mood, not to make a bad situation worse, and I walked on before the temptation to speak overwhelmed me.

I moved to the perimeter, where I stubbed my toe on a building stone, stumbled, swore, and lost the last handful of my lunch. The men around ignored me, except for one fellow who turned and snarled, then marched off with squashed fish cake and sticky sauce attached to his back. It happened every day. The Agora is a building site in which anyone could stumble and fall. It's been that way for as long as I can remember.

I had walked to a highly controversial building, half risen, with a strange circular wall in place of the normal four corners at right angles. It had been designed by an architect, so it bore little resemblance to any normal structure. My father, who has to deal with architects from time to time in the course of his trade, considered it typical of their alienation from all normal sense and taste. This was the Tholos, which, when it was completed, would house the leaders of the Boule: the committee of

five hundred that manages the agenda for the Ecclesia and over-
sees the running of the city. They would live in the Tholos when
on duty, since they have to be available to the people day and
night. The Boule had existed for generations, but because its
members were chosen each year by lot from among the citizens,
and no man could serve twice, it was part of the new democracy. There was talk too, since it was close to the Agora, of placing in the Tholos the standard weights and measures, so that
any dispute in the marketplace could be settled quickly before it
came to blows. That idea alone would decrease the annual murder rate by an appreciable amount.

The workmen had stopped for lunch. They sat among the
formwork, rivulets of sweat making tracks down the dust on
their faces and chests, in the shade of that strange circular wall.
Their hands cupped small bowls of lentils and bread. I sat among
them but heard nothing of value. All they talked about was
women and sport.

Curiosity got the better of me. "Aren't you men interested
in the latest news? Haven't you heard Ephialtes has been
murdered?"

A small, thin man with a hook nose and sparse hair looked at
me as if I were mad and said, "What do I care? I'm a slave. They
treat me the same no matter who's in charge." His friends nodded their heads gloomily. A man in another group spat into the
dust and said, "I'm a free man, but I'm so poor I gotta work for
someone else. You think Ephialtes matters to me? Promising to
cancel debts, was he? No? Thought not. Well, when you find me
a politician who wants to cancel debts, redistribute the land,
and make the poor richer I might care. In the meantime I gotta
work hard to feed my kids." He spat again. "At least the slaves
here get enough to eat. I ain't even got enough for the kids."

I wished them luck and went on my way, coming to the statues of the Ten Heroes, each of whom lends his name to one of
the ten tribes. All the people of Attica—the large region of

mainland Greece that Athens controls—belong to one or the
other of these tribes, and government jobs are shared equally
among the men of each tribe so that no group can have too
much influence.

The Ten Heroes are spread out in a line, each hero in such a
noble pose that I'm sure his own mother wouldn't have recognized him. Eight of the Ten were famous kings of old: Aegeus,
Erechtheus, Pandion, Oeneus, Leos, Acamas, Cecrops, and Hip-
pothoon; then there was Ajax, who fought at Troy, and finally
Antiochus, the son of Heracles, the tribe to which my own family
belonged.

These then were the famous heroes of old, their statues in the
Agora, and not for the first time I wondered why Theseus, surely
the greatest hero Athens ever produced, was not among them.
Theseus, after all, sent himself as a sacrificial tribute to Crete,
slew the Minotaur, and returned to Athens having delivered the
city from subjugation at the hands of King Minos. You can't get
more heroic than that.

As I always did when I came this way, I walked around to the
rear of Antiochus, to check once more on my greatest triumph
as a young boy in Athens. There, scratched deep into the hero's
ass, just below the cloak line, was a large N. It's very hard to cut
graffiti into marble, the other boys had had to make do with ink
that had soon washed off; sometimes being the son of a sculptor has its advantages.

The monument serves as the notice board of Athens; anything of importance, any official proclamation, is announced
by writing it on the plinth. Someone had splashed whitewash
across the plinth, obliterating everything that had been there
before, replacing all those words with a single message in large
letters: EPHIALTES IS MURDERED.

Men had been streaming into the Agora in the time I had
been walking about, so that the normally crowded marketplace was now as fit to burst as a boil ready for the lance.

They had come to hear the latest about the murder or to offer their own opinions to anyone who would listen. I pushed my way with some difficulty to the other side of the Agora, which was open-ended and so had some space for the crowd to spill out to.

This was the site of the new Stoa Poikile: the Painted Porch. Like the Tholos it was still under construction, but it was almost done, and the pressure for it to open was so strong that men were already making use of its wide, cool, covered walkway. Unlike the Tholos, everyone was already remarking how well it looked. The Stoa was a long portico with columns on the side facing the Agora, and a flat wall at the back. Two painters were using charcoal to sketch on the wall, far apart from each other, ignoring the chatter of the excited crowd about them. One had enough detail in that I could see he was about to paint a battle between the Hellenes and the Amazons; the other had barely begun.

"What's it to be?" I asked the second man.

"The Fall of Troy," he said, not turning. His eyes stayed on his work and his arm didn't stop moving.

His lines were simple and direct, no fancy touches, not much detail, I marveled as the strong walls of Troy suddenly appeared beneath his confident hand. Without a pause he left the walls and began on a figure, a woman whom I guessed to be Helen.

I said, "Well, don't put me in it."

That stopped him. He gnashed his teeth and said, "Gah! Why must onlookers always say that?" He threw a dirty rag at me, which I dodged, and I skipped out of the porch.

It was outside the Stoa that the political argument reached a crescendo.

"The Areopagus has murdered Ephialtes!"

"Kill the bastards that murdered Ephialtes!"

"How do you know it was them?"

"Who else would have done it?"

"Serves him right for upsetting traditions. We've always been ruled by the smart men. He wanted to replace them with common idiots."

"Who are you calling an idiot, you pox-faced scum?"

I left them grappling in the dirt and moved on to another argument.

"He was a dangerous revolutionary. We're all safer without him."

"You sound the sort of guy who might have killed him!"

"Me? Don't be ridiculous. That sort of trouble I don't need. Anyway, why would I when it was obvious the Areopagus would get him in the end?"

"You're talking about the man who stopped the oligarchs from taking all our power. You want to go back to the days when the rich told everyone what to do? You don't want to vote anymore?"

"That's a good point. Ephialtes protected the democracy. Who's gonna do that now?"

"Don't forget Archestratus! He wrote the laws, you know. He's still around."

"But for how long? If they killed Ephialtes that means they're gonna be looking for Archestratus too!"

"I don't care about Archestratus. What about Pericles? What's he say?"

"What are we going to do if the oligarchs take up their arms? What if they take back their power by force?"

"Hundreds of rich men against us thousands? Don't be daft!"

"Yeah, but they got shields and good swords. You own a shield, do you?"

"Hades, he's right! We ought to take over the shield factories and pass out shields and armor to everyone!"

If what I was hearing was anything to go by, Pericles' evaluation of everyone's reactions was correct. The one thing everyone seemed to agree on was that Ephialtes was murdered because he removed the powers of the Areopagus. The only difference of opinion centered on whether they were right to kill him for it.

It wouldn't take much to turn this lot into a mob. I wouldn't have been a Council member in this crowd for anything. In fact, the old men of the Areopagus were not to be seen. They had wisely decided to stay safe in their homes, or they would be scurrying through the streets to the homes of their colleagues, to confer. The men who mattered among the populist politicians had not come to the Agora either. I guessed they were banging on each others' doors. There was a power vacuum to be filled. I had little doubt that at least three conspiracies would be underway before nightfall.

I edged my way out for fear the mood might turn to rioting. There was a pile of building stone waiting to be used and I climbed up it. From the top I could see over the heads as if they were so many sheep. I could see the Panathenaic Way, which leads from the end of the Stoa to the Acropolis. It is one of the few paved roads in Athens, and no wonder, because this is the route the people of the city walk during their religious festivals. It was this path I had been walking in the morning. From where I sat I could see it reach to the base of the Acropolis and then curve right to begin winding its way round to the top. The path disappeared from view a hundred paces before the spot where Ephialtes had fallen.

"Hey, Nico!"

An ugly little boy threw himself onto my back. He almost knocked me down but I managed to stagger, reach behind and swing him before me. Like me he wore the chitoniskos tunic but his was filthy, smeared down the front with some kind of dark dirt, and ripped at the bottom.

"Guess what!" he demanded in great excitement.

"Ephialtes has been murdered. He was shot by an arrow and fell from the Rock of the Areopagus."

He gaped. "How did you know?"

"I was there. He came within a pace of falling on me."

My little brother gaped at me in admiration, as if being felled by a falling corpse was a sign of great virtue.

"There you are!" A man elbowed his way through to us, slightly out of breath and frowning. "Your father ordered us to find you; where on earth have you been hiding all morning?" This was Manes, one of my father's slaves. When a boy is judged old enough to wander the streets, his father gives him a pedagogue to accompany him everywhere, to provide a role model, possibly to teach him a little, and hopefully to keep the boy out of trouble, though that was asking too much of any man when it came to Manes' current assignment. Manes had been my own pedagogue ten years ago. Now that he was quit of me, he was landed with my brother. It hardly seemed fair on the poor old man.

My brother said, "There was a boy said I was ugly as a toad."

"So what did you do?"

"He almost killed him," Manes interjected. "I pulled them off each other and sent the other boy running."

It was true. My little brother was as ugly as a toad, but I would never have admitted it to anyone, least of all him or my parents. This was odd, because I conversely was considered quite handsome. We had the same unruly dark hair, the same brown eyes, but where he was short, I was medium height; where his face was squashed like a . . . well, like a toad's, mine was rounded; where he had a bulbous nose pasted into the middle of his face, my nose was typically Hellene; and where he was stocky, even squat, I was the normal build of any young man.

"Did you hurt him?" I asked.

"Yes, Nico."

"Well done. Next time you see him, hit him again." I knew from my own bitter experience what it is like to be a boy in Athens. You either prove yourself with your fists, or you are persecuted by the bullies for the next decade. I had been too quiet to fight, too happy to live within my own imagination, believing the other boys would become bored and leave me alone, and had suffered grievously for my miscalculation. When I was finally goaded into attack they were ready for me and beat me black and blue. I hoped my brother would take the fight to them.

Manes looked from one of us to the other in dismay. "Master Nicolaos! If I had not lived with your family for fifteen years, listening to this I would have said you were the sons of a Spartan, not an artist."

"Nico, I've been thinking—"

"Yes?"

"Is it true the murderer ran away?"

"No one knows who did it."

"Whoever killed him must be a really good shot. And they'd have to practice a lot to be confident."

"What makes you say that?" I was intrigued and annoyed at the same time. This was my case, not his, though he didn't know it yet.

"What if he missed with his shot? The killer must have been far away, because if he'd been close he would have used something more certain, like a sword or a spear. But if he was far away he must have been sure he could kill with a single arrow. If he'd missed with his first, then Ephialtes would have run away quickly. The killer must be an expert marksman."

"Who have you been talking to?" I demanded, angry. Not only had he reproduced the logic I had used to impress Pericles, but he'd gone on to deduce more.

"No one! I swear it, Nico."

"Then how do you know all this?"

"I thought about it, that's all. I'm sorry, Nico—"

"This is my case, not yours, so don't butt in."

"Your case, Master Nicolaos?" Manes asked.

"Mine," I said firmly. "I have a commission from Pericles to discover the murderer."

"Wow! Can I help?"

I ignored my brother.

"But, Master Nicolaos, your father—"

"I will talk to my father," I cut Manes off.

"I was about to say your father is looking for you. He expects you back at the workshop immediately. He said to tell you. That's why we've been out, looking for you."

I groaned. The excitement had made me forget I should have been assisting my father all morning. Father cannot conceive of any better life for a man than that of a sculptor. It was not that he disapproved of my rejecting his profession, it was simply that he couldn't even comprehend such a thing. He was as determined to turn me into a polisher of stone as I was to avoid that fate.

My commission was like a gift from the Gods. I had a chance to learn about Athenian politics from the inside. This could be the start of my proper life if I succeeded, or the end of it if I failed.

"Go to Father, Manes, and tell him I have been unavoidably detained by this murder. I will explain the rest later. Warn him it may be some time before I can return."

"The master will not like that."

"I know. It'll be a long explanation."

"Nico, I've been thinking—"

I sighed. I didn't want to hear any more ideas from my clever little brother. No matter how much I might love him, I was determined this was going to be my case, my success, the making of my name. "Try not to think so much, Socrates. It will only get you into trouble."

"Yes, Nico."

3

I decided my next step must be to do exactly as I had advised Pericles: speak with Xanthippus.

I imagined Pericles' relationship with his father must have been more strained than the usual father-son tension. Pericles was a leader of the party that was destroying the old ways and strengthening the democracy. Xanthippus was a respected member of the power base his son was determined to destroy. Family dinners must have been interesting.

Xanthippus' house would normally have looked like any other, but right now it resembled a small fortress. Two armed men stood at the front door. Others stood upon the roof. The guards would have turned me away but I claimed to have been sent by Pericles. I knocked on the door, and was answered by a house slave, looking scared, who let me into the public room. Xanthippus entered quickly, an old man but lively. He looked me over carefully. "You come from my son?"

"Yes, sir. I am Nicolaos, son of Sophroniscus. You are aware Ephialtes has been murdered?"

"It did come to my attention as one of the day's more important events." He crossed his arms and stared at me, waiting. It occurred to me Xanthippus did not suffer fools.

"Pericles asked me to look into the death of his friend."

"That's a job for Ephialtes' deme, if they care," Xanthippus said. "Let's see now . . . Ephialtes of the deme Oa, of the tribe Oeneides, wasn't it? I suggest you go home and wait to hear what the men of Oa have to say."

I was uncomfortably aware that Xanthippus was correct, but no deme in its right mind would involve itself in what looked like a murky political assassination, even if the victim was one of their own. I wondered if Xanthippus was relying on exactly that. However, I had an out.

"Technically, any man can investigate a crime," I said. "It is merely by custom that the job is left to the demes."

Xanthippus harrumphed. "A custom that has worked for our people for generations."

"Your son is hoping I might resolve the matter more quickly and, if necessary, more quietly," I offered.

"Why you?"

"I found the body, sir, and questioned the slaves working on the Rock of the Areopagus."

"Is that where he was killed?"

"I was hoping you could help me with that, sir. I understand you were there this morning."

"I was there, to meet with Ephialtes, in fact."

"What did you discuss, sir?"

He glared at me. "Did my son hire a simpleton? We talked politics, and matters of state. That's what one does at the Areopagus. Ephialtes was determined to destroy the Council. I was determined Athens should retain the good counsel of her elder statesmen. We met to see if there was some compromise that might avoid a damaging fight at the next meeting of the Ecclesia. There wasn't. I left him after our discussion." He paused. "Alive."

"How are you with a bow and arrow, sir?"

His face tightened in anger and he said, "If you've come here to insult me, then you can leave immediately. I'm a hoplite citizen, young man! I fight in the phalanx with my spear and shield.

I have no use for bows, like some auxiliary from a weak city, nor am I a mercenary."

I nodded gloomily, all too aware that he was telling the truth. There is a hierarchy in the world of arms, and this man was at the top of it: a soldier-citizen who could afford the large, round hoplon shield, armor, and spear necessary in a phalanx. Archers were light troops who couldn't afford better weaponry, and they mostly hired themselves out. Even if I put a bow in his hands, Xanthippus probably couldn't aim it.

"I apologize, sir, but I had to ask. Was there anyone else there as you left?"

Xanthippus needed a moment to calm down before he said, "No one, not even the slaves. I sent them off before Ephialtes arrived. I had to find them to tell them to return to work. They were lounging about atop the Acropolis, enjoying the view and avoiding their duties, as usual."

"How did Ephialtes know where to meet you?"

"I sent him a message, of course. Is this your idea of incisive questioning? I will send a note to my son suggesting he replace you with someone with at least a modicum of intelligence. You are looking in the wrong place, young man."

"I am?"

"I suggest things are not all rosy among the democrats. Ephialtes told me so himself. You could hardly expect otherwise when a rabble thinks it can run a city. Now if you wanted to know who would like to see Ephialtes gone, you might start with Archestratus."

"Archestratus?" One of the men with Pericles had named him future leader.

Xanthippus smiled. "He's Ephialtes' little dog. He likes to nip but he can't hurt you. The man holds delusions of grandeur way beyond his ability. He wants to lead the democrats after Ephialtes, and he's made no secret of his ambition."

"And that might happen now," I said.

Xanthippus became grim. "Archestratus is nothing more than a legal technician. He drafted the laws that emasculated the Areopagus."

"Oh? Then whose idea was it, Ephialtes' or Archestratus'?"

"To give total power to the Ecclesia? That was Ephialtes. Archestratus hasn't the imagination. But these new laws leave the Areopagus as the court for homicide and treason. That, I suspect, was a little whimsy on the part of Archestratus. If it were up to Ephialtes, the Areopagus would have been dissolved altogether. Allowing us some function means we are left to squirm in public. That sort of humiliation is the type of thing Archestratus would enjoy.

"Ephialtes was competent, I'll grant him that. If Archestratus gets his hands on the government, Athens will collapse within months."

I left Xanthippus' home more confused than I'd arrived. He didn't sound like a murderer to me, he sounded like a grumpy old man. Of course there were plenty of other members of the Areopagus who might have cheerfully killed Ephialtes, but Xanthippus had been the man on the spot.

I noticed a young man as I departed, loitering on the other side of the street. Normally I would not have given him a second glance, but I was preternaturally alert to anything that seemed out of the ordinary, and I felt the fellow's eyes on me the moment I stepped through Xanthippus' doorway. I returned his gaze, wondering if I knew him, but he turned and walked away. I decided that my newfound job was already making me overly suspicious, and I told myself firmly not to go chasing shadows.

Some of those shadows were falling across the city and the narrow streets between the crowded homes were already dark. The men of Athens were making their way home to eat with their families, or to the homes of their friends to attend a symposium, with a slave or two in tow to help them stagger back to their beds in the middle of the night. To continue daily business after dusk is not quite a crime, but it is close enough that no sensible man would take the risk. So I did what any sensible young man does when he is hungry, but which I had been putting off for as long as possible. I went home.

I lived with my parents, as most young men do until they marry. Only the sons of the richest men can afford their own place. Like most Athenian houses, the street front of our home was a blank wall with only a door and no windows on the bottom floor. Athens is a crowded city, so the citizens build upward, where a country estate would build out.

I stepped inside to the entrance hall and checked the public rooms to the left and right, which are reserved for the men. Both were empty. Upstairs to the left were my father's private rooms, his study and bedroom; to the right, the women's quarters, which in our household meant only my mother Phaenarete. I had not been up there since I was twelve. I stepped through into the courtyard beyond the entrance hall. This was the main living area of the house, and the place where the men sit if the weather is good. Our family altar to Zeus Herkeios stood in the middle, as it does in every proper household, and I smelled the lovely aroma of a fresh garland that had been placed upon it. The dining hall lay behind the courtyard, also my bedroom and my brother's. I could hear my father's voice.

"Where have you been?" Sophroniscus demanded as I walked into the dining hall. The first things people notice about him are his hands. His right hand is larger than his left, his right arm better muscled. The left hand was damaged where he had struck it with a mallet in his early days, but is still good for doing the most delicate finishing work. The skin of both hands is calloused and scarred, and the rest of his skin seems almost permanently layered with marble dust; even after he's washed, it still seems to cling to him. His face is round, like Socrates', his hair thinning but not balding. He likes to smile. He claims in his youth to have been as thin as I am now, but I have never known him to be anything other than comfortably padded. Our family is not rich or powerful, but it has always been well enough to put food on the table, and not every family in Athens can say the same.

Father was reclining on a dining couch, next to his close friend Lysimachus. Lysimachus was slightly younger than Sophroniscus, I think, but in better condition, barely gray, and certainly better dressed. I never quite worked out why they were friends, because their personalities were as different as the mountains and the sea. Sophroniscus was a practical man with an obsession for stone. Lysimachus thrives on knowing people, and conversation. With those qualities he is a valued dinner guest in many of the best homes in the city.

I heard the quiet laughter of women and the clatter of utensils and crockery in the small domestic area beyond the dining hall, which is reserved for the women and slaves, and is where the kitchen lies and the slaves sleep. Before us, two slave boys were already mixing the water and wine in the krater, to be drunk after the meal. Another slave was bringing out the first courses.

Lysimachus often dined with us, so he knew me. However, since he was here it meant my mother Phaenarete and my little brother would be eating in her rooms, since no proper Athenian household would allow its women and children to dine with visitors. I sighed inwardly. What was to come would have been easier if my mother were present.

"I'm sorry, Father. I was—"

"Your brother and Manes returned with some ridiculous story about Ephialtes being murdered and you doing something about it."

"It's true, Father." I related the day's doings as best I could. My tongue became twisted in his presence because I feared how he would respond. I had spoken easily with Pericles and Xanthippus, great players in the political game of Athens, but I stumbled speaking to this respectable sculptor who was my father. When I drifted to a confused finish he asked sharply, "Have you joined the democrats?"

"No! I'm only doing work for Pericles."

"That sounds like the same thing to me!"

"Would it be so bad if I had, Father?"

"Wait on there, Sophroniscus," Lysimachus interrupted, holding up his hand. "The Gods know your son is your own concern, and may the Friendly Ones visit me before I get between a man and his son having an argument, but I know this Pericles, and he's not such a bad chap."

I blinked. Was Lysimachus taking my side?

Sophroniscus looked at his friend in surprise. "Comes from a good family, does he?"

"His tribe is Acamantis from the deme Cholargos. His father is Xanthippus, you know, the strategos who commanded the army at Mycale and won, and on his mother's side he's descended from the Alcmaeonid family."

I could see Sophroniscus was impressed. The Alcmaeonids are an ancient aristocratic family who have held great power in generations past. But still there was the inevitable question whenever a member of that family is mentioned. Sophroniscus asked it. "But what of the curse?"

The Alcmaeonids incurred a curse more than a hundred years ago when they slaughtered a band of revolutionaries on sacred ground. It wasn't the slaughter that offended the Gods, it was doing it on temple territory that really rankled. The family had been accursed in all its subsequent generations.

Lysimachus waved his hand airily and said, "If it lingers on, it doesn't appear to have settled on Pericles. He's a talented man and he's enjoyed great fortune. But then again, he's only just started in politics, so there's plenty of time for him to be ostracized, executed for treason, bankrupted, or any combination of the above. You know how it goes."

Father nodded. "I do indeed, and that's why I don't want Nicolaos involved."

"That of course is your decision to make, my friend."

Sophroniscus considered, drumming his fingers, then asked me, "I suppose this democratic movement is popular with the young men? It's the latest fashion, is it?"

"I don't know, Father. Uh, I suppose so." In fact I knew many young men were vociferous about the democracy, even those from the better families. However, none of them moved in the circles I had frequented this morning. The young men were the supporters of Pericles, not his colleagues. I thought with great satisfaction that the young men who had run in the streets with me when we were youths would be watching with jealousy when they saw me consulting with important politicians.

Sophroniscus picked figs from a bowl and said, "I see. In my day, son, it was tragedy. All we young men were going to turn our backs on society and become tragedians, actors, or both. We did it to annoy our fathers. No doubt this is the same thing again, the mere trend of the moment and the revenge of the Fates for the anguish I caused my own sire. It'll all blow over when the next fad comes along. As long as it doesn't affect your work, I suppose it can't do any harm yet."

"My work . . ." I didn't quite know how to say what I knew I must. I breathed deep and took the plunge. "Father, this political work . . . I think that's what I want to do."

Even Lysimachus laughed at that one. Sophroniscus said, "Don't be ridiculous. Nobody gets paid for doing politics, son. That's what the rich do because they don't have to earn a living. You need substantial wealth even to begin, and I don't have that sort of money, and even if I did I wouldn't spend it on helping you become yet another opinionated orator." I had expected anger, I was prepared for that, but his scorn was more devastating.

"They are more than mere orators, Father. Among them are men who make real decisions, important decisions."

"Listen, son, politics in this city is not for the faint of heart. The lower men work themselves hard, sacrifice their own time and wealth, and get nothing for it. The leaders, the few who make it to the top after years of effort, they're mostly corrupted by the experience. Let me tell you how badly wrong this could go. Have you ever heard of Themistocles?"

"I don't remember much about him."

Lysimachus put in, "His fall was more spectacular than most. Themistocles led Athens in his day, much as Ephialtes does— did, rather, until today."

"He led the democratic movement?"

Lysimachus shook his head. "Themistocles was no democrat. He was a brilliant strategist. It was Themistocles who saved us all when the Persians invaded."

Sophroniscus added, "But as soon as the people no longer needed him, they got rid of him. First, they ostracized him. Then the Council of the Areopagus saw their chance and found him guilty of treason, guilty of colluding with the Persians, would you believe, when it was he who had defeated them. Then he was condemned to death, and all his property was forfeited to the state."

Sophroniscus stopped to take a handful of olives. I'm sure he did it to leave me plenty of time to contemplate the fate of Themistocles.

One of the oddities of Athenian politics—odd, at least, to the states which don't practice it—is that once a year in winter, the Athenians vote, not for who should be *in* power, but for who should be *out* of it.

If the Ecclesia decides an ostracism should be held, then the people vote, and whoever gets the most votes is exiled for a period of ten years. This is the sort of vote a politician wants to lose! The "winner" is required to depart within ten days, and not return until his ten years have expired. He must leave not only Athens, but all of Athenian-controlled Attica, and if he steps within Attica during his exile then the penalty is death. This was the fate that had befallen Themistocles and, while he couldn't be there to defend himself, the Areopagus had declared him a traitor, effectively making his exile permanent.

Sophroniscus said, "So there you have it. Exiled, criminalized, condemned, and bankrupted. And, son, Themistocles was a *successful* politician. You don't want that to be you, do you? So let's say no more about it. You have enough to learn the art of marble."

"But Father, I'm only doing a job for Pericles. None of that's going to happen to me."

Sophroniscus threw up his arms in despair.

"So Themistocles died?" I asked, desperate to change the subject away from me.

"No, he wasn't stupid enough to hang around waiting to be condemned. He ran to the Persians! If you're going to be damned for something, you may as well get the advantage of it. The Great King set him up as Governor of Magnesia."

"You mean he was guilty after all?"

"The treason charge was rubbish," Sophroniscus declared, pushing away the last bowl and reaching for his wine. "But it served to keep the man away from Athens permanently. The rest of us who aren't as smart as he is are safer that way."

"Where could I find out more about Themistocles?"

"Try his temple."

"His *temple*?"

Lysimachus laughed. "Oh, he built it in honor of Artemis of Wise Counsel, but no one doubted who he really meant to honor. It was such arrogance as this that disturbed the common people so much they were willing to ostracize him. If it hadn't been for his personal faults he might still be ruling Athens today, and Ephialtes would never have led the democrats, nor reformed the Areopagus."

"Nor been murdered," I couldn't help adding.

Lysimachus nodded. "Yes, young Nicolaos, I think you

probably have the right of that. Tell me, what are they saying in the Agora?"

"That the old men of the Areopagus killed him."

"Revenge? Well, it wouldn't be the first time an Athenian killed for that reason, but somehow, in this case, I doubt it. Revenge is stupid, and these men aren't stupid, whatever else people might think of them. Why risk their position for mere satisfaction? No, if the Areopagus killed him, it must have been for a good reason."

"What reason?"

He shrugged. "I know of none. That's why I don't think they're involved."

"Then tell me, Lysimachus, what do you think happened to Ephialtes?"

"I wish I knew! But whatever it is, it will be something to do with power. Power's what drives this city, young Nicolaos. And I tell you, Sophroniscus my friend, if this goes on we could lose everything." Lysimachus rubbed his chin and frowned. "Political destruction is one thing—even my own father was ostracized and took it in good part—but to murder a man for his politics is the next best thing to armed insurrection."

That intrigued me. "Your own father was ostracized, Lysimachus?"

"He was indeed, and the cause was a bitter political infight with the man we were just discussing: Themistocles. This was before the Persians came, lad; you were not even born yet. My father, Aristeides, whom men called the Just for his fairness and honesty, argued against Themistocles on the matter of whether to meet the coming enemy with a large army or a large navy. The argument became so heated that an ostracism was called, and Aristeides lost." He smiled. "My father even had to cast a vote against himself. He offered to help a man who didn't know how to write. The man said he wanted to vote for Aristeides—he was a farmer from out of town, you see, and didn't know to whom he was speaking. My father, intrigued, asked what the man had against Aristeides if he had never met him, and the farmer replied he was sick of all this constant talk of 'Aristeides this' and 'Aristeides that,' and 'Aristeides and all his fine virtues.' So my unfortunate father meekly wrote his own name on the shard and dropped it into the voting box!" Lysimachus laughed. "Themistocles had the right of it, I admit it; the navy he created was what saved us.

"But that's the past, and it's the future that worries me. There's a party in this city willing to kill for power, and that is very, very dangerous. The next logical step is armed coup."

Sophroniscus looked alarmed. "Do you think something like that is brewing?"

Lysimachus shrugged. "Who can say?"

Sophroniscus muttered to himself, "I will move the family treasury outside the city tomorrow."

"When was the last time something like this happened?" I asked, curious.

Lysimachus thought about it while he held out his cup to be refilled.

"The last political killing? You'd have to go back to when the last tyrant was expelled. That's what . . . three, four generations ago?"

I was exhausted by the day and disappointed by the evening. I could not keep my eyes open a moment longer and so asked Father for permission to retire. He gave it, and I departed while Lysimachus continued his discourse on the dangers to Athens. I noticed Sophroniscus glance at me curiously.

The next morning at breakfast, our kitchen slave brought two small bowls of bread soaked in wine. She smiled at me as if to silently say that she sympathized. She would have heard every word that had been said last night. Certainly every slave in the house knew I had disagreed with my father.

Sophroniscus let me finish the meal and then led me into the workshop at the back of our house. Inside was a marble statue of a horse that had won at the last Panathenaic Games, commissioned by its owner as an offering in thanks to the Gods for his victory.

The statue was almost finished. I sighed, picked up the necessary cloth, and began rubbing its rear end. This was the story of my life; great events were happening all about me, I could feel the world was changing, and here I was rubbing the rear end of a stone horse. Sophroniscus began chipping away at another block with mallet and chisel, his preliminaries for another work. He usually left me to finish a piece while he commenced his next job. I continued the tedious rubbing, silent.

Sophroniscus observed my deep unhappiness and said, "Cheer up, son. There's no reason you shouldn't discuss politics in the Agora with the other young men. It's a fine thing for any man to think about the future of the state. It's simply not possible for anyone but the rich to do it full time, and especially not for a man who's destined to be a sculptor."

"But Father, I don't want to be a sculptor."

"You don't—" Sophroniscus put down his tools in amazement and repeated, "You don't want to be a sculptor?"

"No."

"But I always thought . . . that is, you always said you did."

"No, Father, you always talk about how I will."

"Why didn't you tell me before?"

"I did, I tried rather, several times. But Father, you always talked over me."

I had never before seen Sophroniscus shocked. He paced across the workshop, stopped to touch the piece I had been smoothing and ran his finger along it, picking up the dust. "This is a terrible disappointment. You do good work."

"I'm sorry, Father." And it was not a lie; I don't believe I have ever felt such sadness as that moment. But we had been building toward this confrontation for years and I was not going to step back from it now that the moment had come.

"What would you do then? You cannot earn money as a politician, Nicolaos. That's where you spend it. Who ever heard of paying a man to wield power? The idea's ridiculous."

"But Father, what if I can make money doing politics?"

"Then I would say you are practicing magic, or you are corrupt. I hope you are neither. We talked last night of how such men are usually caught in the end."

"This commission from Pericles—if I succeed I will earn a substantial reward."

Sophroniscus scoffed. "Enough to live on? I doubt it."

"Enough to start with. I hope so."

"And what of the next commission? And the one after that? I tell you important politicians aren't murdered every day, my boy. It's not exactly a thriving industry, no, nor even a small trade."

"I see myself acting as an agent to men such as Pericles. It is a trade, Father, a kind of political trade."

"Morally dubious and physically dangerous. Very dangerous."

"More dangerous than serving in the army?"

Sophroniscus considered. "Perhaps not."

"Yet, Father, you served in the army when the Persians came."

"And will again if they return. That is the simple duty of every citizen to protect his city."

"Isn't what I propose the same thing then, sir?"

"We are discussing the difference between an honorable death facing the enemy in combat, and a knife in the back in the dead of night. I know which risk I'd prefer."

"I'm willing to take that chance, Father."

"Humph. The confidence of youth. I can see, son, that you are bent on this course. I could order you to give up this commission and return to your proper work but . . . you wouldn't be happy, would you?"

"No, Father."

"I still believe your thought of a political trade is fantasy, but I will allow it to this extent. Go and do your political work, son—" My face broke into a huge smile. "But! Mark my words. If this commission of yours fails, if you do not win this supposed reward, if you do complete it and Pericles refuses to pay you, if at the end of this bizarre exercise you have not earned a drachma, then you will return and we will continue your training in sculpture as before, and there will be no more words about it."

"You are very fair, Father."

"Stupid is more like it, but I see I must indulge you in this to get it out of your system. Furthermore, young man, even supposing you do earn your first commission, I wonder where the next will come from. I am giving you two years to prove you can make a life of this. If you fail, back you come. I hope there will still be time to teach you a proper trade before you're too old."

"Thank you, Father."

"Now the only problem is, who am I going to find to help an old man in his work. I doubt I can cope on my own anymore," Sophroniscus said mildly. He wasn't really particularly aged, but he liked to pretend that he was in his declining years and sometimes referred to himself as an old man. "There will be times I need you to assist me, son. The heavy work is more than one man can manage."

"Of course, Father! I don't mean that I don't want to help my father, I mean that I . . . er . . ."

"Don't want to do it a lot?" Sophroniscus offered with a smile.

"I'll help!" a boy's voice called from above. Sophroniscus and I both looked up in surprise to see Socrates kneeling on the top of the latest marble block. The little rat must have heard every word of our conversation.

"You, Socrates? I never thought you would be the one to take up sculpting."

"I would like to try, Father. Please may I?"

Sophroniscus made a show of thinking about it. "You are young to start, but if it is your wish you can begin with the simpler pieces." A blind man could see he was jumping with joy at the thought of having a son to pass on his trade. I had hurt the poor man deeply. Socrates had offered a perfect solution. Now I suppressed a smile.

Later I asked Socrates, "Did you truly mean what you said in there? If you didn't, Father is going to be even more hurt later."

"It's okay, Nico. I think I'd like to be a sculptor."

"Very well then, as long as you mean it." I shared Sophroniscus' surprise. Socrates didn't seem the sculpting sort, or any other type of artist for that matter. You never can tell about people.

4

It seemed to me the next thing to do was talk to Archestratus and find out where he'd been at the time of the murder. To my surprise I found him at home. As soon as I said I came from Pericles, I was admitted into the andron, the public room at the front of the house reserved for men. Archestratus was a well-fed man with squinting eyes. He sat in an upright chair, in which he barely fit, surrounded by men, sitting upon couches set along the walls or standing. There were perhaps twenty or more of them, half with the worn faces and skin of middle age, and half younger men. A couple of those standing were jittering up and down on the spot, like runners about to start a race, but most of the men sitting had a slight slump to their shoulders. The air in the room felt hot, despite the open windows looking out onto the courtyard. Bowls of half-eaten food and cups of wine sat on low tables. A few scraps and over-turned empty cups lay scattered about the floor.

The men were certainly citizens, or they would not have been present. Most wore the exomis, a knee-length garment that wraps around the body from the right side, belted about the waist, and tied over the left shoulder, leaving the right shoulder and arm bare. The exomis was the favored clothing for artisans and craftsmen. My father and I wore the same thing when we worked. Only a few men with gray hair had both shoulders and chest covered by the full-length chiton tunic of a genteel citizen, and two men my age wore the thigh-length chitoniskos of an active man. Excepting Archestratus, I doubted there was a landholder among them. Typical, in fact, of the very men the Areopagus wanted to keep from power. They had been talking loudly, but fell silent as I entered and was introduced. Every eye was upon me.

"So Pericles wants to deal, does he?" Archestratus said with satisfaction.

"I beg your pardon, sir?"

"A power-sharing accommodation is possible, but tell Pericles I won't have any of that 'you lead every alternate day' nonsense. We split our interests down the middle. He can have foreign policy and I'll take domestic."

"That's not why I'm here, sir. I'm investigating the murder of Ephialtes."

Archestratus goggled. "You're from his deme?"

"It's a private commission."

"The man's dead. Obviously the old men of the Areopagus killed him, and there's nothing we can do about it. We could hardly arrest the entire Council, and even if we did there's no mechanism for taking them to trial."

The men on the couches sat up straighter. One of the other men said, "What do you mean, Archestratus? Of course there is. Anyone accused of murder can be forced to stand trial. Being a member of the Areopagus is no immunity."

Archestratus smiled and said, "You're quite right. So can anyone tell us, when a man stands trial for murder, in which court is it held?"

I knew the answer to that one. "You wrote the law yourself, Archestratus. They're tried by the Council of the Areop— Oh."

Archestratus smiled and said, "Correct. Our accused murderers are the city's entire set of homicide judges. Imagine the scene at the end of the trial, the accused walk to the front of the court to lay judgment on themselves. What verdict would you expect?"

Archestratus let that sink in for a moment.

"Constitutional crisis, gentlemen," Archestratus said with relish. "Constitutional crisis of the highest order. I think I can say with all due modesty I am one of the few men equipped to deal with it."

He certainly had me impressed, and I could see the other men were admiring Archestratus.

I said, "But sir, what if the murderer wasn't a member of the Council?"

Archestratus frowned and said, "Of course he was."

"Not necessarily. For example, what if someone else wanted to lead the democratic movement?"

"Your implication is clear, but I cannot imagine Pericles resorting to murder."

"Pericles!" I exclaimed.

"Of course. You're not suggesting I am a murderer, are you, young man?"

"Er—"

The men growled.

"No, of course not, Archestratus."

"Good. If it was not the Council that did the deed, then look to his personal affairs." A few of the men sniggered.

"Oh? Can you tell me about that?"

"I don't inquire into other men's personal business. I merely make the suggestion as a man who has seen his fair share of trials. Did you know most murders are over family feuds? Take it from me, young man, if the motive isn't politics, then it's personal."

"Sir, I'm sure you understand the law better than I ever will. Could you tell me what happens now to Ephialtes' house and property?"

Archestratus harrumphed. "If he had sons, or even nephews

or brothers, his possessions would pass to them. I happen to know he had no close male relatives still living. There was a brother, but I believe he died in battle against the Persians before he could sire children. The law requires property to stay within the family. So in this case Ephialtes' widow will be required to marry the closest possible man within his greater family. I have no idea who that is."

"What if that man is already married?"

"Then the law requires him to divorce so as to marry the widow. Keeping property within the family overrides all other considerations. The man would retain his own property and acquire that of Ephialtes. The divorced woman would be sent back to her family."

This struck me as being somewhat harsh. But fortunately that wasn't my problem. My problem would be finding the name of the lucky groom.

"It couldn't have been Cimon who killed Ephialtes, could it?" a man speculated.

Archestratus chuckled. "Cimon? He's an arch-conservative, no man is more aristocratic, and he and Ephialtes hated each other with a passion, but have you forgotten he was ostracized three months ago? We won't see him back in Athens for nigh on ten years. How he could fire a bow on the Rock of the Areopagus when he isn't even in Attica is an interesting question."

Nevertheless, the suggestion was a good one. Cimon was our greatest living military commander, and the son of Miltiades, who led us to victory at the Battle of Marathon. With credentials like those, he was a hero to many, and as Archestratus said, was known for his deep conservative views, so deep that he was friend and admirer of the strange, militaristic city-state Sparta, Athens' greatest rival for domination of Hellas. Yes, indeed, if Cimon were in Athens he would be a prime suspect.

But he wasn't in Athens, nor anywhere in the Attica region surrounding, because the previous year, Cimon had led a party of volunteers to go to the aid of the Spartans when they suffered a slave revolt. The expedition had ended in a farce when the Spartans sent home the Athenian contingent as not required. The people were incensed by the insult, blamed Cimon, and had taken out their indignation by ostracizing him.

I said, "What if Cimon hired an agent to act for him?"

"I don't believe it," another man spoke up. "Cimon wouldn't kill a man like that. He'd face you down." Others around the room nodded their heads.

"Where is Cimon now?" someone asked.

Silence. Nobody knew where he'd gone. That wasn't so strange since he'd only recently departed. No doubt he would surface in a few months after he'd found a new home. Cimon had been the only man capable of stopping Ephialtes. The moment he was gone, Ephialtes had pushed through his reforms.

"Maybe one of Cimon's friends is acting on his own," someone suggested.

"I suppose that's possible," Archestratus conceded. "But if you're right, there's going to be another murder."

"What!"

"Oh, yes. It was Ephialtes who wanted Cimon's political destruction, but the man who prosecuted him after the Spartan disaster was Pericles."

It was only after the door shut behind me that I realized I'd never asked Archestratus the one question I'd gone there to ask: Where had he been at the time of the murder? I shook my head in disgust with myself. How could I have let him get away with that? Xanthippus had called Archestratus a little dog who liked to nip but couldn't hurt, but having met the man I thought there was plenty of bite in Archestratus. The difference between them was, if Xanthippus was a hunting dog that came at you from in front and went for your throat, then Archestratus was the kind that pounced onto your back from behind.

I considered Archestratus' rather clever backhanded suggestion that Pericles might be the killer. But if he was, I had to get around my own evidence that he held no bow, and besides, why would he commission me to catch himself?

It had all looked so simple when I'd questioned the slaves!

Archestratus had dropped a broad hint that all was not well in Ephialtes' private life. I decided to visit his home, where I'd be able to ask about his family, and perhaps even discover if there was a relative who hated him.

The home was easy to find, since such a public figure had a long line of mourners visiting. I pushed my way through the crowd, which began even outside the door.

The public rooms held some decent dinner couches, but nothing opulent. The cups men held were standard pottery. There were murals on the walls, the usual Homeric scenes, but nothing like what I would have expected in the home of such a famous man. Indeed, our own house held better artwork, and that confused me. Ephialtes would not have been a rich man, not compared to an aristocrat like Xanthippus, who owned many estates and probably a silver mine, but he should have been very comfortable compared to most. So where was his money? It certainly wasn't in this house.

Everything was overshadowed by the most important display, the body of Ephialtes. As is the custom, he had been carried straight home from the murder scene. The body had been washed in perfumed water and seawater and laid to rest in the courtyard, with his feet pointing toward the door.

I stepped forward to the body, as was required. An urn of ashes had been placed there. I dipped my hands in, raised them high above me, and poured a handful of ash over my head, felt the soft falling touch against my face, and the harsh burnt smell in my nose. Looking down I could see the pattern of black and white specks on the floor all about me, where every visitor before had done the same thing. I cried and lamented for the shortest time I decently could, inspecting the body all the while. Ephialtes had been dressed in a white shroud. A honey cake rested by his right hand. A strip of linen had been tied around his chin to the top of his head to keep his mouth shut, by which I knew the coin, an obol, had already been placed in his mouth. Ephialtes would give the coin to Charon the Ferryman, who would carry him across the Acheron, the river of woe, on his way to Hades. He would cross the river Cocytus of lamentation, and the Phlegethon of fire, before coming to the river Lethe, where he would dip in his hand and drink of the waters, and so lose all memories of his earthly life, finally coming to the Styx, the river of hate, after which he would be in Hades, and remain there for all eternity.

Death, my death, was not something I had ever contemplated before, but looking down at this man whose death I was investigating, knowing what he was going through that very moment, I wondered for the first time what my own fate might be. The great hero Achilles of Trojan fame had said he would rather be slave to the poorest man living than king over all the dead, and he should know. Achilles' word was enough to tell me being dead was a bad idea.

When I felt I'd lamented sufficiently I stepped back.

Without a son in the home there was no one to greet the mourners, so they wandered, poking their noses about the home of a famous man, talking to each other, and picking up and inspecting anything that took their interest. I wouldn't be surprised if a few items disappeared before the day was out.

We could all hear the wailing from the women's quarters, particularly shrill from one voice, whom I guessed would be the wife. It is against all decency for a married woman to socialize with men, and the husband being dead is no excuse for breaking the rule. Ephialtes' wife and any girl-children would not leave their quarters until all the visitors had left. Equally, the custom was that they must keep the wailing going to show their distress.

It set my teeth on edge, and the men talking to one another had to raise their voices to be heard above it.

I hadn't fully appreciated how confused this house would be. How was I going to get any information here?

A slave was hobbling about with difficulty, serving wine. The slave was thin, almost weedy. His hair was falling out, and he had the look of illness rather than old age.

He was struggling to carry the amphora. It almost slipped from his grasp and I barely grabbed it in time.

"Here, let me help you."

"Oh no, sir, I couldn't do that!"

"Whyever not?"

"What would the master say?"

"Very little. He's dead."

The slave was taken aback. "Why, so he is, sir. I keep forgetting, it doesn't seem real."

I took the amphora from his protesting hands and started to serve. As I walked among them, some of the visitors asked if I was Ephialtes' son. I claimed to be the son of an old friend—explaining why I had not cut my hair in mourning—and moved on.

The cup into which I was pouring jerked, making the wine splash my feet. The fellow holding the cup said, "Now there's a brave man."

For a moment I thought he meant me before I realized he was looking over my shoulder. I turned to see an older man standing by the body, a new arrival since he had no ash on his shoulders. Many in the courtyard had stopped talking to watch him.

A voice called out, "What is it, Lysanias? Come to make sure he's dead?"

Lysanias ignored the implicit challenge, but said in a tone that brooked no argument, "Paying my respects to a good man." The expression on his face was grim, made grimmer by his hair being cut so close that it was barely gray fuzz above his skull.

"Who's he?" I asked the man next to me.

"One of the Council of the Areopagus."

Lysanias stood for a moment, looking down at the corpse, then made his respects, much as I had done, but with more style, lifting the ashes in two hands above his head and letting them fall upon him. His lamentation sounded like he might have meant it.

When he finished, he did not stay. Probably there was no one in the house who would have wanted to speak with him anyway, except for me. Lysanias strode to the front door and out.

It had been an impressive performance. I had to agree with the fellow who'd spilled his wine on me: there went a brave man.

Several more members of the Areopagus arrived late. They too had come to do what was right for the dead man's shade, and they were left in peace. Time passed slowly, but the stream of visitors finally slowed to a trickle, and by dusk they were all gone. I sat down, exhausted. It had been a long day. The slave sat beside me, looking like he might faint. I poured a cup of wine and handed it to him, then one for myself.

"What's your name?" I asked him.

"Achilles, sir."

"Achilles?" I could not keep the surprise from my voice. Never has a name less matched the wearer.

"I believe it was in the nature of a jest, sir, on account of my heels."

Looking down, I saw that both Achilles' heels had been cut deeply. They had not healed clean. The scars ran to his ankles, the mutilated flesh was tight and folded, white and flaky. Walking must have been painful.

"Who did this?" I asked in horror.

"A distant cousin of the master, sir, when they were boys."

"For goodness' sake, why? Did you do something very bad?"

"I believe it was in the nature of a jest, sir."

I sat there with Achilles, trying to ignore the wailing from the women's quarters, which had not let up the whole afternoon, as was proper.

"They're doing a good job up there, but they must be getting tired," I said, as I refilled his cup. "Is that shrill one the wife? She must be upset, her screams almost sound genuine."

"I'm sure I couldn't say, sir," Achilles said and, after a long pause, he added in a low voice, "There's another house will be in mourning,"

"What's that?" I asked, startled.

"Another house, only not so public. His mistress, a hetaera with a special place for the master."

I had to think about that. "When you say this woman's a hetaera, I suppose you mean that as a courtesy title. Surely she's some young girl that Ephialtes took in and gave a home?"

"Oh no, sir! Euterpe of Mantinea was never one of those common pornoi one finds walking the streets. Ephialtes first met Euterpe at one of her soirées, when she was already well established, with her own salon and a respectable clientele."

Euterpe would be her professional hetaera name, not the one she was born with. The name meant "Great Delight." The idea of Ephialtes keeping a highly expensive hetaera didn't fit my image of him as a noble leader of the common man. The hetaera is a courtesan. Unlike most respectable women, she can read and write, and is as versed in poetry, philosophy, and politics as any man. She is able to hold an enchanting soirée in her salon, and the best men of the city will clamor to be invited. Hetaerae are not considered respectable by the wives, but the men who can afford them aren't too bothered by that. On rare occasions, such a lady will form a special relationship with one man. He is expected to keep her in the style to which she is accustomed. She will see no other man.

"How do you know this, Achilles?"

"It was no secret, sir. I went there myself with the master more than once." He told me her address.

"Did they get on, Ephialtes and Euterpe?"

"As one usually gets on with one's mistress, sir. They've been together for years, sir. I understand she sees no other customers. It was almost like a second home for the master."

Well, this certainly cast a new light on the shrill wailing coming from the women's quarters, which was making my ears ring! "And what did his wife think of this?"

Achilles shrugged. "She wasn't best pleased, I should imagine, sir. But then, the mistress is rarely pleased, and we can all get used to anything, given enough time, can't we, sir?" He looked down at his feet.

"Achilles, I am going into your old master's private room to have a look around."

Achilles looked at me with interest and some fear.

"I don't think that would be a good idea, sir. This house belongs to the new master now."

"And who is that?"

He shrugged. "Who's going to tell a slave something like that?"

"I'm not going to take anything. But I need to see if there's anything that could tell me who killed him. Come along and watch me if you don't trust me."

Achilles held up his hands in horror. "Oh no! Then I'd be beaten for sure. No sir, you claimed to be a distant relative, like you said to some of those visitors. You ordered me to the kitchen to clean the place from top to bottom. When I returned, you were gone."

"Thank you, Achilles." I refilled his cup, and he shuffled off into the house. "Good luck," I said to his back.

All Athenian houses are built to a common plan, a fact that burglars must bless, and that I was beginning to appreciate myself. I knew which side of the house held the women's quarters—that's where the screeching was coming from—so Ephialtes' private rooms would be on the other side. From the small entrance hall I climbed the stairs and found what I wanted.

Ephialtes' private room contained a desk, a few chairs, a
dining couch, and boxes and boxes of scrolls and papyrus. The
room felt musty, and it was dim, dark even, because the two
windows which both looked out over the courtyard were in
the wrong direction for the sun. I could see the body of Ephialtes below, lying in his shift. Directly opposite across the
courtyard space, at the same level as me, were the women's
quarters. I would have had to be careful not to be seen, except
curtains were drawn and shutters pulled in. I wandered about,
the floorboards squeaking with every tread, which made me
wince. It was a good thing Achilles knew I was here, or the
household would assume it was the restless psyche of their
departed master. There was a wax note tablet on the desk with
some scratchings. Wax tablets are very popular for making
temporary notes; when you're done, or the tablet is full, you
need only warm the wax and smooth it over to start again.
The writing was small and awkward as it usually is on such
things to avoid having to clean too often. At first glance there
was nothing of interest on it. I picked it up anyway to inspect
later. Nobody was going to miss it. There was a small scroll
rack built onto the wall. Almost every slot was full. I pulled
out a few of these and saw they were all books or treatises,
mostly on philosophy or politics. One row held nothing but
plays, most of them by Aeschylus. Ephialtes must have paid
the famous poet to write out extra copies. I opened one and
ran my fingers across it. The papyrus was smooth to my touch
and consistent in color: Egyptian, expensive stuff. The boxes
of papyrus contained notes, drafts of laws, more notes, letters,
all written on the cheaper, standard material. In short, I was
looking at piles of useless rubbish. I could spend the next
month reading through this and still not find anything that
gave me a hint of why he was killed. And if there was a clue, I
probably wouldn't recognize it. I kicked the table in disgust
and then limped down the stairs and out the door, pausing

only to wash my hands and head at the urn set outside to purify myself after being in the presence of the dead.

I was ambushed the next morning. I left home later than usual because I was on my way to see Ephialtes' mistress, still hoping to find out something about his private life, perhaps a motive for his death, and it would not do to arrive too early on the door-step of a woman to whom I had no introduction.

The way led me through a number of side streets, each a tes-tament to Athens' complete lack of city planning. Not that the city officials don't try—there are ordinances—it's simply that the people completely ignore them. Although there are rules against it, the upper stories of the houses almost universally overhang the street. The owners want a simple way to throw out the rub-bish without having it run down their nice whitewashed walls. And besides, people like having the extra bit of space. Walking the smaller streets in Athens feels a bit like passing through a tunnel. I avoided the center for fear of buckets of slop, or worse, poured on me from above—I have been struck more than once—which was why I was surrounded by half shadows and passing the niches between buildings.

It was from the shadows of one such niche that a man stepped before me. His clothing was worn, making me think of a coun-try worker or perhaps a laborer.

"Hey, you Nicolaos?" he asked.

"Yes, what do you want?"

"Stop asking questions. Hear me? Just stop." His voice was harsh.

"What?" I said, my mind stupid for a moment before I real-ized what he was saying. "You want me to stop investigating the murder? How do you know about that?"

"Not your problem. Leave it alone."

"Who are you?" And, because I could not credit this bump-kin as acting on his own, I demanded, "Who do you work for?"

He punched me hard in the diaphragm and I doubled over, the air knocked out of me. I was still recovering when my legs were kicked out from under me and I went down. Another man ran up and I thought he was coming to my aid, but instead he kicked me in the kidneys.

The first man said again, grunting as he kicked me in the gut, "Stop asking questions. Leave it alone." Then the two of them started on me in earnest. There was nothing I could do but cover my head with my arms and hope they didn't maim me, or did they intend to kill me? The beating hurt worse than anything I remembered, and oddly, the anticipation of not knowing where the next blow would fall was worse than the pain. I cried out for help.

"Hey! You! Stop that!"

They both took to their heels. I remained curled in a ball and felt, rather than saw or heard, several pairs of feet run to me.

I was picked up. I opened my eyes, but I was so dizzy I shut them again. I felt myself swaying, and a pair of hands on either side helped to steady me. I opened my eyes again, and the world was spinning about, but slower than before. When it stopped, I found myself looking into the eyes of Archestratus.

Archestratus poured a cup of watered wine and set it down beside me. "Did you get a look at him?"

We stood in his courtyard. One of his slaves who knew something about injuries was checking me for broken bones. I flinched every time he poked me.

I shrugged. "Not good enough. He came at me from the shadows, and I'd walked from bright sun into the shade. My eyes hadn't adjusted. He had a beard, dark hair, average height, bad clothing. That should narrow it down to half the men in Athens."

"Just so. What about the second man?"

"The best I can tell you is he needs to cut his toenails."

"That would describe almost every man in Athens."

"Just so," I said, imitating his way of speech.

The slave ceased his prodding and stood up.

Archestratus said, "Well?"

"There will be many bruises, sir. But as far as my humble skills can say, the bones are whole. He was lucky we came along when we did; if it had continued much longer, I feel sure something would have broken inside. The young man should see a healer to be sure. Sometimes a man might walk away from such a beating but die without warning a day or two later." Such a cheery fellow.

I immediately said, "No thanks, I have my own resource in that area."

Archestratus raised an eyebrow.

"My mother is a midwife."

Archestratus said, "Terrible as your ordeal was, I don't think you need fear pregnancy."

Another slave came running with a chitoniskos in his arms. I took off the soiled one and tipped a bucket of cold water over my body before putting on the fresh.

Archestratus said, "This will be laundered and sent to you."

"I am in your debt."

"It's my pleasure."

I sat and sipped at his wine. He sat down beside me with his own cup and lay back on the dining couch. A slave brought a bowl of figs, olives, and grapes. You can tell a lot about a man from the way he treats his slaves, and Archestratus thanked his boy, who smiled and departed.

"Tell me, how goes your investigation?"

I hesitated.

"If you would like to repay that debt you mentioned, let me help you if I can. Pericles does not hold a monopoly on revering Ephialtes. I beg you recall he was my friend too, and my leader. His murder affects me and many other men."

That was a hard appeal to deny. "So far, all I've done is ask questions."

"Yet even that small effort appears to have offended some-body," Archestratus observed with some justice. "Are you so objec-tionable in your conversation, or do you think perhaps you are asking the right questions?"

"Let us hope the latter."

"How did a young man like you come to be embroiled in such a murky situation?"

I told him of the falling corpse and of meeting Pericles as he came down the path.

"And you saw Pericles descending? How interesting." He took a handful of grapes, popped one into his mouth, and sat back.

I said, "I know what you're thinking, but it doesn't necessarily work. He could have been coming down from either the Acropo-lis or the Rock of the Areopagus. He says it was the Acropolis."

"Do you believe him?"

"I don't believe anyone yet! Is it possible Pericles used the bow, threw it away somewhere I missed, and then walked calmly down the path? Yes, it is."

"So your employer might be the man you're looking for. What a piquant thought. What would you do if the evidence led to Pericles?"

Panic, most probably. I'd wondered the same thing.

"You feel a little bit lost, don't you, young man? I wish I could sympathize with your plight, but I must be honest and welcome you to the twilight world of Athenian politics, where the man who proclaims friendship in the morning is the one who stabs you in the back over wine that evening. If there is one piece of advice I hope you will take from this conversation, it is trust no one who is a player. Trust their motives least of all. Take Xanthippus for example. I imagine he told you he has the purest motives for opposing Ephialtes. I expect the phrase 'for the good of Athens' came into play?"

"It didn't, but the sentiment was there."

"I am surprised. It's a phrase Xanthippus repeats endlessly, as if he were the only judge of benefice. Xanthippus used to be a man of the people himself. But something warped his spirit; perhaps it was the war against the Persians. The war certainly proved he's capable of killing in cold blood, and with the greatest cruelty."

"It did? But Xanthippus was one of the heroes of the war."

"Do you know the story of the Persian commander? No? There was among the Persian force a commander called Artaÿctes. This man stole great treasures from a Hellene sanctuary at Elaeus, in Thrace, far to the north and east of here. Much later Artaÿctes and his son were captured by a force led by Xanthippus. Artaÿctes tried to bribe his way out of trouble; he offered to restore the treasure, to pay the sanctuary one hundred talents—that's six hundred thousand drachmae!—and twice that amount to the Athenians, if only they would release him."

"No wonder Xanthippus is so wealthy," I said. For surely he would have pocketed some of that.

"You think so? Then let me tell you, Xanthippus had Artaÿctes led to the shore, where they nailed him to a plank and raised the plank high so he could see. Then they chained his son to a pole set in the ground. They stoned the son to death, before the eyes of the father, whom they left to die slowly of crucifixion."

The thought of it made me shudder. Had the grumpy, cantankerous old man I'd met truly done such a thing?

Archestratus continued, "You see that Xanthippus is not a man one crosses lightly. He's been living off his hero reputation and his power base. That base is the Areopagus. It's what gives him the ability to influence policy without having to justify himself to the people. Without it, he'd be nothing."

"You aren't exactly free of that ambition yourself, are you?" I challenged him. "Isn't everyone looking for power?"

"They certainly are! But the difference, young Nicolaos, the important difference, is that I seek leadership of the people, not control over them. So too does Pericles, or at least, that's what he says."

"You think he doesn't mean it?"

Archestratus mused, "It must be difficult, having grown up the son of a wealthy, aristocratic family, groomed to lead Athens from his earliest days. His distinguished ancestors merely reached out to take the reins as their birthright, and yet he must *ask* the people for permission to lead, must persuade, where his ancestors had only to command. The temptation to reach out and take as his ancestors once did must be almost overpowering at times. And then, of course, there's the matter of your employment. Odd, wouldn't you say?"

"What?" I said, startled. "What's odd about it?"

"My dear young man! How many friends do you think Pericles has? How many allies? And how many of those do you think are more experienced than you, more skilled in diplomacy, with a better knowledge of the power game? Yet he chose you, a young man of no experience, to carry out this important task. Why? I speculate, of course, but could it be Pericles wants to be seen to be doing something without wanting to risk an unfortunate result?"

I bristled at that. "Archestratus, I was hired to find the truth, and I swear by the Gods that's what I'm going to do."

"My boy! My boy! I never suggested otherwise; you wear your integrity like a cloak. It's not *your* motivation I question."

"What are you saying?" I demanded.

"Simply this: if you reach the point where you can no longer fully trust Pericles, come to me."

I found the fine artwork missing from Ephialtes' home. It was all in the home of his mistress. One of them had good taste. I decided it must be Euterpe of Mantinea, since surely Ephialtes would not have selected that statue of Apollo cavorting with a nymph? The anatomical detail was remarkable.

The house slave sniffed at me when I knocked, as if I were too verminous to cross her threshold. The name Ephialtes got me as far as the public receiving room, where I had been left to linger long enough to have inspected every art piece in the room, and there were a lot of them. I had never before been in the salon of a hetaera. The murals were short on Homeric battle scenes but gratifyingly long on sporting nymphs, satyrs, and priapic Gods. I peered at them closely, my nose almost pressed to the wall.

"Educational, aren't they?"

I turned, startled, and crashed my knee against a nearby table. Trying not to swear, and clutching my knee, I saw framed in the doorway the most beautiful woman I'd ever laid eyes on.

Euterpe had reddish brown hair that flowed down her lovely neck and over a shoulder to her breasts. She was wearing a dress that, even if it were not made of fabric I could see through, would have been considered scandalously immodest. As it was, she had my body's full and immediate attention. The dress was tied in some way so that the material flowed with her skin. My mind ceased functioning since it was not required for the moment.

"Oh! Are you hurt?"

She knelt before me and touched my knee where I'd banged it. Waves of pleasure coursed up me.

Euterpe looked a little higher, and smiled. She stood, swayed to a couch, and reclined, arching her back so that her nipples pressed out against the material and her legs were exposed.

"So, what may I do for you, young man?"

I collapsed back against the nearest couch, unable to speak and agonizingly aware how I must look to her.

Euterpe let me recover. She clapped her hands. A young woman appeared, whom I barely noticed.

"Diotima, dear, would you bring me wine? And a carafe of cool water for our guest."

The young woman reappeared with an exquisite thin pottery watercooler. I took it and thankfully let it rest in my lap, where it did me a lot of good. Euterpe eyed this arrangement while a half smile played on her lips, and her gaze traveled up and down.

"I understand you've come about Ephialtes?" She used her finger to twirl some of the tresses that fell upon her breasts.

I had to consider the possibility that Euterpe was not doing this to me deliberately. She may behave this way with every man. If so, I found it incredible Ephialtes had lived long enough to be felled by the arrow. He should have died from excruciating pleasure long ago. I supposed she was old enough to be my mother, but the evidence before my eyes suggested not, or else Aphrodite had shared some of her secrets.

"Uh, when did you last see him?" I managed to croak.

"Why, yesterday, the day he died. He spent the night here and departed in the morning."

"He did?" I said, surprised.

"You are surprised."

On reflection I should not have been. "Then at least his last night was a memorable one."

Euterpe clapped her hands in delight.

"A compliment! Oh, do keep practicing. One day you'll be enchanting the ladies and receiving invitations to all the best salons."

"I don't ever expect to be able to afford it. Did you know where Ephialtes was going?"

"I didn't ask. It didn't seem important. Ephialtes sometimes left at dawn to conduct business."

"How long had you known him?"

"Many, many years," she said quietly, as much to herself as to me. Then she recollected the admission and said, "Long enough for us to be great friends, as well as the rest. We hetaerae with special friends are more to our men than their own wives, did you know that?"

"I can well believe it."

"Ephialtes was a rising young politician when we first met. He could barely afford me then, but when he had the funds he would visit. As he rose he became wealthier and could visit more often. Eventually we came to the current arrangement: he kept me in the style I required, and I kept him happy, and saw no other man."

"I've never heard of such a thing before, a hetaera with only one client."

"It's unusual, yes, but it served us both well. Ephialtes posed with the people as one of them. He could hardly do that and visit all the expensive hetaerae! The common men can't afford hetaerae and have to make do with those dirty pornoi. So a quiet, permanent mistress seemed the best idea."

"Are you really from Mantinea?"

"Oh yes! I come from a well-born family. I was given as a girl-child to the temple to be priestess there, where the priestesses are required to be virgins but retire early to marry. Well, you can imagine having done my duty as a virgin priestess I was ready for anything! I married a local well-born citizen many times my age, who died on me the following year. Poor old Alexias."

I had an idea how Alexias had expired, and felt nothing but envy for the old man.

"His lands passed to his son by a previous marriage. The son loathed me—I can't imagine why—and by mutual agreement I departed for Athens with his funding. So here I was in Athens with no husband, and the local wives looking down on me. It was the most natural thing in the world to arrange a few soirées. One thing led to another, and here I am."

She paused to consider me.

"Are you married yet, Nicolaos? Betrothed? No? Then some respectable girl still awaits the pleasure of your company."

"I thought a lady such as yourself would have no time for the respectable girls."

"Oh, respectability is nothing of value. But security, dear man, security is the important thing for one such as me. The wives may be boring, drab, disgusting, but they are secure."

Financial security seemed a delicate subject better avoided with Euterpe. I wondered what it cost to maintain this house and where she would find the money now. No doubt there were rich men would pay well to be with her, but she was reduced to looking for custom again where before she had a certain future and a steady income.

"We seem to have moved from investigating the death of your client to my personal love life."

She came to sit on my couch, leaned against me so that I could feel her breasts against my chest, stroked my thigh, and looked into my eyes with sincerity.

"I often mix business with pleasure. In fact, pleasure is my business. Have you a thousand drachmae? No, I thought not, but if you ever have a windfall, you'll be thinking of me, will you not, handsome Nicolaos?"

This was more than any young man could be expected to bear. I made my thanks and escaped the room, followed by her light laughter.

Back out on the street I felt light-headed and had to lean against the wall for support. I took deep breaths. She was right, if I won that home and modest income from Pericles, I might throw it all away for a night with Euterpe.

A young man peered around the corner onto the street as I stood there. When he saw me notice him, he stepped back out of sight. The light was dim so late in the day and I didn't get a clear view, but I thought it was the same man I'd seen watching me outside the house of Xanthippus. Could he be one of the men who'd beaten me? I hadn't had a good look, but I didn't think so. I sidled to the corner with my dagger drawn, and looked about. He was gone, but it worried me. I was sure I was being stalked.

5

I found Pericles in the Stoa Poikile off the north side of the Agora, in the corridor of colonnades. The two painters I'd seen before were both still at work, and both had moved on to color. The battle with the Amazons was coming out with brilliant, vivid hues, but the Fall of Troy was looking a bit monotone to me.

The stoa was already the favored place for men to meet and talk. The porch was wide and cool, far enough away from the stalls that the dust kicked up by the shoppers didn't hang in the air. The columns were stylish, tapered at the top so they appeared to be straight all the way. Some men sat on the steps of the porch, their clothing tucked up, but most stood within the shady area. There was much angry talking, much hand waving. Pericles was talking, but he wasn't making speeches.

He talked to small groups of men, going from one to the next. He harangued other speakers calling for revenge. He took men aside and spoke to them quietly. He coaxed the doubtful, soothed the angry, cheered the fearful. His message was the same every time: don't jump to action, think first, consider the consequences, wait for news.

Although I needed to speak to him myself, I stood back and watched, not daring to interfere while he worked. Pericles was barely controlling a mob ready to lynch someone, a Councilor of the Areopagus for preference, but any rich aristocrat would do.

He played heavily on being Ephialtes' trusted lieutenant, telling the mob what Ephialtes would have wanted. But his own wealthy aristocratic family told against him, and when someone shouted Pericles was son of the murderer, it all threatened to boil over. Who was he to say what the people should do?

"There will be news!" Pericles bellowed in a voice that could command a battle, jumping upon an empty plinth. That shut them all up for a moment.

"There will be news," Pericles said more quietly, forcing the people to listen carefully to his words. "We do not know who killed Ephialtes, but we will. And when we do, people of Athens, if the murderer is Xanthippus, then I, Pericles, son of Xanthippus, will lead the prosecution against him. And if the killer of my friend was any other man, then too I will lead the prosecution. Our democracy favors no man."

As he stepped down from the plinth I heard him whisper sadly, "Not even me."

Pericles and I had made eye contact some time before. Now, with the crowd breaking up under the force of his personality, he strode over to me where I stood in the full glare of the sun, between the stoa and the stalls.

"There *will* be news, won't there, Nicolaos?"

"There will, sir." I had been feeling a trifle warm, now I began to sweat. I hoped I sounded more confident than I felt. I had intended to tell him of my troubles and doubts, but changed my mind having seen his own load. Instead I detailed what I had discovered to date, neglecting to mention most of the events in Euterpe's rooms.

"I have to emphasize, Pericles, if the point Archestratus made of Cimon is good, and it may well be, then you are in mortal danger."

Pericles stroked his beard thoughtfully. "It's almost as useful if Cimon is behind it as the Areopagus."

"But aren't you worried?"

"Hmm? Worried? No, I'm not." Pericles began to stroll about the perimeter of the Agora, I guessed to prevent anyone from eavesdropping. We had the chaos of the markets to our right and the relative calm of the public buildings on our left. Pericles went on, "Athens is no good to anyone if it's a burning wreck, and the murder of a second democrat now would tip us into civil war, no question. You saw the mob yourself. I am not being arrogant, Nicolaos, when I tell you the only thing standing between Athens and self-immolation this moment is me. If Cimon is watching then he knows that. But surely he must be out of Attica by now. If he were found within the territories during his period of exile he could legally be killed on the spot."

"You forget the agent theory."

"Cimon has many friends, that's true."

"Does he have enough to stage a coup?"

"Take Athens by force? It's been done before, of course. Who have you been talking to, or is this your own idea?"

"Lysimachus mentioned it to my father."

"Lysimachus, of course. I think I said when we first met that your father and I have a common friend. That's him. Lysimachus is prone to dramatize any situation. But in this case it would hardly be possible to overestimate the danger."

"So you agree. Cimon has the ability to foment revolution."

Pericles considered. "Yes, I believe he could; the man is an outstanding military commander, even if he is an aristocratic prig. But Nicolaos, you must remember no one has ever successfully held Athens long-term by force. The people will rise against a tyrant they don't like." We had to stand to the side for a moment while a donkey laden with small pots trundled by. From the spicy sweet smell, it had to be fish sauce. As we watched the donkey's backside recede down the road, Pericles continued, "A tyrant is a king in all but name. If the people like him, no force is required. Peisistratus ruled as tyrant for decades, yet he died an old and happy man, because some men make good kings." He paused. "But then of course, others don't."

I said, "Pericles, you should not assume everyone thinks the same as you about the state of Athens. Political assassination happens; we're looking at it right now. I'd prefer not to have to say 'I Told You So,' while pulling an arrow out of your chest, or a dagger from your back. At least arrange for some bodyguards."

"Certainly not! What would the people think? However, Nicolaos, to appease you I will avoid dark alleys, and ignore dubious summonses to meetings in lonely corners of Athens. Now, tell me of my father."

"If you'd asked me two days ago, I'd have sworn he did it. Now, I'm not so sure."

Pericles long face brightened to a smile. "You have evidence in his favor!"

"No, I have too many suspects, all of whom could be killers." Pericles' face fell once more.

I said, "Ephialtes left his mistress Euterpe that morning. She says she doesn't know where he was going, but we have only her word for that. Of course it's ridiculous to think she could have pulled the bow, but she could easily have sent a man."

"A man willing to commit murder just because she asks? Is that realistic?"

"I see you haven't met her."

"It sounds like I should."

"You see, Pericles, only someone who knew Ephialtes was going to be on the Rock of the Areopagus at that time could have killed him. Euterpe could have known the time and place well in advance. She's one of the few."

"But surely she would be the last person in the world to want him dead. Even his wife has a better motive."

"Yes, that annoying little detail gets in the way of my otherwise sound theory. If Euterpe is behind a murder plot, then I need a very good reason for it."

"What about the wife then?"

"I hadn't thought about her."

"Why not?"

"Because I can't get near to question her, because it's unlikely she might have known where he was going, and because she doesn't have Euterpe's outstanding powers of . . . er . . . persuasion to cause a man to act for her."

"But she might have family. What about a male relative avenging insults to her?"

"Pericles, this doesn't sound promising to me."

"But it's possible, isn't it?"

"Yes," I reluctantly conceded. "But why reach for the top of the tree when there is low-hanging fruit to be plucked?"

"Your meaning?"

"Your father. He knew the time and place. He has the motive, he had the opportunity."

Pericles leaned against the wall and shut his eyes. "Could I bring my own father to trial for murder? Should I? Would it count as patricide?"

"You would have to ask a priest that, or a philosopher."

"Perhaps I'll have to ask Archestratus to act for me."

"On that subject, Pericles, what would you do if Archestratus is the killer?"

Pericles opened one eye. "Are you saying he might be?"

"He did have a reason for wanting Ephialtes dead. Look at the way he's behaved since. I think he already has more followers than you do, Pericles. You need to watch out for him. You don't seem to be doing much to build your position."

Pericles laughed and said, "Ah, Nicolaos, Nicolaos! How we do change! It wasn't so long ago, my young friend, a mere four days, that you had to ask me my name. Now you are my political advisor!"

Our meandering had taken us close to where the fishwives were screeching at the tops of their voices, the aroma of warm fish was not enticing, and somewhere close by someone was cooking goat meat in garlic. Pericles screwed up his face and said, "Come, let's go for a walk elsewhere."

He guided me south along the Panathenaic Way, away from the crowd. Archestratus was speaking to some men on the other side of the Agora. As I looked in that direction a face surfaced among the sea of heads, and I thought I glimpsed the young man who had disappeared at Xanthippus' house and then Euterpe's, but I couldn't be sure. I said to Pericles, "Wait here," and pushed my way through the crowd. But either I was wrong, or the man had spotted me yet again and disappeared, easy enough to do in the noisy, busy crowd. In frustration, I elbowed my way back to Pericles, who lifted an eyebrow but chose not to ask me what I'd been doing. We continued our walk.

Where Pericles walked, men followed. A few came up to Pericles to discuss the killing, urging him to take action. Some had other issues.

"Tell us true, Pericles, will you put your hand on the leadership of the people, or won't you? Do it now!"

"Pericles, there isn't enough corn in Athens, and what there is I can't afford. My children starve while farmers send their corn to richer markets. What can be done about it?"

"Pericles, the tax on imports is ruinous."

"Pericles, what do you say to Archestratus leading the people?"

"Pericles, my neighbor is moving the boundary markers between our farms . . ."

"Pericles, they say you saw your father murder Ephialtes, is it true?"

Pericles abruptly stopped, and turned to face the crowd. His piercing, intelligent eyes looked down on them. They fell silent.

"Was Ephialtes a tyrant, that the city should collapse in a heap without him?" Pericles singled out the importer. "You there! The taxes are the same they were yesterday, and the day before, and the day before that. So why do you come to me now? Taxes are a question for the Ecclesia." Pericles pointed to the farmer. "There is a court for grievances such as yours. If the boundary markers are moved, they will be put back, and your neighbor fined. And while you are about it, sell some of your corn to this man whose children hunger. Perhaps we need a law banning export of corn while any Athenian starves." He looked over the people, who now seemed abashed at the way they had thronged about him. "Neither Archestratus nor I can be your leader, because in our city the people lead themselves. Are you sheep without a shepherd, or are you the men of Athens, living in the democracy of your own making? Talk to each other instead of to me."

Pericles turned to go, but hesitated, then said, "And for the future, I will advise the people of Athens as best I can."

After that we walked silently for some time. We came to the spot where Ephialtes had fallen, and gazed awhile at Ephialtes' blood, which still stained some of the small rocks.

I asked, "What will you do, Pericles, if Archestratus is the killer?"

He hesitated. "Do you have anything against Archestratus other than his ambition?"

I had failed to discover where Archestratus had been that morning, but I wasn't going to admit that.

"Not yet."

"I want you to forget about Archestratus. Your job is to find the link to the Areopagus that we both know is there."

"No Pericles, my commission is to find the killer, whoever it might be."

"It's the same thing," he said.

Much against my will, I was forced to recall the words of Archestratus, that Pericles might be using me to deliver the answer he wanted.

"Pericles, why did you choose me for this investigation?"

"You pick a strange time to ask the question. I explained at the time: you impressed me when we found the body, you are intelligent and energetic, and you don't panic in a crisis." He raised an eyebrow and with an arch tone said, "Are you saying you want to resign your commission?"

"No!" I said, suddenly afraid he might be about to take it from me.

"Then trust me on this, Nicolaos, you are wasting time on extraneous issues."

"There are some who might call that interference."

"Let us say instead that I am directing your energies in the most fruitful direction."

I took a deep breath. "I will pay close attention to any hint of a link to the Areopagus, *as well as* other suspects that come my way."

Pericles said nothing, so I repeated my question.

"What would you do if Archestratus is the killer? Would the democratic movement collapse if the killer was a democrat?"

He said slowly, "I think, though I am not sure, we would have to suppress the knowledge."

I gasped.

Pericles went on. "It would be for the good of the city. I cannot imagine Ephialtes wanting to see his greatest triumph crumble for revenge of himself, and which is more important, the democracy of Athens or punishing one murderer? I think we would take the evidence to Archestratus and offer not to prosecute if he exiles himself for the rest of his life."

I felt like my insides had turned to ice. "I seem to recall a man, not long ago, saying he would prosecute whoever had murdered his friend, without fear or favor."

"There is what a man says to a mob to avert a riot, and there is what a man does for the good of Athens."

"And what, then, if the murder was done by Xanthippus?"

"Him I would prosecute."

"Because your father is a conservative, and Archestratus is a democrat?"

"That's right. Welcome to politics, my new advisor."

I had thought Pericles a good man, and now I realized he was a politician like the rest of them. I was deeply disappointed.

We continued the walk up the steep path to the Acropolis. The giant rock with the flat top had been the bastion of Athens since time immemorial. In ages past it had been the palace of the kings, and later, of the tyrants. In modern times the government had slid downhill, and what remained up high were the sacred temples, or at least, what was left after the Persians were finished with them.

When we reached the top we saw fallen, charred pillars, masonry rubble littering almost every part, and burnt timbers that were mostly charcoal. The old temple to Athena Polias, the protector of our city, once sat here. There had been a temple to Athena on this spot since the city was founded, rebuilt again and again. The one the Persians burnt to the ground had been a hundred years old. The replacement temple was a ramshackle collection of planking and daub mud that rose like a pimple out of the ruins, put together so that the city would still have the presence of our founding Goddess. The rough temple was so small it barely fit its statue of Athena. The plan of the original temple was clear upon the ground: the foundations had proven harder to destroy. There had been other buildings here too that suffered the same fate, notably the old palace of the tyrant Peisistratus, which if the exposed floor plan was any indication, must have been sumptuous.

We sat upon a toppled wooden pillar that lay cracked and rotting in the sun. I broke the silence by asking, "Pericles, what were you doing up here, on the day Ephialtes died?"

"I was wondering when you would think to ask that. I was considering my plans for the Acropolis."

"You have a plan?"

He shrugged. "A new temple to Athena, at the very least." He gestured at the small shack. "Look at that pitiful excuse for a temple. Do you think the Goddess is happy to be housed in there? What does it say about us? The people decided, after the Persians were defeated, to leave the ruins as they were, as a reminder of what had happened. But I say Athens has lived long enough in her past. It's time to build for the future." He paused. "That sounded good. I must remember that phrase for a speech."

He shifted his position on the toppled pillar, then shifted again, in a search for comfort. Each time he did, Pericles edged away from me.

We made desultory conversation about the site, where a new temple might be laid, what should be done for gates.

"There was a second temple here," Pericles said.

"There was?"

"Right next to us is where the new temple to Athena Parthenos had been planned. They were halfway through building it when the city was sacked."

I looked but couldn't even see the outline in the ground.

Pericles abandoned his seat and stood. I noticed the seat of his chiton was smudged and decided not to mention it. I stood too and we walked slowly around the site, avoiding the subject of Ephialtes.

We stopped at the northern edge where we could see conelike Mount Lycabettos, reaching up higher even than me, and directly below, the chaotic Agora. The people looked like ants scurrying at my feet.

The Rock of the Areopagus rose to the west, lower and much smaller. The ground between fell sharply away from the Acropolis, ambled along, then rose almost as quickly on the other side. The seats cut into the rock, upon which the Council sat when they met, stood out in strong relief in the reflected sunlight. The sight of the Rock of the Areopagus before us made me think back over the crowd who had accosted Pericles with their questions, and I realized something that bothered me. He had answered all but one. He had not said whether he'd seen Xanthippus murder Ephialtes.

"Pericles, did you know your father was to meet Ephialtes?"

"Yes, he told me of it."

"And the time and place?"

"Not that."

"Did you see them here, that morning?"

"No! And I did not see my father pick up a bow and shoot my friend, and I did not know he was dead until I came across his body upon the path, with you skulking in the shadows, ready to stab me in the back." He was shouting, the first time I ever saw Pericles lose his self-control.

He turned and walked away.

I watched his back and thought to myself, *I have lost the most influential friend I am ever likely to have, and with him goes my chance of rising in Athens.* I would return to my family's business and spend the rest of my days making statues of men more important than me.

I sat and buried my head in my hands. There was no point in moaning, but that didn't stop me from doing so for some time. However, someone would eventually find me there, and I didn't want to be seen wallowing in self-pity, so I rose.

I walked to the southern edge of the rock. The sea was easily visible in the far distance. It was from here that King Aegeus had thrown himself to death when he wrongly believed his son Theseus had died fighting the Minotaur. I looked down. Yes, jumping off here ought to do the job.

To my right stood the temple to Athena Nike: Athena Victorious. It was a small building because that's all the Athenians had been able to manage at the time. It had been built to celebrate the victory over the Persians and give thanks to Athena for our deliverance. The tiny temple stood where the last defenders of Athens had died.

When the Persians invaded they had swept through Thrace and Macedonia and had come down upon us from the north.

Themistocles ordered the evacuation of the city. The women and children were carried on our merchant boats and trireme warships, mostly to the island of Salamis where the government relocated, but also to the city of Troezen. I was among those who went to Salamis, but I was too young to remember it; a baby who had not yet seen his first year. Had the Hellenes lost the coming battle, the Persians would have taken my small body and dashed me against the ground, or run a spear through me.

But not everyone evacuated. A rearguard of volunteers remained. They were joined by the old and infirm, for whom there was no room on the boats, and some priests who refused to leave their holy places. They held their last stand atop the Acropolis. They used stone and wood to block the only path to the top, then sharpened their weapons and waited to die.

And, of course, they did die. But first they sent a lot of Persians to Hades before them. They held the barricades for longer than anyone thought they could. The Persian attacks broke up against their spears. But the tough soldiers and the old men and the priests died one after another. At the end they were overwhelmed when a few Persians climbed the unclimbable rock face on the far side and surprised the defenders in their rear.

I looked at the ground and imagined how much blood had flowed across this bare rock. Those men hadn't given up, merely because what they attempted was impossible. I didn't know if Pericles would continue my commission, but I would see it through to the end anyway.

6

I decided to go to the nearest tavern and get some food. If there were another way I would have taken it, but there is only one path down from the Acropolis. I stepped across Ephialtes' lifeblood once more. It mocked me as I passed.

The Agora had calmed to normal commerce. There were several stalls selling wine, and I paid for a cup at the first I came to. Two stalls down, an old woman was selling bronzeware: mostly urns and pans. I stopped to admire a mirror. They intrigue me; it seems like magic to be able to see myself as others see me. I was relieved to notice the skin where I'd shaved off my beard was starting to darken to the same olive color as the rest of my face. The haggard look that Pericles had commented on was almost gone, my face was filling out now that I was getting normal, regular meals. I saw a bruise on my left cheekbone—I hadn't realized it was so prominent—that I'd received during the beating, there were abrasions on my chin that had scabbed over, and a small cut above my left eyebrow, all of which my mother had treated and were healing well. I noticed my hair was curling, and I made a note to have it cut. As I tilted the mirror a fraction this way and that, to see myself from different angles, the image of the mysterious stranger appeared above my shoulder. He was peering from around the stall behind me and our eyes met via the mirror.

I turned and walked toward him. "Hello? You there!"

The figure broke from cover, snatched a huge fish from the stall next to him, and whacked me across the face. I fell back with a curse. Everyone but the fishmonger laughed at me. The stranger ran to the right.

He was fast and I was groggy but angry. I couldn't keep up with him, but I knew it didn't matter because someone was bound to trip him up.

No one did. They were all enjoying the show too much. I cursed again and ran faster.

He stumbled into a slave carrying pottery jars. The stranger went one way and the slave went the other. The jars flew up and crashed, shattering on the paving stones. The stranger staggered but kept going.

I had to run through this mess, shouting, "Ouch! Ouch!" as my sandals fell upon the jagged shards. He ran along the walkway, which was terminated by stacked jars of olive oil. He pulled a stack over to force his way. Olive oil flowed across the ground to the wails of the farmer selling it. I, of course, skidded and slipped, falling into the remaining stacks, which crashed down upon me. I flung my arms up to protect my head. I would have bruised arms tomorrow.

The stranger was out of the Agora now and disappearing down a narrow street. I had to be wary of being led into an ambush. I'd been beaten once already and had no intention of being caught again. But nor was I going to let this character go, not now that I had him in view.

I took off after him on my shredded, slippery sandals. I cursed, tore them off, and continued in bare feet. He darted down one street and then another, dodging the pedestrians. I stayed with him like a limpet, determined to finish this once and for all. For the first time I had a good look at him. He was obviously still a youth, wearing clothes slightly too big for him so that they covered him down to his knees, and wearing a headdress in the manner of the barbarians.

He turned another corner and was confronted by a hay cart coming from the other direction, which filled the street from side to side. He looked back at me, then around in desperation. He dived through the window of the building beside him. It was an inn.

I heard the clatter of falling cups and shouts of angry men. I ran through the door to see he had skidded along a table. Every man present pointed at the back door. Half of them were covered in wine. I ran into the back room in hot pursuit of this one-man army of destruction.

The innkeeper had been standing over an open barrel of soaking linen. They use urine in those tubs to get the cloth clean. He'd been pushed from behind and gone in headfirst. He'd hauled himself out, spluttering angrily, when I came through the door and knocked him back in again. I yelled, "Sorry!" but didn't stop.

The stranger hit the back wall running and scrambled over it like a frightened hare. I jumped, grabbed the ledge, and hauled myself over. He was away down the street. We were on one of the major thoroughfares now, it was a clear run for both of us and I would chase him all the way to Megara via Eleusis if I had to.

He must have realized he'd be stopped at the city gates because he turned north back into the narrow streets. He was slowing; I was gaining. He made the mistake of turning into an alley that I knew doubled back. I jumped the wall and landed square on top of him. He collapsed beneath my weight and we both fell into a pile of garbage.

"Now I have you, you bastard!" I turned him over and pulled back my fist to knock him senseless. His headdress came off, and I stared, dumbstruck, my fist hovering.

"Get off me, you oaf!" she grunted. "Well, are you going to help me up?"

I hauled her out of the garbage. Now that her headdress had fallen away it was obvious, despite the loose clothing, that she was a young woman.

We sat with our backs to the wall, catching our breath. I didn't think she had the energy to run any further, but I stayed to the exit side in case she decided to try it.

"And what do you think you're doing running around the streets, a respectable woman like you?" This wasn't some dirty street girl—well, at the moment she was, but that obviously wasn't her norm—she spoke with an upper-class accent, and if you removed the grime she would probably look like any well-brought-up maiden. Her hair was tied back, dark and curly, and washed. Her face was feminine, with a thin nose and full lips. Her breasts were full, and clearly outlined through the material. She had rubbed dirt about her face for disguise, but close up I could see her skin was clean at her hairline. Her hands likewise had been rubbed in dirt, but her clipped fingernails and the lack of abrasions or scars gave her away. Whoever this girl was, she wasn't a slave, and her family wasn't poor. She was also in outstanding condition; I'd had to work hard to run her to ground.

"I'm investigating the murder of Ephialtes."

I laughed. "You? All you've been doing is following me about, and you didn't even do that well. I spotted you every time."

"I've done a lot more than that! Someone has to avenge my father. I have no brother to act for me, and you're not showing any signs of doing it." She glared at me. "My name is Diotima. That's Diotima of Mantinea."

I had a terrible sinking feeling. "You're . . . you're . . ."

"The daughter of Ephialtes and Euterpe of Mantinea, and I'm priestess-in-training to the Goddess Artemis the Huntress."

All I could think of to say was, "You don't look like your mother." That was a mistake.

"Well you'd know, wouldn't you? All you did was sit there and ogle her."

"You were there?"

"I handed you that watercooler. See what I mean? You don't remember me at all, do you?"

"No," I admitted. But now that I thought about it I had a vague recollection Euterpe had called someone Diotima.

"Aren't you ashamed of yourself, the way you behaved around her? She's old enough to be your mother."

"I have an idea she likes it that way, and I'm not sure she'd welcome the reminder about her age."

"Aargh. All right then, let's try and pretend that embarrassing incident never happened. Now, tell me everything you've discovered."

"So you can go tearing around Athens again? I don't think so." I had no reason to trust her, and every reason to think she was acting for her mother, who was a suspect.

She sat there thinking about what I'd said.

"You want the glory of finding the killer for yourself, don't you? Do you have some kind of deal with Pericles?"

This was so close to the truth that I blushed. She grinned.

"Then we trade. I can tell you where Archestratus was during the murder."

"Where?" I asked eagerly.

"Oh no! First, you tell me what you got from Xanthippus. I haven't been able to talk to him."

I had no choice but to deal with her. "Xanthippus was at the scene. He lured your father there."

"I know that. Tell me something I don't know. You say 'lured' as if you think he's involved."

"He says he had nothing to do with it. He might be telling the truth, there's no evidence one way or the other, but if he's innocent he's had incredible bad luck to be in the most suspicious spot. It was Xanthippus who sent me to Archestratus. He suggested a leadership fight."

Diotima pursed her lips and thought about that. I could see the calculations flowing through her mind.

"Archestratus is framing Xanthippus?" she asked.

"Or Xanthippus is the murderer and throwing suspicion on

Archestratus, or someone else is framing Xanthippus, or Xan-thippus is plain unlucky."

"Too many options. But no one carries a bow in town. Father's death was planned. And the planner must have known where he was going to be."

"Which brings us back to Xanthippus."

"Or Archestratus, if Father happened to mention the meeting to him. Or maybe any other high up member of the democratic movement. It could be Pericles."

I shook my head. "I saw him immediately after and he had no bow." Then I pulled myself up. "Wait a minute, I didn't agree to tell you that."

Diotima said primly, "You offered me free product. If you regret it now, that's your problem. But I owe you for Xanthip-pus, so yes, on to Archestratus. He was alone, somewhere out on the streets. He doesn't have an alibi."

"How do you know that?"

"Because I haven't been sitting around doing nothing. A respectable priestess has the freedom to walk around town as long as she's decent." I choked on that last comment, but forbore from pointing out that at the moment she looked more like the worst kind of pornê.

"Yes, I know what you're thinking, but a respectable priest-ess is not supposed to be following strange men, and my posi-tion at the temple means everything to me. The last thing I want is to end up like my mother. I had to dress like this when-ever I wanted to know what you were up to, who you were talking to. It was a shock when you came to visit Mother! I thought I was the only one asking questions. I couldn't let you get information I didn't have, so I had to see anyone you talked to."

"How did you find out about Archestratus?"

"I asked his house slave, of course. Slaves see things about people but they never let on, and no one ever notices them.

He told me Archestratus walks every morning. He always takes a different route."

"That's interesting." But what Diotima said reminded me of something else, something I couldn't quite recall. What was it? Slaves see things. So they do, but what other slaves could have seen something? The slaves at the Areopagus hadn't seen a thing, they'd been atop the— I put a stop on that interesting thought before my expression gave me away to Diotima.

"Can Archestratus use a bow?" I changed the subject.

"I don't know. I asked, but it's not the sort of thing his house slaves would know. Maybe if we can find someone he's hunted with we can ask them."

"Where was your mother that morning?"

"At home, of course. You know that."

"I don't know if she was there the whole time."

"I left the house early myself. I have temple duties every morning."

"And you didn't see Euterpe?"

"Does my mother strike you as an early riser?"

"Point taken. But wait! That means you must have seen your father." Diotima nodded.

"So what was said?"

Diotima hesitated. "What do you mean?" She chewed at her thumbnail. "We just talked. I didn't know he was about to be murdered. I didn't know to say, 'Farewell forever, my father.'" She paused. "I think I complained about the milk. It was curdled. I said I'd talk to the cook about it."

"Did you?"

"Forgot completely."

"It all sounds too domestic. I can't imagine what it must have been like in your household, having a father married to another woman. Did he stay often?"

"Maybe two nights in five. But that wasn't the problem. If you ask me, the unlucky one was the wife. I doubt she saw as much of him as we did—I think he was too busy with his politics to pay her any attention—and at least when he came home to us he brought love with him." Diotima muttered to herself, "If anything, he loved us too much."

"Did he talk about his . . . er . . . other family?"

"There weren't any children. I'm his only child. He never said anything about his wife. But then, if you were with your mistress and the daughter you got on her, would you talk about your wife?"

I didn't bother to ask why Ephialtes didn't divorce his wife and marry Euterpe. In Athens that would have been social and political self-destruction. All marriages are arranged, and if a man doesn't like what was arranged for him he can always find his pleasure elsewhere. What made Ephialtes odd was being fond of his alternative. Keeping the girl-child of a hetaera was unheard of; normally such children are taken to Mount Lycabettos and left there to die. Ephialtes' reputation for kindness must have been deserved.

"Did Euterpe or you ever meet—"

"Never. And I don't want to meet her now either. From what Ephialtes said she's as boring as wash water."

"But there's something I need to know."

"What's that?"

I told her of Pericles' theory that Ephialtes' wife might be behind it. "But, of course, I'll never be permitted to speak with her. I don't even know the woman's name."

"Stratonike," she said absently, considering. To my surprise Diotima didn't reject Pericles' idea out of hand. She was as intelligent as I'd thought.

"You want to know whether she might have asked a relative to murder her husband. Risky business. I don't know what sort of a death they'd impose for that, but it wouldn't be pleasant."

"Stoning, I think, beside the old quarry pit. They tie you to a post and anyone can throw rocks. There's a competition to keep the victim alive as long as possible. So you'll do it, talk to his wife?"

"Are you going to tell me everything you discover?"

"No."

"Then if you want to know what I find, you'll have to trade for it. And I can think of a few other lines I might try as well."

"Diotima, you mustn't continue with this delusion you can find Ephialtes' killer. A woman can't move around Athens the way a man can, and the men certainly aren't going to talk to you, priestess or no."

"I have a big advantage over the men though."

"What's that?"

"I'm smarter than most of them. Come talk to me when you need more help, Nicolaos, son of Sophroniscus."

I stood to go.

"Wait!" she said, raising her hand in alarm. She touched my arm, as a supplicant might, and looked up at me with big brown eyes. "You won't tell anyone, will you, that I was following you dressed as a man? No one must find out, or I'd lose my position at the temple."

She'd just given me the perfect hold over her. I thought of several nasty things I could say, but I swallowed all of them. She seemed genuinely frightened.

"I'll tell no one if I can avoid it." I walked briskly away from Diotima. I had no intention of seeing her again. I'd set her the job with Ephialtes' wife only to get her out of my hair. As soon as I was out of sight, I began to run.

I ran all the way to the Rock of the Areopagus. Thank the Gods, they were still there, the same two slaves who'd been cleaning the day Ephialtes died. Their faces were weathered, old, and lined, their hands gnarled where they gripped their brooms. I suppose this light cleaning was the only job they could do.

I grabbed the first slave and started dragging him along.

"Quick, show me where you sat while you were waiting for Xanthippus to finish."

They took me down and up, to the edge of the Acropolis, not quite directly across from the point where it is closest to the Areopagus. I could see everything: the Agora in all its chaos, the sturdy walls surrounding the city, and close by the top of the Areopagus.

"Men, I don't give a curse about the legal process. I promise I won't tell anyone where I got the information. Now, you are going to tell me everyone you saw while you sat here this morning."

One of the slaves crossed his arms and pouted. "Why should we? There's nothing for us but trouble."

I said, with a quiet but firm voice, "Because if you don't, I will report that you witnessed the murder."

The men turned visibly red, even beneath their weathered skin. "That's a lie!"

"I know it is, but that won't help you after they've finished torturing you, will it? Come now, if you tell me who you saw, I promise on the shades of my ancestors to hide you from the law. Whatever you tell me, I'll confirm some other way before I reveal it."

The slave was glum, but I had left him no choice. "There was Xanthippus first. He told us to clear off. We never saw Ephialtes. He must have come up the path as we were walking to the Acropolis. Some time later there was Pericles. He walked up here to the Acropolis, went behind us, and we didn't see him again. Then Xanthippus left the Areopagus. We saw him leave, but figured we'd stay here until he found us. No point in lining up for work early, is there? That was all we saw until you came along."

"That's it?" I asked, disappointed.

"Oh, and there was a city guard loitering about."

Dear Gods, a guard! How could I have been so slow? In Athens, it is illegal for any citizen to lay hands on another for any reason whatsoever. This makes arresting citizen-criminals something of a problem. How do you arrest someone you're not allowed to touch? So to get around this silly rule, the city owns a force of three hundred Scythians—northern barbarians—who keep the peace, do crowd control, and arrest Athenians when an archon orders it.

Everything about the Scythians made one of them perfect for this crime. Their barracks lies at the side of the Areopagus, where they can defend the Council in an emergency, and they're known for their favorite weapon: the bow.

I rushed to the barracks immediately. Pythax, the chief of the Scythians, was there watching some young men exercise with swords: a tough, leathery, scarred man with bulging muscles, who looked as if he would as soon squash me as talk to me. This was a man who regularly intimidated archons.

He looked me up and down. "We don't take piss-poor little mama's boys in this outfit. So if you've run away from home, go find some other place to cry," he greeted me.

"You misunderstand, sir! I'm on an errand to ask you something, from Xanthippus, sir." I decided immediately, if I didn't embellish my authority I was going to be kicked out.

"Xanthippus, eh? Well, ask away then."

"Who of the Scythians were here four mornings ago?"

His eyes narrowed. "That would be when Ephialtes bought it. Is that what you mean?"

I nodded.

"No one."

"*No one* was here?" I was amazed.

"Every Scythian not on duty in the city was with me on a field exercise. We ran to Piraeus and back, in full armor."

I winced. That would have hurt.

"Could one of the duty Scythians have returned to barracks?"

"Not unless he was injured, and there were no injuries that morning. What's your problem, boy?"

"Someone reported seeing a man looking like a guard in the area that morning."

"On his own? Then he wasn't one of ours. We patrol in pairs."

How hard would it be to impersonate a Scythian? Not that hard, as long as you avoided speaking. The accent is unmistakable. The Scythians mostly wore light leather armor and a rather odd, noticeable peaked leather cap. Anyone wearing the leather jerkin and cap, and carrying an unstrung bow, would go unnoticed in Athens.

"Oh, and by the way, little boy?"

"Yes, sir?"

"It's funny Xanthippus should have sent you to ask that, because he was the one who ordered us away on the exercise. His memory must be slipping. I'll mention it next time I see him."

I felt the blood rush to my face, but managed to croak out, "Yes, sir," before disappearing.

It was only after I was well away that I realized I'd been calling a man "sir" who was technically a slave.

I walked slowly up the path to the Acropolis and took a seat among the ruins. Perhaps Athena would grant me wisdom, here where her temple had once stood.

Xanthippus had been on the spot, and his actions were suspicious, but he couldn't use a bow. The Scythians could use a bow, but they hadn't been there. Pericles might be able to use a bow, but I myself had seen him immediately after the death, and he hadn't been carrying one. Then there was the mysterious man who looked like a guard but wasn't. Who was he, and where did he go?

Yes, indeed, where did that man go? I knew he hadn't returned down the path to the Agora, because Pericles and I blocked the way. But a man pretending to be a Scythian could hide in their empty barracks. He would stay there until the excitement of discovering the body was over, and then walk back into the city with no questions asked. The safe thing would be to change clothes and return as a normal citizen. A citizen carrying a bow and leather armor? Definitely not. Therefore the armor and bow were still in the barracks, where no one would notice an extra set.

I thanked Athena for her wisdom. "When Pericles rebuilds your temple, I'll make sure it's an especially nice one," I promised.

"You again?" Pythax growled.

"Do your men use their own armor and weapons?"

"Armor is issued by the city. Some men prefer their own weapons, but the city provides a serviceable sword and bow for the men who can't afford their own. Every man looks after his own kit until he's freed or dies. If he returns the kit in anything less than perfect condition, the reason for return had better be death."

"Any objections to me looking through your armory?"

"Be my guest, little boy."

The armory was a dank room that smelt of sweaty leather. I sifted through the pieces, and quickly found what I wanted. Underneath the first layer was a leather jerkin, recently oiled. I searched carefully but could find no clue as to the owner.

There were stacks of short, composite reflex bows, made of reinforced horn. They looked identical. I shoved them aside. At the back, out of sight, was one longer than the rest. I pulled it out to study it closely. On this one the reinforcement of the horn was quite different. It was heavier, but the grip was noticeably more comfortable. They all had the same maker's mark at the base, even this odd man out.

I went back to Pythax. "Who supplies your bows?"

The workshop of Brasidas the bowyer was at the rear of his home, in the smithy and armorers' section of the city. Hellenes generally avoid bows, so Brasidas was outnumbered by forges, many to one. I found him bent over his workbench; a middle-aged man of middle height, wearing an exomis that was covered in sawdust and flecks of wood, we stood exactly eye to eye. We also shared the same dark hair, though his was straight and hung long. He had large hands and remarkably broad shoulders. His right arm was noticeably better muscled than his left. I held out the bow to Brasidas and asked, "Did you make this?"

He glanced at it and nodded. "It's my work. Is something wrong with it?"

"No, if what I suspect is true, then it works very well indeed. I found it in the armory of the Scythians."

"Impossible," he said shortly.

"Why?"

"For two reasons. The first is, the Scythians don't like that kind of bow."

"But it looks much the same, only a bit bigger," I commented.

"Only to someone ignorant of bows." He snorted. "Here, I'll show you."

Brasidas took out a bow from below his workbench. It was unstrung and curved forward from the grip.

"This is a bow I made for the Scythians. Scythians like their bows short and powerful. No good for any distance farther than you can spit, but what you hit with this bow will go down and stay down. They don't aim well, but the Scythians don't care because they're quick to draw and so can loose three arrows to your two. In a close fight that gives a man an edge." He took the bow I was holding. "Now this is a marksman's bow," he said lovingly. "The stave is longer, so the arrow doesn't pack as much punch, but it will travel farther with accuracy. It's longer and harder to draw, but you don't care, because this isn't a fighting arm. This is a hunter's weapon."

"I'm convinced! But you said there were two reasons this bow couldn't be Scythian. What was the second?"

"I recognize that bow. I sold it to a man from Tanagra not long ago."

I grinned like a madman. This was wonderful news, exactly what I'd been hoping for. I mentally vowed to sacrifice to Athena, Zeus, and Apollo in thanks.

"What was his name?" I held my breath.

Brasidas shrugged. "He didn't say."

"You mean you don't know?"

"Look, when I sell a weapon, should I care who buys it?"

"Do you know where I can find him?"

"Sorry."

I canceled the sacrifices. "If you don't know his name then how do you know he was from Tanagra?"

"He tried to pay me with their coins, and he sounded like he was from there. But I only take good old Athenian owls. That's money you can trust. We argued about it, but he gave in."

Every city mints its own coins, and few traders willingly take the risk of accepting the coins of a foreign city; the chances of being shortchanged are too great. A visitor anywhere would normally be expected to exchange his coins for the local currency with a money changer at the Agora. The sole exception to this rule are the coins of Athens, which are all stamped with the picture of an owl, the sacred bird of Athena. Athenian "owls" are the only currency accepted across all of Hellas, because *everyone* trades with Athens.

"Can you at least describe him?"

"I'll bet his friends call him Scarface. Looks like he's seen a lot of sun. I'll tell you one thing: the man knew his business. He insisted on testing every hunting bow I had, and the way he handled them, I could tell he knew what he was doing. I gave him five test shots with each one, and then he selected the best in my shop." Brasidas waved the bow he held. "This one."

"Did he say anything? Anything outside of bows and archery, I mean."

"He was the close-mouthed sort."

He would be. I sighed.

Brasidas considered me through suspicious eyes and said, "Why are you asking all these questions, and how did you get this bow?"

I debated how much to tell him, then realized it wouldn't be long before he put the pieces together himself.

"Listen, this is very important. That bow you're holding was the one used to kill Ephialtes. You want to think about that. Do you want people to know you're the man who made the weapon that killed him?"

His knuckles whitened on the stave. "The bow didn't kill him, the guy holding it did. No one's got any cause to blame me. And if that was a threat you just made then you can get out of my shop right now."

"Relax! I'm only trying to point out it's in your interest to help me find this man." I picked up a potsherd and scratched my name into it, then dropped it on his workbench. "Come see me if you think of anything. I'm willing to pay a reward if you can tell me where to find him."

That got his attention. "How big a reward?"

"Big enough." I was being a trifle free with Pericles' money.

Brasidas guffawed. "You're paying, are you?" He looked me up and down, and I knew what he was thinking. I looked a mess after the chase through the Agora after Diotima, and my chitoniskos was patched and stained.

"Pericles is paying."

Brasidas threw the bow back at me and said, "Oh, I get it! You're going to take a cut for *my* information. Well, I might just go straight to him, and what will Pericles pay if I bring in the man himself?"

That alarmed me. "Brasidas, do yourself a favor and tell me if you know anything."

Brasidas stood mute, and folded his arms.

"This is dangerous. You'd better be careful, or you could find yourself dead."

"You're not going to hurt my father!"

I turned, surprised. The lad standing in the doorway behind me was three or four years younger than me.

"That's not what I said."

"Yes it is. I heard you."

My head was aching, I was sure Brasidas knew more than he'd told me, I was exasperated by his attitude, and I was disappointed and frustrated at having victory held out before me and then snatched away.

I pushed past the boy and walked down the street.

7

The messenger boy from Pericles had asked me to come. That pleased me because we had last parted on poor terms. I wanted to mend fences with Pericles, and delivering important progress would smooth my way.

Pericles was busy with another visitor so a slave left me to wait in the courtyard. Paths formed a cross, splitting the courtyard into four quadrants, each grassed and with vines running about the entire space. The fragrance of the vines was sweet and so intense that even I, who normally ignored such things, was drawn to walk over and sniff. The mandatory statue of Zeus Herkeios was placed in the most distant corner, with flowers growing about it and a step placed in front for the daily sacrifice. There were a number of couches placed to form a large circle, and beside each couch was a table carved from marble. The grass was patchy; it was easy to see the spots where men commonly placed their feet when walking from one couch to another. This was a working courtyard for a man who regularly held large symposiums.

What the slave could not have anticipated was the raised voices, and the way the sound floated down to me from Pericles' study.

"You *will* go to the estates," Xanthippus' voice roared.

I looked up to the second floor, startled, to see two heads

framed within the window, facing each other, as if they were putting on a show for me.

"With the greatest respect, Father, I must say again that I decline. There are too many issues needing my personal attention here in town. I'm sure you understand that. Perhaps after this crisis has died down—"

"You must leave Athens, for your own sake, at least for a few months. The family estates need more attention than we've given them. This is the perfect time for you to learn the management of our property. I am sending you as your father, I expect you to obey as my son."

It was going to be embarrassing if they looked down and saw me. I moved to stand directly underneath the window, where I wouldn't be noticed if they glanced out. Besides, this was interesting and I didn't want them to stop.

"I'm not a child any longer, Father."

"In law you are."

"I owe you all the loyalty and obedience a son owes a father, but I will not run away from Athens like a coward. We both know this has nothing to do with managing the family wealth."

"You're right, it doesn't. I've done my best to protect you from your actions, but I can't keep it up much longer."

There was a lull in the conversation. I edged closer to the window.

"Son, I made a mistake when first I walked in here. I should have asked you to go, not told you outright. If you wish, I will apologize. But the fact remains it's in your best interests to leave Athens for a while."

"I disagree." Pericles' tone could have frozen water. "My interests lie right here. May I say, Father, how disappointed I am that we cannot seem to have any conversation these days without it turning into an argument."

"I wonder whose fault that might be?"

"Both of us, I should imagine. I remember when we could

discuss almost any subject, and even if we disagreed, it never became an issue for personal antagonism. I wonder what changed?"

"You became obsessed with this democratic movement."

"I think rather had you been born at the same time as me you would have become a democrat yourself. You were a reformer as a young man. You were a champion of the people before the time of Themistocles. Where did it all go wrong?"

"It didn't *go wrong,* young man. I still champion the best interests of the people. What I realize is the people cannot be trusted to champion themselves. Under this democracy of yours Athens will make mediocre decisions at best, and sometimes very bad ones."

"Are you sure, Father, that that is not the opinion of a man accustomed to wielding power?"

"No, it is reality. When you are fighting in the ranks of the army, do you want the smartest, most experienced man to command, or an incompetent, the least experienced?"

"The answer is obvious."

"Just so, it is obvious. Yet as soon as we start to talk about the leadership of our city, a subject of infinitely greater importance than any one battle, suddenly the idea of choosing the best man for the job disappears."

Their voices had calmed, and were quieter. I edged my way up the stairs to a position where I could hear more clearly. Pericles was speaking.

"The Ecclesia can be persuaded by the wisdom of our best men. Men like you, Father. Trust them to respond to good advice."

"Pericles, I am going to say something I don't think I have ever said to you before: you are a fine man. I'm proud of you, son. But intelligence makes conservatives of us all in the end. Young men should have a social conscience. Old men must work with reality."

"If you were proud of me you'd at least consider my words before you reject them."

"I could wish you were prouder of me, and listen to the wisdom of my old age."

"I will not leave Athens."

"If you stay here, you will die."

"If I leave, I might as well be dead."

The door flung open without warning and Xanthippus stamped down, pushing me out of the way.

"You again!" he shouted. Then he stopped and turned to me. His face twitched into a bleak smile. "I think my son is looking for you." Xanthippus continued on his way in a cloud of anger.

Pericles was not in a good mood.

"You again!" he shouted, sounding remarkably like his father. "What in Hades is this?" He snatched something from his desk and waved it in the air.

"It looks like a bill," I said.

"And this?" He picked up another, which lay beside a rotting fish. The fish was propped up so that one eye stared at me accusingly.

"Er—another bill?"

"You *trashed* the Agora? What were you thinking?"

"Actually, the man I was chasing was doing the trashing," I muttered. I didn't think I'd be doing Diotima any favors if I told Pericles a priestess was stalking the streets, destroying everything in her path.

I shifted uncomfortably where I stood. My mother Phaenarete had bandaged my feet, both of which were cut to shreds. I had a black eye where the fish had hit me. I could barely move my left arm; the right was black and blue but at least I could use it. My head ached. This was not a good time for Pericles to be offering a critique of my work.

"He had information to do with the murder," I said.

"And you know this how?"

"I caught him. Archestratus has no alibi for the time of the murder."

"That's the information I get for the price of one large fish, twenty-four jars of figs, and a small farm's worth of olive oil?"

I didn't think this would be a good time to mention the wine and the well-washed innkeeper, so I said meekly, "Yes, sir."

"If you catch this killer, *when* you catch him, I will be deducting the cost of this mess from your reward."

"I have other important information." I gave Pericles the story of the bowman and the bowyer. Pericles' reaction to this news was predictable. "It's the Areopagus, of course. They must have hired this man from Tanagra."

Pericles' determination to implicate the Areopagus was starting to irritate me. Of course it would suit him politically for it to be true. But we hadn't a scintilla of evidence to prove it.

"Find this man, Nicolaos. We must be able to prove who he's working for."

"I will. There are some things I need to know, Pericles, about politics."

"Ask."

"Ephialtes was killed by a man from the city of Tanagra. I think that very likely. But what does a man of Tanagra want with an Athenian populist politician? Could this be a political killing?"

"You are asking whether Tanagra has a reason for wanting Ephialtes dead; could the assassin have been sent by his city?"

"Precisely."

Pericles considered for a moment. "Tanagra is a minor city, of no political power. I cannot imagine the Tanagrans doing anything that might bring the wrath of Athens upon them. No, the Tanagrans' best strategy is to keep their heads down and hope no one notices them."

"Then the odds are the Tanagran is a hired assassin. His city had nothing to do with it, and I am searching for his employer."

"You'll have to find the assassin first."

"I doubt I can come to his master any other way."

"You overheard my argument with Xanthippus?"

"Yes."

"My father has become my enemy, Nicolaos, because of who-ever is behind this plot. When you find him, you will come to me immediately. Tell no one else first."

"So that you can hide the truth, Pericles, if it doesn't suit you?" Archestratus had invited me to see him should I ever lose trust in Pericles. At the time I'd been sure it would never hap-pen. Now I dismayed myself by contemplating the possibility.

"So I can extract revenge, regardless of whether my revenge must remain hidden for the good of the city."

I turned to go, but Pericles stopped me.

"And Nicolaos?"

"Yes?"

"I hope you like fish."

He picked up the rotting fish and threw it at me.

I started on my way home, pondering the relationship between Xanthippus and Pericles, and couldn't help comparing it to mine with Sophroniscus. Did all fathers object to their sons' careers, and if so, why? Was it some sort of initiation ceremony they gave you after your firstborn? It seemed no matter how much wealth, power, and privilege a family had, you still got the same argument.

I must have been deep in thought, because two Scythians appeared so quickly they might have been shades rising up from the earth at my feet, one on each side of me. There were beads of sweat and street grime on their faces and they were panting slightly. That and the dank, warm aroma wafting from beneath their leather jerkins told me they'd been running about for some time. I recognized them as having been in the exercise yard when I visited Pythax.

I grinned and greeted them. "Hello! Has Pythax been mak-ing you run again?"

Without a word they grabbed an arm each, picked me up so that my feet barely touched the ground, and marched me down the street. Men talking to one another stopped and stared as we passed.

I said, "Hey, what is this?"

They didn't answer.

"You know it's illegal for a citizen to lay hands on another!"

One of them spoke at last. "We're not citizens, we're slaves."

That shut me up. So they were, and this was precisely why we had the Scythians: to manhandle citizens when they needed it.

I thought of fighting back, but decided I didn't need my fellow citizens to see me being beaten by slaves. So I acquiesced to the ride and let them guide me where they would.

We wound our way through the narrow streets that make up most of Athens. Citizens were going about their business along the sides, we three abreast filled a lot of the width, and my captors were in a hurry, so they marched me straight down the center where no one walks, because that's where the sewage always pools. Streets in Athens are raised at the edge and low in the middle, so when people throw their buckets of slop out the window it flows away from their walls. If they're lucky, the street is on a slope and the sewage flows away; if they're not lucky, it doesn't. Either way, my feet were dragged through the muck; all manner of vile objects became lodged between my sandals and the soles of my feet. Some of the things were squishy. I had to hop on one foot so I could shake the other loose of rubbish, then swap feet and do the same again.

The guards stopped at a small crowd of people at a crossroad. A herm, a bust of the God Hermes, rose above the crowd, upon a tall, narrow plinth, looking down upon the confusion. Besides being Messenger of the Gods, Hermes is also, logically enough, protector of travelers; every cross street in Athens has a herm as a charm for passersby. My guards demanded the crowd part to let us through. Men shuffled back to reveal what all the fuss was about.

Unfortunately the herm at this cross street had failed Brasidas. He lay faceup in the dirt. His throat had been slit from side to side. I'd seen pigs slaughtered, and this looked just the same. His eyes were dull but wide open in horror, telling me he'd known what was happening to him. The blood had spurted, but a pool had encircled his head and then trickled to the center to mix with the garbage lying there. I saw some paw prints that suggested a couple of dogs had licked at it.

Pythax crouched over the body. I shook my arms free, and now the guards let me go but stayed at my back. I walked over, careful to avoid the blood, until my shadow crossed Pythax. He looked up and grunted. "Oh, it's you. You took your time getting here." He sniffed twice then screwed up his nose. "Zeus, your feet stink! Don't you ever wash?" I tried to think of something witty to say, but failed, unable to take my eyes off the corpse. Brasidas was staring straight up at me.

"Hey!" My gaze shifted from Brasidas to Pythax. He looked into my eyes. "Is this your doing, little boy?"

I had a horrible feeling it was, but not in the way Pythax meant.

"I had nothing to do with it, Pythax."

He grunted again and rose, wiping his hands on his tunic.

"I found this lying beside him." Pythax held out a potsherd.

I recognized it immediately and nodded. "Yes. I scratched in my name myself. I left it with Brasidas to come to me if he remembered anything else. I guess he was carrying it."

"Sure. Or else you didn't notice dropping it when you were here cutting his throat."

There were splashes of blood high on the wall next to us. I noticed one drop had landed on the nose of the herm.

"He was killed standing up," I said.

Pythax said, "Way I see it, whoever did him came up behind,

probably covered Brasidas' mouth and pulled his head back, and then killed the poor bastard with one stroke. Real neat. I like his work."

"Well, that proves it couldn't have been me then, doesn't it?"

Pythax glared at me but said nothing.

There may have been more clues on the road, but if so they'd been trodden in by the feet of the crowd. A few men had stood in the blood, which was still gooey enough that they had tracked bloody footprints all over the place. Any hope of finding the killer's prints was gone.

Pythax asked, "Could he have been going to see you?"

I thought about it, then shook my head. "I don't think so. My father's house isn't in this direction if he was traveling from his own home."

"So what do you reckon he was doing, little boy?"

I had a feeling I knew. He was heading in the right direction for Pericles' house. I cursed silently. Brasidas must have found the man from Tanagra. And the man from Tanagra had found him.

"I couldn't say, Pythax."

"What I don't like about this, little boy, is I tell you where to find Brasidas. You go straight there and threaten to kill him, and the next day he's dead. It don't look real good, does it?"

"That's a lie! Who says I threatened him?" I demanded.

"He does." Pythax pointed, and for the first time I noticed the son of Brasidas, standing apart, head bowed, with a guard beside him.

"He says his dad left before dawn, and didn't say where he was going. When he failed to return to meet customers, the son went looking for him, and found him here. He called the guard."

At mention of this, the son looked up, and his dark, angry eyes stared straight into mine.

"Murderer! Murderer!" He started toward me but the guard held him. Every eye present turned to me. I knew the crowd was waiting to see what I would do.

I stood my ground and said quietly, "The best I can say is I didn't kill him, Pythax. Are you going to arrest me?"

"I can't do that. It's for the man's relatives to charge you, if they think they can prove it."

"The son?"

"He's not of age. They say there's a brother."

"So I'm free to go."

"All the way to Hades if you like."

I made to go but Pythax called to me. "Hey!"

"Yes?"

"Watch your back, little boy."

"I'll do that."

Several men stood in my way as I tried to leave, silent but plainly sympathetic to the boy now fatherless. I wasn't willing to give them the satisfaction of turning away, so I pushed my way through. It was reckless, but I calculated that with the city guard watching, they wouldn't make anything more of it. Luckily for me, they didn't, but once around the corner I departed at a trot.

I didn't stop moving until I reached my door, berating myself every step of the way. How could I have been so stupid as to let Brasidas go searching without me? The moment he reacted to the mention of a reward, I *knew* he had more than he'd told; why didn't I force him to tell me? I shouldn't have lost my temper. I should have assured him he could have all the reward. I should have waited outside and followed to see where he went. I should have done any number of things other than what I did do. For the first time, I wondered if I had the skills to do this, and contemplated failure.

A messenger boy was waiting for me in the anteroom.

"Are you Nicolaos, son of Sophroniscus?"

"Yes, that's me, what do you want?"

"My mistress sends this." He handed me a note, and disappeared. The note said, "Come to the house of Euterpe. News."

Now what could she want? Then I noticed the name at the bottom, and I worried.

I was back at the home of Euterpe once more, but this time I gave the house slave the name of her daughter Diotima. In any decent household I would have been thrown out for daring to ask after a maiden. In this highly unusual home, the slave raised his eyebrow and led me to the courtyard, where I was left standing. I gathered the public room I'd been taken to last time was reserved for Euterpe's clients.

I admired the frescoes on the surrounding walls, which were predictable and rather interesting, while wondering whether Diotima would come with a chaperone, and if so who in this house could possibly be appropriate for the job. Euterpe as a chaperone would be like throwing oil on a fire.

Euterpe must have seen me through one of the upper-story windows, for she came gliding down the staircase wrapped in something tight.

"Have you come by your fortune then?" She smiled at me.

"Not yet, Euterpe. It's only been a few days." I said, backing away.

She laughed, and stepped closer. I was starting to feel distinctly uncomfortable, and absolutely determined Diotima would not see me with Euterpe as I'd been last time.

"How then can I serve the young man this time?" she breathed.

"Actually, with your permission of course, I would like to speak with Diotima," I said. "About the murder of Ephialtes, that is."

Euterpe's face froze for a moment, then transformed into a mask of incredulity. "You've come to see my *daughter*?"

"Does that surprise you?" a voice within the rooms said. Diotima emerged, looking more smug than I thought good for either of our futures with her mother.

Euterpe composed herself and asked sweetly, "And what does Diotima have to do with Ephialtes' death?"

"You don't know?" I was surprised. I'd thought Diotima was acting on her mother's instructions, and the fact that she wasn't was very interesting.

"Know what?" Euterpe asked suspiciously, looking at Diotima.

"I'm investigating his murder," Diotima announced.

Euterpe turned to me and accused, "You've dragged her into this. How dare you!"

Diotima was defiant. "I dragged myself into it long before this idiot came by to gawk at you."

"Idiot, is he?"

"I'm judging by results."

Euterpe looked at Diotima, then to me, and back to Diotima with a calculating look in her eye.

"Ah well, run along and play, children." She swept out of the courtyard in an indignant cloud of expensive perfume.

"Come with me," Diotima said shortly, and led me to a set of small rooms at the back of the house. Unlike everything else I had seen, these were practical and furnished in a simple style, with not a rampant satyr or orgasmic nymph to be seen. I deduced I had come to Diotima's private rooms. She sat me opposite her on couches.

"We can't be heard here. There are no spy holes or listening tubes," she said as a matter of fact.

"You mean there are elsewhere?"

"In all the public rooms."

I decided I was not going to inquire into that any more closely. "Why am I here?"

"I have information."

"Good, tell me."

"Oh no! First, what do I get in return?"

"You cannot be serious. Do you want the murderer of your father caught, or don't you?"

"Are you going to tell me everything you know?"

"No."

"Then you'd better have something to trade."

"All right, we take turns, like last time."

"Go ahead."

"My mother taught me better than that. Ladies first."

"*My* mother taught *me* better than that. Don't give a man anything until he's paid."

"Can't we even start a conversation without arguing? Who went first last time?"

"I did."

"I thought you might say that. But I remember the conversation quite well."

She said in disgust, "Then why did you ask? Oh, very well then. You recall Stratonike is the name of Ephialtes' wife?"

"Yes."

"She's insane."

"You mean that, or is this a figure of speech?"

"She is a genuine cursed-by-the-Gods lunatic."

I thought for a moment. "And that wailing I heard at the wake?"

"I imagine it was genuine, though she might not even be aware her husband is dead. I don't know. She spends her days hiding in fear of her life, because she's convinced Ephialtes is trying to kill her."

"And he's failed to do it in twenty or so years?"

"Yes, I know. But the bad part is, she's been trying to kill him in deluded self-defense for years."

Diotima slumped against the whitewashed wall. "I know now why he refused ever to speak of her. Poor Father. I discovered this from her nurses. They have to keep knives away from her, or she uses them to attack him as soon as he appears, and if she doesn't have a knife, she throws pots."

"Is she sane enough to arrange for his death some other way?" I thought to myself, an arrow is a sharp implement too.

Diotima shrugged. "I asked the nurses the same question.

They said she does have periods of apparent lucidity when she can be surprisingly cunning, but they don't recall her talking to anyone outside the home."

I gave that some thought. "What about Achilles?"

"I don't think he did it. He's been dead since the Trojan War."

"Not that one." I told her of the slave and his heels. "You said Stratonike has seen no one outside the home, but he's inside, and he might bear a terrible grudge. Stratonike might have used him as a middleman."

"Could he have pulled the bow himself?"

"I doubt it, he looks weak. But he has the freedom to walk the city. He could have paid an assassin."

"I will find out what I can about the slave Achilles. Now it's your turn."

I hadn't expected Diotima to turn up anything with Ephialtes' family. I wasn't sure she had, at that, but what she'd told me was worth something. "I have a very important piece of information worth more than you've given me. You can have it in return for one more question answered."

Diotima frowned and she spoke quickly. "Nicolaos, son of Sophroniscus, if you are not willing to share information with me, then why should I tell you anything?"

"I am sharing, a great deal. That's why I want more in return. Priestess, believe me, you want to hear my questions. Unfortunately I think you'll get more from this than me, but I need the answers."

"Ask away then, but this had better be very good indeed, or I'll tell you nothing else."

"Tanagra."

"That's a noun. Even if you put a question mark at the end it still wouldn't be a question."

"Does the name mean nothing to you?"

"Tanagra is a city in Boeotia. Beyond that it means nothing. I've never been there."

"Did Ephialtes meet anyone from Tanagra?"

"No."

"Did he correspond with anyone there?"

"Not that I know of."

"Has your mother had any visitors from Tanagra? Does she know anyone there?"

"How should I know? She could have slept with half their statesmen in her younger days. I don't keep records."

"You have earned one question."

"I answered four."

"If you ask me the right one I'll give you much more than you gave me."

Diotima thought carefully. "If this is a trick I'll ask my Goddess to put a curse upon your hunt. Very well, why are you asking me about Tanagra?"

"Ephialtes was shot by a man from Tanagra."

Diotima leaned forward, her brown eyes wide. "Tell me how you know this."

In more detail than I had for Pericles, I repeated the story of the Scythian who wasn't a Scythian and the bow in the barracks. "So I went straight to the bowyer, a man you won't have heard of called Brasidas."

"I certainly have. He made my bow."

That stopped me in total amazement.

"Say that again?"

"He made my bow." She paused. "Your mouth is hanging open like some dead fish. I realize there's a close match in personality, but you really shouldn't advertise it."

"Show me your bow," I ordered.

"Not until you tell me why."

"I'll tell you that *after* I've seen your bow."

"Wait," she said in a frosty tone. Diotima rummaged through a small storeroom next to the room we were in. She started pulling out things and leaving them in the corridor.

Pretty soon there was enough junk piled up to fill a small house. I looked at the pile in some interest. There were several balls, a couple of old writing slates, children's wooden toys, well used, a doll, a box of material of some sort, rolls of wool, countless scrolls.

"It seems to be missing." She picked up two more boxes and suddenly stopped. "Oh, of course!" She dropped the boxes, which scattered more scrolls, and went to a cupboard where she removed two dresses to reveal a bow.

I inspected it closely, to give the impression I knew what I was doing. It certainly resembled the other bows I knew Brasidas had made.

I repeated the bowyer's description, trying to sound as professional as possible. "Hunting weapon. Accurate over long distance but slow rate of fire. It should be hard to pull, how do you manage it?"

"Brasidas altered the material slightly so it isn't so stiff. See here? The bow is thinner at the curve and the reinforcing is wider. But the length is the same as a man's bow. I lose some power but it's still accurate. I see you know something about weapons."

"What's a nice girl like you doing with a weapon like this?"

"I'm a priestess of Artemis, remember? What is the favorite weapon of the Goddess?"

The bow, of course. Artemis is always drawn hunting with a bow. "Can you use this thing?"

"Oh, I'm fairly good, but I'm out of practice," she said, in the sort of tone which in a man would mean, "I can put out your eyeball at a hundred paces; you pick the eye."

"Can all the priestesses do this? Why haven't I heard of mobs of deadly women?"

She looked embarrassed. "The priestesses are all supposed to be the daughters of citizens. Ephialtes was my father, of course, but not of his wife, so I was excluded. I wanted to be a priestess more than anything else in the world. I begged him to help me.

Father wouldn't allow it at first, but in the end he relented. I think he was hoping I'd get it out of my system. He used his influence to have me appointed a trainee. The older women who run the temple were not entirely pleased because of who my mother is. They resented Ephialtes forcing me upon them. So I thought if I could do the things Artemis did then the older women would look on me more kindly. There's a ceremony we hold once a year, when one of the women shoots an arrow at a deer. I was the chosen one last year. I hadn't seen the ceremony before. So I learned how to shoot."

"I'm beginning to see where this is going." And I was beginning to understand this girl. Being Diotima, she turned herself into a crack shot, because perfection was her normal standard.

"Yes, how was I supposed to know they had a flimsy little toy in the temple for the initiates?"

"So you turned up with your marksman's recurve bow with the reinforced horn . . ."

"The deer never knew what hit it. It was flung sideways and landed on the high priestess, who fell in the mud. Then they told me I wasn't supposed to hurt the animal. Father had to buy them a new sacred deer. I was scrubbing the temple floors for months after that."

We both laughed.

"Are you sure you want to be a priestess?"

"Absolutely. I'd rather die than become like Mother, and the life of a wife shut up at home and never allowed out doesn't bear thinking of. Priestesses are the only women with even a hint of freedom to do as they wish." She paused, then demanded, "So now you are going to tell me how Brasidas comes into this."

"He sold the bow that killed your father to a man from Tanagra."

Diotima jiggled in her seat in excitement. "Good! What else did you learn?"

"That's it. Brasidas shut up when he thought he might get a

big reward later. That's why I have the word Tanagra and nothing else. And now he's dead."

It was her turn to look like a gasping fish. "Brasidas? He's dead?"

"Couldn't be deader." I described the scene of this morning.

"But this is wonderful!"

"It is?"

"Don't you see? If Ephialtes' killer was here to silence Brasidas this morning, then he's still in Athens."

"You do look on the bright side, don't you?" But here was a thought I hadn't considered. "Why would a hired assassin stay in Athens after doing his work?"

I answered my own question. "Because he hasn't been paid yet, or because he is so obvious he can't safely be seen in public, or because he has more work to do."

"You can forget about number two. Those slaves took no particular notice of him when they saw him walking to the Areopagus."

"And whoever heard of not paying a successful assassin? They're not the sort of people you want to annoy."

Diotima and I looked at each other. "There's going to be another murder," we said in unison.

She asked, "Did Brasidas keep a list of all his customers?"

"I doubt it. Why would he bother?"

"Then we must search Athens looking for anyone from Tanagra."

I laughed. "And how long do you think that would take? Besides, it isn't possible."

"So you're going to sit there doing nothing, are you?"

"I'm certainly not going to run around wasting my energy on fruitless exercises. The killer is still lost."

She covered her eyes and groaned. "What a disaster! Brasidas could have told us the name, or at least where to find him. You fool, Nicolaos, how could you let this happen?"

"What do you mean, let this happen? I didn't kill him," I sputtered.

She sighed. "It's too late now. We'll just have to mend the damage you've caused as best we can."

I said heatedly, "I suppose you would have done better?"

Diotima nodded. "Almost certainly," she said as a matter of fact. "You shouldn't have put the idea in Brasidas' head he could be in trouble for selling the bow. You should have put money down on the table right away. You should have waited outside to see if he went anywhere and followed him."

This evaluation was so close to what I'd been saying to myself that I squirmed, but I had no wish to hear it from an inexperienced girl.

"It's all very well thinking of these things in hindsight."

"But you thought of none of them at the time. I expect then you were dreaming of the glory of catching the killer, and Pericles' reward."

I felt my face flush with embarrassment. I had been thinking of precisely that, but nothing was going to make me admit it. I said, feeling somewhat testy, "Why don't you go walking the streets investigating if you can do it so much better?"

"I may have to at the pace you're going."

I was instantly horrified. "Don't! I was only joking. What will you do if a mob attacks you?"

"I'm not an aristocrat."

"You look as if you could be, and you're a woman, and it's getting lawless out there. A mob's not going to stop and think until after they've raped you."

"Who is going to attack a poor, modest, defenseless maiden, and a priestess at that?" She held up a small knife with a curved blade that looked sharp enough to split a hair. "We use this for sacrifices."

Defenseless was the last word I would have used to describe Diotima.

I had been relating my adventures each night to my family over dinner. This wasn't merely for entertainment. I was showing Sophroniscus that I had become my own man. So far I had skipped only a few items, such as the episode with Euterpe, Pericles' offer of reward, and all mention of Diotima. If my family discovered I was talking to women in the street I'd have a marriage arranged for me before the month was out. Tonight, for the first time, I found most of the day required careful editing. I certainly could not speak of the argument between Xanthippus and Pericles, and I was too embarrassed to relate Pericles' lambasting me with the bill of damages. But I was able to make a great tale of tracking down Brasidas and his dramatic death. Father looked troubled at this but did not say a word.

Sophroniscus was an unusual head of family; in most households the women and children eat in a room separate from the men, but he allowed my mother Phaenarete and Socrates to dine with us. She and Socrates sat at a low table in the middle of the floor while Sophroniscus and I reclined on couches. Socrates was plunging his fingers into the dishes as fast as the kitchen slave could bring them. He was sopping up the last of the lentils with the barley cake when the slave came in carrying a large plate of eels, which she deposited as far from him as possible. That didn't stop Socrates from stuffing the last of the cake into his mouth and reaching for the eel, and Phaenarete was moved to tell him to slow down, and eat less, or people would think she'd raised a barbarian. Phaenarete was a small woman, fair, with brown hair that she tied back out of the way when she worked. She scooped out a good handful of eel into a bowl for Sophroniscus and then another bowl for me. Resting as we were on the couches, he and I could eat with only one hand.

As she handed me my bowl Phaenarete said, "Tell us about Pericles, Nicolaos, what's he like?"

"Smart, assertive, charming, and persuasive. I like him, I think. Or it may be he wants me to like him because that suits his purposes, I'm not sure which. He looks like someone you'd want for a model, Father, except for his head. It's strangely long."

Phaenarete nodded. "Yes, it happens often in birth that a babe will be born with a head that is pointed. It flattens in a month or two. But sometimes—rarely—the head does not entirely flatten. The bones set as they are. And so the child grows with a head that is shaped like a cone."

There may be a creature in this world more irritating than a younger brother; but if there is, I am not aware of it. Eight years lie between us, but this has never prevented him from giving me advice, nonstop since the day he learned to speak. Not even when his mouth is full.

"Nico, I've been thinking—" Eel juice dribbled down his chin.

"Try not to think too much, little brother. This is a matter for adults. What could you possibly say that would help?"

"How did the assassin know the barracks was empty?" he asked.

My jaw dropped. Phaenarete looked puzzled. Sophroniscus laughed heartily.

"The boy has a point. Your man with the bow must have known about the Scythian exercise. Who could have told him?"

Who indeed?

8

Diotima's news that Stratonike was mad posed an interesting conundrum. Archestratus had said Ephialtes' wife would be forced to marry Ephialtes' nearest male relative. But who would marry a madwoman? Maybe someone else stood to inherit his property. I had to find out, and there was only one man who could tell me: the Eponymous Archon, the chief executive of Athens, in charge of all business relating to citizens, including the estates of orphans, widows, and heiresses.

I found the Archon the next day in his suite in the row of offices in the new Stoa next to the Agora. I had to sit on a low stone wall with the other men who wanted business with the busiest executive in Athens. Some of the men whiled away the time playing games, using boards that had been scratched into the stone, and pebbles of different sizes for the pieces. It was close to midday by the time a man with a paunch, tired eyes, and garlic on his breath came to tell me the Archon would see me.

Conon was balding, with a few thin strands of hair surviving above his ears. He had a rounded, lined face. "What do you want, and it better be simple," he snarled.

"It's about Ephialtes' death—"

"*Everything's* about Ephialtes' death," he interrupted me. He pointed to the low stone wall where I'd been waiting with the other suppliants. "Every accursed man sitting out there wants something done *right now,* before the civil administration collapses in the fighting."

"You think there's going to be fighting?"

"What do you think? The only line longer than that one out there is the one before the courts for disorderly conduct. I've already had three wealthy men from good families in here this morning demanding action because their sons and slaves have been assaulted by rioters. One of the sons is dead. Two of them insist the army be called to attack the next mob that appears. They forget the mob *is* the army. Oh Gods! I can't believe I volunteered for this job." I suppressed the temptation to pat him on the back and make soothing noises.

"I think my problem might be simpler," I encouraged him.

"I hope so."

"Who inherits Ephialtes' estate?"

"Simple, you think?" He paused to shout through the door. "Tiro! Get your ass in here!"

Conon's secretary entered with barely a raised eyebrow. "Yes, Conon?"

"This young fool thinks Ephialtes' estate is simple." They both shared a good laugh at my expense while I sat there.

Tiro relieved my ignorance. "The case is one almost beyond any experience of the law. Ephialtes had no male issue, so the wife should be forced to marry the nearest male relative. The problem is she's insane, mad as a crazed cow, and it is impossible to force any man to marry such a woman. In fact there's an ancient edict that forbids it, since the mad are cursed by the Gods, and no man may be forced to incur a curse he doesn't deserve."

Conon added, "Besides which, if what I hear is true, any man who did marry her is likely to get a knife between his ribs, or his head cracked in."

I said, "So on the face of it Stratonike gets the property herself."

Tiro shook his head. "No. It is absolutely impossible for a woman to own property."

"But wait! What happens if a man dies and there are no male relatives of any distance?"

"Then the state takes control of the property and administers it for any girl-children until the time they marry, after which the property is sold and the sum goes to the state, after allowing for suitable dowries. But that doesn't apply here, because there is a distant male relative. What's his name, Tiro?"

"Rizon. And we must find a way for him to inherit."

"Then it seems to me there's no solution at all."

"That's because you don't credit me with doing my job well," Conon said. "It's radical and controversial, but I found a way out. Ephialtes had a daughter by his mistress. She's a metic, so we can do whatever we like to her. She will be allowed to inherit and be forced to marry in place of the insane wife. Her name is . . . here, let me see . . . ah yes, Diotima of Mantinea."

I stumbled from the Archon's office in a state of shock. What sort of man was this Rizon? I had to find out.

I banged on his door harder than is polite. When his house slave answered I demanded an immediate interview on a matter of importance to the state. This got me to his public room.

I saw quickly that Rizon was a man of low means. His house was of the smaller sort. I spotted only two slaves, both men. His furniture was wooden but rough.

Rizon walked in. He was a middle-aged man, perhaps in his mid-thirties. He had a thin face and was balding, but I could see he was reasonably fit. The puzzled expression on his face turned to startlement as soon as he saw me. I was startled too. I had seen Rizon before, in the company of Archestratus, when I first interviewed him. He had been one of the men present when Archestratus explained the laws of inheritance.

He said, "I know you, but I can't place where."

"We met at the home of Archestratus."

"Ah yes, Pericles' agent. What do you want with me? I assume

Pericles is not asking for an alliance with an unknown sandal maker."

"That's what you do for a living?"

"It is. Would you like a new pair?"

"I'm more interested in what you were doing with Archestratus."

"The same as everyone else you saw there, sucking up to the next leader of the people. Unlike your master, I believe in the democracy."

"Pericles is not my master—"

"Oh?"

"And in any case Pericles is more a democrat than Archestratus, if what I've heard from Archestratus so far has any meaning."

"Or Pericles hides his aristocratic leanings better."

"I'm not here to bandy words about politics."

"Then I wish you would tell me why you are here, so I can get back to my work."

"When Archestratus said he didn't know who inherited Ephialtes' estate, why didn't you declare yourself?"

Rizon held out his hands palms up and said, "For a very simple reason. I had no idea then. Of course I knew I was distantly related to Ephialtes, but it came as a shock when the secretary to the Eponymous Archon came to me the next day and informed me that not only do I inherit, but I am the only male relative of any sort."

"Where were you on the morning Ephialtes died?"

"In my workshop, of course. Are you suggesting I might have shot him?"

"You inherit. It's a motive."

"Only if I know it."

"There's only your word you didn't."

"Then accuse me before the judges and we'll see what evidence you've got." He threw down the challenge confidently.

Unfortunately I shared his confidence. An accuser whose charge fails pays a heavy penalty to the accused, and I couldn't afford it.

"Do you know about Stratonike?"

"His wife? I gather she's mad. But it shouldn't be a problem. They tell me I have to marry the daughter of some whore he got a child by. Frankly I'm looking forward to it. I hear she's a decent-looking tart, and her mother's probably taught her all the tricks of the trade."

I pushed my way out of the house, desperate for some fresh air. Behind me, Rizon's slaves were picking him up off the ground. I hoped his jaw hurt as much as my fist.

I felt completely drained, I could feel the investigation slipping away from me, and I'd lost the will to continue. I decided to go to the Agora and find somewhere I could sit quietly and drink.

I never got the drink. A mob was pushing and jostling about. I thought, rolling my eyes, that it was another riot by men angry at the death of Ephialtes and fearful of a coup, and expected Pericles to arrive at any moment to quell the disturbance. The crowd was too dense for me to see what was happening at the center, but I could see Archestratus on the other side, standing upon something to give him height and shouting at the crowd. I couldn't hear a word he said, I could only hope he was having some effect.

A man on the fringe told me two dead men had been laid out on a trestle table in the Agora. I pushed my way through with a terrible feeling in my heart, and looked down to see the two old slaves who cleaned the Areopagus. Their throats had been cut. Their faces were masks of horror. They'd seen their fate coming to them, but had been too old and weak to resist.

They had given me the most important clue I'd discovered, and I never even knew their names. I whispered to them, "I told no one. No one!" But then I realized that I had. I'd told Pericles, and Diotima, and my family. And someone had known to kill them before they could testify.

I tried to search their bodies for any clue who might have done this, but the crowd were having none of it.

"Here, you! What are you doing?"

"He's doing something to the bodies!"

"Sacrilege! Stop him!"

I became fearful and stopped. In this ugly crowd, anything might happen.

I don't know who started it; the mob surged like cattle into the streets. I was carried along in the center whether I wanted to go or not. The men stopped outside a place I knew, the home of Xanthippus.

The guards were still on duty, but they were swept away like flies. Ten men in the face of hundreds would have been fools to stand and fight. They ran through into the house and slammed the door behind them and barred it shut. The mob began forcing the door. Fortunately Xanthippus was no fool, he had had the door reinforced when the troubles began, and the angry men couldn't batter it down. Someone broke into a nearby home— the women inside screamed as they were invaded—and emerged dragging a dining couch. Others helped him carry it to the door and used it as a battering ram. A few men grabbed torches hung outside for night time, and lit them. They threw the torches high onto the roof of the two-story building. Arson is a terrible crime punishable by death, but no one saw who threw the torches and even if they had, I doubt anyone in that crazed riot would have done anything other than cheer.

Men appeared on the rooftop carrying buckets. They tossed water on the torches before they could set the building alight, but they were targets and the crowd pelted them with stones and several daggers. One man was struck on the head. He let out a loud groan and fell backward into the courtyard below. I don't know whether he died.

The pack had dispersed enough now that I could force my way out. No one was thinking, they just wanted to kill Xanthippus. I ran around the block to the back of the building. Slaves were pouring out, carrying whatever valuables they could. It was like watching ants escape a damaged anthill. A young woman was shepherding three slave children out of the house and down the street. They were crying in fear. The guards who had escaped the front of the house were now cordoning the escape route. They stopped me from continuing.

"Let him through!" Xanthippus was standing in the courtyard, calmly overseeing the withdrawal. The old man, thin but lively and alert, reminded me of a General commanding in the heat of battle, which was no coincidence. Xanthippus in his younger days had been a General, and had given Athens victory at the Battle of Mycale. I noticed the statue of a dog, sitting straight and proud, alongside the altar to Zeus Herkeios. I had never seen its like before. It was such an odd thing that it stuck in my mind. I went to Xanthippus.

He said, "Tell Pericles what is happening, and for all our sakes find Pythax and order him to quell this mob!"

I nodded and ran off without saying a word.

I banged on the door of Pericles' home and pushed my way in the moment the house slave pulled back the bolt.

"Quick, where's Pericles?"

The slave pointed upstairs.

I crashed through the door to his inner sanctum and stopped. Pericles was leaning forward, in close conversation with Conon the Eponymous Archon.

He looked up in great annoyance, but before he could speak I said, "Your father's home is being attacked by a mob. He's evacuating out the back."

I'll say this for Pericles, he doesn't waste time in a crisis. He jumped up and raced downstairs, calling for slaves to come with him.

Conon stood and said, "What are you waiting for? Fetch the Scythians at once. Do you know where to find them?"

I nodded and left. Fortunately someone had already had the sense to alert them, because I was running out of breath. I met them coming downhill, dressed in their leather armor and carrying their unstrung bows to use as wooden staves, long loops of rope, and heavy buckets of something. Pythax was in the lead. He saw me and said, "You were coming to us?"

I gave him a rapid description of the riot as I had last seen it. Pythax didn't break his quick march for a moment. When I finished, he barked orders to the men behind us. We broke into a trot.

As we approached the street, half the men peeled away and took off down a side alley. Those who stayed with Pythax unrolled the rope and pulled it tight to make a barrier. Other men took rags and dipped them into the buckets, then wiped them along the rope, which I saw was now heavily covered with paint. The remaining men stood behind the rope line wielding the staves.

The Scythians commenced a slow, steady march down the street. I saw the Scythians who'd broken away appear at the other end, doing the same. The rioters were trapped between the two lines. Most shied away from the painted rope, falling back and causing confusion for the more aggressive men coming forward. Those who pushed past tried to break through. Their hands became smeared with the paint and they were beaten back by the staves. The men in the center of the mob became aware they were trapped and turned their attention from attack to escape.

In the time I'd been away, the door had been broken down. It lay hanging off its hinges in pieces. I suppose a few men had entered the building, but now everyone realized the only escape from the Scythians was through Xanthippus' house. The mob surged and pushed. Men tripped and fell and were trampled. I could hear their screams beneath the feet of those still pushing.

Pythax shouted orders, and the rope men at both ends of the street closest to the door started to edge toward one another, supported by the stave men who hit out over and over again. They met at the entrance and joined the ropes, so it formed a semicircle protecting the entrance. They took two steps toward the center of the street. The mob saw that they were well and truly trapped, and became docile. The only way out for them now was to wait to be let out.

Pythax ordered again, and all but a few of the Scythians armed with staves filed into the house. I followed them in. I could hear Pythax shouting at me, but I ignored him.

Broken furniture was lying about, pottery and statues were smashed. The rioters were fighting with anything that came to hand; anyone the Scythians caught was being hit hard. A few men had snatched spears off the wall. Those the Scythians took on three to one to suppress any chance of anyone being hurt, any Scythian that is. A quick glance into the courtyard told me Xanthippus and his household had all made it out. A few rioters had taken that route too. They were the smart ones.

I stepped around struggling men and ran up the stairs. Xanthippus had cleared his private papers off his desk before fleeing. I cursed the man's foresight. I scanned the room for anything that might help me. There were small bags made of soft, thin leather on a shelf. They were empty. A few papers were scattered about the floor, dropped in the rush. I picked them all up and stuffed them into my tunic, then made my way downstairs again before anyone noticed where I'd been. The fighting had finished, the Scythians held the field. They were dragging the unconscious into the street.

I surveyed the mess that had once been the home of one of our premier citizens. All the internal rooms would have to be rebuilt, and the door and all the furniture was in splinters, but the outside structure was solid and the fires had been extinguished quickly.

I could see that outside Pythax was processing the men within the rope barrier; each was being taken straight to a magistrate. I hoped they'd enjoyed their riot, because now they would each be paying a very substantial fine to the state. The ones caught inside would be paying compensation to Xanthippus for the damage. It would probably drive most of them into bankruptcy, which meant Xanthippus could legally sell them as slaves to recoup his losses. I wondered whether he would take that drastic step, which would make him even more unpopular with the people than he already was, or whether he would absorb his loss so as to be seen as magnanimous. Personally, looking at the damage they'd done, I'd have shipped them straight to the slave market at Piraeus.

I didn't read the papers until I had them safely back home. Unfortunately none of them was a receipt for payment of a new bow. Most of them were notes or bills of the usual household kind. One did look different though. I read it again. It was an old order for a box of fragrant herbs. That didn't sound like Xanthippus to me; he had no women in his household. The handwriting appeared different too. I turned it over. Scribbled on the back, in the same handwriting as the front, was a note. "I will meet you at the Areopagus at dawn." I stuffed that note back into my tunic and went back out onto the streets.

The temple of Artemis Agrotera, the Huntress, is to the southeast of the Agora, across the river in the deme of Agrai. The way took me down Tripod Road, one of the busiest roads in Athens and always crowded, despite being so broad that two large horses could pass each other and not touch. Not that there was room for the horses; as usual, Tripod Road was overflowing with merchants and their donkeys, and men traveling to or from home. The donkeys were kicking up an uncomfortable amount of dust, so that my nose itched. Every now and then one would brush by me, and its rough coat would leave a smear on the material of my chitoniskos.

Bordering both sides, like soldiers standing to attention, were the many bronze tripods that give the road its name, too numerous to count without making an effort I had never bothered with. Each tripod was a simple bowl, held aloft by three legs, with a chain running between the midpoints of the legs to hold them in place; each stood upon a stone base, some tall and ornate, some low and elegant, each different in design or style. Most of these monuments were so old that they had tarnished with neglect and gone green. Others were well cared for, and a couple were shiny new. No matter its condition, each proclaimed a victory in the choral competition at the Great Dionysia. Every tribe enters a chorus of boys and of men for the choral event, and the choregos who produces the winning performance is awarded the bronze tripod with which to record his triumph. He places it along this road, so men forever after will be able to read of his success from the plaque he attaches, which records the name of the choregos, his tribe, the name of the poet, and the name of the musician who accompanied the singing on the aulus pipes.

I noticed one tripod so old it had fallen over, and that no passerby had stopped to put it right. I picked it up, being careful not to cut myself on the broken, corroded leg that had caused the fall, and reset it as best I could, though even when I finished it was still somewhat at a lean. I tried to read the plaque to see who had won this victory, but the words had faded to nothing. Such is fame.

I passed the turnoff to the right that would have taken me to the Theater of Dionysos and continued to the Illisos River crossing, where there was a low stone bridge.

The dry stone wall that marked the border of the temple sanctuary was in poor condition. I stepped over the tumbled stones and asked for Diotima of Mantinea by name and waited for her to arrive. A man was sacrificing upon the altar which stood in the sunshine at the foot of the steps to the temple. A dozen or so men and women were watching the rite. When he turned, I saw it was the Polemarch, the archon in charge of everything to do with the city's many metics.

"Nicolaos!" Diotima stood beside me. She wore a full-length chiton of fine, light linen that stretched all the way to her ankles, clasped at the shoulders with the decorations of a priestess, brooches in the figure of Artemis and her deer. She had tied a belt around her waist and a rope beneath her breasts and wore a silver necklace. Both sides of her dress were open and patterned down the hems with intricate design in blues and greens. Her dark hair was tied back and held with a bronze clasp, which didn't stop the curls from escaping. All of a sudden I was very aware of my heart beating fast. She smiled warmly.

"What's he doing here?" I asked, to get the subject right away from what I was thinking.

"The Polemarch? He's the sponsor of this temple."

"The Polemarch, not the Basileus? I thought the Basileus is the official in charge of ceremonies and rites?"

Diotima nodded. "You're correct. This is an exception. They tell me the Polemarch has been in charge of this temple since time immemorial, for some important reason that happened so long ago, everyone's forgotten what it is, but no one dares change the rule for fear Artemis might be offended. For all we know, maybe it was the Goddess herself who decreed it."

The Polemarch held down the sacrifice, which was a goat, while speaking the prayer. The goat must have felt her doom, for she bucked and tried to run. I thought the Polemarch had her under control, but then the animal twisted under his hand and slipped away.

"After it!"

The goat ran straight for the orchard beyond. Two attendants jumped in front of her. She tried to bounce around them but one dived and got an arm over her back and dragged her down. The people sighed in relief. For a sacrifice to escape would be the worst possible luck. The attendants grabbed her by the feet and hauled her upside down back to the altar, where the Polemarch stood waiting, embarrassed.

This time there was no mistake. The attendants held the animal in place while the Polemarch pulled back her head and made a quick, practiced slash. The blood splashed into a bowl held below the throat by one of the attendants, yet still the goat kicked in a vain attempt to escape with her life.

"The sacrifice did not go willingly," Diotima observed. "It is a bad sign."

"Does that surprise you, given what is happening?"

"No."

The Polemarch washed his hands in a basin. A junior priestess closed in on the carcass with two men alongside. They carried the animal to the rear of the temple, where it would be butchered and roasted. The meat of a sacrifice is never wasted, not in a city where there are too many mouths to feed and not enough food. The Polemarch was a hard-looking man with a square face, short hair, and intense blue eyes. He stopped as he passed and looked at us closely.

"Diotima," he said shortly. She nodded.

"You are Nicolaos," he stated. I agreed, puzzled how he recognized me. "Come to see me later today, for a chat." He stalked out of the sanctuary without saying another word, heading the way I'd come, back toward the Agora.

Diotima said, "That's strange. An invitation to chat with the Polemarch is as good as a summons, and it's not as if he has nothing better to do."

"I saw the Eponymous Archon this morning. He must have told the Polemarch, but I can't imagine why."

"What did you want to see him for?"

"I'll tell you later."

"Have you visited this temple before?"

"I'm afraid not."

"Then let me show you around!" Diotima said. She took my arm and led me to the fore steps.

The outside walls were covered in plaster that had been recently applied, and painted in bright colors. Unfortunately, the paint couldn't hide all the cracks in the underlying mud brick of which the temple was built. Straight wooden columns swept around all four sides. They held up the wooden roof, which was in the normal temple style, sloping to both sides. The building was so old it originally had had no decoration at all within the metope, the triangular forepart that the roof formed. Someone had climbed up and attached a terra-cotta plaque that displayed the Goddess hunting. The Temple of Artemis didn't look particularly special to me, or rather, it may have been a special temple, but despite their best efforts it was in a sad state of disrepair.

Diotima said, "This is an ancient temple. The Goddess Artemis herself hunted on this very ground when she came to Athens from Delos. The area has been a sacred hunting ground ever since. Our temple survived the Persians, I suppose because it's so far out of town and on the south side of the river."

"Would you like a new one?" I asked.

"I think it would be nice, but I don't know what the High Priestess would say. I've generally found whatever I think, the women in charge think the opposite. But who wouldn't want a new temple?" Diotima sighed. Then she looked at me strangely. "You said that as if you have a spare temple in your bag."

"As it happens, I might." I thought of Pericles' promise to rebuild the Acropolis.

We walked inside between the pillars and to the end of the room as far as we were permitted for a closer look at Artemis. It took a moment for our eyes to adjust. When they did, the cult statue of the Goddess was before us.

"The statue is very ancient too," Diotima said in half pride, half apology. The sculpture wasn't up to modern standards: to start with, she was made of wood. She was stiff in her pose, standing upright like an ephebe before his commander, and archaic in style. My father could have done better with one hand, but that didn't matter, because this statue was sacred. The spirit of the Goddess could reside within this ancient wood, and on occasion did. Someone had placed a real bow in her clenched hand. She'd been dressed in a modern chiton, with a himation of good quality draped over her shoulders.

Hung about the inner walls were all manner of things; clothing, bronzeware, tools, some children's toys. These were dedications to the Goddess, brought by people seeking her favor, or perhaps simply to express their devotion.

Two older priestesses were watching us from the side and whispering to each other. "Let's look outside."

At the back of the temple were the working buildings. A place such as this has many practical requirements. There are animals to be kept, both sacrificial and sacred, maintenance to be done, fields to be tended, implements to be stored, slaves to be housed. The Temple of Artemis the Huntress was nothing short of a holy farm.

Diotima led me to the field beside the temple where goats and a horse browsed. I took out the note.

"Do you recognize this?"

She looked at it carefully. "I don't recall the note, though it looks to be one of ours. The handwriting is Father's."

"I thought you might say that."

"Where did you find it?"

"In the study of Xanthippus."

"What! How did you come to be rummaging in there?"

"You've missed a lot of excitement out here at this peaceful temple." I brought her up to date with the latest Athenian riot.

"That was quick thinking," she approved.

"Diotima, I'm going to tell you something I think you need to know."

Diotima smiled. "For free? No trade? That isn't like you, Nicolaos."

"I know. Uh, I think we might need to be somewhere we can't be heard."

"We're somewhere we can't be heard now."

"Somewhere even more can't-be-heard."

She looked at me warily. "Is this a trick or a joke?" She saw that it wasn't. "Come with me."

We stopped in an orchard grove that grew by the river Illisos. The trees grew tall here, the branches were thick and the leaves gave cool shade. The temple must have harvested much fruit from them. Diotima stopped beneath the spreading branches and said, "Go ahead."

"Congratulations, you are going to be a bride." I told her everything the Archon and his secretary had told me. I did not tell her of my visit to her future husband. I felt this was enough bad news for one day.

At first, Diotima simply stood there, white-faced.

"Those bastards," she whispered. "Those scum. Those vermin. Those . . ." She shouted a stream of vitriol in ever-increasing volume.

"Don't scream," I said urgently, "or there'll be people running out here."

"They can't make me do this."

"Actually, I think they can."

"I won't let them. I'll stop it. I'll kill myself first."

"Running away would be better," I advised.

"Do you think this is funny?" she flared in a screech.

"No," I said shortly, and turned away. Diotima was beating the trunk of a tree with her fists. I let her. It would help get it out of her system. I went for a walk to give her time alone, and because I was shaking.

When I returned Diotima was sitting. Her knuckles were skinless and bleeding, her face bloated from sobbing.

"Thank you for telling me, Nicolaos. I'd like to be alone now. You can go back without me." She was watching the waters of the river.

I had a terrible premonition. "I think that would be a very bad idea. Come along." I helped her up. "You haven't found your father's killer yet. Isn't that still important to you?"

"Yes."

"Then worry about the rest of it later. If the worst occurs you can always run back to Mantinea."

Diotima laughed bitterly. "Didn't you work that out? Mother was a common whore. There wasn't a good family, there wasn't a former husband, and she was never a priestess, virgin or otherwise." She stood up. "Now you can escort me home."

9

We met Pythax as we turned onto Diotima's street. He was look-ing as big and as tough and as mean as ever, and he didn't look happy.

"You!" he growled at me in greeting. "As if the city weren't in enough uproar, do you know that kid of the bowyer's is in the Agora, swearing you killed his dad?"

"Am I under arrest then?"

"No one's paying any attention to the boy . . . yet. Think of this as a friendly warning. You better avoid the Agora until the kid's gone. I don't need any more trouble than I already got."

"Okay, thanks."

"And another thing, there's some guy called Rizon been has-sling the archons. He says you knocked him down in his own home. It seems to me you've been at one murder, close to another, arrived late for two more, and been in the middle of the worst riot we've had in years. You want to watch yourself, little boy. You don't want to go getting a reputation for violence." He cracked his knuckles.

"I'll remember that."

"See that you do."

"Who's Rizon?" Diotima asked me.

"No one you want to know," I growled.

Pythax studied Diotima for the first time.

"You Ephialtes' girl?"

"Yes."

Pythax grunted. "Sorry about your dad."

"Why, hello there!" a voice purred behind us. Euterpe had walked up while we were speaking with Pythax and I hadn't noticed. A slave stood behind her holding her purse and another held an umbrella to keep her in the shade.

"Hello, Mother," Diotima said unevenly.

"Who's your friend?" She swept her eyes up and down Pythax and smiled.

Since I wasn't the recipient of her undivided attention I was able to keep myself under control. Pythax was not so lucky. I find it hard to believe to this day, but Pythax actually blushed. His bulging muscles seemed to expand even more and he stood taller. He eyed Euterpe with the same level of interest she was displaying. The grizzled warrior and the smooth, sophisticated woman made an interesting contrast. In her case, I assumed it was professional interest.

I said, "May I introduce Pythax, Chief of the Scythians."

"A barbarian! I love a he-man." She tore her attention from the big man enough to notice me. "You brought two of them, dear? That shows ambition."

Diotima said through gritted teeth. "We're talking, *Mother*."

"Ah, well. You must come for a cool drink. It's so hot and dusty in the street, don't you think?" She took Pythax by his unresisting arm and led us into her receiving room. She sat him down and offered him wine. I watched with amusement as his eyes tracked her form when she swayed to the wine cooler.

"I can tell you're the strong, silent type. Do you speak?" she teased him.

All too frequently, I wanted to answer, but instead I smiled inwardly as Pythax struggled to work out what one should say to a beautiful woman. Diotima leaned over to me and muttered unhappily, "This is cruel."

Pythax said gruffly, "Yes, I do, lady, when there's something to be said. But not to a lady who mocks me." He put down his wine and stood. "I'll be going now."

Euterpe was astonished. So was I.

"What was that? What do you mean?"

"We never met before but you're pawing me all over. I know you can't mean that with a rough old man like me. I ain't that pretty, so I reckon you're mocking me on purpose. Well, Euterpe, you might be a highborn lady, and I might be a peasant ruffian, but I don't take that from anyone."

Euterpe was flustered. She took a step back and put her hands to her mouth as if she were genuinely upset.

"I . . . I'm sorry, Pythax. I didn't mean to offend you. It's just my way of dealing with men. I don't know any other." She put a hand lightly on his arm. "Please stay a moment."

Diotima said quickly, "Yes, please stay, Pythax."

He looked at Diotima with narrowed eyes, then at me. I nodded encouragement. Then he sat and picked up his wine once more. He muttered, "Sorry, I'm not used to . . ." and drifted into silence.

Euterpe sat on a couch apart from Pythax. Not only did she not lean back, she didn't even cross her legs. She looked particularly uncomfortable.

I thought it was a good time to change the subject. "Euterpe, since we're here, I have some questions about Tanagra. Did Ephialtes know anyone there?"

"We have had this conversation before. I didn't involve myself in politics."

"Did anyone from Tanagra come to visit?"

"He never received any visitors here."

"Did he ever speak of enemies?"

"Constantly. How many would you like?"

"Any from Tanagra?"

"No. All conservatives."

"And you didn't see Ephialtes the morning he died? You didn't come out of your rooms before he left?"

"Not during that argument! I wasn't going down there and getting involved. I'd had enough of it the night before."

"What argument?" I hadn't heard this before. I looked at Diotima, taken aback, who in turn was staring at Euterpe in fury.

"Mother, must you bring that up *again*?"

"I didn't, dear, your boyfriend did."

"He's not my boyfriend. You couldn't wait to say it, could you, Father wanting me to marry?"

"Well, he did, dear Diotima. Really, I don't know what's wrong with you. It's not as if you seem to have any objections to men." She glanced at me slyly and winked.

"Marrying for what I can get out of it is no different than selling my body."

Euterpe turned to Pythax and me. "Diotima has invented a philosophy of love. Apparently this means she must never have sex unless she does it from her own heart. So she refuses to take advantage of any man and instead must be taken advantage of. Both Ephialtes and I wanted her to marry. Ephialtes even began the negotiations and could have had the whole thing arranged months ago. But the ungrateful wretch refused to cooperate, and since she wasn't his legal offspring he couldn't force the issue like any sensible father would. Really, she was most stupid. She could have been a citizen by now."

"And be a whore like you? I'd rather die!" Diotima shouted in fury.

"I am not a whore, and you will kindly remember the difference between a hetaera and the common pornoi," Euterpe said between gritted teeth.

"Ah yes. Hetaerae get paid more."

From the way Diotima had made the accusation I could tell this was a sore spot for her mother.

"I am what I am, and you will remember it is what I did to look after you, you ungrateful, pompous, righteous little ass of a child. You know nothing of what it takes to survive. Nothing! You've never been hungry. You've been pampered from the moment you were born. I gave you the best of everything. And, yes, to do it I had to lie on my back and spread my legs, but I did it for you."

Diotima said sweetly, "I think you have that the wrong way around, Mother dear. You spread your legs, so you had me to look after. The spreading comes before the child."

"Is that what you think? Then let me tell you something, wretched ingrate. The moment you were born your father picked you up. He was taking you away. Yes, that's right, Ephialtes was taking you to Ceramicus. He said he had no place for a girl-child, a son might have been different, but an illegitimate girl was good for nothing but the urns. I begged him not to, *begged*. I offered him anything in the world, everything I had, if only he would leave me my child. And so he did, and the price I paid for you was to be bound to him for the rest of my life."

Diotima swallowed and said nothing. There are two ways to dispose of an unwanted child, either leave them on the hillside to die of exposure, or drop them in a funeral urn in the cemetery and walk away.

"He let you live for love of me. Dropped you on the bedclothes and walked away. And when he took an interest, arranged that marriage, I thought, no one will ever be able to do to my little girl what he did to me. The wife of a citizen can keep her children, some of them anyway. She doesn't have to watch them all be taken away to die. She has a place, some security. And then, when you refused to marry, I saw the look on his face and I remembered the day you were born and I think he was thinking he should have taken you away after all."

Diotima was crying. "Oh, Mother!" Diotima threw herself into Euterpe's arms and the two of them sobbed.

Pythax and I let ourselves out. We were both feeling some-what glum and embarrassed by the women's emotions.

"Pythax, did any of that make sense to you? I mean, the way they got so carried away?"

"No, lad." He hesitated. "This Euterpe, she was Ephialtes'?"

"Yes."

"But she's a hetaera."

"She was, years ago. I don't know if it counts if she was only seeing Ephialtes for years."

Pythax grunted. "You think she only saw Ephialtes, do you? I guess she's got trouble now, her man's gone. Or is she happy he's dead?"

"I don't think so."

"She ain't exactly dressed like a grieving widow."

"Euterpe isn't the sort to display emotion, or rather not that particular one. There are other emotions she does really well. She might go back to her trade."

Pythax grunted.

We parted. I went to the Polemarch, whom I found at his office in the Epilyceum.

He bade me sit and sat himself beside me in a manner wholly alien for an important public citizen dealing with a young man of unimportant family. He looked at me with blue eyes, but nothing softened the square face or the hard lines around his mouth. He smiled, but there was something intellectual about his smile, it was the smile of a man who wanted to be seen smiling, as sincere as the priest who apologizes to his sacrifice.

"Now, Nicolaos, son of Sophroniscus, I have been hearing good things about you."

I doubted that mightily, but didn't know how to say so with-out causing offense, so I kept silent. The Polemarch's face was not naturally expressive. I had no idea what he was expecting from me. After a pause, he resumed.

"Not everyone can be born to the best families, and we older men have to keep an eye out for talented youngsters and help them to rise in the service of the state. One of my secretaries is ill—I have two, you know—he's unable to continue to the end of his term of office. The post of secretary is a public one, but unlike other public posts I can nominate my own man for the job, no need for a messy election, and as long as he passes a simple review, there should be no problem.

"That's why I want to offer you the position."

I could barely believe I was hearing this, let alone credit that the Polemarch meant it. The job he offered was that of a functionary, full of hard work and plenty of blame when anything went wrong, but it was also far beyond the experience of my years. It was a job you offered to a coming man to give him experience in executive government before he took on an archonship.

"I . . . I can't believe you're saying this. Thank you, sir!"

"So you accept?"

"I would love to—"

"Fine, then I'll get the process in motion—"

"Sir!"

"Yes?"

"I was going to add, sir, I have a commission. I have to complete it before I could start with you."

Silence fell across us like a blanket. The Polemarch sat rock still for a handful of heartbeats, I could count mine quite clearly, then said, "This commission, is it of a public nature?"

"No, sir."

"Do you think your private interests should come before service to the state?"

"No! Of course not, sir."

"Then I don't see the problem. You can continue this private affair when your work for the state is done."

"This commission is in the public interest, sir, and I don't see how I can stop now, having said I would complete it."

"Integrity is an excellent thing in a young man. I applaud you. Many would have accepted my excellent offer without a second thought. Have you been paid for your work?"

"Not yet."

"So again, there is no problem. Not having been paid, and delivered nothing, the contract is easily terminated. Your employer can find someone else at no loss to either party."

"It's still in the public interest, sir," I persisted.

The Polemarch let the smallest touch of irritation show in his voice. "Are you working for a public official?"

"No, for Pericles, son of Xanthippus."

"Then no matter what you might think, you are not at this point in service to the state. Xanthippus I know well, his son less so. And let me give you some advice on that score, from a man of greater years and hence greater experience in public affairs. Nico—I can call you Nico, can't I?—associating with the more radical democrats is not likely to get you marked by the men that count as anything other than a troublemaker. I am right, aren't I, in reading you as an ambitious young man?"

"Yes sir, I suppose that's true."

"Nothing wrong with that! I remember feeling the same way as a young lad. Right now, Nico, you have a feeling that you are contributing to the state. Because you're talented and ambitious and have dreams, you magnify the significance of what you do, and in the process you overestimate its importance. Any young man would do the same. But what, after all, are you doing? You're not working for an elected official. You're not fulfilling the wishes of the Government, nor the directives of the Ecclesia."

"I am investigating the murder of Ephialtes, sir."

"There you are then, my point exactly! That's a matter for the man's deme, if they want to pursue it. The Government can't spend its time catching criminals, or we'd never get any work done. That's why we leave it to private individuals to do the leg-work and make the accusation, and we in Government supply the courts to judge the results."

"Surely the death of this man matters far more than the aver-age murder!" I protested.

The Polemarch raised an eyebrow and leaned back in his chair with a smile. "Was Ephialtes a public officer when he died? No? A strategos or other officer of the army? No? Then are you suggesting in our democracy we should treat one man as more important than another? Surely not, that would be quite contrary to what the democracy stands for, wouldn't it? So it is quite impossible to do anything other than treat Ephialtes' death the same as any other citizen."

I pleaded, "Isn't it common sense that his death means more? What if he was killed by an official?"

"I quite agree with you. All the more reason for his deme to get on with the job. You can search high and low throughout Ath-ens, Nico, and you will not find a single official whose job it is to investigate crime. There never has been, not if you search back to the time of Draco, not even if you go back to King Theseus.

"I can see you feel confused. I understand. I am going to give you a while to think about what I've said, Nicolaos, a short while. I hesitate to say it, but there are other young men of tal-ent who perhaps are as deserving of recognition as you. I can-not leave my offer open for long: say, for another three days. If you have not accepted within that time, I will be forced to con-clude with the greatest sorrow that you have turned down the chance to boost your career far beyond what you could hope to achieve on your own in the next decade. Good day to you."

I walked onto the street almost sobbing. I was desperate because everything the Polemarch had said was true. Murder was a private affair. Pericles' commission was a private one and nothing to do with the state, even though he and I were sure it had everything to do with the state. And the greatest truth the Polemarch had told struck me to the core: I *was* desperately ambitious to succeed. It seemed to me in that short conversation the Polemarch had destroyed my life, because I could do nothing other than continue Pericles' commission, and when I did, the Polemarch would slam his door in my face.

I tossed and turned all night thinking about what the Polemarch had said. The temptation to abandon Pericles and throw in my lot with the Polemarch was almost overwhelming. At some point in the darkness I decided to do so, and composed several speeches I might use to tell Pericles. I discarded every one of them when I imagined the disdain on Pericles' face as I told him what I was doing. I realized with some shame, I hadn't the courage to tell Pericles I was leaving him, but nor did I have the strength to turn away the Polemarch.

I temporized with the dawn. If I completed my commission quickly, then all my problems would disappear. I could have both Pericles' reward and the Polemarch's job by finding this hidden Tanagran within the next three days, and wringing the truth from him. I hoped to Hades he hadn't already left town.

It may have been a fantasy, and it was certainly driven by moral cowardice, but it was the decision I made, and, of course, it was no decision at all. I rose immediately to perform that urgent task.

But where do you go to find a man in a city as big as Athens? There must be tens of thousands of men.

I rose to the predawn naked from my bed, and reached for my chitoniskos hanging on its peg. What a pleasure to be wearing civilian clothes again. I'd had to buy new clothes after my army time, and I preferred the smaller chitoniskos because it gave me room to move quickly; besides which, it was the fashion among all the young men. Mine was made of two rectangular sheets of light linen, sewn together down the right side and open down the left. I wrapped it around me, pinned the front and back sheets together over my shoulders, and stuck in an extra pin along the left to hold it all in place. I belted with a piece of rope and pulled the material up so that it bloused a little and brought the hem above my knees. I wrapped a short chlamys cloak across my shoulders and then added one more item many Athenians don't carry—a dagger, which I lodged under my belt and within the material where it would not be obvious.

I had risen early, but my twelve-year-old brother had risen earlier still. He found me in the courtyard as I nibbled on a bowl of yesterday's bread dipped in wine and pondered how to find one particular grain of sand on a beach.

"Nico, I was thinking. I suppose you're going to look for that killer this morning?"

"Yes, but don't even think about asking to come along. Our mother would kill me."

"Of course, there aren't many places you need search."

"What! There are countless men in Athens."

"But most have work, or live outside the walls on their farms, or will be in their homes. An outsider has none of those things. Where would they go? There're the Agora, the streets of the tradesmen, the public buildings, the inns, and Piraeus. I know it's a lot of area to cover, Nico, but surely if you ask for any man from Tanagra in those places, you must find him quickly."

I said confidently, "Exactly what I was about to do. But you did well to think it for yourself."

"Thanks, Nico!"

I wasn't yet ready to admit my irritating younger brother was smarter than me.

It was harder than it seemed. I eliminated the Agora quickly—visitors are noticed, often questioned, and it's a small area to cover—then began a trek through the inns. There are many of these. The temptation to stop at each for a cooling drink was strong, but I controlled myself. I had to be sober if I found the man.

The good-quality inns close to the Agora had never heard of him. There were men from Tanagra all right, but they had either come as a group, or were merchants known to their innkeepers for years as regular customers. I assumed an assassin brought in to kill a man would be on his own, and wouldn't be a regular visitor. So I started on the low dives. These are to be found in the narrow, muddy backstreets close to the main gates. I commenced with the ones by the Dipylon Gates that led to the west and north, thinking my quarry was more likely to have arrived by foot if he came from Tanagra. This drew a complete blank. It was only when I finished at the end of the day that I realized my foolishness. If the man wasn't acting for Tanagra then he probably didn't come directly from there. So I hurried to the inns closest to the two gates that lead to Piraeus, the port town of Athens. If he didn't walk here, then the Tanagran must have come by boat. That was going to make it harder. A lot of boats come to Athens.

"Do you have anyone from Tanagra staying here?" I asked of yet another innkeeper, a beaten-down looking fellow with crooked legs. It was early in the evening and the local custom was just starting to arrive.

"The man has more visitors than a whore," the innkeeper muttered.

My jaw dropped. "You mean you do?"

He shook his head. "Nah. Did have, though. Gone now."

My heart fell. For a moment there I thought I'd found my man. "When did he leave?" I asked.

"Expensive business, running an inn."

"I'm sure."

"Takes a lot of time too."

"I can imagine. Now about that man from Tanagra—"

"Can't afford to spend time talking when I got work to do."

He moved to the next table, where a drunk was already slumped over. The innkeeper pushed him aside, wiped the dribble where the man had been lying, then pushed him back into place.

"Isn't it a little early for him to be drunk?" I asked.

"Ephron? Nah, that's just his hangover from lunch. He'll be better when he's had something to drink."

I pulled out a few drachmae, having worked out the hint. "These for what I want to know."

The innkeeper glanced at my offering and snorted. "Hope yer don't want to know much."

"This Tanagran, when did he leave?"

"Two days ago." He reached for the coins. I pulled my hand back.

"Not yet. When did he arrive?"

The innkeeper thought. "Last month? Maybe a bit before or after."

"What was his name?"

"He said he was Aristodicus."

"You doubt it?"

The man shrugged. "He seemed the type to have a few names, yer know what I mean? He said his name was Aristodicus. I got no reason to think otherwise."

Better and better. "Had you seen him before?"

"Nah."

"Had he been in Athens before?"

"How in Hades should I know? He never been at my inn before, I can tell yer that."

"Who are these men who came to visit him?"

The innkeeper held out his hand. "Yer got your money's worth. Yer want more, yer pay more."

I dropped the coins in his hand and pulled out another handful. I wondered if I could bill Pericles for this, and decided I wasn't brave enough to try.

"I dunno who the guys were that came to see him."

I put the coins back in my bag.

"Wait! I can tell you they were Athenians from the way they talked. And they were rich."

To this man, almost anyone would look rich. "How many visits?"

He shrugged. "Four, five, six. Maybe three times for each of them?"

"Them?"

"Two guys with their slaves. It's hard to tell a slave from a citizen in Athens, you know? Everyone dresses the same. But definitely two men came here, and they both had slaves. And always they asked for Aristodicus. That's unusual for some out of town drifter, yer know? And I don't think they knew about each other. At least, they came at different times."

I had no idea who the two visitors were, but I was sure I'd found my man.

"Describe Aristodicus."

"Drifter, like I said. Tough man, kinda grizzled-looking. He's been a mercenary some time or I'll eat my own bar food. Scar down his face, left side, like can happen if a spear catches yer in the helmet."

That agreed with what Brasidas had told me.

"Okay, catch." I tossed him the coins and turned to get out of this cesspit.

"Funny thing though, this guy never left."

"What was that?" I asked, startled.

"He never left. I mean, he left the inn, said he was leaving town, but I saw him in Piraeus yesterday when I went to get more wine."

"Maybe he didn't like the bedbugs here."

"Then he made a bad deal. Compared to the inns in Piraeus, my place is a king's palace." He spat into the mud of his floor.

I think I danced all the way home. Aristodicus of Tanagra was still in Athens, or at least he had been until yesterday. But he'd changed inns, and I was sure I knew why.

Aristodicus wasn't planning to leave town. If he had been, he would have left from where he was already staying. Why shift inns for just a night?

No, Aristodicus had moved because he didn't want at least one of his two visitors to find him. And he'd moved after the murder. How interesting.

There was a man waiting for me when I returned home. The house slave ushered me into the public room, where a rather pale, ill-looking fellow sat drinking our wine. Sophroniscus had met the fellow, as is proper, discerned that he was a citizen wanting to see me on business, and had left him to it. This meant whoever he was, my father didn't like him. Otherwise, Sophroniscus would have been drinking wine with him and boring the man with talk of sculpture.

"You want me?" I said as I entered.

He looked me up and down and said coolly, "Not I. The Polemarch, who happens to be a friend of mine."

"Oh." I sat before him. "You've come about the secretary position."

"Indeed. My name is Tellis. When the Polemarch was allotted his office he asked me, his old friend, to be one of his two lieutenants. I am ill, as I have no doubt you've already observed, and whether I shall survive to next year lies with the Gods. The Polemarch asked me to see you, to convince you his offer is genuine. He thinks, you see, that you might not have believed him when he offered you the position I now hold."

"I confess the thought occurred to me later that perhaps the Polemarch would be quite happy if I had to abandon my investigation."

Tellis waved his hand as if fending off a minor irritant. "I cannot speak to the Polemarch's motivations, and nor, I suspect, can you. What I can tell you is that the offer is genuine, and the offer expires in two days. You see me before you, so you know the Polemarch spoke truth when he told you his secretary is ill. Having told that much truth, might the rest not be true too? The Polemarch sees you as a coming man. It is better to have such men in your camp than on the other side. Therefore he offers you a position far beyond your years. I remind you that unlike the archonship—a position of infinitely greater power— the secretariat does not prevent you from holding higher office in the future."

"I'm afraid the Polemarch overestimates the depth of my arrogance. I have never imagined myself as an archon." I think I blushed lightly as I said this, because in my dreams I had imagined myself before the people, leading them in the Ecclesia. In the cold light of day, having observed the likes of Pericles, Xanthippus, and Archestratus in action, I knew it would be long before I had that ability, if indeed I ever would.

"Be that as it may, the position is open and the offer is made. If it will not make you a great man, and I can promise you from personal experience it will not, the job would certainly put you in the public eye, be a springboard for higher public office. What do you say?"

"The same as I said to the Polemarch: that I must think about this before giving an answer."

Tellis rose to go, steadying himself with a shaky hand on the end of the couch. He picked up a walking stick that rested alongside, and said, "You are either remarkably cautious, which for such a young man is an admirable trait, or else you are a fool, which for such a young man would be quite normal. I wish you joy of your deliberations. Goodbye."

Sophroniscus was jovial at dinner that evening. He had studiously ignored my activities unless I spoke of them, but tonight he said over the wine, "I notice your business is becoming more popular. You're even starting to receive clients at home. Who was that man who came to see you today?"

"His name is Tellis. He was secretary to the Polemarch."

"Was?"

"Yes. He fell ill and had to retire."

"What would the Polemarch want with you?" Phaenarete asked. She ordered the slaves to clear the courtyard of dinner bowls.

"Uh, he offered me the secretary position Tellis vacated."

"Congratulations, my boy!" Sophroniscus beamed. "I confess, I thought you were overreaching when you said you wanted to try this—well, I made myself clear at the time, I suppose—but to pick up such a position so quickly speaks of good prospects."

"I haven't said yes, Father."

Silence.

"You . . . you *turned down* the Polemarch's offer?" Sophroniscus spluttered. "Are you the same son who was so desperate to make a name in public affairs, he spurned his father's trade?"

"Yes, but—"

"Then you go right back to the Polemarch, thank him kindly for his offer, and accept the job!"

"But—"

"There are no buts about it."

"I haven't said no, either!" I almost shouted.

Sophroniscus paused. "What do you mean?" He held up his cup for more wine and a slave boy immediately refilled it from the krater between us. Phaenarete ordered sweetmeats to be brought. That was a sign she thought this conversation might go on for some time.

"I mean if I take the job I would have to abandon Pericles."

"You feel loyalty?"

"I'd feel like a rat fleeing a sinking ship."

"I see." Sophroniscus drummed his fingers on his dining

couch. "Has it occurred to you, when the rat jumps off the ship it is acting quite rationally in its own best interest?"

"It's still a rat, Father. And . . . I think perhaps what I'm doing might be important for Athens."

"There speaks egotistic youth. Beware hubris, son. The Gods punish it."

"I have three days to accept the offer, Father. If I can find the man who killed Ephialtes tomorrow, or the day after, then I can make Pericles happy and still have time to say yes to the Polemarch."

"Impossible. You haven't succeeded so far, what makes you think you can do it quickly now that you really need to?"

"I've made important progress. I know that the assassin is still in Athens, and I know where he was staying until a few days ago." I basked in the glory of my own cleverness as I described my success in detail.

I boasted, "It's only a matter of time now before I solve the entire problem. All I have to do is track down this Aristodicus and force him to tell me who he's working for."

My little brother hung on my every word, looking up at me in adulation. Even Phaenarete looked mildly pleased. Sophroniscus frowned and said, "Do not risk the anger of the Gods, Nicolaos. The Gods hate hubris in a man almost more than any trait. Remember the boastful words of Odysseus to Poseidon after the fall of Troy? He paid for it with ten years of his life, and the lives of all his men. Retract your boast before something bad happens!"

"You are right, Father, and if Aristodicus eludes me tomorrow I shall."

He said urgently, "Do it now, right now."

"But what could possibly go wrong right now?"

The door flew open. Every head turned, startled or in fear, for there'd been no warning of a disturbance.

Our head slave stood there in shock and blurted, "Master

Nicolaos, there is a young woman in the public room. She says she must speak with you immediately."

Diotima stood in the public room, tears streaming down and a look of horror on her face.

"Wow! Where did you find her, Nico?" my little brother asked in admiration. My entire family stood behind me. I didn't dare turn around to see the expressions of Sophroniscus or Phaenarete, for if I did I would probably die of embarrassment.

Diotima had run here in bare feet. The mud was caked on past her ankles. She was wearing a tunic which was definitely supposed to be inside wear; her hair was down. She stood wringing her hands.

"I'm . . . I'm sorry. I didn't mean to upset you, but . . . but I didn't know who to . . . Nicolaos, they say I'm to bury Ephialtes!"

"You?" I was surprised. "But you're not—" I broke off, unwilling to continue more of this highly interesting conversation before my parents.

Phaenarete said angrily, "Nicolaos, you will tell me who this girl is before I take her to the women's quarters and have her escorted back to her home."

Trapped. No way to get her out of the house and then explain her away as a distraught witness.

"This is Diotima of Mantinea, priestess-in-training to the Goddess Artemis." I was not going to say the rest even if Sophroniscus ordered the slaves to beat me.

Sophroniscus demanded, "And what does she have to do with you? Have you any idea what her father is going to say when he finds out—"

"My father is dead! Murdered!" Diotima blurted.

And all the while Phaenarete was muttering, "Diotima. Mantinea. Diotima? Mantinea? Mantinea!" Phaenarete shouted in triumph, "You're the daughter of Euterpe the hetaera!" Phaenarete looked Diotima up and down. Diotima nodded meekly.

"You know Diotima?" I asked, incredulous.

"Of course I know her! I delivered her all those years ago, didn't I? Don't look so shocked, son. I am a midwife, you know."

Sophroniscus and I were banished to the dining room while Phaenarete took Diotima to be washed and given warm clothes. My brother was dragged to bed by slaves with orders to tie him down if necessary.

Sophroniscus raised an eyebrow. "I told you so," he said.

"But she must already have been running here when I made the boast," I protested.

"But if you hadn't boasted, she wouldn't have been running here."

I decided not to argue the illogic of that, since nine out of every ten men in Athens would have agreed with Sophroniscus wholeheartedly. Phaenarete opened the door and led in Diotima, who looked somewhat more composed, though her eyes were red and bloated from crying. Phaenarete sat her down on a couch and sat beside her, as a good chaperone should.

"You will now tell us why you are here," Sophroniscus ordered.

Diotima looked at me. I nodded. Phaenarete followed that little exchange with her eyes but said nothing.

"The secretary of the Archon came to our house tonight. I am to lead the funeral procession for Ephialtes alongside his wife Stratonike. They say I must because she is mad, and I am to be made his heir."

Sophroniscus said, "You aren't his daughter though, not legally that is."

"I am now," Diotima said through clenched teeth. "I was adopted this morning by his estate, on the orders of the Eponymous Archon."

So that was the radical idea Conon had mentioned. A man could adopt someone in their will. But Conon had gone one step further.

"That's rather clever," Sophroniscus murmured. "So what does this have to do with Nicolaos?"

Diotima looked confused. "Why, who else would I tell? He's investigating the murder."

"That doesn't explain why you ran through the streets at night," Sophroniscus said. "You might not like what's happening, but what do you expect Nicolaos to do about it? And I will point out you now have a promised husband who will not be at all happy to hear of this, not happy at all." He looked at Phaenarete, who understood and called for slaves.

Sophroniscus said in a voice that brooked no argument. "I and two stout slaves will escort you to your door. You will walk through that doorway. You will stay there, or at least, if you must run through the streets it will not be to here." He turned to me. "And you will stay away from Diotima from this point on."

"But—"

Sophroniscus talked over me. "A man caught in adultery can legally be killed by the husband as long as the couple are found in the act and there are witnesses. Did you know that? And being betrothed counts."

"But we're not—"

"However, in the case of the wife, she can be killed by her husband if he so much as suspects. It might not be perfectly legal, but I've never known any man be charged for it where the woman's reputation was dubious. Did you know *that*? Nicolaos, you are risking this girl's life. Now say goodbye to her."

10

"Heave!" Sophroniscus shouted. The slaves, all eight of them, took hold of the rope and dug their heels into the dirt. They leaned back and pulled, with determination and copious sweat all over their faces, the muscles in their arms and backs bulging with effort. None shirked; they wanted this over as much as we did. Just when I thought nothing was going to happen, the sledge they were pulling, bearing a huge statue, edged forward yet another small distance. The rope slackened while the men took a breath before doing it all again.

We'd been breaking our backs since first light, and when I blinked at the sun, high overhead, I saw it was almost midday. I'd breathed in so much dust I could no longer smell anything, I was hot, sore, and hungry, and I had no doubt everyone else was too. But there would be no rest until the job was done. Fortunately the end was finally in sight—literally so, just down the end of the street in fact.

Being the slave of a sculptor has its advantages, particularly if the owner is a man as mild as my father. Sculptors are not war-like people, so as a slave, you are not likely to find yourself in a battle camp except in time of war. Nor are sculptors major estate holders; a sculptor's slave isn't likely to find himself toiling from dawn to dusk in a shadeless field, tending olive trees under a hot sun. And you certainly won't find yourself down a mine, or pulling the oars of a ship. No, the slave of a sculptor has it easy, most days.

But sometimes a sculptor needs to move large, heavy blocks of solid stone: raw blocks to the workshop, and finished pieces to the estates of rich men. Right now, the slaves of Sophroniscus were paying their dues.

The men rested, and while they did Socrates raced to the front of the sledge carrying a bucket filled with pig fat and the cheapest olive oil. He scooped out a dripping lump of the revolting mixture and began smearing it all over the undersides of the boards. The sledge itself was an old one, which had been in the family for years. It was made of solid oak, strong enough to hold up any weight of marble, and thoroughly weathered. The undersides were stained a deep, rich color from years of oil, and the boards were smooth as a girl's skin.

We were taking this finished piece to a sanctuary for Sophroniscus' client, Callias, who was said to be the richest man in Athens. Callias was descended from an ancient Athenian family, despite which he controlled a vast business empire. Unlike other well-born citizens, he was only too happy to sully his hands with sordid trade, which no doubt explains why he was rich and they, for the most part, weren't. He owned his own silver mine, but everyone knew he made most of his fortune by renting out his excess slave labor to the silver mines run by the city. This was tough on the slaves, whose lives were short and painful, but since most of them were prisoners of war nobody cared.

The work was a racehorse, larger than life, commissioned by Callias to thank the Gods for his victory in the races at the most recent Panathenaic Games. It was done in a single block of marble which Sophroniscus had especially ordered for this client and shipped in from the island of Paros, where the quarries produce the best marble in the world. This block was of the highest standard—it had cost Callias a fortune to acquire—and was a beautiful white with virtually no blemishes. It seemed almost a pity to paint it, but of course that would have to be done. No one with any artistic taste would want to stare at a statue in a monotonous marble color—if nothing else you would never see the fine details unless they were highlighted—and Callias, who had bought from Father in the past, unquestionably had excellent taste. Nevertheless it seemed a pity to cover such good stone. I was reconciled to it only because I knew Callias would certainly hire the best painter, and a good painter with such material to work on would certainly keep his dabs light and enhance the stone, not hide it from view.

The finished piece was not only a thing of fragile, delicate beauty to behold, a study of elegant movement in stone, it was also damned heavy.

I helped haul on the harder sections, but spent time too overseeing the men, in particular making sure everything was done safely, and that the statue never shifted in its stand. This was a job I knew well from long experience. Atop the sledge was a wooden stand and brackets, which had to be built anew every time, so that the statue being moved fit snugly in its hold. Few things are more dangerous than a piece of marble toppling sideways, so to reduce the chances of an accident the pieces are always transported lying lengthways.

At that moment the road was sloping ever so slightly downhill, and Sophroniscus and I stood side by side, watching the slaves hauling, and Socrates dashing in from time to time to smooth their way.

"So tell me, son, what is it about sculpting you don't like?" Sophroniscus asked without warning. To put it mildly, I was startled by the sudden question. There was an edge to his tone that I rarely heard from my father. I guessed he'd had to nerve himself up to ask the question. I thought for a moment about the best way to express how I felt.

"There's nothing wrong with sculpting—" I began.

"Is it that you don't like me? Is that it?" he said sharply. "Be honest."

"No! No Father." I was shocked. I hadn't realized how much he took my rejection of his profession as a rejection of him.

"No Father, it's nothing like that at all. I just find sculpting . . . boring." There, I'd said it at last.

"Boring?" he repeated, as if I'd uttered some absurdity.

"Yes sir. Boring."

"But . . . you used to love it as a child! All those hours you spent in the workshop, watching me. I remember it so well. You would sit on the blocks, with those big round eyes of yours, watching everything I did. You loved it."

"No Father, I loved you. Still do, in fact. I wanted to be with you, and the only way to do that was to be in the workshop, because you never left it."

His eyes widened, I think in surprise. But he said nothing. I was glad, because the conversation was making me feel distinctly uncomfortable.

Not once had Sophroniscus taken his eye off the work. He may have been concerned for his precious statue, or he may have been avoiding my eye. So I saw him in profile, and not for the first time I remarked the similarity between him and my younger brother. Both of them had a bit of the look of a satyr about them. I on the other hand took after my mother's side of the family, and I wondered if the dissimilarity extended to our personalities as well. Perhaps that was the reason we couldn't agree.

"Socrates, get out from under there!" Sophroniscus roared. The little fool had taken to jumping through the gaps between the formwork holding the statue and the sledge as it moved. Socrates jumped out of the way and let the men get on with their work.

"I see," Sophroniscus continued. "Well, lad, I'm glad you had the guts to stand up and tell me to my face, but it doesn't mean I'm reconciled to what you're doing. Our family has a poor enough record when it comes to dealing with the powerful that I can only assume disaster will come of this adventure of yours. You know what happened to our illustrious ancestor when he got himself entangled with great men."

I did indeed, since Father never tired of telling us. Family legend had it that our line was founded by Daedalus himself, who built the Labyrinth for King Minos of old, and who had to flee in fear of his life with Theseus, after the hero slew the Minotaur. As Father said, a fine example of being caught between two powerful men. Daedalus lost his son, Icarus, on that adventure, and had to remarry and beget more sons when he arrived in Athens.

"Well, it won't be a problem for me, Father," I said in jest. "I don't have a son to lose!"

Transporting a statue always attracts an audience, most of them stopping to watch the fun, some to offer helpful suggestions that we could live without, and some to critique the artist's work, which if Father overheard might result in litigation or violence. Nobody ever offers to help by pulling, unless they're down on their luck and want to be paid.

A woman in priestess robes came walking down the street, attended by two slaves. Men moved to let her pass, but she stopped to watch us. I glanced in her direction, distracted by the movement, then did a double take and looked again.

It was Diotima, dressed as I'd never seen her before. She seemed older in the robes, more mature, and looked as if maybe she really was a priestess and a respectable member of society.

I was suddenly and acutely aware of my own appearance. I was wearing nothing but a loincloth. I was as filthy as the slaves, the dust and the dirt covered my bare chest, and you could see where the sweat dripping down me had formed tiny rivers in the grime.

I knew she'd spotted me, there was no point trying to hide, so when she gestured I walked to her.

"Nice chest!" Diotima murmured, low enough that no one

else could hear. Her dark eyes looked me up and down in a way no one could miss; she smiled, and I had to order myself not to blush. I wasn't used to being ogled in public; the women in Athens aren't supposed to do such things.

She diverted her eyes to our job. "Looks heavy. Why don't you use wheels?" she asked.

I smiled. "Ha! There's someone in the crowd asks that, every time."

"No doubt the intelligent, curious ones," she said, trying to look stern. "And what do you reply? Feel free to avoid any phrases that might hint this is a stupid question."

"If we had wheels, there'd be only four points holding up the block of stone. The moment we tried to cross anything other than solid rock the wheels would sink into the dirt and we'd never get it moving again. And you've probably noticed the streets in this city are fundamentally—"

"Mud!" we said in unison, and laughed.

I finished, "But with a sledge, the weight is carried across a wide surface, so we don't get stuck."

"I didn't think of that," she admitted.

"Don't take it hard; if you didn't have to do it yourself, you'd never know."

"Rizon has no alibi for Father's death," Diotima said.

"And you know this how?"

"Same as for Archestratus. I asked his slaves while I was in my boy clothing."

"Does it matter? Don't we know the man from Tanagra killed your father?"

Diotima shrugged. "I thought it better to know. But, Nicolaos, Rizon does have an excellent alibi for when the bowyer died."

Sophroniscus called to me, and I had no choice but to leave Diotima.

"I saw you, son. I told you to stay away from her," he said.

"Yes, sir."

"This girl . . ." Sophroniscus spoke in a quiet voice, almost whispering, then he paused.

"You mean Diotima?" I automatically looked in her direction, and Sophroniscus followed my gaze. She noticed our attention and waved.

"Her. Your mother has spoken to me. It's Phaenarete's view, given the mother's . . . er . . . position in life, that there's very little can be done to sully the daughter's reputation more than it already is, and the talk in the Agora is that the man she's betrothed to would hardly notice the difference between a virgin and a pornê off the street. They tell me he's been boasting to anyone who'll listen about what he intends to do with her."

My hands clenched and I gritted my teeth, but Sophroniscus was still speaking. "So I've decided to withdraw my objections to you associating with the girl." Sophroniscus frowned. "And of course the near certainty that you would completely ignore my order makes the decision easier. Still, I wish you wouldn't be seen talking to her in public."

"It was business, Father."

"Then that's even worse," he said. "You allow a woman to work for you?"

"It is her father who died, sir. I could hardly stop her."

Sophroniscus shook his head. "You need to learn how to control women, son. Remember, her behavior should be seemly, which it certainly is not if she's conversing with men in the street."

"She stopped and talked to me, Father. I didn't ask her."

"Then order her to keep walking. You're a man, she'll obey."

"Is that how it works with you and Mother, sir?"

"Er . . . pay attention to the load, son. It's your responsibility if it tips."

It was just past midday when we finally reached the sanctuary. The staff had been expecting us. The site was leveled to perfection and swept of loose stones. Sophroniscus checked it, nodded in satisfaction, and ordered the back end of the sledge to be adjusted so that the feet of the statue would slide into the correct position. This was done by the men with crowbars and much swearing.

The base block had been delivered the previous day, and placed in precisely the right spot. It remained only to pull the statue up and onto its base. A small A-frame tower of tall wooden beams was raised, blocks and tackles hanging off it, and ropes were threaded through pulleys hanging from the top of the A-frame and attached to the horse at points Sophroniscus knew to be strong enough to take the strain. The ropes would pull the statue off the sledge—now tilted back—so that the stone would touch land with its hind feet first, and then while still supported from above rotate over to a standing position.

Sophroniscus waved his arm, and the men hauled for the final effort. The horse's hind feet slid to the ground as expected, and his body slowly rose into the sky. This was the moment of maximum strain for the men and the grunting was loud.

Socrates jumped onto the platform, directly underneath, pressed his hands against the horse's belly, and pretended to be pushing the piece upright. He laughed.

Sophroniscus roared, "Socrates! If I have to tell you one more time—"

A rope snapped.

The horse lurched away from the men, directly down on top of Socrates. It all seemed to happen in slow motion for me. I could see his face turn from laughter to horror in an instant, he put his hands up, as if to try and hold the statue for real, before he fell backward with the immense block of stone toppling on top of him. The dust flew up in a cloud, obscuring the disaster. Something cracked. The sledge jerked beneath the sudden weight.

"Oh Gods." I ran through the cloud, waving my hand to clear the air before me and coughing.

I expected to see a pool of blood, and the crushed body of my brother. I found him lying flat, his face turned to the side, unable to move, the statue upon him. He was having trouble breathing, but, miraculously, he was still alive.

"Help me, Nico," he whispered.

The wooden framework used to hold the statue in place during transport had protected Socrates. The support struts were still attached to the stone, and had fallen to each side of him. The struts should have splintered in an instant, but they had held enough that, bent and broken as they were, enough of them remained to afford Socrates the tiniest gap between the statue and the platform of the sledge. But the frame which had saved his life also trapped him in a cage which would collapse at any moment. To pull him out I would have to remove some of the struts encasing him, and when I did that, the only thing keeping the statue off him would be gone.

"Hang on, little brother, we're going to get you out of there." The woodwork creaked. Both Socrates and I eyed it suspiciously.

"Hurry, Nico," he said unnecessarily. A tear rolled down his cheek, which he tried to blink away. I refused to notice it.

"Don't move, son," Sophroniscus ordered. He was already eyeing the setup. To the men, who had all gathered around, upset and shouting, he yelled, "Get back, you fools! Get back now!" He was worried a man would knock the fragile structure and cause it to collapse. Sophroniscus and I both stepped back carefully.

"We could pull him out from the head end, directly along the line of the statue," he said to me. "The problem is, even pulling him out might knock a strut, or shake the frame enough to collapse it. We have to get something else under there, now."

I nodded. "The base?" I suggested. It was the obvious thing to use.

Sophroniscus shouted to the men to pick up the round base and wedge it under the horse's head. They heaved it up, all eight clustered about it, and carried it around the statue from the feet to the head. They placed it as close as they dared underneath the head, but with the best will in the world they could not jam it in; the angle was simply wrong, leaving a small air gap the breadth of two fingers between head and base. It wasn't much, but Socrates hadn't any room to spare, and if the statue came down even a finger's breadth it might be enough to break bones inside him.

There was only one thing to do. I took our heaviest mallet, lined up my stroke by eye with the greatest care, and, praying to any Gods that would listen, struck the base with every bit of my strength.

The base moved enough to wedge itself underneath. I struck again. The statue might have risen by a fraction, but it might also have been my imagination.

"Hold," Sophroniscus ordered.

I put down the mallet. He pointed at the upper hindquarter. Cracks and fissures had appeared about the leg joint. The fall must have damaged the stone at that point, which was not surprising now that I came to think of it, because that was the point of greatest pressure when the statue fell. The jolt must have been terrific, and my hammering had completed the damage.

Sophroniscus put both hands on the leg and pulled, gently at first, then harder. The leg snapped off and fell to the ground. Sophroniscus ordered the slaves to take the leg around to one side of the statue. While he directed, crouching low and watching everything with the greatest care, the men jammed the snapped leg underneath the chest of the animal, and wedged the broken end into the dirt at their feet. One of them—the largest and strongest man—ran to where they'd been working, took up a crowbar lying on the ground, and raced back. He plunged the crowbar into the place where the leg met the ground, further blocking it from any movement. He leaned into the crowbar, bracing his bare feet against the dirt, his toes searching for the best purchase. Sophroniscus nodded approval. "It's time," he said, and stepped into the shadow of the broken horse.

I put my hand on his shoulder and gently held him back.

"No, Father, this is my job. You're in charge," and I was quick to step around him and squat beside Socrates before he had a chance to object.

Socrates had lain there without struggling and without panic, not wasting our time with questions when he knew we were hurrying to save him. He hadn't even stirred when the base had been hammered in, and the great weight above him had wobbled. It occurred to me that, for a young boy, he had amazing self-control. "Are you all right, Socrates?" I asked him, keeping my voice as slow and calm as possible.

"Do I look all right?" he responded, his tone telling me I'd asked a stupid question. I repressed a smile. Mortal danger hadn't changed his attitude one bit.

"I'm going to pull you out." The broken-off leg angled upward directly above me. I would have to be careful not to stand up, nor to hit the leg with Socrates' body when I pulled.

I said, "As soon as you're on the ground, clear the area, get right away, all right? Because I'll be coming after you, and I won't be looking where I'm going."

"Got it." He paused. "Thanks, Nico."

"Right, on the count of three." I held fast to his arm and leg, and braced my foot against the side of the sledge. I noticed, irrelevant to the crisis, that the timbers were cracked. It had seen its last service for the family.

"One . . . two . . . three." I yanked on his arm and his thigh simultaneously. Socrates' body was pulled into the remaining struts, which resisted for a moment before popping out. I fell backward and Socrates landed sideways on my lap. The statue fell the breadth of two hands before jerking to a stop, held up on our side by nothing except the support of that one marble leg. I could hear loud grunting behind me and knew our slaves, leaning into the leg, were saving our lives with every breath.

I practically threw Socrates out from under the shadow of the stone. He was a sturdy, thickset lad, but men who watched told me later they saw a boy flying like a quoit. The force of the throw sent me the other way, and my back hit the wreck of the sledge. I looked up. The stone horse was staring down right at me, we exchanged eye contact for a moment, and I wondered how he could be so impassive when we were both about to die. He lunged down at me.

I don't remember diving out of the way, but I must have, because when I came to my senses I was lying facedown, and I wasn't screaming in pain. I raised myself onto my elbows, spitting out dust, and looked behind. The horse had rolled and landed at my feet, on its back, its three remaining legs in the air and the amputated fourth beneath it. If it had been alive, we would have put it out of its misery straightaway.

Someone helped me up, I think one of the slaves, but I don't know because immediately Sophroniscus wrapped me up in his arms and hugged me. There were tears in his eyes.

"Nicolaos, my son—" he began.

"What in Hades is going on!" A man was marching toward us, trailed by a small cloud of slaves. It took no intelligence to realize this was Callias, the richest man in Athens, and by the look on his face, a very unhappy customer. He was an older man—I knew that he had to be at least fifty or sixty years old because he had famously fought at the Battle of Marathon, wearing no armor but the robes of a priest. I knew too that in his younger years he had won the horse race at the Olympics, come second in the chariot race, and had been a victor at the Pythian Games.

For all that he was getting on now, Callias hadn't the paunch one often sees, and nor was he stick thin. The speed at which he walked toward our debacle was impressive.

He stopped short at the scene, stared at the wreck of his expensive artwork, and swore roundly, finishing with, "What in Hades happened?"

Sophroniscus explained—his voice wavered enough to tell

me he was rattled—and Callias' headman, who had been watching the entire fiasco, confirmed it.

Callias grunted and asked, "Is the boy unhurt?" Which I thought showed compassion and I took a liking to him, a feeling that instantly dissolved when his next comment, after hearing that Socrates was only scratched was, "Sophroniscus, much as I value you as an artist, I am bound to say this is down to your incompetence. The men were yours, the equipment was yours, and you were paid to deliver and install the work. I hold you responsible, and you will pay me the cost of the marble. I needn't add I won't be paying you your fee."

Disaster. The block had been paid for by Callias directly, and it was worth more than all my father's wealth put together. He would be a ruined man, unable to pay his debts. If Callias pressed his claim, Father would be forced to sell his home and workshop and tools and slaves and be reduced to the life of a common laborer. For a master craftsman, it would be total ignominy, and to maintain the family I would have to labor alongside him.

Socrates, who was sitting on the ground nursing his bruises, shouted, "That's not fair, it was an accident!"

Sophroniscus waved a hand at him and said, "Quiet, son. I'm afraid Callias has the right of it."

I've never been prouder of my father than at that moment, because he said, with a quiet, matter-of-fact voice, "It is true what you say, Callias. The fault must be mine, though I can't imagine how this happened, I've never had such a problem before in my entire career. I stand ready to pay the loss."

I said, "But Callias, you still have a statue."

"A horse without a leg is worthless," Callias said mildly.

Sophroniscus was too strong a man to beg, so he said nothing. I was simply aghast.

"Master!" a man shouted. He was one of the slaves who accompanied Callias, and he beckoned to us from where our equipment lay. Callias strode over to him, and we all followed.

"There is something here you should see." The man knelt by the block and pulley system used to raise the statue. He held up the rope that had snapped.

"You see, Master?"

I saw it in an instant. But Callias said irritably, "No, I don't see, Koppa, that's why I have you. Tell me."

The slave ran his fingers across the break. "The rope is thick, strong," he said. "See? It is as thick as my wrist. It needs to be for the weight it holds. But look at the break, Master. It is smooth on the inside, a clean cut, but here, around the circumference, these few threads"—his finger traced the outer skin of the hemp— "here it is all frayed."

Callias frowned. He wasn't a stupid man. He said to us, "This is Koppa. He understands mechanical things. Stand aside and let him inspect."

We all stepped back and watched in silence as this odd man walked about the entire mess, humming to himself. He was a small man with thinning white hair and a slight paunch, and spoke with an accent I couldn't place. That a slave was fed well enough to put on weight told me Callias valued him highly. Koppa paid particular attention to the pulleys, blocks, and levers.

"There's no doubt about it, Master. This equipment was sabotaged," Koppa reported back to Callias. "The rope was cut inside, as I showed you." He held up more of our equipment for everyone to see. "In addition, this pulley I hold was weakened where the pin meets its container. With a little more pressure, it would have snapped."

I said, excited, "Both the rope and the pulley would only be under pressure while we were raising the statue, and before we had it upright."

Koppa looked at me in surprise and slight distaste. He must have thought I was a lowly slave from the way I appeared, but he agreed. "Master, this man is correct. The purpose of this crime was to smash the statue."

"Thank you, Koppa." Callias turned to my father. "Well, Sophroniscus, it seems you have an enemy. At least you have the small satisfaction of knowing it was not your own negligence that undid you."

"But this means Father doesn't owe you anything," I said in triumph. "It's the man who sabotaged us who owes you."

"It alters nothing," Callias replied. "Your father allowed his tools to be damaged. He remains liable to me. If he can find his persecutor then the sum might be recouped."

Sophroniscus said nothing, which meant he knew Callias was in the right again. I had only one more try.

"Are you sure, Callias, this wasn't aimed at you?"

"Your loyalty to your father does you credit, young man." He considered for a brief moment. "No, it's most unlikely. I have enemies aplenty, but anyone smart enough to think of this is certainly bright enough to know they could only hurt the sculptor."

Sophroniscus nodded glumly. "I will have to think on this."

"I expect your payment before the end of the month. Do not fail, or I shall take further action." Callias strode back toward his mansion.

Father hadn't an enemy in the world. I, on the other hand, like Callias, had plenty. A murderer out there somewhere didn't want me to catch him. Someone had ordered me beaten. The political futures of many men rode on the identity of whomever I uncovered. And if I was forced to answer my family obligations, I would have no time for anything else. There wasn't any doubt in my mind who this was aimed at.

My brother had almost lost his life because of me. And worse, I, Nicolaos, son of Sophroniscus the sculptor, was the cause of my father's downfall.

"Callias!" I shouted at his back.

He stopped and turned. His unsmiling face showed impatience. "Yes?"

"Whoever caused this, whyever it was done, it was not my father."

"Yes. And your point is?"

"If I can prove who it was, will you sue them instead? They say you have a reputation for liking justice; well, if you do, shall we see some?"

Callias stood silent for a moment before nodding. "You raise a reasonable point, young man. Very well. Bring me the name of this enemy, and proof good enough for a court, before the end of the month. If you fail, the responsibility falls on your father." And so saying, he turned on his heel and walked rapidly away.

To put it mildly, the atmosphere in our home that night was despondent. Father blamed himself for almost losing a son. He left dinner early and shut himself in his office, to ponder his finances for some way to pay Callias. I was not hopeful and nor, I suspect, was he. Socrates blamed himself for playing silly games underneath the statue, forgetting that Father would be facing the same financial ruin regardless. I was the only one to receive any praise—for pulling Socrates from danger—and that served only to make me more miserable because I was sure the sabotage had been directed at me.

The only one carrying on any semblance of normal life was my practical mother.

"That's because there's nothing else I can do to help," she said, when I asked her. "Your father will work it out; I have every confidence. When we returned to Athens after the Persians sacked it, we'd lost everything and had to start again, and then we had a small baby to care for—you."

The revelation that Ephialtes had considered exposing Diotima to die as a child had kept niggling at me. Was it really true, or was it something Euterpe had made up to gather sympathy? I couldn't be sure; I decided to put the matter to rest by asking the one person who could tell me what had really happened.

"It was a close call," Phaenarete admitted. She was instructing the slaves for their household duties, but I interrupted her to ask the question. "I remember it was an easy birth; Euterpe suffered little compared to most women, for all the fuss she made." Phaenarete grimaced. I had no trouble imagining the drama Euterpe would have created.

"When it was over I cut the cord and tied it, and put the baby into Euterpe's arms. Euterpe did what every new mother does, check the sex of her child. She saw, but said nothing. As custom required, Ephialtes was called, and when he entered the room Euterpe held up the baby to him, still without saying a word. I remember he just stood there and stared.

"Euterpe said, 'I present your daughter,' and she cringed a little.

"Ephialtes was silent for a moment, while he considered. Then he said, 'Expose the child.'

"Well, Euterpe went into hysterics. You can imagine! I think at that moment, maybe for the first time in her life, she must have developed strong feelings for someone."

"You didn't say anything?"

"This happens every time a child is born, and I never say anything. It isn't my place. The mother has no say either, only the father decides whether to keep the child.

"Euterpe must have been sore and in some pain, but she threw herself on her knees and begged for the child's life, making all sorts of promises. I won't go into the details of *that* conversation! It was torrid, I must say. I was embarrassed to have to listen, but I could hardly walk out." Phaenarete shuddered.

I said, "Wasn't she taking a terrible risk, a woman in her position? He might have walked away and simply never returned."

Phaenarete nodded. "I thought so too. But he took the baby from Euterpe's hands, which meant he accepted her, and said, 'Very well, you may keep the child, but only so long as you keep your bargain,' referring to all the promises she'd made. He handed the baby back to Euterpe, turned his back on the whole scene, and walked out of the room. I helped Euterpe back into bed, cleaned and washed her, made sure she and the baby were comfortable, and left. Later I recommended a wet-nurse. Ephialtes paid my bill on time but didn't send a bonus. I expected that; men only pay a bonus if it's a boy. I suppose Euterpe's been bound by those promises she made ever since."

"You think that was hard on her?"

"I think she's had a remarkably soft life. I'm almost jealous." Then she laughed. "Don't look so shocked, my son! But it's true enough that the hetaerae have much freer lives than we respectable married women. They're permitted to walk the streets whenever they want. They can go to the theater. They can talk with men. They can even socialize with men." She laughed once more. "Of course, that rather goes with the job."

"Wouldn't you rather have a husband?" I asked, amazed.

"Oh, I'm happy enough! I have a good husband, even if one that's absentminded and covered in gritty marble dust. There are worse fates to befall a woman, dear boy, much, much worse. And every day I thank the Goddess Hera that I have what I have. A girl's father decides whom she will marry, and it's the luck of the draw, my son, what husband a woman gets. He might treat her well, he might beat her, though if he beats her and the neighbors know of it he might be excluded from public office until he behaves better, but that's the only punishment for a wife beater."

I think I must have gone quite white.

"It's not so bad, dear. The women, after all, are in charge at home, whatever the men might think. The slaves work for me, not your father." She paused. "I have spoken freely with you, perhaps more freely than a woman should, but I've done so because you are a grown man now, my son, and when the time comes for you to marry, I wish you to remember what I have said about the lot of a woman."

"I will," I promised. "You shocked me, Mother, when you said you'd been midwife at Diotima's birth. You've been called out to so many births, but somehow I've never thought of the babies you deliver as being real people. I've never met one before."

"You've met several; you just didn't know it. They're *all* real people, Nicolaos, all those babies, even the ones that are exposed."

"What happens to them?" Exposing babies was something everyone knew happened, but no one ever talked about.

"The ones that the father doesn't want? They die, for the most part; rarely a passerby will take an abandoned baby to raise as a slave. But most are stuffed into clay pots and left, still crying, at the cemetery by the Dipylon Gate. Some are thrown down old wells. The babe is killed by cold, or hunger, but not directly by the father, so the Gods won't hold him responsible. The baby just cries and cries, until eventually there's silence." Phaenarete's voice was harsh and it was obvious who she held responsible.

This conversation was making me squirm, but, having started it, I was determined to finish. "Have you ever . . ."

"Killed a baby I delivered?" She grimaced. "Never a healthy one. I wouldn't dare offend Eireithya, the Goddess who controls childbirth. What might she do to the next baby I had to deliver, if I killed one that she allowed live? No, I leave the killing to the men."

A sudden thought came to me, a startling one I'd never had before. "Uh, Mother, did you . . . or rather, did Father . . . that is, did Socrates and I . . . ever have a sister?"

Phaenarete said, her voice firm, "No, you never have, Nicolaos. And if you had, she would be with us now. Your father has never been so poor that we could not feed another mouth."

I'd been sure that would be the answer, but I was surprised how relieved I was to hear my mother say it.

Phaenarete sent two men to fetch water from the nearby well, and ordered the girls to sweep out the public rooms. As the slaves left for their duties she said, "One thing I'll tell you, my son: I know it's important for you to find Ephialtes' killer, but I saw him prepared to let a little girl die, and I'm not sorry he's dead."

11

The funeral procession began at dusk, as is the tradition, so that Apollo the Sun God would not be offended by the sight of the dead man. I would have attended the funeral in any case, to see the reactions of everyone involved, but with Diotima as one of the main actors I had a double reason to be there.

I stood outside the house of Ephialtes, among many men. They had come to pay their respects, or perhaps they had simply come to see the fun. I knew some men were laying bets there would be a riot at this funeral. Pythax obviously thought so: he had Scythians grouped in pairs throughout the crowd. He and I caught each other's eyes. I nodded, Pythax looked away.

The door opened, and Stratonike stepped outside, wearing a dark shift and walking barefoot. She was a thin woman, almost bony, and her face was drawn; her hair was cropped and untidy, but that of course was as it should be for a woman in mourning. Her eyes were a little wild and she looked back and forth, as if she couldn't quite comprehend what was happening.

A woman stood to each side of Stratonike, and I knew these must be her nurses. They were large, middle-aged, and appeared strong. They weren't Hellene; perhaps they were sturdy mountain stock from Thrace. They would be slaves for sure; no free woman would willingly do their job. I wondered why a man like

Ephialtes would have kept Stratonike when he could surely have disposed of her and married elsewhere.

Diotima stepped through the doorway, dressed as Stratonike was in a dark shift. I saw that sometime since I last saw her she had taken shears to her hair, which now was ragged and short.

With the body about to leave, libations were to be poured to cleanse the entire building. A nurse dipped a cup into the urn that I had used days ago to purify myself, and pressed it into Stratonike's hand. She looked as if she was about to drink it, but the nurse grabbed her hand and gently turned it until the water fell into the dust. The nurse said something and encouraged Stratonike to repeat her words.

Diotima stepped forward with a face set like stone and dipped her cup into the urn. She spoke the words of the ritual in a clear voice, calling for the house to be cleansed of evil. She too spilled the cleansing water upon the doorstep.

Now Pericles, Archestratus, Rizon, and men I didn't know walked inside, and emerged with the bier. They laid the body upon a wagon that had been dressed in black. The crowd was completely silent. Stratonike, held by the nurses, waited behind while Diotima stepped to the fore carrying a jar of libations. Rizon stepped to the fore too, carrying a spear. Diotima was surprised by this, and went to Rizon and took hold of the spear in its middle.

He refused to let go, though I could see her tugging. They had words while the crowd watched, said low so no one else could hear, but there was no doubt in my mind what was happening. The spear represented vengeance for the man who had died by violence; it was always carried before the body of a murder victim, and Diotima was quite certain that she and not her future husband was going to carry the burden. This was so far beyond reason that most of the crowd didn't understand what was happening.

I think Rizon realized he was starting to be the centerpiece of a very public show. He let go in order to avoid a spat at his first public appearance as the heir of Ephialtes. I smiled, realizing something he probably did not: he had also acquiesced to his future wife in public and at their first ever meeting, a precedent I was quite sure Diotima had knowingly engineered. She had made two important points in one action.

Diotima set off, carrying the libations in one hand and the spear in the other. The musicians hadn't been expecting the abrupt start. They were slow to commence playing, so that Diotima was well on her way before the crowd could follow. The procession wound its way through the streets of Athens to the cemetery by the Dipylon Gate, mourners wailing and tearing at their hair.

Diotima led us through the gates of the cemetery and up the path to the place where the pyre had been raised. The same men who had loaded the body onto the cart now removed it, and placed it upon the wooden platform; a path had been cleared for them through the kindling and old wood.

Diotima took items from a bag and placed them around the body. I saw a stylus and a scroll, no doubt his favorite. She took a torch and circled the pyre, then lowered the torch to the tinder. The flames rose quickly.

Stratonike had been watching all this standing between the protective arms of her nurses, her face slack and uncaring, as if she were almost infinitely bored. Now she reacted as the flames reached up to her husband. She turned swiftly to one nurse, then the other. She was saying something I couldn't hear. One nurse said something to her gently.

Stratonike laughed, great gutfuls of loud raucous laughter that carried across the crowd. This was a terrible omen. The nurse said something urgently, then ordered her to be quiet loud enough that we could all hear it. Stratonike continued to laugh. The nurse slapped her, once, twice, across the face, to shut her up. But Stratonike kept on laughing and laughing, and the nurse kept on hitting until the laughter turned to screeching and then screams of fear. She began to shout, "No! No! He's coming back, he's coming back!"

Stratonike cowered before the nurse, who now was shouting, "Be quiet! Be quiet, you horrible woman!" And she struck Stratonike until the older woman sobbed and held her arms above her head.

The crowd was fearful, glancing at one another in doubt. Ephialtes' shade was sure to return with a disaster like this in the making. There was no way the shade could be placated with his own wife joyous as his body burned.

A man sidled up beside me and said, "There must be plenty of wives think it, but I do believe that's the first honest woman I've ever seen." Archestratus smirked. He was the only man present enjoying the spectacle. "So, how goes your investigation, young man?"

I didn't answer but looked around the crowd. Pericles and Xanthippus were both here, standing on opposite sides of the pyre, and I could see they were both making an effort not to notice the other. Pythax and the whole squad of Scythians had accompanied the crowd. Pythax ignored the spectacle and kept his eyes roaming across the faces of the younger men. If there was going to be trouble that's where it would start.

The nurses grappled Stratonike under control, each holding an arm. The flames were well above Ephialtes now; what was left of the bier was hidden by the flames and smoke. The men watched silently. Diotima stood at the head, silent and respectful. She had ignored the ranting of her stepmother. Now as the flames died she took a ceremonial amphora, filled with wine. She walked around the mound and poured the wine, which hissed as it touched the hot remains and leavened the smoky air with the sweet aroma.

Diotima put down the amphora, picked up a fine cloth bag, and with a small ceremonial trowel scooped up the ashes of her father and poured them carefully into the bag.

From behind us rose a paean, a victory song of the sort raised when the enemy has been vanquished. It rose and lilted and the woman who sang it danced a small dance of victory in place as her nurses tried desperately to hold her down. She raised her face to the sky and called upon Zeus to witness the defeat of her enemy, and she screamed over and over, "I killed him! I killed him! I killed him!"

Rizon, who technically was now master of Stratonike, shrank back from dealing with it. It was too much for one of the nurses. She covered her eyes to blot out the evil and cried. The other became desperate. She punched Stratonike, once, twice, hard in the head. Stratonike was knocked to the ground.

Funerals are held at night so that the body won't defile the sun, but that meant any shade unhappy with its sending-off would be free to register its displeasure, and if Ephialtes' shade was still with us then it would not be happy at this spectacle. The murmurs began in the ring of spectators; a few men decided they were more fearful of staying than the disrespect of leaving early. I suspect more were scared to leave and scared to stay. Those ones were looking around, trying to judge what everyone else was going to do, looking at the fleeing men and back to the stalwart ones.

Someone hissed, "She's saying she did it. She killed him!"

This was taken up and passed around the crowd in wonder.

"She killed him!"

"She says she did it!"

Everyone could believe anything of a madwoman, cursed by the Gods. I could feel the waves of relief wash across the crowd. Of course she was acting strangely, the spear had promised vengeance, and now the Gods were exacting justice even as Ephialtes departed for Hades.

All thoughts of the Areopagus being responsible fled their minds. Somebody called out, "Kill her!" But no one was brave enough to take the first step. There was something about Stratonike that was positively evil.

Diotima was doing her best to ignore the terrible sacrilege. She didn't raise her eyes, nor did she hurry her gruesome task to get it over with. She would make a fine high priestess one day.

When she was finished, she placed the cloth bag with the ashes into the funerary urn, which was Ephialtes' final resting place. Then she picked up a cup and poured honey upon the urn. She followed this with a cup of milk, then water, wine, and oil in succession. When she had poured this final libation she placed her fingers to her lips, kissed them, and slowly touched the urn. Her final kiss was not part of the ceremony, it was the only act that had been truly Diotima's.

Diotima turned and began the slow march back to the house. She passed me, but took no notice. Her face was blackened by the soot of the fire. Her hands were filthy and clenched. I saw that there were tears in her eyes.

There should have been a banquet for the relatives, but with only Rizon qualified to attend, such a thing would have been a farce. Diotima was now required to purify Ephialtes' home, room by room, with seawater. She would be doing that at dawn tomorrow.

"That was an outstanding performance," Archestratus said to me approvingly. "So many of these young women feel the need to make an emotional ordeal of the whole thing. That young lady knows how to carry off a funeral with dignity."

Stratonike was dragged past us by the grim-faced nurses, not caring if she stumbled. Two of the Scythians had held her down while a third looped rope around her. Stratonike cursed them with every step, shouting vile obscenities interspersed with hysterical laughter. Blood was dribbling from her mouth where the nurse had struck her.

Archestratus stared at this spectacle. "She, on the other hand, is entertaining for a short period, and then becomes merely grotesque. When I see that, I wonder if poor Ephialtes might not be better off dead. He had to live with that every day? Still it's a huge relief."

"It is?"

"We've saved the constitutional crisis, my boy. The wife confessed. The constitutional crisis is averted. She isn't a judge, she isn't a conservative or a democrat, or a member of the Areopagus. No one cares if it was her that killed him."

"Do you think she was telling the truth?"

"I know she confessed!"

"But it might not be true."

Archestratus sighed. "Truth is not a major component of most court cases, young man. Public opinion—what the jury thinks—is much more important. And here we have a truth far too convenient to be lightly disposed of. At last we have someone we can try, judge, and chain to the pole to be stoned to death without offending anyone. And Athens will breathe a sigh of relief when she's gone. Democrats will stop blaming the conservatives, and the conservatives can stop looking over their shoulders in fear."

I thought back to what Pericles had said, should the man beside me be the murderer, and had a horrible feeling Pericles would agree with Archestratus. And I had to be honest, Archestratus might be right. Stratonike had confessed after all, and she might have known Aristodicus of Tanagra.

"So you think the city will calm?"

"I hope so. All we politicians can get back to business as usual, and openly backstab each other in the Ecclesia, rather than secretly on the Areopagus. I'm looking forward to it."

"Archestratus, will the people make you the new democratic leader?"

"It's my right. I had a right to the position after Themistocles left, he favored me, you know, I should have been leader after him. But Ephialtes was popular, more so than I who had always worked quietly in the background for the good of the people. I didn't make that mistake again after Ephialtes took power, I can tell you."

"Then Pericles came along," I said, not as a question but as a fact.

"Ah yes, Pericles, son of Xanthippus. Xanthippus was a democrat in his youth, did you know that? The power corrupted him."

"But Pericles?"

"Should the people trust a man whose father has already gone over to the oppressors of the poor? Xanthippus leads where Pericles will follow given half a chance, once the power corrupts him too."

I thought back to what I'd overheard Xanthippus say to Pericles. After removing the political bias in each case, both men were actually much in agreement on Pericles' future.

"But Ephialtes favored Pericles, didn't he?" It was a stab in the dark.

Archestratus scowled. "You're his agent, I forget that. Yes, of course you'd say such a thing. Have you thought upon what I said to you before, young Nicolaos, when I rescued you from that beating?"

"Yes, I have, Archestratus, several times."

"And?"

"My faith in Pericles has not been broken, but it's been sorely tried one or two times. I cannot honestly say I trust him completely."

"Some sense begins to penetrate!"

"But nor has he betrayed me, nor done anything to hurt me."

"Waiting until he does is not a sign of high intelligence."

I decided to bore on. "It provides you with a motive, doesn't it? Remove Ephialtes before he can declare for your rival."

"The leadership is rightfully mine. I worked for it. I *slaved* for it. I *earned* it." Archestratus' eyes were wide, he was breathing heavily, and his voice became harsh. "I will not listen to ridiculous propaganda put about by the stooges of my, as you put it, rival.

And you forget one thing: if I were going to kill for the leadership, the man I'd remove wouldn't be Ephialtes, it would be Pericles. Then Ephialtes would have had no choice but to support me."

Archestratus stalked off in a huff. I trudged along more slowly, feeling drained. Archestratus would have made the perfect suspect, except that everything he said in his defense made perfect sense.

"What do you think of him?" Pericles walked up to me. "I saw you talking to Archestratus."

"What do I think? He's a bitter man beneath a pose of elegance and urbanity. I don't know if he's the master legal technician everyone says he is, but I do know he's going to do everything in his power to get the leadership of the democrats."

Pericles nodded. "Yes, I think you read him correctly, but I would add that he's a man who hates, but doesn't want to advertise his hatred. He's also an incisive logician."

"Dangerous enemy?"

"Very much so."

"He has similar thoughts about you."

"I don't doubt it."

"And I wouldn't be surprised if he was right too."

Pericles chuckled. "So nice for all we democrats to be of one accord, even if it consists mostly of mutual suspicion and nastiness. Let me add another suspicion to your already teeming collection, Nicolaos. I was talking to my father during that appalling spectacle of a funeral. He mentioned to me in oh-so-casual innocence that he will propose a bill before the Ecclesia to promote Pythax to citizen."

"Why?"

"Inestimable services to the state."

I considered. "That might be a fair judgment."

"There's no such thing as altruistic fairness when it comes to my father."

"So what do you think?"

"I don't know, but I'm going to ponder it."

Pericles left me for other men waiting to speak to him. I took the path home.

A form I barely recognized ran out of the nearby bushes, grabbed my arm, and dragged me out of sight among the branches.

"Euterpe, what in Hades do you think you're doing!"

"Silence!" She put a hand over my mouth. "If you must speak, do it quietly."

I nodded and she removed her hand.

"What are you doing here?" I hissed.

"Did you think I would let them bury the man who was the closest I'll ever have to a husband without seeing him off?" She was dressed in mourning but her hair was uncropped.

"All right. That doesn't explain why you dragged me in here."

"Do you want Diotima married to that weed Rizon, and bound to the same house as that revolting madwoman?"

"No, but you should be happy. You're the one who was insisting she marry. Now she has no choice."

Euterpe hissed, "Not him! Ephialtes would never have chosen Rizon. He was going to find a sensible older man from a good family."

"What do you expect me to do about it? You need to talk to the Archon."

"I did," she surprised me. "He told me he hadn't much choice. I offered him *anything* he wanted if only he would marry her to someone better."

My mind dwelled on the contents of *anything*.

"Nicolaos, are you listening to me?" she demanded.

"I'm considering your words very closely indeed."

"The bastard took the *anything* and then walked out, saying he still had no choice."

"There's nothing I can do, Euterpe. I'm a nobody in this

game. Everyone I'm dealing with is a high official or a powerful politician, and I'm just a young man."

"Yes there is, there's something I didn't tell you before. Ephialtes was planning to prosecute the Eponymous Archon and the Polemarch as soon as they left office. He believed they've been stealing public funds."

"Ephialtes told you this?"

"Yes. Days before he died."

"Did he have proof?"

"He must have. He couldn't take them to court without it. He wouldn't have talked of it to me unless he was certain."

Footsteps approached, two men talking. Euterpe and I remained silent while we waited for them to pass, which to my relief they did. If I was discovered under the bushes with Euterpe I would never hear the end of it from Diotima.

When we were alone once more I said, "Then Ephialtes was going to hit the Archon and the Polemarch with this when they went for their public review after their year in office?" It wouldn't be the first time Ephialtes had prosecuted a high official for corruption or negligence, and he'd nailed quite a few of them.

Euterpe nodded. "That's what he said. He said the scandal would at least destroy them politically, and perhaps a jury might fine them heavily."

"What about the Basileus?"

"Ephialtes only mentioned the Archon and the Polemarch."

"Do they know what Ephialtes had planned for them?"

"I don't know. They might have. When Ephialtes prosecuted in the past, he told the men beforehand and gave them a chance to withdraw."

It all made a certain amount of sense, though given what I knew of Euterpe, one thing surprised me. "Why didn't you blackmail Conon with this? You could have stopped the marriage."

Euterpe laughed, not her usual light tinkling laugh, but a sound full of scorn. "My word against his? Don't be ridiculous, I'm not even allowed to testify in court. But I know that somewhere there's something to prove it. There has to be."

"You searched your home."

"Of course. Nothing. I wouldn't expect it, he never brought work to my house."

"But he had another home, and that's where it would be."

"It's not a home I can enter, and I thank Aphrodite for that small mercy."

"But Diotima can. She's there now."

"Yes. Tell her, Nicolaos, when she purifies the house, to take every piece of paper, every scroll she finds. Tell her quickly. I don't know how long she'll be allowed to remain there."

I grimaced and shook my head. "I've been warned if I compromise her, Rizon might declare her an adulteress."

"I accept the risk of my daughter's death in return for not having her married to that man."

"Are you going to offer me *anything* to help her?"

Euterpe smiled and leaned forward so that I could feel her breasts pressing against my chest. She put her lips close to mine. "I made that mistake before, but I know you now, Nicolaos, son of Sophroniscus. I don't need to offer you anything."

I hurried along to Ephialtes' house in a state of anxiety and sexual frustration. It was nighttime now, and surprisingly quiet after the morning's tumult. I put my hands on my hips and stared at the front door. Diotima was in there somewhere, I couldn't go in, and she didn't know to come out. I went round the back of the house. The back gate was open, with buckets lying beside the entrance. This must be where the slaves were storing the seawater for the morning's ritual. I stood by the gate and waited. I waited a long time. Eventually Achilles came shambling out to set up things for the night.

"Achilles!" I called softly. He looked up, startled and fearful, and squinted. I realized he didn't recognize me in the dark. "It's me, the one who helped you with the wine."

Achilles hobbled to the gate and looked at me closely. "So it is. I hadn't thought to see you again, sir."

"I have a favor to ask, Achilles, a simple one."

"The new mistress is in the house, sir. I won't be letting you in."

"Of course not, I wouldn't ask that of you, Achilles. Instead I want you to bring the new mistress to me out here."

"Oh dear, sir. Is this in the nature of a jest?"

"Not at all, we're acquainted, believe me."

"That is not necessarily a reassuring statement, sir. The new mistress is to be married, sir."

"Achilles, I know what you're thinking, and you're right."

"I am, sir?"

"You are. You're thinking that you work for the new mistress now, at least until she marries, and she will reward you greatly if you do the right thing by her."

"Is that what I'm thinking, sir?"

"It is," I said firmly. "And reward you she will if only she receives the message I have for her."

"As to that, sir, I have spoken to the new master and I suspect he is not one for rewards, sir."

"All the more reason to get in now before he takes control."

Achilles thought about that. "Tell me your message, sir."

Diotima marched across the courtyard to the back gate; I could hear her teeth grating all the way. She halted in front of me and put her hands on her hips.

"Before I kill you, answer one question."

"My pleasure."

"Why did you send Achilles to tell me my mother has just dragged you into the bushes?"

"I thought it would get you here fastest."

"So you couldn't wait to brag about your sordid activities."

"So I could tell you what she told me." I repeated the entire conversation.

"That's it?" she asked suspiciously. "That's everything that happened?"

"I swear it," I lied. I'd left off the bit about asking if Euterpe would offer me *anything*.

I was shy about mentioning the funeral, but I thought it needed to be said. "I thought you did exceptionally well during the ceremony. So did Archestratus. He said you pulled off a difficult job with dignity."

"The Gods know I could have killed that bitch."

"It must be tough, having to bury your father and deal with that at the same time."

"Has it occurred to you I left my father in an urn in Ceramicus, exactly where he wanted to leave me when I was born?"

There wasn't anything I was going to say to that!

Diotima continued, "I hope you never have to do it."

"How is she?"

"Do you care?"

"You have to deal with her tonight."

"Those two nurses gave her a sleeping potion. I haven't gone near her and I don't intend to. Nico, do you realize once I'm married I'm going to have to live with that thing, every day?" There was a catch in her throat, I wondered if she was about to sob. In her place, I would have.

"We just have to hope your mother's plan works."

"Nice of her to worry about me. I can't remember her ever doing that before."

"You know, she might care for you more than is immediately obvious."

"You mean beneath that exterior of professional lust and obsessive self-regard there lurks a compassionate, loving, maternal woman?"

When she put it like that, my suggestion did seem mildly

ridiculous. "I wouldn't go quite that far, but you must admit she's gone out of her way to save you from Rizon."

"Tell me about the papers, where do I find them?" Diotima asked, bluntly changing the subject.

"I know what his office looks like. There're a lot of scrolls, and there's a box of papers. You better check all the scrolls to make sure I didn't miss anything, but my guess is any evidence is going to be in the box."

"Wait here."

I waited, and waited. I strolled up and down the lane. I tried not to look like someone waiting to collect stolen property.

Diotima returned carrying the box. "The scrolls are all books. Here's the box of papers. Keep them safe until I'm out of here tomorrow afternoon. Don't you dare read them without me. The only reason I'm not keeping them here is that I fear the Archon will arrive in the morning and forcibly remove them. He seems to be able to do whatever he likes to me, so I wouldn't put that past him."

"I'll keep them at my house. No, better still, I'll keep them at Pericles' house. Conon wouldn't dare raid him, and if Pericles has to replace me my successor will have them."

"What do you mean?" Diotima asked, alarmed. "Are you in danger?"

"No, quite the reverse." I told her of the Polemarch's offer, what it would mean for Pericles' investigation.

Diotima chewed her lip. She said doubtfully, "I don't think you should do it, Nicolaos. I don't trust the Polemarch."

"I don't see a problem. He wants me because he thinks I have ability."

"Maybe he isn't making the offer to have you working for him, but to stop you working for Pericles. It doesn't sound genuine to me."

I had had the same thought, but I didn't need Diotima reinforcing my own fears.

"So you don't think he's judging me by my ability."

"Yes, he is. He might be worried you'll do too good a job for Pericles."

At least that was a more pleasant way of looking at it.

"You make the offer sound like some sort of bribe."

"Yes, precisely. I wonder what he has to hide?"

A man passed by. He paid us no attention, but it put me in mind that we were in a somewhat exposed position to be discussing such things.

"I must return to my family, and you'd better get back inside that house."

Diotima hesitated. "Uh, didn't your father warn you not to come near me?"

"I think the way your mother phrased it was that she is willing to risk your death if there's a chance of avoiding Rizon."

Diotima grimaced. "I think I agree with Mother for the first time in my life. I'll be done by lunch. Bring the box to me at home, in the afternoon. Pericles can't have me at his house, and no one can accuse us of adultery if I'm being chaperoned by my own mother." We both laughed.

Diotima continued. "But give me a few hours first to get some rest, I'm going to be exhausted."

"Why exhausted? You don't start the purification until dawn."

"If you had to spend the night in the same house as Stratonike, would you go to sleep?"

"Good point."

12

I was woken early next morning by the house slave. I groaned, rolled over, and opened one bleary eye to peer through the window. It was still dark outside, not even dawn.

"What is it?" I mumbled. "Go away."

"Messenger for you," the slave said quietly to avoid waking my brother.

I groaned again, pulled on my tunic, and shuffled down the corridor, trying not to step on the planks that I knew creaked, through the courtyard and into the vestibule.

The messenger was a young slave boy. His hand was shaking when he handed over a piece of torn papyrus and he stuttered the words, "Fr-fr-from the new mistress." On it were scribbled two words: *Come quickly.* The finger marks where Diotima had held the papyrus were marked out clearly in drying blood.

I grabbed the slave boy by both shoulders and shook him. "Is she alive? Is she hurt?" I demanded.

But he fainted, and even slaps to the face could not bring him around. I let the fool fall to the floor and snatched the sword Sophroniscus had presented to me when I'd commenced ephebe training. It's illegal for a citizen to carry a sword through Athens except on military duty, but I wasn't going to worry about that now.

I ran all the way and crashed through the door. Fortunately it was unbarred, because it never occurred to me to check. If it had been locked I would have broken my shoulder. The silence in the house was ominous. I saw bloodied footsteps leading both up and down the stairs to the women's quarters. I bounded up and pushed through the upstairs door with my shield arm forward and my sword in ready thrust position.

But there was no one to attack me. Blood lay everywhere. The floorboards were awash with it. Blood spattered two walls and lay across the couches. One of the nurses was slumped back across a couch, the wide, red streak of a deep slash wound in her forehead. I saw it had been either a sword or something like a butcher's cleaver wielded by someone who hadn't hesitated to kill brutally. The other nurse lay along the opposite wall, curled into a ball. The pool of blood thickest about her middle told me I didn't need to look any closer. Stratonike lay on her back in the middle of the room, her head thrown back and her throat slashed open. Most of the blood pooling on the floor came from her.

Diotima was in the middle of the room, like an island rising out of a sea of blood. She looked at me with tears in her eyes and forced a tiny smile. "I've had a lot of bad days recently. I wouldn't mind having a good one for a change."

I helped her downstairs and called for slaves, but the only one there was Achilles. He told me the others had run. I couldn't blame them, but I was angry they'd left Diotima behind. I was torn by priorities. I had to get Diotima back home to her mother's house, but I didn't dare leave the scene upstairs. There was no telling what might happen while I was gone. I had to find out who had done this and how Diotima had managed to survive. That would have to wait, though. Diotima wasn't yet fit to talk.

"Oh yes, I am," she protested in gasps, when I said as much to Achilles. I had ordered him to escort Diotima home. The two of us had wiped her face, but fixing her soiled and bloodied dress was a problem we couldn't solve without a female slave. "Anyway, this is my home now."

I raised an eyebrow at that. "You've only just moved in, and that was supposed to be for the night only. I didn't think you'd become proprietorial."

"That was before someone dared to murder my household. I could have been in there!"

"Why weren't you?" I asked.

"Remember the last thing I said to you last night? I resolved I was not going to spend a night in the same rooms as a madwoman who had danced around her husband's grave. So I walked about the house. I walked a lot. I looked into every nook and cranny. There was nothing else to do. I know this house as if I've lived in it. This place belongs to me now. *Me,* Nicolaos. I am mistress of this house."

Aha. Diotima had finally found somewhere she could be free of Euterpe. Granted, it had a few disappointing features. It was recently vacated by a murdered man—her father—it housed a violent lunatic, and to possess it, she would have to marry a loathsome creature. But even with these domestic inconveniences it was a place away from her mother, and that counted for a lot with Diotima.

"I realized, I don't know when, I couldn't stay awake all night. I could barely stay on my feet. So I slipped into Father's bedroom and slept in his bed. I barred the door so the slaves wouldn't discover me in the morning. I thought I would slip back into the women's quarters before dawn."

"The door to the women, did you bar it behind you?"

"No. Stratonike was out cold. The nurses' sleeping draft worked."

"So anyone could have walked in."

"The house was shut up tight."

Achilles spoke up, "If I might say, sir, the young mistress is quite right. I checked the doors myself before retiring, front and back. All was barred as it should be, sir."

"Windows?"

"Downstairs shutters locked, sir."

Diotima said, "And besides, Nicolaos, remember I was walking the house for half the night. If someone had broken in I would have known for sure."

"Who found the bodies?"

Diotima shuddered and went pale again. "I did, when I returned before dawn."

"Wait here."

I had left Diotima and Achilles as much to give myself a moment alone as to investigate. While I was out of sight I took the time to lean against a wall and feel sick. I was shaken by what had happened here. I stayed until my stomach had settled, then continued my work.

I went around the doors, front and back, and every window. Every bar but the front door's was in place. None showed the least sign of cracking.

"When you sent the messenger to me, did you have to unbar the front door?" I asked on return.

"Yes sir, I noticed that particularly," Achilles said.

I looked at him closely, unsure whether he understood the implication of what he said.

I said slowly, "I should think the person who did this was a man. It must have required strength."

Diotima asked, "What do you think happened?"

"You heard no screams?"

"None. But then, by the time I fell asleep I was dead to the world, utterly exhausted."

Achilles said, "It may help you to know, sir, the old master Ephialtes had special work done to the women's quarters. The workmen made double walls and pushed cloth within the gap. I think they did the same to the floor. One couldn't hear what happened within."

"Why in Hades would they do that?" I asked, astounded.

"It was on account of the old mistress, sir. For when she was having one of her . . . turns. She could scream fit to wake the dead. The neighbors complained, sir, and the slaves couldn't get a night's rest."

"I see." That would explain why no one heard anything. And even if they did, everyone would assume Stratonike was having one of her screaming fits. What a beautiful opportunity to murder someone.

"Sir? May I ask a question? I haven't seen the room. I thought the old mistress must have taken to the old nurses and then killed herself. Isn't that what happened?"

I looked at Diotima meaningfully. She nodded. "Achilles was downstairs when I screamed and ran for help. He didn't go up."

I looked at his bare feet. The crippling scars were there to be seen, and not the slightest trace of blood. They were perfectly clean. Very well then. "Achilles, it is most unlikely that your old mistress killed herself."

"Oh dear, sir." I left them again and stepped outside into the street. The sun's rays were strong now; the day had begun. There was a single set of bloody footprints going out the door and down the street. I squinted and studied in hope, but it was easy to see they'd been left by the boy who'd come to me. The back lane was even worse, the only obvious prints were my own from the night before. If an outsider had killed the women, he'd left without dripping blood, a feat I considered to be impossible.

Was Achilles capable of this? There were two other men slaves; they'd been among those who'd run. But the slaves had left no blood in their wake. Achilles was clean.

Hmm. He was clean. So was everyone else who'd left the house except the messenger boy. Diotima was the only one covered in blood, and I refused to believe she could have committed this crime. I returned once more to Diotima and Achilles.

"Where do you wash yourselves in this house?"

Achilles said, "The men slaves douse themselves back of the slave quarters, sir. The women do the same only they have a large basin they sit in, and there's a screen for them. The master liked to use the baths at the gymnasium, of course. The old mistress and the nurses had water carried to their quarters. I believe there's a copper tub."

Diotima nodded. She had a bit more color in her face. "The tub's in the room beyond the bodies."

"Did you look there?"

"This morning? No."

I went first to the corner behind the slave quarters. It was as Achilles described it. There was not a drop of blood to be seen. Also, it was perfectly dry. Whoever had killed the women hadn't washed themselves here. Next I went back up the stairs, took a deep breath, and opened the door. I stepped through as quickly and gingerly as I could, trying not to step in the mess. I had to jump over the largest pool. Fortunately it was almost dried. The room beyond held beds, three chests, a cupboard, and a tub. One of the beds had metal rings bolted to the wall above it. There was stout rope hanging from the rings. I guessed this was where Stratonike slept. She was probably tied when she was being particularly difficult. The other two beds would be for the nurses. All three had been slept in.

I looked closely at the tub and the floor between the tub and the door. Not a drop of blood to be seen, and these too, were dry. This was rapidly becoming irritating. My fine theory as to how the murderer managed to leave clean was being destroyed by lack of evidence.

I put that aside for the moment and considered another question: how had the bodies ended in the common room? Had they been dragged from their beds? No, that was inconceivable. There was no blood in the bedroom. Had they been knocked unconscious in bed and then dragged? But then why didn't attacking the first woman wake the others?

So all three women had left their beds, and willingly walked to the common room to be murdered, like lambs to the slaughter. My imagination rebelled. I thought of the big, strong nurses with their muscled arms. I thought of the homicidal Stratonike. Any one of them would have scared me in a dark alley. All three together would be like facing the Furies. I shuddered to think what would happen to any man who took them on all at once.

Stratonike's arms were bruised, but there was no telling if that was the work of the murderer or the nurses handling her during the funeral. I could see from the stains that the blood had poured from her throat down both sides of her neck. She must have been lying as she was now when she died.

How could the killer have persuaded her to lie still while he cut her throat? She might have been mad, but she wasn't that far gone. Besides which, Stratonike was the homicidally inclined of the three. Why hadn't she fought? The answer came to me immediately. Diotima had said the sleeping potion had put Stratonike out completely. Looking down at her now, I could see her face appeared calm and peaceful, possibly for the first time in many years.

So if Stratonike was unconscious, why would anyone bother to murder her? The two nurses might have been disturbed by an intruder and walked into the common room to investigate, but that didn't explain the death of their mistress.

There was only one possible answer. The purpose of the intruder was to murder Stratonike. The nurses' deaths were merely necessary because they'd been woken.

I was quite pleased with myself. I'd made quick progress on these murders, faster than I'd managed with Ephialtes. I had a simple picture in mind.

The murderer had crept into the bedroom, picked up the comatose Stratonike and carried her into the common room where he proceeded to open her throat. This woke at least one and possibly both nurses, who came out to investigate. They probably saw that Stratonike had left her bed, and thought she was making the noise. So they walked in unprepared for what was happening. The murderer took a swipe at the first nurse from his crouching position over Stratonike. That's why the nurse was struck in the stomach. She fell to the side. The murderer, now standing, swung at the next nurse, taking her in the head. She was flung onto the couch where she quickly died, spurting blood up the wall.

The scene was perfect in my mind. It explained the state of every corpse.

Then the murderer, who must have been dripping in gore, walked out of the room leaving no trace, no track, no drops of blood on the stairs or on the ground floor.

No, it was impossible. Yet my theory fit so well, I felt I had the right basic idea. So the killer had cleaned himself before leaving. He must have. But there were only two ways he could have done that, and both were pristine dry.

I set that problem aside once again and considered who would want to murder Stratonike. The nurses sprang instantly to mind. I glanced at their mutilated bodies and decided I could eliminate them as suspects. Who else? Diotima. And she was the only one covered in gore. If Diotima killed the women, it would explain everything and eliminate the need for the killer to be clean. My mind rebelled at the thought and I had to force myself to stay on track. I'd thought at first only a man would have the strength, but could I be wrong? I recalled our race though the city. She was definitely fit. And she loathed Stratonike—with good reason. Would her hatred supply the strength and will to cut her throat? It might . . . maybe. But if Diotima was the murderer, where was the weapon?

I choked back my distaste and searched the women's quarters thoroughly. I didn't find a cleaver, nor a knife, nor a sword, nor any other weapon. There weren't even the small knives anyone would have. I supposed that was to be expected, given the presence of Stratonike.

I returned to Diotima.

"What took you so long?" she demanded. "I don't have to ask where you've been."

My investigation had taken its toll. My sandals were red. I was spattered from my feet to my knees, and my palms were smeared.

I ignored her comments and asked, "Where's the kitchen?"

"Hungry?" she asked sarcastically.

"Not particularly. I don't think I'll be eating meat for a while. I want to see the knives."

"I'm coming with you this time," Diotima said.

She led me to the kitchen, next to the slaves' quarters. It looked much like the kitchen of my home, with the oven placed outside to avoid fires and the preparation bench and food stores inside. The knives were hung on hooks. Every hook had a knife.

Diotima frowned. "How strange."

"What is?"

"The knives are all there."

I nodded unhappily. "Yes, I was expecting one to be missing."

"No, Nicolaos, you don't understand, there *was* a knife missing."

That startled me. "Say that again?"

"Last night, as I wandered the house, I came in here and I noticed there was a knife missing. That one." She pointed to the meat cleaver.

I stepped close to the cleaver and stared. "I can see the slightest trace of blood on it, in the crack between the handle and the blade."

"Of course you can, it's a meat cleaver."

Achilles coughed. "Excuse me, young mistress, but I think you must be mistaken. All the knives were there yesterday morning."

"Nonsense," Diotima said brusquely. "The cleaver wasn't there last night."

"It was there in the afternoon. I saw it."

"Are you sure, Achilles?" I asked.

"Quite sure, sir. I looked over the kitchen especially because we all expected the new master to stay for the funeral feast."

"Didn't he?"

Diotima said, "He did. But being the only male family member, it was a depressing affair even by the usual standards. Stratonike was alternating between wailing a cacophony and hysterical laughter. Rizon shouted at the nurses and me to shut her up. He was in a foul mood after what happened at the funeral. He walked up to the nurses and shrieked at them that Stratonike was to be silent or he'd have them beaten."

"Did he beat them?" I was thinking of the bruises on Stratonike.

"No. He and Stratonike ended up face to face, him shouting that she belonged to his household now and she's to do what she's told or else, her mouthing obscenities and ignoring everything he said. He stalked back to the table and stuffed his face with Ephialtes' food and wine. Stratonike picked up a knife and threw it at him. She missed, but the knife flew past his face. Rizon went pale, shouted that he was a fool to let a self-confessed murderess anywhere near him, not to mention the bad luck and the curse of the Gods that falls upon a woman who murders her family, and that in her case it was too late and now she was doubly cursed. That was when he ordered us to get her out of his sight."

"Then he left?"

"He left some time later. I didn't see, I was upstairs with the women. I had a choice between staying with Stratonike or Rizon."

"What about you, Achilles?" I asked.

"I didn't see him leave either, sir. I was clearing the table. The new master departed while I was out back at the midden."

"And he didn't do anything else? Anything important, I mean."

"He struck—" Achilles glanced at Diotima, who ordered, "No, Achilles."

But I'd heard enough, and with the hint I could see the bruise forming along the side of Diotima's face.

"He *struck* you?" I was enraged.

"He was unhappy I'd grabbed the spear of vengeance from him during the funeral march. He hadn't known how to exert his authority over me in front of other men, but he knew what to do afterward."

"Rizon and I are going to talk," I said grimly.

Diotima tossed her head to the side and refused to let me examine her bruises. "There's no point, Nicolaos. I belong to Rizon now and it's all perfectly legal. He can do whatever he likes to me. I suppose I'll have to get used to it, and learn how to keep out of his way."

The funny thing was that the wrong person had died. If someone had murdered Rizon it would have made perfect sense. There was a houseful of people who hated him, plus me. But everyone in the house was used to Stratonike. Why kill her now? I was unwillingly drawn back once more to Diotima as a suspect.

I made another round of the kitchen in search of inspiration, but I saw nothing except the cleaver, which I took down. There was nothing special about it I could see, except I was sure I was holding the blade that had killed three women. I hung it back on the wall. I looked out the window into the courtyard. Someone had come in here, in the dark, having to be careful not to awaken the slaves. That person had taken the cleaver off the wall and then in the dark walked up to the women's rooms. He would have to be careful not to trip over anything on the way.

Diotima and Achilles were restless during my silence, but I ignored them. I had to think this through. Presently Achilles muttered to Diotima, "Mistress, what about the purification? Should we do it now?"

Diotima replied, "I don't know, Achilles. I'm a priestess and not even I know the rules for this situation. If there's ever been a time when the house of a murdered man sustained another murder before it was washed, I've never heard of it."

"That's it!" I exclaimed in excitement. I almost jumped for joy. "Achilles, tell me, how many buckets of seawater did you bring for the purification?"

"Sir? Ah, seventeen."

"Are you sure?"

"Yes sir, we had the seawater brought here from Piraeus. I loaded seventeen buckets on the wagon because that's as many as we had plus the ones we could borrow from the neighbors. I carried each one in when the wagon returned. I was most particular to make sure none were stolen."

"Go count them."

I grinned at Diotima until Achilles returned. He looked puzzled.

"Sixteen, sir. I can't imagine what happened to the other one."

"I can. The murderer carried it upstairs to wash himself after the crime. Athens might be dark and lonely in the middle of the night, but no murderer could risk dripping blood all the way back to their home."

Diotima said, "There was a bucket in the corner of the room. I remember it."

"So do I, but I assumed it was used for night stools."

We went up the stairs once more. Diotima and Achilles stayed at the entrance, where Achilles gaped at the scene for the first time, while I went to the corner beside the door in which stood the bucket. Now I knew what to look for. The floor in that corner was ominously clean, though the wall behind was spattered. I put my nose to the empty bucket.

"Seawater." The salt smell was obvious.

Who would have known the house of Ephialtes had seawater that night? Depressingly, every man in Athens who attended his funeral the day before. That would be about half the population, including everyone implicated by Ephialtes' death. Most people could have guessed the seawater would be kept at the back of the courtyard, anyone with a bull's-eye lantern could have found it. Anyone could have guessed there'd be a cleaver in the kitchen.

We retraced our steps downstairs. The runaway slaves had come to their senses and sheepishly returned. They were waiting for us in the courtyard. If they'd kept on running, they could have been executed. Diotima forbade them to go up any stairs, ordered them go about their business, and sent the kitchen girl to make us something light to eat. It was almost midday and we'd been on the go and under stress since before dawn. We invited Achilles to sit with us: after the morning's trauma he was more like an assistant to us than a slave. I was aware he'd stayed with Diotima when he could have run. I was sure she'd be mindful of the same. Achilles was a man I could trust with her.

The kitchen girl returned with heavily watered wine, olives, and bread. Diotima said to her, "Thank you, Criseis, that will be all. Oh, and please wash the meat cleaver. Do it now." Criseis stared at Diotima. "Be thorough," Diotima ordered. Then she turned to me and asked, "Who would have wanted Stratonike dead?"

I could answer that one immediately. "You, Rizon, anyone in this house who couldn't take any more of her screaming, and whoever killed Ephialtes."

Diotima nodded glumly. "Well, I didn't kill them! And even if I was going to murder the wretch I would never have hurt those poor nurses. Do you think it was the same man as killed Father?"

"It's possible."

"That leaves us with the slaves. I don't suppose you killed them, did you, Achilles?"

Achilles held his hands up in horror. "Please, mistress! Never jest about something like that. I know you don't mean it, but that's the sort of comment that could get a slave like me killed."

"Sorry," she said. "But what do you mean, a slave like you?"

He said sadly, "There are some slaves, mistress, who get by

almost as if they were metics, some are almost like members of the family. Then there are the ones who are treated like working drudges, as most of us in this house. But at least those are ignored by the owners. Then there are a few slaves that seem to be the butt of every cruel jest. No matter how well they serve, they always seem to be noticeable when it's time to play a joke on a slave. That's me."

Diotima said, "I'm sorry, Achilles. I never knew you before, but you belong to me now. Can I make it up to you?"

"Don't free him," I said quickly. "He's the only one here you can rely on."

Achilles looked at me, hurt. "Well, thank you very much, sir."

"Ignore him, Achilles. I tell you what, when this is over I'll free you if that's what you'd like."

"I take that very kindly of you, young mistress. May I think on it? I'm not sure what I would do if I was free. How would I earn a living?"

"We'll work on it later." She patted his hand.

I pointed out, "Of course, in order to make good on that promise you have to be alive later."

"What do you mean?" Diotima asked, startled.

"Has it occurred to you, the murderer might have had two targets?"

"No, it hadn't. Are you suggesting he was after me?"

"He was looking for at least Stratonike. That must be so since, not having found you, he went ahead and killed her anyway. She was killed either because of who she is, or who she was married to. If the former, then it's going to be an esoteric form of a domestic quarrel. If the latter, then whoever is involved in the death of Ephialtes is afraid he might have said something important to her, or is afraid she might have seen something, or perhaps have observed someone visiting this house."

"That seems preposterous." Diotima snorted. "She was a lunatic who barely knew the people around her. I'm sure Father would never have discussed anything with her." She thought about it with her head tilted to one side and staring into the distance. "How about this," she suggested at last. "What if Father wasn't murdered for politics? What if it was a personal reason? Then it might make sense that they also would want to kill Stratonike."

"And you thought my idea was weak?"

"Let me know when you have a better one."

"I do. Right now, I would very much like to get my nose close to Rizon and have a big sniff."

Diotima grimaced. "Gah! Even the thought turns my stomach."

It was impossible of course. I could not go anywhere near the man without it being clear I'd been tramping about a murder scene with his fiancée.

Fortunately someone had to inform him of what had happened. Ordinarily a messenger would be sent, but it would be reasonable for Diotima to go personally. Once there she would see what she could of his clothing, appearance, and, most importantly, get close enough to smell him for the aroma of the sea. Diotima shuddered in distaste. "The thought is appalling but I suppose I must." Diotima rose to wash and change her bloodied clothes with the help of the returned women slaves.

"Go with her to Rizon," I ordered Achilles. "Don't let her out of your sight once she's in the house with him."

Achilles trembled. "The master may have a different view, sir."

"I know, but do your best." It occurred to me that Achilles ultimately would belong to Rizon, and he could earn whatever favor there was to be had by reporting the morning's actions. "I'm going to offer a variation on what Diotima said to you before, Achilles. If Diotima is unhurt when all this is over, then there'll be a reward for you. If I can, I'll buy you and set you up with a comfortable existence."

"Thank you, sir. And if the mistress is regrettably hurt, sir, despite my best efforts?"

"I'll buy you anyway, but if you were negligent then I'll kill you."

"That would not be in the nature of a jest, sir?"

"No, Achilles, it wouldn't."

"And I had thought you such a nice young man, sir," he said in an aggrieved tone.

"Concentrate on the happy part where she isn't hurt."

I left Diotima and Achilles to clean up the mess. Diotima remained a ward of the state until the wedding, and so in addition to telling Rizon of the deaths she would have to send a messenger to Conon. I regretted not being there when he learned of this latest thorn in his backside, as if Ephialtes' death wasn't complicated enough already.

13

I returned home to wash and change clothes before continuing. Sitting in our public room was Tellis, waiting for me. For a moment, I wondered what he was doing there, until I realized how many days had passed. I had failed to find Aristodicus in time.

"Ah, Nicolaos. I noticed this morning you had not made an appearance at the Polemarch's office. The Polemarch noticed the same thing, and he's wondering why. Have you an answer for him?"

I pondered Diotima's position. I thought I could live with Pericles' contempt, but if I left him now, I would also be leaving Diotima with her father unavenged, three corpses in her home, and in an unknown degree of danger. Also, I was as convinced as ever that whatever lay behind the murder of Ephialtes was important to Athens, Father's words notwithstanding, and if I gave up now, we might never know the truth.

But the offer was so tempting.

"I would like another day."

"You do not have another day, the terms were clear. Tell me your words to the Polemarch."

I took a deep breath.

"Firstly, that I am enormously flattered that the Polemarch should consider me; secondly, that it is impossible for me to accept if it means I must abandon my investigation; thirdly, that I think that is precisely what the Polemarch wants to achieve with his offer; and fourthly, that I look forward to finding out why."

Tellis rose. "Then I shall leave you to your fate. I cannot say that I am disappointed; I tell you frankly I advised the Polemarch against his course. You and I are of one mind on one point only: you are not the man for the job. However, in my case it is because I judge you to be a cocky young man with too much regard for your own importance. Good day to you." Tellis left in a fit of coughing.

I paused to mourn the future that might have been, then returned to the hunt. The main game was finding Aristodicus of Tanagra. I knew, or at least I thought I knew, from the innkeeper who'd hosted him, that he'd moved to Piraeus. That made sense for a man worried about discovery. But why was the man still in Athens at all? I'd have to ask when I found him.

So I put the chaos of Ephialtes' house out of my mind and walked to Piraeus, which lies to the southwest of the city. I took the south road, which is encased between the famous Long Walls of Athens. The Long Walls stretch from the city, down both sides of the road, all the way to the fortress walls of Piraeus, and so protect the entire southern route. The Long Walls are high and strong, made from the toughest timber and with support posts dug deep into the earth. They turn Athens and Piraeus into a single combined fortified site, so if the city is ever besieged again, the Athenians will still have access to the sea, and their mighty navy.

The road was crowded, as it always is, even during the heat of midday. I had to watch my step from carts rattling uphill to the city, pulled by braying donkeys and pushed by slaves. The owners walked alongside, swearing with every step. Most of those carts were loaded with corn. Athens can never have enough corn; no matter how much arrives, it's never enough to fill all the mouths. Carts were rolling downhill too, most filled with our best export to pay for the corn: the famous Athenian red-figure pottery. The owners of those carts were swearing with every bump in the road.

The walk to the coast is an easy one, and it wasn't long before the smell of the sea was strong enough to overpower the odor of donkey and donkey droppings. The three harbors of Piraeus were spread out before me, the large commercial harbor to the west, with countless merchant ships waiting to dock alongside the Emporium, the smallest harbor to the east, where the fishing boats and the local craft had their anchor; and in the middle harbor, a flotilla of triremes. There were perhaps two hundred triremes anchored in that bay, and at least another hundred out serving Athens on various missions. Long, thin, tall enough to accommodate three rows of oars and oarsmen, wet and wooden, fast and tough, they were the reason Athens dominated the civilized world, because a hundred triremes dropping anchor off your city is probably not going to be good news.

I wished I could have used some of those forces for myself, because facing me was the same dreary march from one inn to the next that I'd already made in Athens. I couldn't bear the thought on an empty stomach, and stopped for lunch first.

That innkeeper had been right. The places in Piraeus are worse than the lowest slums in Athens. Much worse. I'd never paid attention to the local inns—only the taverns and drinking bars had piqued my interest in the past—but now that I was paying attention, I realized it made sense. The sailors looking for a bed more comfortable than a wallowing deck would want a place to stay close to their work. The wealthy would be arriving off ship to visit the city.

By late afternoon I had checked three-quarters of the inns in Piraeus. Who would have thought there would be so many? I felt like searching myself for fleas as I left each one, and I had learnt the subtle art of stepping around drunk, hungover, or simply bellicose sailors.

I asked the question yet again at an inn situated in a dim, tiny alley behind the corn exchange, a bit better than most I'd seen. This time the innkeeper raised an eyebrow, and pointed me to a man seated in the corner, his back to the wall.

Aristodicus was an observant man. Before I had taken a step he had risen, turned, picked up the table before him, and charged me. The table was a ram that pushed me backward through the doorway and out into the street. Men cursed and fell away from us. I ignored them. I whirled to the side and he lurched forward, swung around, and threw the table. It was a bad throw, but I didn't know that then and jumped clear anyway, giving Aristodicus plenty of time to draw his knife. I did too.

"I only want to talk!" I said, crouching into a defensive position.

He drawled in a low voice, "Sure you do! I was warned you were asking questions." That made me blink.

Aristodicus was middle-aged, but looked the kind of man for whom knife fighting in the street was an occasional inconvenience. There wasn't a trace of fear in him. A younger man like me should be faster, possibly stronger. But I was sweating.

Experience told. He made a sequence of feint, lunge, twist, and stab that left me with a bleeding wrist and my knife on the ground. Aristodicus stamped forward and left his foot firmly planted on my knife. He grinned.

It was clear how this would end unless I changed the rules quickly. Trying not to betray my move, I threw myself at my opponent, intending to wrestle him into submission.

My own incompetence saved me, because while I might be a neophyte, Aristodicus certainly wasn't. He knew exactly what I was about to do even before I did, and stabbed at my chest as I pushed forward. His knife would have punctured my heart if I hadn't tripped over my own torn chitoniskos and crashed to the ground.

I grabbed the only thing I could, his feet, and heaved upward, desperate to keep his knife out of my back. He fell backward and I crawled across him to grab his knife arm. He slipped the blade downward, aiming for my eyes. I had to grab the blade to save my sight. I shouted in pain but found a grip on his wrist and came level with him as he turned the blade upward to slit my stomach. Now it was a matter of main strength whether he could drive the blade home, or whether I could turn his blade against him. We were both gritting our teeth with the effort. I could smell his breath and hoped it wouldn't be the last thing I remembered.

Aristodicus hooked a leg around me and rolled us both. With him on top, I couldn't hope to keep the blade out of my belly. I tried the same trick.

Those backstreets are muddy due to the straightforward sanitary arrangements. Aristodicus and I rolled over and over, struggling for control of the knife, and covering ourselves in substances I didn't want to contemplate.

Aristodicus stopped the roll and straddled me so he could put all his weight into the drive home. I felt a thud, something sharp pressed my stomach. I closed my eyes.

But Aristodicus didn't finish me. He'd gone limp. It was a moment before I realized I could no longer smell his rancid breath. I pushed him away, astonished to see an arrow embedded in his back. I looked down, and saw the arrowhead protruding out of his belly. The point I'd felt had been the arrow, driven straight through him and cutting into me.

Pythax was standing in the street, slinging his bow.

"Thanks, Pythax," I said, and meant it. But I couldn't resist adding, "A little harder and you could have had two for the price of one."

Pythax was having none of this jollity. "Where's your backup, boy?" he demanded.

"My what?" I asked stupidly.

"Your backup! Your backup, you stupid son of a poxed Persian whore." He reached down to his calf and pulled out a wicked-looking knife. "Listen to me, little boy. If you're going to play with the grown-ups, then never walk the street without an extra blade hidden somewhere you can reach in a hurry. Think you're the first man to lose his weapon in a fight? Hades is full of idiots like you. Learn, boy. Learn, or join them. Your choice." Pythax grunted and looked me over with a hard eye. "Be at my barracks first light tomorrow for training, and every day from now on."

"I finished ephebe training last year," I objected.

Pythax spat into the mud. "Ephebe training is learning how to be a soldier, to fight in the ranks of a phalanx. You think that's going to do you any good, boy? The way I see it, you're the kind who's going to be doing his fighting on your own, in the dark, or rolling in the mud in a disgusting street. I'm not going to teach you how to fight like a soldier, boy. I'm going to teach you how to kill like a man, any way you have to." He eyed my dripping wrist. "To start with, you've got to learn to use your blade in either hand."

"Okay, I've got the message. I'll be there. Thanks, Pythax."

He spat into the mud again. "Don't thank me. I figure Athens is going to be a safer place if you stop blundering around."

And with that warm vote of confidence, Pythax turned and sauntered away, leaving me with the body, and numerous questions I didn't think of until he was gone.

"Who was he?" the innkeeper demanded.

"That man with the bow was Pythax, chief of the Scythians."

The innkeeper nodded, and started up the stairs. "I'll turf out Aristodicus' things."

I immediately turned to the body. I had to search it before the locals stripped him of everything of value. This was my fourth corpse examination of the day. I wondered if a priest would have predicted it if I'd asked for an augury that morning.

I picked up the dagger that had come so close to ending me.

It seemed standard issue from any smithy. Next I put my hands down his tunic to see if he'd carried anything there. Men watched this from the inn and a few muttered, "Pervert . . ." I felt myself blushing but finished the job. I found a sweaty piece of papyrus lodged under his belt. It said, "Areopagus at dawn. Eastern edge." I put it in my bag. There was a bag of coins tightly strapped round his waist. It felt heavy. I hesitated to bring it into the open for the same reason Aristodicus had strapped it down, but I had little choice. I cut the knot with his dagger and transferred the belt to me and retied it. At least twenty pairs of eyes followed this action.

I followed the innkeeper upstairs without waiting for an invitation. He glanced at me and continued stuffing clothing into a bag.

"So that was Pythax, was it?"

"Yes."

"So I guess this was an official killing? It's okay if he kills someone?"

"I guess so."

"Good-oh then. So long as it's official."

"You have a relaxed attitude toward dead tenants," I commented.

He grunted. "It happens from time to time, in this business. I just don't want any of those officials from Athens wandering about the place, scaring off the customers. I know they've got all those riots keeping them busy, but that won't go on forever."

"I hope not. What do you do with the belongings?"

"Sell them for back rent, of course."

"What about the body?"

"Nah. Can't sell that."

I wandered about the tiny room. The place was a pigsty. The innkeeper sighed. I quickly spied a scroll case that looked oddly familiar next to the bed, and hid it beneath my chitoniskos before the man could notice.

I looked around, with the quiet satisfaction of discovering someone untidier than me. I picked up a rag from the floor, realized it was a soiled loincloth, and quickly dropped it.

"I wonder he didn't buy new ones when he was in Persia," muttered the innkeeper.

"Say that again?" I asked.

"I said, he should have replaced his old clothes when he was in Persia," the man said loudly. He must have thought I was hard of hearing, or an idiot.

"How do you know he was in Persia?" I asked.

"Simple. See these sandals?" He picked up one that was lying on the floor. "These straps are embossed with figures, right? When was the last time you saw a Hellene sandal embossed with figures of Persian soldiers? Never, right?"

I squinted, and saw that the innkeeper was probably right. The figures looked vaguely Persian to me.

"How did you spot that?" I asked him, intrigued.

"I'm an innkeeper, and this is Piraeus. We see all sorts shipping in, from all over the world. You get to know people by what they wear and the things they carry."

I took the sandal from him, inspected it. The sandal was worn, but not so much that the sole had become uneven. I took off one of my own and compared it. The wear was about the same, and I had bought mine three months ago.

"What else can you tell me?" I asked.

The innkeeper eyed the sandal, and said cautiously, "It was probably made somewhere in Asia Minor. The style is Hellene, the design Persian, and the leather is light. They tan the leather darker in the farther parts of the Persian Empire, you know. So I'd say this sandal was made by a Persian tradesman living in a Hellene city inside Persia."

I thanked the innkeeper profusely, and left him a handful of coins.

The body was lying there, minus his dagger, the rings he'd

been wearing and, no doubt, everything else of value I'd left behind. Piraeus was that sort of place. They probably would have taken his clothing too except he'd soiled it as he died.

I tried entering a nearby tavern for a drink to calm my nerves, and to read the scroll. They wouldn't let me in. One look down the front of my chitoniskos was enough to tell me why. I was covered in mud, feces, and blood, and my hand was still bleeding freely.

I walked—staggered—back to Athens and slipped in the back entrance of our home, hoping to wash myself and burn the clothing quietly, but a house slave screamed when she saw me, bringing Phaenarete running. Mother didn't panic, being a midwife, but her voluble description of my numerous intellectual defects was quite vivid as she personally stripped, washed, and bandaged me. All the while my little brother was watching, wide-eyed. This excitement brought Sophroniscus from his workshop, covered in dust. He took one look at me, ordered Phaenarete away, and led me into his private room. He ordered a slave to bring wine and had me down two cups unwatered as I told him everything that had happened.

His only comment was, "Have you accepted the Polemarch's offer yet?"

"No, Father. I turned him down this morning."

Sophroniscus gripped his own cup tightly. His face paled.

"I knew you were young, and rash as all young men are, but I had not thought you foolhardy." He sighed. "Son, I hope you know what you're getting into. You have now aligned yourself irrevocably with Pericles. Politics in Athens is rough, the mob is fickle, and there's no mercy for losers."

"I'm not doing politics," I said.

Sophroniscus raised an eyebrow. "No? You have a commission from Pericles, the victim is Ephialtes, Xanthippus and the whole Council of the Areopagus is suspect, the killer is a mercenary foreigner, and you don't think this is politics?" He shook his head. "You might not be standing before the people making speeches, but you've become a politician all the same. One working behind the scenes, like some men do during a play, so everything works for the actors out front. Do one thing for this old man, Nico: make sure your play is a comedy, not a tragedy."

"I'll have to discuss that with the author, if I can find him."

Sophroniscus smiled. "Use this room whenever you need privacy." And with that he returned to his work.

I sipped at the wine and inspected the things I'd taken from Aristodicus. I was sure he had killed Ephialtes, but was none the wiser who had instructed the assassin.

The door opened slightly, and a little head poked its way in. "Can I help?"

"No."

"Can I watch?"

"No."

"I promise I'll be quiet!"

"You can come in if you stop interrupting me," I grated, thinking this conversation could go on forever otherwise.

I opened the two notes and began to read. Instantly two little eyes were reading over my shoulder.

The first seemed straightforward to me. It gave the time and place of the murder. Obviously someone had told Aristodicus.

The handwriting wasn't familiar to me. I pulled out the papers I'd taken from Xanthippus' study and laid them out flat beside the one from Aristodicus. None of these bills and notes had anything to do with the murder, but I didn't care. I picked through them to find one that had certainly been written by Xanthippus. I compared the handwriting of Xanthippus to that on the note. I was hugely disappointed. They didn't look the same to me, and I'd been so sure I'd been about to solve the killing. I took out the note Ephialtes had sent to Xanthippus, setting the meeting at the Areopagus. Ephialtes' writing didn't match the note from Aristodicus either, but then, I'd never expected that it would.

Next I examined the shipping note. It was an agreement with a merchant to give Aristodicus a place as passenger on one of his boats leaving Athens. It was marked with what I guessed to be the seal of the boat owner. Aristodicus had paid in advance. This was so unusual, I frowned. No one ever paid a captain for passage in advance. The chances were the captain would take the money and leave early.

"Nico, what does this mean?" my little brother asked.

"I don't know. Maybe he thought he wouldn't have time to negotiate passage when he wanted to leave."

"Like people were chasing him?"

"That's right."

"But Nico, how would you know days ahead that someone was going to be chasing you?"

I read the note again. "It doesn't give a departure date. It only says, 'When Aristodicus says to Telemenes he wishes to sail from Athens, Telemenes will give Aristodicus space on his first departing boat. If Telemenes has no boat within the two days then Telemenes will buy immediate passage for Aristodicus on the boat of another man.' And for the amount he paid, I'd say Telemenes is getting a good deal. It says here Aristodicus paid three times the going rate. Even if Telemenes had to buy space from a competitor he would still make a profit." I threw down the page. "It doesn't make sense. Why go through this bizarre arrangement when for the same money Aristodicus could simply stand at the docks and shout out what he wanted? There'd be half a dozen captains sailing the same day who'd take him for that price."

My little brother said, puzzled, "But Nico, isn't that because Aristodicus doesn't want anyone to know about him? If he did that everyone in Piraeus would know about it right away, and he wants to hide. Isn't that why he moved to a different inn?"

I said grudgingly, "All right, that might be true. But then you have to explain why he's still in Athens at all. If he felt he needed to hide, and he had this get-out-of-Athens agreement with Telemenes, why didn't he use it?"

"Because he hasn't finished what he was doing."

I thought back to what Diotima and I had deduced long ago, after Brasidas had been shot: that there was another murder to come. But since then the slaves and the women of Ephialtes' household had met violent deaths. Did they count in the equation? The innkeeper had proven Aristodicus had been in Asia Minor, and the evidence of the sandals suggested it had been not more than three months ago. That was very important because Cimon, the brilliant General recently ostracized by Pericles, champion of the conservative party and bitter enemy of Ephialtes, was *not* in Asia Minor. I didn't know where Cimon was, but I was quite sure Asia Minor would not be it. The Persians controlled Asia Minor, Cimon had spent most of his life fighting them, and the Persians were none too fond of Cimon either.

Could Aristodicus be working for the Great King of Persia? It was certainly possible—many Hellenes did—and the Great King was rumored to have an extensive spy network. The idea of the Persians sending a Hellene to assassinate a Hellene was totally believable. If this was a Persian plot, then it meant the Persians were on their way again. That was a possibility I had to take to Pericles right away. Every political squabble, every conspiracy, every other consideration paled alongside the prospect of another Persian invasion. They had almost beaten us last time, and only the cunning of Themistocles had saved Hellas.

I paused. Themistocles was in Asia Minor. After being accused of treason, he had fled for his life and washed up at the palace of the Great King, who had made him Governor of Magnesia, Lampsacus, and Myus. Was Themistocles, the deep strategist who had preceded Ephialtes as leader of the Athenians, the man behind the death of his successor?

I picked up the bag of money. I spilled the coins across the table. What Aristodicus had hidden were tetradrachmae minted in Athens, with Athena on one side and her sacred owl peering out at us on the obverse. Aristodicus had placed bits of rag in among the coins to prevent jangling when he moved.

"Nico, is this what people usually get paid for killing other people?"

The coins were wealth, but not a fortune. "I don't know, little brother, but I doubt it. It doesn't seem enough to me, considering who Ephialtes was. Father is paid more for a large statue." I picked over the coins. In among them was a token I didn't recognize. I held it up to the light. It was a piece of board, fitting easily into my palm, with a design on it of some form. The board had been cut in two, slicing through the design with a zigzag edge. I couldn't make head nor tail of it, but I knew Aristodicus had thought it important.

I returned my attention to the bag the coins had been in, which seemed familiar to me although I knew I'd never seen this bag before in my life. Now where had I seen one similar?

At the house of Xanthippus! In his study there was a row of bags identical to this one, I was sure of it. I could have leapt for joy. At last I had a connection between Xanthippus and Aristodicus. I would have to find out where the bags had come from. If they were bought then someone else might have the same, but if they'd been made by Xanthippus' slaves, he would have a hard time evading the implication. I imagined myself prosecuting Xanthippus before the people of Athens and tearing apart his defense with ease.

"Nico, I've been thinking."

"What now?" I demanded, exasperated.

"The man who gave Aristodicus his orders must be in Athens."

"Why do you say that?"

"The note about the meeting. No one outside Athens could have written it."

It was so obvious it made me ashamed. I gave up all thoughts of Persian spies, Cimon, and Themistocles.

"All right then, you've made your point. Anything else to add?" I asked sarcastically.

"Whoever wrote the note probably ordered Aristodicus to stay in Athens. He probably has someone else to kill."

My little brother had reproduced almost everything I'd worked out, but with only half the evidence.

"Nico, I've been thinking—"

I sighed. "Try not to think so much, Socrates. It will only get you into trouble."

"Yes, Nico."

14

Pythax screamed, "Again!"

I thrust again with the blade in my left hand. And again I missed. It was astonishing the difference in strength between my left and right wrists. It was my first morning of training with Pythax. With my right still bandaged, Pythax was starting by teaching me what to do when my normal fighting arm was out of action.

The Scythians thought it terribly amusing that a citizen should be fighting in the dirt with them, but they took it in good part because Pythax treated me not one whit different to them. In fact, if anything he treated me more harshly. When I asked him why, he replied, his expression grim, "Because my men keep the peace and do crowd control, but you go looking for trouble."

Antigonos and Euphrestes, the two Scythians I had been practicing with, laughed, and poked me in the ribs. The first thing I had discovered about the Scythians was that very few of them were, in fact, Scythian. The true Scythians are tribes of barbarians who live far to the north. They are tall, fair, and ride like centaurs. Their people have no towns or villages. Instead they travel from place to place and erect tents for the women and children whenever they stop at a place for more than a few days. Perhaps the original Athenian force was truly Scythian, but that was farther back than anyone remembered. Now the

Scythians of Athens came from almost any of the northern hill tribes, and they were Hellenes for the most part, if primitive ones. I was even introduced to a "Scythian" from Crete!

At the end of training I stripped, poured a bucket of water over myself to clean off the dirt, and put on a fresh chitoniskos. I intended to go straight to Piraeus from the training ground.

As I rounded the path to the south, I ran into someone I knew coming the other way.

"Oh! Hello, Nicolaos. That is, I was just going for a walk," she volunteered quickly.

"Hello, Euterpe," I said.

She seemed to be peering around my shoulder. "Tell me, are they the Scythians over there?"

"Yes, they are. Pythax has been running early morning training. You might want to say hello if you're passing by."

"Yes! Yes, I might do that. Thank you," and she stepped past me nervously, but then stopped and said, "Oh, ah. You won't tell Diotima you saw me, will you? If she learned I was exercising, she would tease me about it."

"My lips are sealed, Euterpe."

I discovered quickly that Telemenes was well known in shipping circles. He owned more than one boat, which marked him as very wealthy indeed. He was a metic, of course; it is almost unheard of for well-born citizens to indulge in anything as disreputable as trade.

The man I asked was distinctly nervous when I approached him, and his hand shook as he pointed to a building by the quay, which he said was the office of Telemenes. I asked why he was so nervous and discovered that news travels fast. I had gained a certain reputation in Piraeus since the fight with Aristodicus the previous day.

The building was typical of the sort found near the docks, where everything looks like a warehouse, with wide doors and cool, dark interiors. What was less typical was the emergence of Rizon as I approached. We ran into each other. He looked frightened and angry.

"Get out of my way!" He raised his arms, probably to push me out of the way, but I wasn't taking any chances. I stepped back to draw my dagger.

He sneered, "So you're going to attack me again, are you? You're a violent man, I've warned the magistrates about you."

"I haven't fought anyone who didn't attack me first."

"Oh, is that so?" he asked, rubbing his nose.

"You don't count. Striking you is an act of public beneficence."

"Proof enough of what I say. Well, if you want to strike me down in public where there are plenty of witnesses, go right ahead." He pushed past and stalked away.

"Rizon!"

He turned. "What?"

"I'm sorry for your loss."

"What loss?"

"Stratonike and the nurses. They were members of your household when they died."

Rizon laughed. "No loss at all. Whoever did that was really doing us all a favor." He went on his way.

I entered the building Rizon had exited. There was a slave sorting through accounts. This wasn't your average slave who did the menial jobs around the house or manual labor on a farm. This slave could read and write, and Telemenes obviously trusted him to add the numbers. Such a man would be worth a small fortune on the market.

He looked up at me and said, "Can I help you?"

"I'm looking for Telemenes."

"Are you buying?"

"What?"

"Are you here to purchase cargo from the master?"

"No."

"Selling? I warn you, we rarely export for other merchants."

"No, I'm not selling."

"Booking passage then. We do take occasional passengers on our ships. Where would you like to go?"

"Nowhere, I just want to speak with Telemenes."

"Then I'm afraid he's not here and won't be until you go away."

"Oh no, that won't be necessary at all!"

A fat man stood in a doorway beyond the slave. He beckoned me inside. I stepped around the slave as ostentatiously as I could manage.

"Do excuse my slave. It's his job to keep me from being interrupted by unimportant personages, but that certainly doesn't apply to *you*." He beamed at me like I was his favorite nephew. His face and body were enormous. Telemenes didn't walk—he waddled from side to side. I wondered how any man could find enough food to get himself into that condition. In body-conscious Athens, which prized physical beauty above all things, Telemenes was unique. If he'd been a citizen, he would have been shunned by his fellows. As a metic he probably didn't care, especially since he was apparently rich enough to buy any number of citizens. Besides which, Telemenes gave the impression of being almost terminally jolly.

"You . . . you know me?" I stammered, suddenly unsure of myself.

"But of course! You are Nicolaos, son of Sophroniscus. It would be a poor merchant who didn't keep up with the latest developments in politics."

"I'm not a politician."

Telemenes raised an eyebrow. "Not too many days past, you formed an arrangement with Pericles, a man who, if I read the signs right, will soon be a powerful presence in Athens. You are acquainted with his father Xanthippus, a powerful member of the Areopagus. Indeed, I'm given to understand you helped save his property when the mob became violent. It's always pleasant to have favors due from the powerful, don't you think? You were seen to speak convivially with Archestratus at the funeral of Ephialtes. You visited the Polemarch—lovely man—at the time one of his secretaries was forced to retire due to illness. The rumor is you *turned down* his offer of a post, which bespeaks a man of enormous confidence of greater positions on the horizon. My dear boy, let's not be unduly modest in this room. I understand it is seemly before the mob, but between men such as us we can dispense with pretense. So, what can a fat old merchant do to assist you?"

And all this time I'd thought I'd been investigating a murder. Was this how other people saw me? Or was this slimy dealer trying to flatter me for his own unspeakable purposes?

"First of all, you can tell me what Rizon wanted."

"The gentleman who was here a moment ago? Surely that is his business. You should ask him."

"He's most unlikely to tell me. You, however, are likely to assist a rising politician. Do you trust your own judgment? Let's reflect on your words about the joy of having favors owed you."

"I see." Telemenes reflected for a moment. "The gentleman in question has occasion to make business trips. Most of our passengers are traveling on business. There is nothing unusual in that."

"It depends on the destination. Where does he go?"

"Ephesus."

"Anywhere else?"

"Always Ephesus, there and return. Three trips."

"So Rizon was here arranging another business trip."

"Indeed."

"Why in Hades would a sandal maker need to travel?"

Telemenes raised his eyebrows. "Now it truly would be necessary to ask the gentleman. I don't inquire of my passengers what they intend when they disembark my boat."

"I'm sure you don't. You had an arrangement with Aristodicus of Tanagra. I want to know about it."

"Who?" He looked bemused. I maintained a steady silence, determined to wait him out. Telemenes finally acquiesced and clapped his hands, and the slave came in. Telemenes whispered something to him and the slave departed, returning a moment later with a thick pile of parchments. He sifted through these before picking out one and handing it to Telemenes, silently departing with the remainder.

Telemenes studied the parchment. "Ah yes, Aristodicus of Tanagra. A minor matter that was taken care of directly by my slaves."

"Your seal is on the document."

"Ah yes, I am a busy man, Nicolaos. I have many things to attend to. Sometimes a busy man will allow a slave to affix a seal. It's a minor peccadillo, I know, but you know how it is. In the world of business, there are many worse things a man could do."

"Do you have many arrangements like this one?"

"Offering passage? Why, of course."

"How about passage for three times the going rate in return for anonymity and a fast boat on a moment's notice?"

"Does it say that here?" Telemenes made a great show of inspecting the note closely.

"I am reading between the lines."

"My dear Nicolaos, you should not make too much of the loose language you come across in notes such as these."

I made a stab in the dark on a sudden inspiration. "Was there a similar note when you brought Aristodicus to Athens?"

"There you are, young man! A fine example of loose language yourself! I did not arrange for Aristodicus to come to this lovely city."

"But he came on one of your boats, didn't he?"

"We are predominantly an import-export fleet, but we do have numerous passengers."

Talking with this man was like wrestling with an eel. "I suppose you must be pleased now that you won't have to deliver on your agreement."

"What do you mean?" He was either genuinely puzzled or an excellent actor.

"Aristodicus is dead."

"He is? Why, the poor man! I sorrow. I do hope it was not a painful illness that carried him off."

"Rest easy. The arrow that took him in the back was quite quick. Forgive me for mentioning it, but for a merchant who likes to keep up on political developments you seem remarkably behind the times about spectacular local deaths."

"I was speaking of the high politics of one of the world's most powerful cities, and you, unless I mistake your meaning, are talking about the sordid activities of a criminal underworld."

"I'm not entirely sure there's a great deal of difference. But even if there were, I am sure you would still know about it, Telemenes."

"My dear Nicolaos! I am a legitimate merchant. I have five boats plying the waters between all the Hellene ports, plus Crete, Asia Minor, Phoenicia, Egypt, and sometimes all the way to Massalia if the profit is right. We export ceramics and other manufactured goods, we import corn and some luxuries. I give you my most solemn promise I make more profit from such ventures than I ever could from passengers, no matter how well they pay."

I decided I could keep asking questions all day, and Telemenes could keep deflecting them as if he had some kind of verbal shield. "Where was Aristodicus planning to go?"

"Syracuse," he said. "Would you care to consider taking his place? As you pointed out, it is paid for."

"Thank you for the offer. If things continue for me as they have been, I might need a fast ship out of Athens some time soon, but I'm not that desperate yet."

Telemenes looked at me with interest. "Ah well."

"Now tell me where Aristodicus came from, and don't try and tell me you don't know."

Telemenes made another great show of inspecting his notes.

"That would be . . . let me see now . . . ah yes, Ephesus, the famed city of marble. Beautiful place, Ephesus."

Beautiful perhaps, but on the coast of Asia Minor under Persian control and, if my memory served, the closest major port to Magnesia, where Themistocles was Governor. So Aristodicus came here from Ephesus, and Rizon travels to Ephesus. What could I make of that?

I said, "Let me take a shot in the dark and ask if Rizon traveled on the boat that brought Aristodicus."

"For that information I will need to consult records."

"I'll wait."

Telemenes clapped his hands and the slave appeared once more for another whispered conference. This resulted in a flurry of activity that terminated with a small scroll placed before Telemenes. He ran his finger down the writing, hesitated, and sat back with a chuckle.

"Indeed they did. Quite a coincidence, wouldn't you say?"

I had time to make it back to Athens before lunch, which was good because I'd promised to take the box of Ephialtes' papers to Diotima so we could search them together. I carried these to the home of Euterpe, where the house slave let me in without a whisper. I dropped the box outside her door. Diotima arrived, looking tired and unhappy. Before we began, I said, "I have news for you, the man who shot your father is dead." I told her the story of his death. This cheered her up.

"Thank you, Nicolaos. You have given me half of the vengeance my father's shade demands." She didn't have to tell me the other half: the man behind Aristodicus. But I couldn't take credit when it wasn't due.

"I didn't kill him at the end. Pythax did."

"It would never have happened if you hadn't tracked him down, so thank you. Revenge for my father means a great deal to me."

She leaned forward and kissed me, and I was not surprised to discover this was highly pleasant. As the kiss went on, she moved into me and I held her tight. I could feel her breasts against my chest and her tongue between my lips.

We were committing a crime. If Rizon walked into the room this minute and killed us both, a court would approve his action as justifiable homicide, as long as he had witnesses.

Diotima probably had the same thought because she broke off the kiss.

"Mmm," she murmured, feeling downward. "So that part works for me as well as Mother!"

The part she referred to instantly deflated. "Did you have to mention her?"

"I thought it would work faster than a bucket of cold water."

"You were right," I complained.

"Oh, but I'm forgetting, you were hurt in the fight. Are you in pain?"

"Not now." I remembered she had had her own trauma recently. "How are you feeling now, Diotima?"

"Very happy." She smiled.

"I was actually referring to the brutal murder of three women in your household. You might recall the event."

"Oh, I'm fine. Now that the shock is over I'm relieved in a dreadful sort of way. I would have had to live with her, you know."

"I would not go about saying that too often if I were you. Stratonike's killer might be relying on exactly that to shift the blame to you. Tell me about Rizon."

"I did my best, believe me, but I couldn't smell any seawater on him."

"Curse it."

"It doesn't mean anything, Nicolaos. Rizon could easily have washed off the sea smell."

"But a positive result would at least have told us we were

heading in the right direction, even if it couldn't be used in a court case. What about his slaves?"

"His slaves are too frightened to say much, but the doorman confirmed Rizon came home late that night. That isn't necessarily suspicious though. He could have been at a symposium."

"I don't suppose the doorman noticed anything?"

"Rizon had red wine spilled down his clothing and he was drunk."

"Red wine would mask the smell. He could have been acting the drunk."

"I had exactly the same thought. Nicolaos, you don't think Rizon is behind Father's death, do you?"

"If you'd asked me yesterday I would have said it was unlikely. Now I'm not so sure." I told Diotima what I'd discovered from Telemenes. "Rizon certainly has a decent motive. Look at the wealth he inherits."

"But why would he have to travel to Ephesus several times to find an assassin? Surely once is enough."

"I don't know, Diotima. Their arrival on the same boat might be a coincidence."

"And a husband and wife murdered within days of each other for different reasons by different people? It beggars belief."

We turned to sifting through papyri containing notes, drafts of laws, more notes, and letters. We were looking for any evidence that Conon and the Polemarch had been stealing or misusing the public finds in their trust. We didn't find a thing. There was plenty about past cases Ephialtes had prosecuted, and if we'd wanted a fast course in Athenian politics we'd come to the right place, but there was nothing about the misdeeds of our current archons.

"Here, what's this?" I held up a sheet with a list of names. We put our heads together as we studied it, and the pleasant smell of her hair was distracting.

Theagenides
Lysistratos
Lysitheos
Archedemides
Tlepolemos
Conon

"I recognize some of these names," Diotima said. "Father prosecuted them for corruption."

"What! All of them?"

"Not Conon, of course, but the others . . ." She chewed her thumbnail. "Yes, I'm sure. These men are all members of the Areopagus, except for Conon, and he'll be a member too by the end of the year. In fact, every one of these men was Eponymous Archon."

"Did Ephialtes win all the prosecutions?"

"No, but he had evidence against every one of them."

I sat back, shocked. "Is the democracy so corrupt that every single man who holds office cheats the state?"

"How should I know? But surely this can't be everyone."

"Isn't it? Who's missing?"

"I'm not sure." It took us a moment to recall the past archons.

Diotima said, "Lysanias is the only one missing from the last six years." Lysanias was the man I'd seen at the mourning for Ephialtes.

"Five out of six abused their power. Dear Gods, Diotima, why am I trying to serve the state if this is what happens?"

"Father didn't win every case, you know! The courts decided some of them were innocent."

"Oh, sure they were!"

She ignored my sarcasm. "Conon's on that list. Nico, there has to be something against Conon, somewhere!"

Alongside each name was a short note. We studied them. Against Theagenides it said *box in corner,* beside Tlepolemos, *scrolls on third shelf,* and so forth. Ephialtes had drawn a line through each, all except for the last line bearing Conon's name. Conon's note said *wax tablet.*

We'd already checked the tablet, but Diotima picked it up again and read everything on it once more. Nothing. She held it so close that the wax was almost rubbing her nose, and peered at the tiniest scratches. Still nothing.

She put down the tablet and sighed. "This is so frustrating."

"Was this everything?" I asked.

"No, it wasn't," she said, and I knew from her tone that she'd found something that worried her. "I also found this, Nicolaos." She handed me a parchment. "I wasn't sure whether to show you or not, but I suppose I should."

The material was new, or almost new, the writing on it was small and careful. I read it through, my uneasiness growing with every word. When I was finished I put it down and said, "You found this in his room?"

Diotima nodded unhappily. "In his private papers."

"Zeus!"

. . . the problem of the leadership . . . while I am strong I must see to the succession, before a successor is forced upon me, or worst of all, there's a faction war after my death . . . Archestratus and Pericles . . . Archestratus intelligent . . . understands the system . . . worked hard for his chance . . . lacks the leadership qualities . . . Pericles . . . natural leader . . . family . . . arrogant . . . cannot be trusted . . .

"Cannot be trusted . . ." I echoed Ephialtes' words. "Pericles can't be trusted—"

"With the leadership, and to continue supporting the democracy," Diotima finished for me. "Well, it's true, isn't it? Look at his father."

"Zeus!" I said again. "Do you think anyone else has seen this?" Diotima snorted. "What do you think?"

Not a hope in Hades. If they had, they'd be standing in the Agora this instant, shouting it out to the world.

"But Nico, what if Pericles knows what Ephialtes wrote? What if he so much as suspects?"

It was enough for a motive, it was *more* than enough.

"You still have to get around the fact Pericles held no bow. I saw him! I know . . . oh . . ."

Diotima nodded grimly. "Right. He didn't need to, because he hired a mercenary to do the actual killing. Pericles was only there to make sure it went according to plan."

I shook my head. "I don't know, Diotima."

"I knew you'd say that," she said in disgust. "I suppose now you're going to tell him."

"Pericles? No, I'm not going to tell him." If I did, he would order me to destroy the evidence, which I would refuse to do, and then we would have a major and final falling-out. For Pericles, this was all about politics. He didn't really care who killed his friend, as long as it was someone convenient for his plans.

"Thank the Gods for that," Diotima said, plainly relieved. "I was worried you were becoming a politician." She paused for a moment, then said, in a gentle tone, "Nicolaos, what would you do? If we find Pericles killed Father?"

"Then it would be back to sculpting for me, wouldn't it?" I said with an attempt at a laugh. "Do you think he did it, Diotima?"

She chewed on her thumbnail. "I don't know, but I think he might."

"We'd never prove it, not in a court, not even if we had solid evidence, which we don't."

"And if Pericles is the killer, it wouldn't save me anyway. I need it to be the Eponymous Archon if I'm to escape my fate. I'm to be married next month."

That shook me. "So soon?"

"It's an arranged marriage for inheritance, not family alliance. It has to take place as soon as possible, and there's no dowry to negotiate." She laughed humorlessly. "Did I tell you what's happened at the temple? I'm scrubbing floors, just like a common girl. I complained to the high priestess, who told me the Polemarch has taken a great dislike to me—he says he doesn't think I'm priestess material—and I'm to be given all the worst jobs until I get sick of it and leave. The high priestess isn't cruel, even if she does look like a withered prune. She advised me to leave now and avoid the hardship."

"What did you say?"

"I told her I would scrub floors for the rest of my life if that's what it took. The Polemarch can't persecute me forever. But he doesn't have to, you know. He only has to persecute me until the Archon has me married to Rizon, then Rizon can forbid me to leave the house."

"Run away," I told her.

"We've had this conversation before, in the orchard, remember? I can't go back to Mantinea."

"Then run to another temple. What about the temple of Artemis in Brauron?"

"It's within Attica. They could easily drag me back."

I thought for a moment. "I have it then! The Temple of Artemis at Ephesus! Father tells me it's the most beautiful building he's ever seen."

"You don't give up, do you? Has it occurred to you temples like that aren't in need of destitute volunteers of doubtful origin? The girls from the best families fight tooth and nail to be accepted. Their fathers pay bribes to get them in."

"I'll pay the bribe with the reward money I get from Pericles."

"You're assuming you'll win it, and anyway, I swore I would never take money from a man."

"Then you're going to starve. Women can't own money."

"Mother does."

That stopped me. Mother did indeed, and obviously a great deal.

"That's a good point, Diotima. How does your mother manage to own her money?"

"The same way all hetaerae do, I suppose. Men friends give them presents, pay for most of their expenses, and give them money. When a hetaera needs something done she asks a client to do it for her. She returns the favor in kind."

"That explains the cash. Now tell me who owns this house."

That stumped her. She looked puzzled. "I never thought about it. There must be someone's name on the title deed."

"I can think of an obvious answer."

Diotima stared at me in horror. "Father kept it in his name?"

I nodded.

"Wait."

I waited. I knew Diotima had her answer when a piercing cry cut through the air.

"What do you *mean* Rizon owns this house. It's *mine!*"

It took Diotima some time to calm down an agitated Euterpe. I didn't go near them, but I didn't need to know most of it. When Euterpe was reduced to mere sobbing, Diotima returned to me.

"Well, I guess you heard that," she said.

"I'm sorry to be the source of bad news."

"Oh, it's not all that bad, Nicolaos. I mean, I know we could lose almost everything, but do you realize this is the first time my mother has ever needed me?"

"That pleases you? I thought you wanted to be free of her."

"Let's say it's rather pleasant to have the boot on the other foot. It is now extremely urgent to Euterpe to prevent my marriage to Rizon, to blackmail the Archon and the Polemarch, and to protect her wealth, and she can't do any of that without me. Despite appearances my mother is not particularly a woman of business. She always left those details to Ephialtes. When I walked out of her room, she was begging me to help her."

"Gloating is rarely pretty, Diotima."

"You can deal with the ugliness for a little while. I'm enjoying myself. What are you doing?"

While I'd been waiting, I'd picked up the wax tablet and was examining it closely.

Diotima said, "We've already checked that. There's nothing on it."

"I might have worked out what your father meant. Do you have a stylus and a scraper?"

She handed me a stylus used to write in wax, and the scraper used to smooth the surface again when the owner wanted to start over. Smoothing was usually done after slightly melting the wax, but I didn't want to risk holding a candle to it. I carefully scraped the wax back along one edge, letting the wax shavings fall to the floor. Diotima peered over my shoulder in interest. She exclaimed as the wax disappeared to reveal a piece of linen. I finished removing all the wax and peeled back the linen protecting–cloth to reveal parchments.

Diotima snatched. So did I. We got half each. We scanned eagerly and called out the interesting parts.

"They've been selling public contracts for kickbacks." She flipped through the parchment. "From the looks of this a dozen or so building contractors are inflating their prices by about a third, and splitting the profits with the Archon and the Polemarch. That must come to a tidy sum considering they're rebuilding the Stoa."

"It happens all the time," I said. "Everybody knows that."

"But not everyone leaves evidence like this lying around. These letters are the deals they struck and records of sums paid. That's enough to kill for."

"Yes, but you haven't proven anything. All you have is motive."

"But I don't want to prosecute them for murder, Nicolaos. All I want to do is blackmail them."

"That's a dangerous business, Diotima," I warned her, suddenly worried.

"I'll take the risk."

"I don't suppose you'd care to leave those with me?"

"Don't be ridiculous." Diotima paused, and sat back down on the couch. "Nicolaos, do you think it's possible Conon or the Polemarch murdered Father? I mean, they might have paid this Aristodicus."

"It's possible," I conceded. "Using an agent, they wouldn't have to be there, so there's no point checking their alibis. But, Diotima, how would they know Ephialtes was going to be on the Rock that morning?"

"That's always the problem, isn't it?" She sighed. "Maybe Father mentioned it to one or the other of them the day before. But you can't be sure, can you?"

15

I left Diotima and walked to the house of Pericles. I had to wait because he was in a meeting upstairs. The house slave put me in the courtyard while I waited.

Pericles came out looking tired and unhappy.

"Tell me some good news," he demanded.

"The man who killed Ephialtes is dead." I began with the most important point. I explained the story in detail, and Pericles listened, asking few questions. When I finished he shook his head. "I can't say I'm entirely happy, Nicolaos. We needed this man alive."

I said in anger, "I know you're under pressure, Pericles, but your habit of ignoring my successes and criticizing my failures is not going to inspire me to my best efforts."

A slave brought us cups of wine. I sipped mine and, when I realized it was thrice watered, drank it down fast. Investigating is hot work. I put the cup down and said, "There are other matters of importance to report." I told him of the murder of Stratonike.

Pericles sat back and frowned, then stood and began to pace back and forth along the paths. "Is it possible, do you think, these are connected?"

"They must be, but I rather think Stratonike died because Ephialtes died."

Pericles pondered, "Yes, I can see that, but what of the two slaves?"

"Almost certainly murdered to prevent them testifying to what they saw."

"Or because they had more to tell."

"You might be right." That thought bothered me.

"This Aristodicus, did he kill the women?"

I shrugged. "The best I can say is, maybe. It's not impossible." I pulled out the thin broken board Aristodicus had carried and asked, "Do you know what this is?"

Pericles looked at it, obviously wondering what it had to do with the murder. I delighted in not telling him. He handed it back and said, "No, unless the answer is a broken piece of board."

I put it away.

"You were going to meet Ephialtes after he spoke to Xanthippus, weren't you?"

Pericles jerked as if I'd hit him. "What makes you say that?"

"Ephialtes didn't leave the Rock of the Areopagus after Xanthippus left. It's been bothering me why not; he had nothing else to do there. Instead he stood waiting to be shot. It makes no sense unless he was waiting for someone. You may have been at the Acropolis thinking about architecture, but you were killing time before seeing him. You must have waited for the appointed time, then walked across from the Acropolis to the Areopagus. You would have looked for Ephialtes and not seen him, decided that he had left and departed yourself. When I saw you walking down the hill you were coming from the Areopagus, not the Acropolis, weren't you?"

Pericles laughed. "I see that I chose the right man for the job. You have it right. Ephialtes asked me to meet him there. He implied he had an important meeting beforehand. I didn't know it was with Xanthippus."

"Why didn't you tell me this before?"

"I didn't want to confuse you with extra details. I know I didn't kill him, why put the idea into your head?"

"Are there any other little details you decided not to confuse me with?" I asked. Diotima's theory that Pericles might have arranged the murder was almost throbbing in my brain.

"None that spring to mind."

"You didn't see anyone while you were up there?" I described Aristodicus in detail. "Did you see anyone looking like that?"

"If I had, I would have told you."

I spotted some of the same bags that Xanthippus had in his study, sitting atop one of the tables. It reminded me of a question I needed answered. "Pericles, those bags Xanthippus has in his study, I see you have some too, where do they come from?"

"They're made on our country estate from leftover bits of sheep leather when the tanning's done. Father swears by them as utility bags. He's forever sending things in them."

"Your family doesn't sell them?"

"No, why? If you want a few, you can have them."

"One will be fine, thanks."

Pericles handed me an empty bag. "Is this relevant?"

"I think it might be."

A man came running. I could see the damp sweat in his chiton. I could smell his fear. "Pericles, Archestratus is in the Agora. He's demanding the recall of Themistocles!"

Pericles stood still for a heartbeat, then, "WHAT!" he thundered. "That's as good as a vote of no confidence in my leadership. Did it occur to anyone that as soon as Themistocles sets foot in Attica, he'll be executed?"

"Archestratus says Themistocles' conviction should be dropped. The people are cheering him."

Pericles turned to me. "The people are losing their nerve. Finish it, Nicolaos, and do it quickly." He strode out the doorway, through his hall, and into the street.

———

I passed through the Agora on the way to see Xanthippus. In fact, I trailed Pericles all the way there; he came as close to running in public as I had ever seen him, yet still he managed to maintain his stately stride.

The friends of Archestratus were clustered about the man himself. I avoided them, but took the opportunity to pass among the citizens, to gauge their reaction to Archestratus' startling proposal to recall Themistocles. From what I overheard, most were intrigued with the idea. Everyone praised Archestratus for putting the good of Athens above his own interest. Pericles too was walking among the people, stopping to talk, and although he was maintaining his famous composure, I was sure he was not liking what he was hearing.

Archestratus saw me as I passed by, and called for me by name.

"I thought you wanted to lead?" I said to Archestratus as he stepped away from his admirers. "Wouldn't recalling Themistocles set back your ambitions even further?"

Archestratus shrugged. "What we have now is an impasse that does no good to anyone. I haven't the support to assume control while Pericles is on the scene—you see, I am a realist—and Pericles won't have the full support of the people while so many questions hang over his involvement in this affair. What I propose is a compromise."

"I see." A spoiling tactic then. If Archestratus could not have the leadership, he would make sure his rival Pericles didn't get it either.

"I called you over, Nicolaos, to congratulate you on your own triumph. The word across Athens is Ephialtes' murderer is dead."

I nodded. "I tracked him down."

"We will all breathe easier for your success. I suppose that now your work is done, Pericles has paid your reward?"

He read the answer in my face and smiled.

"There's still the question of who's behind the killer," I said, feeling somehow embarrassed.

"Of course, I understand perfectly." Archestratus' face showed no expression. "But, might you be looking for shadows where there are none?"

"There are still a few loose ends. Can you tell me what this is?" I showed him the broken piece of board, with not much hope of a useful answer.

"A broken piece of board?" he suggested, meeting my expectations. He looked at me, curious. "Have you taken to carpentry?"

I saw out of the corner of my eye that Pericles had broken off his conversation with one group, and was stamping in our direction with a scowl on his face.

I decided there were safer places to be than standing between Pericles and Archestratus, so I said, "Excuse me, Archestratus, I must move on."

Archestratus waved his hand with an air of nonchalance and said, "Of course. Weighty matters call you." And at that he was swept away by his friends before Pericles could reach him.

I walked on to the house of Xanthippus. The guards recognized me and let me pass. Slaves were swarming over the place, rebuilding what the rioters had damaged. This was the home of a wealthy man, so it was made almost entirely from strong wooden beams and solid timber walls. If Xanthippus had been a poor man, or even one of only average means, the walls of his home would have been constructed from daub and mud brick, perhaps so thin that a determined man could punch his way through from the street. The stronger construction had worked for Xanthippus—his house was still standing after all—but meant rebuilding was going to be more costly, take longer, and be more expensive; any support that was fire damaged could no longer be trusted, and I saw several places where workers had pulled down smoke-blackened veneer to inspect the struts behind. I doubted Xanthippus would be able to recoup the cost from the men the Scythians had taken up.

Since the andron was in ruins, the house slave led me to the study, where Xanthippus sat.

He glanced up as I entered and said, "You again." He stood. "I didn't thank you for your assistance when the mob came. I thank you now."

I was uncomfortable considering what I'd come to say. "Any citizen would have done the same."

"Many citizens would disagree with you. The ones attacking my home, for instance."

"The man who shot Ephialtes has been killed."

"So Pythax told me. He also told me he saved your life."

"I'm very grateful." It was no surprise to me that Pythax had reported to Xanthippus.

"Good. Now we can put this whole sorry saga behind us and get on with the vital job of ruling Athens."

"You think so? Then what of this proposal from Archestratus to recall Themistocles? Doesn't that upset the Areopagus?"

Xanthippus, for the first time since I had known him, looked less than sure of himself. He fidgeted in his seat and crossed his legs.

After a pause he said, "I'm no hypocrite. I regret the death of Ephialtes, but I can't deny it's an opportunity to restore some imbalances."

Xanthippus stopped speaking to watch some slaves carry out a broken table.

"It's a compromise," he said, oddly echoing the words of Archestratus. "Themistocles was a member of the Areopagus, but he was also extremely popular with the people. Perhaps Archestratus has the right idea."

"But what if someone hired the killer? It's inconceivable Aristodicus could have been acting on his own. What possible reason had he for killing an Athenian politician?"

Xanthippus shrugged. "Not every killing has to have a reason. In all likelihood, he was a madman acting alone. I understand he later ran amok in Ephialtes' home and slaughtered all the women. Perhaps he had a personal grudge against Ephialtes. We'll probably never know."

I placed the bag I'd taken from Pericles on the table, then the other alongside it. "One of these was found around the neck of Aristodicus of Tanagra. Would you care to explain what your money bag was doing around the neck of the assassin?"

Xanthippus' eyes widened. "But that's impossible! I have no idea how he got it."

"Someone gave it to him. The obvious person is you."

"I would be foolish to deny it. I am the obvious choice for your suspicions. Yet I will swear by any God that I didn't. I've sent these bags to many people in the past. Any one of them could have passed it on to this assassin." Xanthippus picked up the bag and examined it. He muttered to himself, "How interesting."

"You see something?"

"What? Oh, no. I merely mean how interesting that this should have happened."

"Your claim that Aristodicus was a madman acting alone is refuted. It is obvious the coins are the mercenary pay for his crime, and it is equally obvious the man who paid him was not just an Athenian, but someone you know, or you yourself, sir. Who else has these distinctive bags?"

"Any time I need to send money or a scroll to someone, I place it in one of these. The less honest among my acquaintances, or to be generous about it, the more forgetful, don't always return the bag. It might be possible to list most people I've sent something to in the last few months, but I doubt the slaves would remember everyone." Xanthippus thought for a moment. "Ah, I have it! It was not long ago that I had cause to send a scroll to Ephialtes. No doubt this assassin stole the bag from his house when he was slaughtering Ephialtes' womenfolk."

"What a very convenient explanation. Are you sure you sent a bag to Ephialtes?"

"I feel quite sure that when I check, I will find that a bag was sent to Ephialtes."

Once more I pulled out the broken token. "Do you recognize this?"

Xanthippus examined the jagged edge with interest. "No," he said curtly. "Does it have something to do with the murder?"

"Yes." But I didn't tell him what, because I didn't know.

I left Xanthippus to the joys of restoring his ruined home. I felt sure that for all the glibness of his replies, he'd be spending a sleepless night. This pleased me. At last I was putting pressure on my suspects.

My next stop was the home of Lysanias, the only Eponymous Archon of the last six years whom Ephialtes had not targeted as corrupt. If Ephialtes, who had been active in trying to discredit every archon he could, had not been able to find anything against him, it probably meant Lysanias was honest. His slaves told me Lysanias had left for the new gymnasium at the Academy.

I walked northwest, out the Dipylon Gates, through the deme of Outer Ceramicus, past olive groves, orchards, and small, elegant estates, then to a walled park. Everything was green, the air tasted of life, beautiful trees provided shade, and olives grew for the picking. Statues and the occasional fountain lined the way. Three of the statues had been commissioned from Sophroniscus and I stopped to admire them as I passed. When I walked through the low gates, it was like stepping into the Elysian Fields.

The Academy had been built many years before my time, the third gymnasium of Athens, but its reputation had been so poor, and it was so far from the Agora, that almost no one used it until Cimon had virtually torn the whole place apart and started again. He had funded the entire enterprise out of his own pocket, using wealth he had taken during his many successful battles against the Persians, and it had cost him a fortune.

The gymnasium, like the grounds, was a thing of beauty. I passed through the entrance into a quadrangle lined with porticoes. Most held naked men giving and receiving massages, bathing, or anointing themselves with oil, so much oil in fact that the whole gymnasium smelled of it. I walked around all four sides but did not see Lysanias, so I passed through into the next courtyard. This was squared off into patches of sand for wrestling practice, jumping, exercises, and playing quoits. As I walked in, I was sprayed with sand as one man threw another, who landed on his back before me. I walked around the unconscious body and walked briskly to the other side, where I saw Lysanias about to throw a quoit. His body was so wiry I could see the cords of muscles move beneath his skin as he prepared.

Lysanias grasped the thong from which hung a heavy ball made of twisted rope. He swung the thong back and forth a few times, getting a feel for the weight, then made a series of rotating steps forward before hurling the quoit with all his strength. I shaded my eyes to look for the fall. I saw it in the distance, the ball struck and bounced thrice before stopping. For an old man it had been an excellent throw.

"Excuse me, Lysanias, could I have a word with you?"

He looked me over with clear blue eyes, which I was entirely unable to read. "You are?"

"Nicolaos, son of Sophroniscus, sir."

"Ah yes, Pericles' little attack dog. I've heard of you. Every member of the Council has been warned about you. Well, young man, I haven't killed anyone this month, so I'm probably not of much interest to you."

That was not the most flattering description of me I'd ever heard! I marveled at the different views of me going about. First the influential young politician from Telemenes, now the dog from Lysanias. And still I thought of myself as a mere investigator looking for a chance to show what I could do. As the philosophers say, no man can ever truly know another.

"I'm doing what I can to uncover who killed Ephialtes, sir. As for the rest, it is true my commission is from Pericles, but that won't stop me from publishing the names of the killers when I have them."

Lysanias humphed. "Likely story. So you're going to prosecute them, are you?"

"I could hardly afford it."

"No, you couldn't. Will Pericles?"

"I can't speak for him."

"Then your assurances lack credibility. The reality is, if you found the killer was a democrat, Pericles would bury the truth quicker than you could blink."

This was so close to what I knew to be so that it was embarrassing.

"I thought as much," Lysanias continued, reading me perfectly. "Very well, young man, what do you want to know?"

His offer surprised me. "You've decided my job is a political exercise aimed against the Council, but you are willing to answer my questions anyway?"

"I am an extremely unusual recent member of the Council. Do you know why?"

"No, tell me why."

"Because I am competent. That surprises you, does it? That I admit the reality, or that I am not one of the usual dross we see as archons today."

"Your forthright manner is certainly refreshing."

"Delicately put. The current Council of the Areopagus is a group of no-hopers."

He waited for my reaction, so I prompted him with, "It is?"

"I have been a Councilor for three years, young man. Supposedly I am doing this to guide the future of Athens, but what you hear at most Council meetings has much more to do with old men protecting their privileges. I tell you it turns my stomach."

Lysanias drew himself up for an important announcement. "I am disillusioned. Therefore I am going to help you, for the good of Athens."

"Did the Council of the Areopagus plot the death of Ephialtes?"

Lysanias snorted. "If that's your style of subtle questioning then the plotters have nothing to fear."

"Since you're being so honest I thought I would try."

"You mistake honesty for stupidity. No, the Council as a whole did not compass the death of the man we hate most in the world, but then, the true Council could have done so and I would be none the wiser."

"The true Council? What's that?"

"The Council is made up of former archons. These days the candidates for the archonships are selected by lot, but long before you were born the archons were chosen based on their personal merits. It means the new members are mostly idiots, because that's usually what you get when you choose a man by chance. But there's a core of old men, from the days of merit, and those old men know what they're doing. If you were to sit in on a meeting, you would hear that the older members have everything discussed, weighed, decided, and stitched up before ever the issue makes it to the Councilors. Most of the lot men are too stupid to realize this. I am not."

"This Council within a Council, they could have plotted the assassination?"

"I have no way of knowing."

"If you are competent, sir, isn't it likely they will invite you into the inner circle?"

"They have had three years, and not done so. I conclude all the lot men are tainted with the same prejudice."

"Can you tell me who the ringleaders are of the inner circle?"

"They are all men of intelligence and experience, but I

should say the three who lead are Calliades, Timosthenes, and Xanthippus."

"Tell me, what was the reaction of the Council after the news of the murder came out?"

"Consternation and fear from most of the members. They saw as clearly as your friend Pericles what the likely result would be. Xanthippus called a special meeting. Aha! I see you didn't know that. I asked the same question you did a moment ago. I demanded that if anyone had knowledge of this murder then they should reveal it forthwith, while there was still time to avert the crisis. None admitted to it, as I expected."

"Then why did you ask the question?"

"Do you know so little of politics, you fool? To judge their reactions of course. The lot men were simply scared. In any case, if one of those idiots had planned this you would have caught them long ago. The reaction of those of the inner circle was much more interesting. They were surprised." Lysanias paused.

"All right, at the risk of having you bite my head off again, I will ask the leading question. Why was their surprise surprising?"

"Because they were surprised, not scared and not shocked. I had the distinct impression that they'd been prepared for something, but what had happened wasn't what they were expecting."

"Thank you for your help, sir. I have one last question."

"Ask it."

I gestured at the quoits lying at our feet. "Aren't you a little old for this?"

Lysanias scoffed. "Excellent! Spoken like a truly brash young man. Pick up a quoit."

"Me?"

"You. Or are you too young for this?"

I'd asked the question to discompose Lysanias. I would have to follow through. So I stripped and performed some warming up exercises. Lysanias waited patiently. When I felt as ready as I was ever going to be I stepped forward and took hold of the thong of the nearest quoit. I swung this back and forth for a while, to understand how the weighted ball would fly. I had thrown discus before, but never the quoit variant.

Lysanias covered an ostentatious yawn.

I stepped behind the line and commenced a twirling pattern of steps, much as I would have done for the discus. I whirled faster and faster until the whole world was a blur and my entire focus was on the speeding quoit straining to leave my grip. I let go of the thong with a stupendous grunt and the quoit was hurled into the sky.

It was a massive throw. The quoit had no doubt left Attica by now and was halfway to Thrace. Shepherd boys would be looking upward, wondering what that thing was passing overhead. I stopped my gyrations and looked skyward for the ball.

Instead, I saw the dust come up as my quoit landed slightly short of the one Lysanias had thrown.

"Not bad," Lysanias allowed. "If you practiced you might amount to something."

"How old are you, sir?"

"Fifty-five, if my old, senile memory isn't failing me."

"You've made your point, Lysanias. I'm impressed."

Lysanias preened.

I dressed myself. As I made to go, he put a hand on my shoulder and said, "Don't take it hard, lad. I practice every day. You seem better than most of the dross we're rearing these days. Come back again and I'll teach you how to throw properly. I could show you how to get extra distance."

"Thanks, Lysanias, I might take you up on that offer some time."

The inn by the gates on the road to Piraeus was empty when I walked in the next morning but for the innkeeper who still had crooked legs, looked more ragged than ever, and moved as if the weight of the world was on his shoulders. I was feeling more than a little sore myself; Pythax had had me practicing extended lunges since dawn. My thighs, calves, and lower back ached.

"Remember me?" I asked. "I'm the one who was looking for Aristodicus."

The innkeeper was bent over an amphora of wine, struggling to lift it to his bar bench. He winced up at me as if the sight were painful. I picked up the amphora and settled it for him in a hole in the wooden top. "Thank you." He belched and straightened. "Ah, that's better. Damned onions. Never could take onions. What do you want this time? I heard you found Aristodicus. How was he?"

"Dead when I left him."

The innkeeper nodded. "Yeah, that's what I heard. Down at the Piraeus, wann't it?"

"Right where you told me to look. I thought I'd drop in and express my gratitude with a jar of your best wine."

He looked at me uncomprehendingly, as if the concept were foreign to him. "Best? Yeah, okay." He shuffled off into a back room and emerged with a dirty cup and liquid inside that I thought it best not to contemplate.

"My thanks to you, innkeeper." I threw enough coins on the bar to pay for several amphorae of this pig's swill. My generosity was unparalleled. The excess coins would go straight into the innkeeper's pocket.

A man staggered in, still more or less conscious as I'd hoped he'd be at this hour. It was Ephron, the drunk the innkeeper had shoved aside when I'd visited before. The man who was always here.

"Why, Ephron! I was hoping to see you."

"Yeah, what for?" He squinted at me as if he were looking into the sun. "I don't think I know you. Do I owe you money?"

"No, but if my hopes flower then shortly I am going to owe you money."

"Yeah, what for?" he asked again. Clearly not a vivid conversationalist.

"Our host tells me you are a great customer of his."

"It's an okay place to get drunk. Any place you can get drunk is an okay place when you can't work."

I looked him over, but he didn't seem sick or lame to me. "What's the problem?"

"I was a sailor. Ran away from home when I was a lad and signed up on a cargo boat, 'cause all I ever wanted to do was sail and see the world. Sailed some good trips, even down to Egypt and back. Then I couldn't sail no more. Couldn't see."

"You're blind?"

"Nah, but everything's a blur. Started years ago, when I was a young man, got worse and worse, 'til I couldn't see what I was doing unless I was up real close. That's a bad thing in a man who has to avoid rocks and put his boat alongside a wharf."

I'd heard of this happening to other men, but not as bad as this case. "That's too bad," I sympathized. "Couldn't you do something else?"

"Sailing's what I know. I tried to get work as a laborer, you know? But it's just as bad. The boss says to move a sack, and I can see something that's probably a sack, but when I carry it I trip over stuff and run into things. No one's going to pay me to drop their sacks, and when I dropped an amphora it was real bad. My woman ran away, got no slaves. So now I do what work I can, I don't care what, as long I have enough to get drunk so's I don't remember."

I said, "Let's hold onto the remembering for a little while longer. Do you recall a gentleman by the name of Aristodicus? Tough-looking man, came from Tanagra, maybe didn't talk much."

He struggled mightily to perform a feat he probably had not attempted in years. Eventually he said in triumph, "Yeah, I remember him. He owe you money?"

"Not anymore. I want to meet his friends. He had two. They used to visit him here. Do you remember them?"

He struggled once more, then, "Yeah, there were two."

Now for the all-important question. "What did they look like?"

He squinted at me with eyes so bloodshot there was barely any white to be seen.

"Okay, scrap that question. What did they sound like?"

"Sound like?"

"That's right. They talked, didn't they? What were their voices like?"

"Posh."

"Posh? Both of them?"

"Yeah. Only one was older posh—you know how you can tell from a voice?—and the other was sort of middle-aged posh. The middle-aged guy talked a lot, sounded sort of slimy. Used lots of big words too."

"What about you, innkeeper?" I asked. He shook his head.

I held up five tetradrachmae. "For a decent description." He stared at the money and licked his lips, but regretfully shook his head.

"Here! Is that money?" Ephron demanded.

I clinked the coins together.

"Let me think . . . the middle-aged guy . . . he had on a pretty good chiton and one of those big himation cloaks, sleazy sort of guy. Two slaves. The slave carrying his purse wouldn't sit down near me, thought I had fleas or something, uptight little bugger. The second slave had a purse too, but he didn't do any paying. Maybe his bag didn't have coins, it dinn't make any noise."

"Are you sure it was the middle-aged man who came with an extra bag, a bag that didn't clink?"

"'Course I'm sure."

"The *middle-aged* man."

"Said so, dinn't I?"

"If you saw him again, maybe heard him, would you recognize him?"

"Nah, I can't see too well you know? But I can tell there's a man standing in front of me."

"Now, Ephron, what about the first man?"

"The old guy? He was angry, I reckon."

"Why?"

"I dunno, he just sounded angry is all. And he was scarier than the other one. Sounded like he was used to ordering people about. He only had one slave, and the slave paid Aristodicus."

"What!"

"Yeah, and that slave wann't scared of me like the other bastard."

"The *older man* paid Aristodicus?"

"Yeah."

"The older man."

"You got a hearing problem? I said yeah."

"And the *middle-aged* man came here with the bag that didn't clink."

Both men looked in silent agreement that I must be dim-witted to repeat their sentences. I was inclined to agree with them.

"Tell me, who came first?"

"The middle-aged man."

"Did anyone hear what either of them said?"

"Nah."

I spilled the coins before Ephron, who scooped them up hungrily. I would have been happy to leave behind the revolting liquid in the cup, but as I rose the innkeeper said, "Here! You ain't drunk my best wine."

If it came to a prosecution, these men would be witnesses. So I held my breath and drank it down. It was mostly vinegar, with a hint of alcohol and all the pungent aroma of a dead rat. I put down the empty cup and said, "I thank you, innkeeper, for a unique experience."

16

A slave approached me as I sat in the Agora, trying to wash down with olives and real wine the taste of the vile concoction I had swallowed.

"Are you Nicolaos, son of Sophroniscus?"

I looked up at him. "Probably. What do you want?"

"I come from Callias, son of Hipponicus. He desires to meet with you."

I didn't bother to ask what about, the man was only a slave. Instead I rose immediately. It wasn't yet the end of the month, not time to ruin Sophroniscus for debt, so what could Callias want with me now?

I was led to his city house. Much of the lower floor was made of stone, an extravagance since every other home I'd been in was wooden or mud brick throughout, but at least it meant he was safer from fire. The house plan was expansive. The courtyard was a perfect square—someone must have measured it off—surrounded by carved wooden columns and a covered walkway. I looked up and turned around. The upper story of the house was made of wood, painted in rich blues except where murals showed the cavorting of the centaurs, Theseus defeating the Minotaur, and other scenes of our past. I noticed most of the slaves were young and beautiful and went about their work serenely.

I had never been particularly ambitious for wealth. Political importance was my dream. Now I quickly revised my estimate of the value of money. If I ever became the richest man in Athens, this was the sort of home I wanted to own.

Callias sat in the courtyard conducting business. At least, he was being read to by one slave while another wrote to his dictation. What the slave was reading and what Callias was dictating seemed to be unrelated. It was a remarkable performance, and I wondered if it had been put on for my benefit or whether Callias normally worked like that.

It was over soon enough and Callias turned his attention to me. He looked me square in the eye and said, "Thank you for coming, Nicolaos. I have been speaking to Pericles."

If he expected a reaction, all he got was, "What about?"

Callias frowned. "You probably don't think too well of me, young man, and I wouldn't blame you for that. But I understand you are stepping into the world of politics, so let's see if you can manage the first rule of the diplomat: separating your personal feelings from business."

I felt chastened, precisely as he intended. He himself had been an ambassador for Athens on more than one occasion, and I knew he had just given me professional advice.

I said, "I apologize. It's obvious you know I'm investigating the death of Ephialtes. I hope to prosecute the murderer regardless of who he is, so I like to think this is not a matter of politics."

To my surprise I saw him smile. "Ah, I thought as much. I am speaking to an honest man. Perhaps there is a touch of idealism too, so appropriate to the young, and of course a trifle brash. I too, young man, have tried during my time to cleave to the path that leads to the greatest good for our city. I caution you it is not an easy path to tread. One finds there are necessary detours."

"Thank you for the advice. That is quite close to something my father said."

"Your father is a wise man, for all that we have our issue at the moment."

"You're not really going to bankrupt him, are you?"

"That remains to be seen, young man. You will have noticed even your father didn't dispute the fairness of his liability. If the culprit isn't brought to light, I suspect he'll bankrupt himself without any pressure from me."

I decided to avoid that delicate subject, as a good diplomat should, and said nothing.

Callias continued, "You may not be aware my dear wife Elpinice is sister to Cimon. Ah yes, I see that's a name you know. Cimon was ostracized last year and has been residing in the north ever since. Word of the tragic death of Ephialtes has only now reached him, and he sent to me straightaway to act on his behalf. Cimon seeks to reassure anyone looking into the matter that he had nothing to do with it."

Callias sat back, and I could see him relax as he placed his fingertips together and said, "I went to see Pericles and he, much to my surprise, suggested I talk to you. I did not realize, when you were here with Sophroniscus, that you were involved in politics, and a supporter of Pericles. This changes things."

For the better, he meant to say, and I felt a surge of hope. Was my association with Pericles going to save my father?

"Do you believe Cimon?" I asked Callias.

"I am a supporter of Ephialtes and the democracy; if I thought Cimon had a hand in his death, I would prosecute him, family or no."

I nodded. Callias didn't know it, but his innocent comment that Cimon went north, and not east toward Ephesus and Magnesia, virtually eliminated Cimon as a suspect.

"What do you need to complete your work, Nicolaos?"

If Callias had made his offer earlier, I might have asked him for men to search the inns for Aristodicus, but that problem was solved.

"What I need more than anything else is information. And I need to find the people who know the things I want. I don't think it's anything you can help me with, Callias."

"Is there anything more I can tell you?"

I decided it was worth trying. "You can tell me what this is." I handed over the broken token.

Callias took it from me and said instantly, "It's a banking token. Or rather, it's half a banking token."

I was suddenly excited. "What's a banking token?"

"There are men in the Agora who will exchange coins of different currencies, that is, minted in different cities. You know that, don't you?"

I nodded. "Sophroniscus sometimes has to go to them when he's paid in foreign coins. He calls the changers thieves."

Callias laughed. "He may not be so wrong. However, they only take money from men who want to deal with them, Nicolaos, and that makes them legal. Now, these men do more than change coins. They also keep your money for you, which can be useful if you have a lot, or they can lend you money at a rate of interest, or they can transfer your money to another city, so that you can travel there and collect it without the risk of having to transport your own gold."

"How do they manage that, to move the money?"

"Ah, good question. They do it by not moving any money at all."

"Eh? That doesn't make sense."

"Oh, but it does! Let's say you have a lot of money and you want to send it to somewhere, let's say—"

"Syracuse."

"Fine choice. You want to send your money to Syracuse, where you will use it to buy a country estate. You take your thousands of drachmae to a banker in Athens. He puts it into his strongbox. In return he writes you a letter, saying that he has taken receipt of your funds and that you will collect an equivalent amount of Syracusan coins when you arrive in that city at an agreed exchange rate. You take your letter and a banking token, and leave. The banker immediately writes to a friend of his in Syracuse, another banker. He tells the Syracusan banker to expect you, and assures the man that your funds are on deposit. When you arrive, you see this Syracusan banker, and he gives you the agreed sum. You have now transferred a large sum of money across the world at no risk to yourself. I use this service myself for my own business dealings."

"That's clever." I was genuinely impressed. "But isn't the Syracusan out of pocket, and the Athenian has made money he hasn't earned?"

"Just so. However, it won't be long before a rich Syracusan wants to send money from Syracuse to Athens. Then the obligation goes the other way. These things tend to even out over time, and you can be sure the bankers keep a very careful count of who owes whom, and how much."

"But wait! The Syracusan has never seen me before. How does he know I'm not an impostor?"

"Pull out your token. Look at it."

I did as he bid.

"There's a pattern on the token. Each banker uses his own pattern and varies it a bit too, so these tokens are unique. The Athenian has told the Syracusan what pattern to expect on the token. The only way to impersonate you is to steal that token."

"I see." I hadn't found any letter among Aristodicus' effects. "Then tell me, why is this one cut in half?"

"It does rather look that way, doesn't it? I can only suggest that two men who don't trust each other have deposited a sum together, and they've split the token between them. The banker would only release the funds if both pieces were presented."

"That's interesting. Would you believe that none of Pericles, Archestratus, nor Xanthippus recognized this board for what it was?"

"In the case of Xanthippus and Pericles that is wholly believable. Both are traditional men—yes, Pericles too!—and they have nothing to do with trade. In the case of Archestratus, I find that very difficult to believe, considering this token belongs to the Antisthenes and Archestratus Savings and Loan Company."

My jaw dropped. "You are not joking? You mean that?"

"Certainly I do. I recognize the pattern."

"*Archestratus* owns a bank?"

"Not your Archestratus; his son, whom he named after himself instead of taking the name of the grandfather." It is traditional in Athens for a man to name his first born son after his own father. A second son would often be named for the maternal grandfather. Consequently names tended to repeat with alternate generations. But the rule was not universal, and some families used the same name every time.

I was stunned by the implications, but some part of me was still thinking because I asked without conscious thought, "By any chance do you know a metic called Telemenes, who runs an import-export business?"

"Why, yes, of course. Telemenes is well known in business circles."

"You wouldn't happen to know his bankers, would you?"

"As it happens, I do."

"It's the Antisthenes and Archestratus Savings and Loan Company, isn't it?" I guessed.

"Yes. But what does Telemenes have to do with this? Is it important?"

The bankers in the Agora are called trapezai because of their oddly shaped tables, which are themselves covered in trapezoids and other irregular shapes. I watched bemused as a seated banker ran knotted string here and there about the top of his table. His practiced fingers moved swiftly, measuring the string against the sides of some shapes. It took me a moment to realize he was calculating money, and that the length of the string, measured by the number of knots, told him how much. He came to some conclusion, nodded, and counted coins to the man standing before him. The client departed, and the banker made marks in a scroll.

It never occurred to me for a moment that the firm of Antisthenes and Archestratus would be anything but obstructive, so I picked my moment, waiting for the one who looked most like Archestratus senior to leave.

"I want to make a withdrawal," I said to the man behind the table. He was dark-haired and young but rather weedy looking. I suppose sitting at a desk all day is bad for you. In fact, I had seen to my surprise that both Antisthenes and Archestratus were young men. Banking is a new idea so I suppose anyone practicing it is likely to be young too. I held up the token.

He glanced at it and said immediately, "You need the other half or I can't help you."

"Can you tell me who has it?"

"If you don't know that, then I *definitely* can't help you. Who are you, anyway?"

His question told me instantly the banker who'd dealt with Aristodicus was Archestratus, son of Archestratus. "I'm Aristodicus of Tanagra. Where's your partner? It was him I was dealing with."

"He's had to leave unexpectedly. I am Antisthenes."

"Archestratus mentioned you."

Antisthenes opened a scroll and ran his finger along a column. He murmured, "Aristodicus . . . Aristodicus . . . ah, Aristodicus of Tanagra, yes, here you are." He peered at the numbers and words written alongside.

"Archestratus noted we are holding funds for you in escrow pursuant to completion of a contract."

"The contract's done. I want my money."

"I am delighted for you. I look forward to seeing you and your other party together with both halves of the token."

"What if my friend gives me his half and I come on my own?"

"I give you the money. We don't care much about people in the banking business. Coins, letters of credit, and account tokens are what get us excited. Oh, and if you want to take money out you'll need to prove you're who you say you are." He looked at me closely. "You *are* Aristodicus of Tanagra, aren't you?"

"Trust me."

"Trust is not a major element of banking. Bring a witness willing to swear to you, particularly since you asked me the name of your other party. That sort of question makes a banker suspicious."

I departed, angry with myself for handling the interview so badly. I should have realized he wasn't going to tell me the name of the other party. I had wanted the name so desperately I'd forsaken all caution. I groaned in frustration. The name written in that scroll was the man behind the killer, unless of course, the bastard had used a false name.

I pushed my way through the Agora, lost in thought. I stumbled into someone.

"Hey!"

"Oh!" The man I'd stumbled against was Sophroniscus' friend Lysimachus. "I'm sorry, sir, I wasn't looking."

"You certainly weren't, young Nicolaos. I saw you looking black as thunder with your head down and thought I'd come over to see if you're all right."

"That's kind of you. I'm having a little trouble, but it's something I need to sort out for myself."

"Your investigation?" he sympathized. "I won't ask how it goes, your expression tells me everything. Come sit down." He ordered the slave carrying his coins to bring us wine. The slave walked to the nearest stall, took a few coins from his mouth, and bought two cups while Lysimachus led me to a seat in the shade of the Monument to the Ten Heroes.

As we sat sipping he asked, "How is Sophroniscus?"

"Father's well in his body, but very disturbed in his mind. We had a disaster while delivering a statue." I related the story to Lysimachus, who shook his head in dismay as I talked, finishing with, "He spends his days selling everything not essential, to raise the money to repay Callias, but I don't know if it will be enough."

Lysimachus frowned. "Thank you for telling me this, Nicolaos. I will go see Sophroniscus at once. I am cross with him for not coming to me. I'm sure I can lend him what's required."

"You can? If you did, I would be eternally grateful, Lysimachus, it would be a huge weight off his mind—and mine too!—but I don't know if he'll accept your money."

"I will be persuasive."

"Well, I hope I can make the whole problem irrelevant, and your generous offer unnecessary. It's up to me to name the man who sabotaged us."

"Your father worries about you, out on the streets like this."

"I know. He thinks I should be a sculptor like him. I haven't thanked you, Lysimachus, for supporting me that evening."

He dismissed my thanks with the wave of a hand.

"In his younger days, your father was something of a rebel too."

"I find that hard to believe." Sophroniscus is the most solidly middle class of men.

"It's true. You'll recall he spoke of annoying his father by threatening to become an actor."

"I thought he made that up."

"No, he was speaking the truth. And I'm sure there are some things he's never mentioned to me. Now, tell me what was upsetting you so much when you ran into me."

I explained, finishing with, "It's the frustration. Every time I think I've cleared the last obstacle something else gets in the way. I don't know how many times I've said to myself this is the last problem to solve."

"I see. Was Callias able to help? Do keep in mind, young

Nicolaos, there are men in Athens with considerable resources who want to see the city come out of this in one piece. Callias is such a man."

"That's all very well, but how can Callias help me with a ba—" I put down my cup. "Thank you for the wine, Lysimachus. I have to get back to work."

I hurried back to the home of Callias and beat on the door. The doorkeeper wouldn't let me in until Callias himself heard the disturbance and came to see what it was about.

"You asked me how you could help, Callias, and I find you have been a greater assistance than I could have imagined. There is one more thing I ask."

"Name it."

"As much money as two men can carry."

He blinked. "I suppose you are going to explain that?"

I explained my problem, and what I proposed to do about it. When I finished he was laughing. Callias clapped his hands for slaves and issued orders.

I found him not in his workshop, but in his private room. Sophroniscus sat sweating over a scroll, squinting at the tiny figures covering it.

"Ah, Nicolaos, I've been looking through the finances, and I think, if we sell down most of the assets and move to a smaller house, we might just be able to manage it. Of course it's going to be tough, and we'll have to—"

"Father?"

"Yes Nicolaos?"

"How would you like to relive the rebellious days of your youth?"

I explained what was needed.

"Have you told your mother about this?"

"No sir."

"Good. Don't." He smiled. "You know I don't approve of this job of yours, son, but I say if you're going to commit yourself to something, then be excellent at it, and besides which, if by some miracle you find this man then it might relieve me of this crushing debt." He wiped his forehead. "Well, if Callias agreed to your plan, it can't be as harebrained as it sounds. I'll help you."

"Thank you," I said. I felt closer to my father than I ever had before.

"And you're right, son. It does take me back to my youth. Ah, those were the days. I envy you, lad."

I smiled. Only two more crew members to recruit.

"When do we start, Nico?" Socrates asked loudly.

"Shhh! Shut up, you idiot, or people will hear you. Do you want to rob a bank, or don't you?" That convinced him. Socrates trailed along beside me without saying a word, a condition entirely unlike him. I picked a spot in the Agora where I would have a good view, then sent Socrates to his starting position, and raised my arm as the signal to begin.

Sophroniscus ambled up to the trading desk of the Antisthenes and Archestratus Savings and Loan Company. He was covered in marble dust. Walking meekly behind him were two slaves carrying bags of money. The slaves belonged to Callias and they were actually trained bodyguards. He might be willing to lend me a fortune, but he wasn't an idiot.

The jangling of those money bags received the full and instant attention of Archestratus and Antisthenes. There was no doubting what they contained.

"Can we help you?" they asked as one.

Sophroniscus said, "Hello. I, uh, I have some money."

"So I see," Antisthenes said smoothly. "Could we offer to take care of that for you?"

"Uh, I've received an inheritance from my dear old uncle. I used to be a poor man—we artists generally are, you know—I don't know much about money . . ."

"That's all right, we do," Antisthenes reassured him.

"Oh, good!" Father didn't have to act his part. He was genuinely and sincerely ignorant on any subject that didn't involve sculpting. Fortunately what he had to do was simple. "Can I give it to you now?"

"Certainly."

They began to count it out under the casual but observant eyes of the slaves, who knew to the drachma what the total should be. Antisthenes and Archestratus themselves had two guards standing behind them. These men appeared to be mercenaries too old for field service, but scary enough to keep away any but a determined attacker. The sudden appearance of so many coins caught their attention too. They went from sleepy to watchful, their eyes searching the crowds for any threat.

When the count was finished, Sophroniscus was handed a token. "I have to insist you take the money to your vault at once."

Archestratus and Antisthenes looked at each other. It was a reasonable demand, more than reasonable. Common sense would be telling them to get this large deposit to safety immediately. They already had enough coins on the table to handle daily business, the day had barely begun, and they hadn't any profit on the table to protect.

Archestratus said, "You take the bags, I'll be fine here on my own."

So Antisthenes stood and ordered their own guards to pick up the bags. They did so and followed their master out of the Agora to a vault, the location of which I had little doubt would be a closely held secret. That was fine with me: it wasn't their money I wanted to steal.

Father signaled his two slaves and walked off in the

opposite direction, mopping his brow as he walked. I turned on my heel and walked briskly to the nearby corner of the Agora, where I nodded to a woman admiring herself in a bronze mirror.

Euterpe put down the mirror and swayed deliciously in the direction of the Antisthenes and Archestratus Savings and Loan Company. At least a dozen nearby male eyes helped her on her way.

"Oh!" she gasped. She suddenly leaned forward and grabbed a nearby table for support. Her position meant that her cleavage was directed straight at Archestratus, not more than an arm's length distance. He seemed to have some trouble raising his eyes to ask, "What's wrong? Can I help you?"

"I think I've twisted my ankle. Oh, the pain! I think I'm going to faint . . ." She put a hand to her head and began to sway. The table rocked and the coins threatened to roll.

"Don't!" Archestratus was around the table in a trice with his arm around Euterpe, who slumped gently against him, tits first. He helped her walk slowly to a nearby bench, perfectly willing to extend the time.

I waved my arm as if to a distant friend. Socrates saw my signal and walked behind Archestratus. He picked up the record scroll as he passed the desk, leaving in its place another that looked at least vaguely like the original. He stepped briskly around the corner to a disused stall where Diotima waited with papyrus and ink pot. There was only one entry that interested us. I prayed to her Goddess that she would be quick.

She was. Socrates was back before I could repeat my prayer to Artemis three times. He paused at the corner waiting for my signal. I waved again and Euterpe, who was reassuring Archestratus that she was feeling much better, asked him to check her ankle to make sure it wasn't broken. I imagined he was only too happy to oblige, he certainly bent to his task quickly enough, and spent plenty of time about it, no doubt to make sure the lady would be able to walk safely.

Socrates replaced the scroll.

Containing my excitement, I walked as quickly as I could without running to the home of Euterpe. She arrived last. Diotima and Socrates were already there. Sophroniscus had gone straight home.

As soon as she saw me, Diotima shouted, "It's Archestratus! Archestratus!"

"The father, not the son?" I asked.

"Archestratus, son of Antimachus, together with Aristodicus of Tanagra, jointly deposited two talents into the bank, the transaction handled by Archestratus, son of Archestratus." Two talents came to twelve thousand drachmae, a very considerable sum. For that amount I could have the house and income promised me by Pericles. You could buy more than a hundred slaves with that sort of money.

Diotima continued, "The token was broken—I gather that isn't unusual—half to be held by Aristodicus, and the other half by Archestratus the Elder. With Aristodicus dead, Archestratus must be thinking he's got away with keeping his money. And listen, Aristodicus left instructions that once released to him, the money was to be transferred to a bank in Syracuse."

"That gels with his sailing ticket from Telemenes," I mused. "They all link together, don't they? Themistocles sits in Magnesia, close to Ephesus. Rizon travels between here and there, transported by Telemenes, whose bank is the Antisthenes and Archestratus Savings and Loan Company. The Archestratus of the firm just happens to be the son of the politician Archestratus, who covets Ephialtes' position, and is the man to whom Rizon carries messages from Themistocles. The assassin arrives from Ephesus, carried on the same ship that returns Rizon. He is paid via the Antisthenes and Archestratus Savings and Loan Company with money from Archestratus Senior."

"Sounds like a conviction to me." Diotima smiled.

"Pericles will be furious when he learns the Areopagus didn't do it," I said in happy anticipation.

"But what about my house?" Euterpe demanded.

Diotima said patiently, "Mother, if Rizon is executed they can't make me marry him, can they?"

"Oh!" Euterpe smiled. Then she had second thoughts, "But what if he isn't convicted?"

"That could happen," I put in. "We have ample evidence to prove the guilt of Archestratus, but there's nothing to say Rizon was aware of the plot. He could claim he was a simple courier of political deals."

"But they traveled on the same boat!" Diotima said.

"Coincidence, that's what he'll say. Yes, I know he's up to his teeth in it, but nothing's been proven."

"Then Mother and I still have a problem. But I've taken steps to deal with that."

The way she said it made me uneasy. "Diotima, you haven't—"

"Yes, I have," she interrupted. "You can leave that to me. It isn't your problem." I opened my mouth to reply but thought better of it. There was nothing to be gained having an argument about it.

Euterpe drifted off to bathe "after her ordeal." Socrates was forcibly removed from the house and told to go home.

As soon as we were alone, I said, "Diotima, blackmail is a dangerous game."

"But not one that has anything to do with you, Nicolaos. This is my problem to solve. Mother is relying on me. I'm relying on myself too, for that matter. I don't want to be married to that man."

"Well, who do you want to be married to?" I hadn't meant to ask, the question slipped out while I wasn't watching.

Diotima didn't answer.

I hurried on. "Listen, Diotima, we talked before about you needing money to get away, to live on your own at Ephesus."

She thought about that, and added, "And you have to prove to your father you can make a living as a political agent."

"That money is sitting in the bank, and Aristodicus is never going to collect it."

"I'm starting to see what you mean. Besides, it's not as if I don't deserve it for the loss of my father," Diotima rationalized.

I said, "Archestratus has the token. If we can take it from him when we arrest him, that would be perfect. I'd be willing to bet Antisthenes isn't aware of what his business partner's been doing on the side. He thinks I'm Aristodicus. He would give me the money if I presented him with both halves of the token."

Diotima frowned. "He probably has it in his house. We'd never get it if it's there. We can arrest Archestratus but whoever heard of being allowed to search someone's home? It's unthinkable."

"I wonder if we could trick him into bringing it out?"

But try as we might, we could think of no way to finesse the token. We gave the idea up as a pleasant fantasy, but unworkable.

"I have to get the evidence to Pericles immediately," I said. "I expect we'll be ready to charge Archestratus first thing tomorrow morning."

Diotima walked with me to the Agora. It was on her way to the temple. We were relaxed for the first time since we'd met, and we idled along.

Pythax and a troop of Scythians approached us, coming the other way, with the Eponymous Archon in their midst. They stopped before us. Pythax seemed glum and refused to look at me.

"Nicolaos, son of Sophroniscus, you are under arrest," the Archon said.

"What am I charged with?" I demanded.

"Let's see now," said the Archon. He pulled out a parchment that he held close to his eyes, then far away. He squinted at it and pretended to read it, the bastard. I don't know if Conon had bad eyesight, but I was quite sure he knew exactly what it said. "It says here the murder of Brasidas the bowyer." I wasn't surprised; I'd been expecting that, though I'd put it out of my mind. "Destruction of state property—"

"What state property?" I demanded.

"The two slaves. You killed them."

"I never went near them!"

"And . . . oh yes, the murder of Ephialtes."

That left me openmouthed, shocked. I turned to Pythax.

"But you know I didn't do that, Pythax. Brasidas sold the bow to Aristodicus of Tanagra."

Pythax said sadly, "And who's the only one who heard Brasidas say that? You. So why should anyone believe you, considering you slit the man's throat the next day? Here's how Conon reckons it works, little boy. You killed Ephialtes, you killed the slaves because they saw you. You killed Brasidas who sold you the bow, and invented this story of the Tanagran to shift suspicion away from the obvious suspect. Then you searched around for the first man you could find from Tanagra and fought him to death to make it look like you'd killed the murderer in a fair fight. Conon noticed you claimed not to get the Tanagran's name from Brasidas. That's because you hadn't picked your victim yet. Anything to say?"

"I didn't kill Aristodicus, you did."

"You were trying mighty hard when I happened along. You duped me into doing your work for you."

"I didn't have a bow when Ephialtes was murdered."

"You looked for a bow Pericles might have thrown away. Pericles never looked to see if you'd hidden one."

When he put it like that, the whole thing was simple, obvious, and ingenious. Maybe I *did* kill them all.

Conon said, "I would stand away from that man, if I were you, Priestess. He murdered your father."

"Goat shit," said the Priestess, and added bitterly, "I suppose you're going to arrest him for Stratonike too."

Conon turned to her. "No, Nicolaos didn't kill Stratonike. You did."

"Really? Are you going to arrest me?"

"No need. Yours is a straightforward domestic murder. It happens all the time. Your husband can deal with you. But this man you're with is a serial killer. He's a danger to the state. Take him away, Pythax."

Diotima stopped him. "Wait! You can't take him to jail, Athens doesn't have one."

She was right. An accused man stays free until the moment he's convicted, and if he runs, that's an admission of guilt and he's condemned to death in absentia. My first thought the moment Conon accused me was that I'd be taking up Telemene's offer of that fast boat to Syracuse.

But Conon destroyed that plan when he said, "No jail for those charged, perhaps, but we do have a cell for condemned prisoners awaiting execution."

"Oh, so has Nicolaos been condemned without trial?"

"Not at all, but he is a serial killer. There's no telling who he'll slaughter next. As Archon, I judge the state is unsafe while he is walking the streets. Therefore he will be guarded until he can be brought to trial. Priestess, I wish to speak with you in my offices. Guards, take the man away."

17

My cell was unpleasant. I suppose that's to be expected since it was normally only occupied by men awaiting execution, and in Athens that period's rarely longer than a day. The cell was a small room carved into rock, with a stout wooden door to prevent me wandering off. A boulder lay five paces in front of the door. This wasn't so much to give me privacy as to hide the unsavory cell and its equally unsavory occupant from public view. The effect was to provide two short walkways to my door. A guard stood at each one. A thin layer of sand had been thrown on the floor. I had a rickety low cot made of pinewood with old straw heaped upon it. A basin served all sanitary needs. If I wanted to eat, my family would have to bring me food.

The thought of my family made me wince. My first visitor had been Sophroniscus. Of course, he had to be notified that his elder son was imprisoned for serial murder.

"So, this is what comes of your grandiose ambition, is it?" He stood at the door, peering in through the barred hole. I could see the flecks of marble dust in his hair and the deep lines in his face.

I stood immediately, ashamed to be seen but determined to show some dignity. "Hello, Father."

"Don't 'Hello, Father' me, you fool. By rights I should disown you."

"I didn't do it, Father. I didn't kill anyone."

"Of course you didn't. I know that. It won't stop a jury finding against you. Did they tell you the Archon himself is leading the charges? How many jurors do you think will go against his word?"

"Sorry, Father."

"I *told* you this could happen. Didn't I say politics in Athens was a rough game? Didn't I warn you losers are killed or exiled?"

"You told me, Father. I knew the risks."

Sophroniscus sighed. "I've been to see Conon. It's normal in these cases to give the accused a chance to run; exile for life rather than execution. Conon refused, wouldn't even listen to me. He's determined to see you dead. You've made yourself a serious enemy, son."

"Sorry about that."

"You'll be even sorrier when they pronounce sentence." He pushed a parcel through the hole. "Here, eat this."

"Thank you."

"Don't thank me, thank your mother. Personally, I thought a little hunger might remind you not to play political games when there's proper work to be done. Phaenarete is distraught, by the way. She's refused all food since we heard the news and shut herself up in her quarters, says she won't eat until you're free. I don't know when I'll be able to see you again. I'll be preparing the way for your exile."

"I thought you said Conon wouldn't allow it."

Sophroniscus looked left and right and lowered his voice. "We might be able to bribe the guards. I'm trying to raise some money, we don't have many relatives to help, and there's the debt to Callias, but perhaps I can borrow."

"Avoid the Antisthenes and Archestratus Savings and Loan Company," I advised him.

"As to where you go, I know a man in Corinth who might be able to take you in. He's a decent sculptor who should be able to start you in the trade I failed to teach you.

"Goodbye, son," he said gruffly. He reached through the door and gripped my hand.

"Thank you, Father. I . . ."

"Yes?"

"I've been a disappointment."

"That would be putting it mildly. Oh, by the way, that girl you were chasing came to see us."

"I wasn't chasing her."

"She apologized and said the whole thing was her fault. I told her not to worry, you were an idiot long before she met you."

"Oh Nico, it's all my fault!" Diotima sobbed. She was the next to come to see me. She had dressed in priestess regalia and I heard her tell the guards she had come to deliver an oracle. They stepped aside, and as she passed, one said he wouldn't mind if she could do him a service too. She walked on with her nose in the air while they laughed.

"It's all my fault!" she repeated.

"Yes, I know." I tried not to be too obviously upset about being imprisoned for a capital crime because of her blunder. "You went ahead and tried to blackmail the Eponymous Archon and Polemarch, and their instant response was to arrest not you, but me."

"The Archon says he'll drop the charges if I hand over all the incriminating evidence against him and swear by my Goddess never to breathe a word."

"Which means you would have to marry Rizon, and your mother loses her house."

Diotima nodded silently.

"So it's a choice between my life or your future."

"I'm afraid so. I told Mother. She said you were a bad influence on me, and extolled the virtues of a married life." Diotima paused. "You know I couldn't let them kill you, Nico!"

"So you'll hand over the parchments?"

She chewed at her thumbnail. "I can't let Mother lose her house. There has to be a way to get both. I don't know what it is, but don't worry, Nico, I'll find it."

"Why would I worry?" I asked sarcastically.

"Take this." She passed through a parcel. More food.

She left me to my thoughts, which consisted mostly of worrying about what she was up to now. With Diotima, there was no telling.

I unwrapped the food and placed it alongside the parcel sent by Mother. I wasn't hungry but I picked at it anyway. I would have to keep up my strength if I was to defend myself in court.

No one had told me when the trial was to be. I assumed it wouldn't be the next day, but Athenian justice is speedy, and I needed to be prepared. The prosecution would be given the morning to make their case. I would have the afternoon to defend myself. The jurors would make their decision on the spot and I would be a free man or a condemned one as the sun set.

What defense should I use? Should I defend myself by declaring the real murderer? Or should I stick to the much simpler plan of proving it couldn't have been me? I considered the difficulty of taking 501 jurors through the labyrinthine logic of the case. It didn't seem possible to persuade normal men with that, not when they hadn't been living with the case for days as I had. There were too many details to absorb. I wondered if a straightforward, "It wasn't me," would be enough to get me off. I thought back glumly over the case for the prosecution as Pythax had put it in the street, considered Sophroniscus' words about the Archon leading the prosecution, and concluded I was probably doomed. I decided then and there that if I had to die, then at least it would be telling the truth. I would tell the jurors of Athens what really happened to Ephialtes.

Oddly enough, accepting that there was nothing I could do

to avert my fate gave me a feeling of calm. I was able to lie down and sleep.

"Move over, little boy."

I was awoken rudely by Pythax, shaking the rickety cot. He held a wineskin in his hand. He gave the cot another shake, and it was sit up or be rolled off.

"What time is it?" I moaned.

"How should I know? It's the middle of the night. Move over."

Pythax plumped down his heavy behind and for a moment I thought the pinewood was going to shatter. It held. I put my bare feet on the cold stone floor and sat beside him.

"Gah!" I choked in horror. A swarm of rats covered the food parcels. And I'd been sleeping right beside them. I kicked out and the rats ran away to the dark recesses. I could see their eyes staring in the dark. The food was a rotten, half-eaten mess.

Pythax barely seemed to notice. He had always been tough and menacing. Now he was maudlin and menacing. He held the wineskin out to me. A certain aroma drifted across.

"Are you drunk?" I asked in amazement.

"Not yet," he grunted. "Drink."

I took a swig, a small one, in case this was some form of exotic trap, and handed back the skin. Pythax showed no such reticence. He upended the skin and gulped.

"To what do I owe the honor? Come to gloat over the condemned prisoner?" This wasn't perhaps the most diplomatic thing I could have said, but I'm always grumpy when I'm awoken in the middle of the night by a drunk barbarian.

"Don't be more of an asshole than you have to be, boy. You've already got more enemies than most men twice your age." He shook his head in wonder. "Shit in Hades, you did it all in a month. I admire that, boy, I really do."

"So you're a friend, are you? You have a strange way of showing it then. You're the one who put me in here."

"Orders, boy, orders. A soldier's got to follow orders."

"You don't think I killed them then?"

"Hades, boy, I know you didn't kill one of them." He hesitated. "It was me popped Aristodicus. I dunno if you did the others. I doubt it."

"What makes you think that?"

"Whoever did for Ephialtes was a professional. Professionals aren't usually smartasses."

"Gee, thanks, Pythax."

I held out my hand and he gave me the wine. This time I took a decent swig before handing it back.

"Tell me something, Pythax. Why are you here?"

"I don't like to drink alone."

"No, I mean, why are you here in Athens?"

"I'm a slave, or hadn't you noticed?"

"You are a slave in the same sense I am the King of Persia. If you decided to walk through the Dipylon Gates tomorrow morning who's going to stop you?"

Pythax took another drink and contemplated his feet for so long I began to feel embarrassed. I was on the verge of telling him to forget the question when he suddenly said, "I did that once, walked through the gates, then I walked back again.

"I used to be headman of my village, up to the northwest of Macedon." Pythax sat back so that he leaned against the damp wall, and he turned his head to look at me as he spoke. "It wasn't anything special, just the usual huts, we had pigs, goats, a few sheep, a cow. The men would raid the neighboring villages, they'd raid us back. There was always a border dispute. I was the biggest man and the toughest fighter, so I was in charge. My father had been headman before me. I settled the disputes between the families before they came to blows, encouraged the odd raid to keep the men's spirits satisfied, and had nothing else to do but hunt, scratch my ass, and watch the women and kids tend the animals. It was a good life.

"Sometimes we'd see armies come close, but I kept the men well clear of them. Even the toughest dog hides when there's a lion about.

"Then the Persians came. There wasn't no hiding from them. You never saw such a river of men! But locusts was more like it when it came to victuals. They stole everything in their path. We slaughtered the cow and salted the meat and buried it. We set the pigs free, figuring we could catch them later. Then I took the people and the remaining animals, and hid up in the mountains where only the goats could follow us.

"Only it turned out some of those Persians had goats for mothers. They knew we had food and they climbed after us. They'd already reaped our fields for the corn. They found where we'd hid the meat, the bastards. I guess they did it by looking for fresh-dug dirt. Now they wanted the sheep and the goats.

"I couldn't let them have it. We were already facing a tough winter, and if we lost the last animals we wouldn't have enough to feed everyone, we'd starve for sure. What we do then is, we boil a large pot of hemlock, and the old men and women, and the mothers with grown children and the small children and the girls all drink it, and then the rest of us have a chance of making it through to start afresh. We'd had to do that once when I was a boy, when the crops failed and some disease killed a lot of the animals. I don't remember much about it but I remember my ma holding me and crying, and then walking away, and that was the last I ever saw her.

"I didn't want to do that. My woman had been with me many years, and she'd even survived having four kids, and three of them were still alive, a boy and two girls. If we had to brew the hemlock they'd all be gone but for my son.

"So I took the strongest men, and told the rest to go high, really high, so high I knew the old ones and maybe a few of the kids wouldn't make it back, and then I took our best men and staked out a position where I knew the Persians had to come, 'cause it was the only good route up.

"We took the first few easily. We were above them and they were easy meat when they reached up. After that, they learned. Two of them were shooting arrows at us, not so much to hit us as to pin us in position. We threw rocks back. I hit one of the bastards and he rolled down the mountain. Didn't do any good though, because those bastards did find another way up. I'll never know how they did it, they must have climbed a vertical cliff face. Next thing we know, we've got Persians above us and below us. I shouted at my son to retreat to our people and take command there—we were going to die, you see—and he shouted something back I didn't hear, and then the man beside me goes down with a spear in his throat and I think a rock must have knocked me on the head, 'cause the next thing I know I wake up bruised and cut with my arms numb 'cause of how they tied them behind my back, and I'm told now I'm a slave of the Persian King.

"Well, you know how the war went. When the Persians were beaten at Plataea there was a lot of confusion. I managed to escape the chains and wrung the neck of our guard, then I made off. I was picked up later by an Athenian patrol and they brought me back here.

"I was happy enough at first. They made me a member of the Scythian Guard, and that seemed good enough for me, seeing as I figured my village and my woman and my children must all be dead. I rose in the Guard, I was good at it, and the man who was chief told me when he retired he reckoned I'd be the man to take over. But I was homesick, you see. Before I did that I had to know what had happened. So I walked through those Dipylon Gates, just like you said.

"There was a village there, same place it used to be, but when I walked in I didn't recognize but one or two of the men, and none of them knew me at all. Then my son comes out of the largest hut and stands before me. He knew me, all right. He says, 'Father . . .' and then stops like he ran into a wall. So I asked where was my woman, and what had happened to his sisters, and he says, 'The Persians took all the animals, there wasn't anything we could do.'

"That's when I realized I couldn't hear any kids crying, and the only women in the fields were young.

"I took a long look at my son, standing there like I would have when I was his age. I knew I could take him. He knew it too. But he stood his ground, and he was proud. So I turned and walked away. I walked all the way back to Athens. I didn't want to kill my son, you see."

Pythax shrugged. "Besides, I like it here. I learned to speak Greek like they speak it in Athens. And I like those plays, not the sad ones, the ones that make a man laugh. And here I have a whole city to look after 'stead of a small village."

There wasn't much I could say after a story like that, so I kept silent while Pythax drank. I thought, compared to him, my life had been shallow.

He handed me the wineskin, now only a quarter full.

"Problem is, little boy, who am I working for, really? Am I looking after Athens, or the people who live in Athens?"

"It's the same thing."

"No, it ain't," he said earnestly. "Listen, if I'm looking out for the city, then who tells me what the city needs?"

"Er, the government?"

"Right. And who's the government?"

"Well, the Ecclesia decides what will be done."

"But you know what? Not one of those common citizens has ever given me an order, and if they did I wouldn't be supposed to take it."

"All right then, the Council of the Areopagus. Aren't the Scythians supposed to protect them in time of riot? That's why your barracks is on the side of the rock."

"Yeah, that's right, but none of them are the government, are they? They used to be archons, but they aren't anymore. And then Ephialtes took away their powers, so they got nothing to do now but scratch their asses and find idiots like you guilty of murder. Doesn't sound like no government to me."

"Okay then, the archons."

"Yeah, the archons. But they get chosen by a sort of gambling, and Zeus, boy, you should see some of the idiots we get. Give me back that wine." He drained the remainder of the skin and crushed it to get the last drops.

"You know about these things, boy. You reckon there's going to be a break between the Ecclesia and the Areopagus?"

"I don't know, Pythax. If we don't tell the people a story they can believe about what happened to Ephialtes, the riots are going to get worse."

Pythax nodded. "There was another riot today. We squashed it. But that's the problem, boy, about who I'm working for. Am I supposed to defend the Council, or should I tell my men to join the people of Athens, who happen to be the ones tearing apart the city in fear of what the Council might do?"

"When you put it like that, I understand your problem much better, Pythax." I thought for a moment. "I think it's like when the Persians attacked your village. Sometimes you have to do things that will be bad now, but are the right thing to do for the future. Only it's not the archons or the Council that has to decide what's right. It's you."

Pythax stood, remarkably steady on his feet.

"I'm not sure how it is, little boy, but somehow you remind me of me."

As soon as Pythax left I lay back on the cot and stared up at the rock ceiling. I found myself wondering how they would they do it, if they were going to . . . kill me. What it would feel like to die was beyond my imagination. I knew there were different ways of executing criminals, depending on the crime. The death of Brasidas was serious, but not of course as serious as the death of Ephialtes, who was a citizen. The slaves amounted to little more than destruction of public property. So it was the death of Ephialtes that would determine the manner of my own death.

Probably I'd be taken to the execution ground outside the Dipylon Gates, along the northern road to Piraeus, off to the side, behind trees. The executioners would clamp a metal collar around my neck. Then they would slowly screw it tighter while I strangled and struggled for breath and my tongue stuck out and my face turned blue. But I wouldn't suffocate, because before that happened the collar would probably snap my neck.

I decided I would have to quickly stop this train of thought before it sent me into a blind panic. I told myself to think of something else, and drifted off to sleep thinking of Diotima.

I woke before the dawn next morning feeling distinctly queasy. The wine had gone to my stomach and I hadn't slept much for fear the rats would come back and crawl on me.

My little brother squeezed his way past the legs of the guards.

"What are you doing here?" I asked, surprised. "How did you get in?"

"They said I could come in and say goodbye to you since you're going to be executed," he explained.

"Terrific."

"Nico, are they really going to kill you?"

I bit my lip, uncertain what to say. "I don't know, little brother. I hope not."

"I hope not too." He scuffed his feet in the dirt. "Nico, are you going to be all right?"

"Don't worry about me, little brother. There's going to be a trial, and then I get to explain everything about what really happened, and then the people who listen to the evidence— they're called dicasts—will realize I did nothing wrong and vote to let me go."

"You mean you'll prove you didn't kill Ephialtes?"

"That's right."

Socrates announced, "I'm going to think of all the reasons why it wasn't you. And then I'll work out who really did it."

I said urgently, "Socrates, do *not* go wandering about trying to solve the murder. Don't worry about it, Pericles will help me." I wondered if that was true. Pericles hadn't come to see me yet, though he must have heard by now I'd been arrested. A great deal hinged on how Pericles reacted.

"What happens if they say you only killed the slaves?"

"That's destruction of state property. They'd only fine me a lot of money. But that won't happen because I wouldn't have killed the slaves unless I also killed Ephialtes. The killing of the slaves doesn't count for much in the trial. It's like an extra piece of sweets at dinner."

"But what if they find out you took that stuff from Ephialtes' home?"

"Shh!" I hissed, horrified. I looked about to see if the guards had heard, but they seemed to be ignoring us.

"How do you know about that?" I demanded in a whisper.

He grinned. "I followed you after the funeral. I saw your girl-friend hand you the box."

"She's not my girlfriend!" I said quickly. "And don't say that to anyone else or you might get her killed."

"Aren't they going to kill her anyway, for murdering the madwoman?"

"Maybe." I winced. "I don't think so though. I think they only accused her to get at me. They need her alive to marry Rizon or he can't inherit."

"I heard Father say Rizon could marry her when they buried her. Mother said that would be an awful thing to do."

I gasped in shock. It was true. Sometimes if a betrothed died before a wedding, the body was buried with the wedding clothes, wedding songs were sung by the graveside, and the families treated it as if the marriage had taken place. Conon could choose to view Diotima's death in the same light.

"I think you'd better go home, little brother," I said gently. "Father doesn't know you're here, does he?"

He shook his head.

"Goodbye, little brother."

"See you later, Nico."

His departure left me plenty of time to feel sorry for myself. I thought upon my impending death and decided I didn't want to die. Not now, not any time. I began to sob. Once started, I couldn't stop. I'm sure the guards heard but they didn't look around. No doubt they'd heard it all before.

I calmed down eventually, or rather, I managed to stop the noise. I was still as miserable as I'd ever been in my short life. I wondered if anyone was trying to save me. I wondered what Pericles thought.

"You've made a complete mess of it," a voice said brusquely. I looked up to see Pericles there.

"Sorry," I muttered, wiping my face with my hands.

"Sorry isn't good enough. How could you have done this to me? I'm disappointed, Nicolaos, very disappointed."

"As I see it, you're the one standing outside and I'm the one awaiting execution."

"You must be tried first, but I agree it's a foregone conclusion. And we still don't know who killed Ephialtes. It's not the result we were hoping for, is it?"

That raised my hopes. "So you don't think I killed him. Are you going to get me out of here?"

"I don't know if you're the murderer or not. I didn't see you with a bow, but then, as I said to Conon when he asked me, I didn't look either. And don't get your hopes up. Has it occurred

to you the men who will be your judges are the ones who probably did arrange his death? They'll be more than happy to influence the jury against you."

I'd had the same thought; the Council of the Areopagus would
be the judges of my case. Irrational as it was, I'd kept some hope
that Pericles might find a way out for me. Now he destroyed me
utterly.

"I don't even dare be seen with you. That's why I'm here, to
warn you not to say anything about our association when they
take you to trial."

I stood to the door and grabbed it. If I'd the strength I would
have torn it off its hinges on my way to throttle Pericles. Instead,
I put my head to the tiny slots and shouted, "Thank you very
much, you bastard! What happened to loyalty?"

Pericles said coldly, "I promised you great reward for success.
Failure wasn't mentioned in the agreement."

He had a point, but it was the clinical way he abandoned me
that rankled.

"Your commission is revoked. You have no way now of com-
pleting it."

"Unless I did kill Ephialtes."

"Did you?"

"No, of course not."

Pericles nodded. "I thought as much, and you have no reason
to lie now. I will give you this much, Nicolaos: if you do not mention me in your defense except insofar as I was present when the
body was discovered, which all men know anyway, then I will
use my influence to protect your girlfriend."

"I'm not his girlfriend," a voice said behind Pericles, who
turned, startled. I looked up. How much had she heard?

Pericles said, "As you wish." He turned his back on her and
said to me, "She must marry Rizon, but I think I can save her
from stoning."

I looked at Diotima and said, "I accept."

"No you don't!"

"Yes I do. Stay out of this."

"You think your noble sacrifice is going to impress me?" she sneered. She pulled out a piece of papyrus and practically slammed it into Pericles' face. "Read it and weep," she snarled.

As Pericles read his face became ashen. "Where did you get this?"

"The papers from Ephialtes' room. We found this."

"We?" Pericles looked at me accusingly. I, of course, had never told him about the note he was holding. I knew what she must have handed him, the parchment in Ephialtes' own handwriting that said Pericles could not be trusted with the leadership.

"This isn't the original," Pericles stated.

"No, of course not. You might have forced that from me. This is the copy I made. The original is well hidden."

Pericles thought for a moment. "Very well, it's obvious you want something from me. What is it?"

"You will free Nico."

"Impossible. I only just finished explaining that to him."

"Then I suggest you be very persuasive when you talk to the people who can."

Pericles was quiet for a long moment, during which I held my breath. Eventually I could stand the suspense no longer and asked, "Well, is it yes or no?"

Pericles said, "Be quiet, I'm working out how to save your life."

He thought some more. Then he said to Diotima, "It's a condition of any agreement between us that you will not reveal the contents to anyone. To anyone, you understand?"

Diotima nodded. "Agreed. But if Nicolaos is executed, if they touch so much as a hair on his head, then this will be sent to the people who would most enjoy reading it."

Pericles nodded reluctantly. "I will receive the original."

"When the danger has passed."

"I see. I was speaking the truth when I said I cannot prevent a trial. Conon has committed himself too far to back out without loss of face."

"But you can have him freed until the trial starts."

Pericles paused. "Possibly."

"And you can get him off. You have to, unless . . ." She dangled the papyrus.

Pericles turned to me. "Congratulations. It seems I will be speaking in your defense."

The moment Pericles left, Diotima asked, "Nicolaos, will you run if Pericles has you freed?"

"Into exile? I don't know. Father talked of it, but I hadn't any hope of being let out until now so I haven't thought about it. He said I might go to a sculptor friend of his in Corinth, but I think instead I might take that fast boat to Syracuse. Telemenes offered me the passage."

"Syracuse? It's better than being dead. I hear it's a beautiful city. I'd miss you."

"You could come with me," I said without thought.

She was startled. "Go with you?"

I'd taken the plunge, I might as well try swimming. "You don't want to marry Rizon. Blackmailing Conon certainly didn't work. Come with me." I paused. "I'd like you to come." I could feel my face burning bright red.

"But that would be terrible, Nico. Mother would never send me money so you'd have to earn for both of us. I've told you I would never be a whore like my mother, and that's what I would be, unless I married you."

"That was the idea." I was in such agony; I understood for the first time why they leave it to fathers to arrange marriages. Doing it for yourself is worse than a trip to Hades.

"Oh," she said in a small voice. "Are you sure?"

I said quickly, "It's all right, I understand if you don't want to. I wouldn't have anything, not even a place for you to live. Father would disown me of course. I don't even know if I could feed us. At least if you stay here you'll have security and enough to eat."

"Okay."

"The sensible thing is for you to stay and— What was that?"

"I said okay. I'll come with you."

My jaw dropped. "Are you sure?"

She smiled nervously. "No, but I just said yes and my heart feels good about it, so I guess the answer is yes."

If it's possible for a man to be locked in a condemned cell and ecstatically happy, then I was that man.

A message boy appeared. He handed me a scrap of papyrus. On it Pericles had scrawled, *Conon refuses to free you. The only way out is to win the trial. It's set for tomorrow.*

I silently handed the parchment to Diotima. She read, then crumpled the message in her fist. "Oh well, so much for that plan."

18

I spent the rest of the day reviewing the case with Pericles. He refused to have Diotima present, so she departed for the Temple of Artemis. He dismissed the entire edifice of our discoveries as too convoluted to convince a jury.

"To prove your theory, you would have to take the jury through the inner machinations of the Council of the Areopagus; expose divisions within the democratic movement; denounce Themistocles, whom many still believe was the savior of Hellas, and explain our banking system to men who've probably never had enough money to save a drachma. To top it off, you need to rely on the testimony of a low innkeeper, a drunken shortsighted sailor, and three men who are dead, two of whom are slaves and whose testimony would have been invalid except under torture."

This matched my own gloomy view so closely that I could only nod and ask, "So what do you propose?"

"That we take the opposite course, and demonstrate merely that the murderer could not have been you. Above all else, everything must be simple. Take care to remember, Nicolaos, men rarely make decisions with their thoughts. It is their emotions that guide their actions. And in a criminal trial, it is how they feel about the accused that matters far more than the facts. You must ensure you come to trial as a presentable young man and

a fine upstanding citizen. Make sure you are washed and properly dressed. Be modest in your manners. You must speak on the
second day, but then you are permitted to hand over your
defense to a friend." Pericles winced. "That will be me."

The first day consisted of witness depositions, and would have
been boring had my life not hinged on the outcome. The presiding archon was one of the lesser of the nine archons. He looked
at me as if I were a curious object. "Ah, so you are the infamous
Nicolaos. Both the Eponymous Archon and the Polemarch have
spoken of you, frequently. I must say, you don't look like an evil
spirit sent to harass Athens. I'm rather disappointed, really. Well,
let's hear what the witnesses have to say. Thank the Gods I
won't have to hear the full case. I leave that to the Council of the
Areopagus."

Conon called the son of Brasidas as his first witness. I discovered the boy's name was Phomion. He looked at me in anger
and spat at me. He recounted the end of the conversation he
had overheard, my words, ". . . or you could find yourself dead."
The father was found the next day with his throat slit, the only
evidence a shard of pottery clutched in his hand with my name
scratched upon it. He asserted only I could have murdered his
father. He was now required to support his mother and sister. To
that end he had taken over his father's business, but the takings
were poor because the customers of his father had fled to more
experienced bowyers and the family was starving. He ended with
a demand for compensation of ten talents.

The next witness for the prosecution was Rizon. He testified
to my proclivity to senseless violence. I had struck him down
without the slightest provocation within his own home and later
had manhandled him at Piraeus. Rizon offered up his slaves for
torture to confirm the account.

The stallholders of the Agora came forward to testify to the
damage I had done while chasing a poor defenseless boy, whom

I had suddenly turned upon. He had sprinted off in fear of his own life. The boy hadn't been seen again, no doubt his corpse was rotting in a secret grave.

The innkeeper who'd been pushed into his laundry tub testified I had tried to drown him, holding his head underwater. Only his valiant struggles had saved him from the demented lunatic. He demanded compensation of five talents.

Piece by piece, Conon built the picture of a man given to sudden murderous attacks against anyone unlucky enough to be nearby when the madness took him.

"The evidence of the son of Brasidas is damaging," Pericles whispered to me. "The rest can be dismissed one way or another. Fortunately the key is Ephialtes. If you did not kill him, then you had no reason to harm Brasidas or the slaves. We will concentrate on showing you could not have murdered him."

I nodded my understanding. I hadn't truly believed this was happening to me. Now that the trial had begun I was struck down by the seriousness of it all. Pericles knew more about the workings of Athens than I ever would, and I was more than happy to leave the strategy to him.

"You will claim you went to see Brasidas about a bow. You have no idea why he was killed but it was certainly nothing to do with your investigation. The son misheard your words."

I objected. "But that would be lying!"

"Yes, that's the usual way to win a court case. Don't talk so loudly, they'll hear you."

For the defense we had but two witnesses. The first was Pericles himself. He gave a simple account of the discovery of Ephialtes.

The second witness was Pythax. He gave an accurate account of my appearance at the barracks and the discovery of the bow, and certified it had been made by Brasidas. He ended by describing my struggle with Aristodicus and the ending of it.

The next day the trial began in earnest at dawn. It was held fittingly upon the Rock of the Areopagus, within the chamber of the Council. For a crime of this type, and given the importance of the victim, there were more than the usual number of dicasts assigned to hear it. Pericles scanned them as they filed in and said to me, "A thousand and one in the jury."

"Is that good?" I asked anxiously.

He shrugged. "It's both good and bad. The more dicasts, the bigger an audience we have to play to, and the more the trial hinges on who can entertain them the best. That's good for us because Conon is a boring pedagogue whereas I am a great speaker," said the modest Pericles. "On the other hand, large juries often provide closer results. Whether your notoriety will work for or against us I don't know."

"I'm notorious?"

"You should hear what they're saying in the Agora."

The dicasts sat along both sides of the chamber. Tiered wooden benches held them all, though barely.

Spectators stood at the back of the room. I nodded to Lysimachus, who looked grave. Archestratus stood in the front row, standing next to his son.

The judges sat at the front. This being a case of homicide, the judges were all chosen from the ranks of the Council of the Areopagus. I didn't need Pericles to tell me that was bad for me. The entire Council filed in and took their seats. The full Council were essentially spectators at the proceedings. There were three seats placed at the fore for the chief judge and his two assistants. Now Xanthippus marched in and took the position of Chief Judge. That shook Pericles, who muttered, "He never told me. They must be doing this because they think I'll be more restrained with my own father in the chair. Well, they have something to learn."

The second seat next to Xanthippus was taken by Lysanias. I felt good about that, I thought Lysanias liked me. The third and final seat was taken by a man I didn't recognize. Pericles snorted.

"Demotion. He's a toady to my father, we can expect him to agree with anything Xanthippus says."

The dicasts were sworn in, repeating in unison the words, "I swear to vote according to the laws of Athens. I will never vote for a repudiation of debts, nor to restore before their time those who have been ostracized. I will not accept any bribe or offer for my vote, and if any man offers me such I will report him. I will not accept or take any bribe on behalf of another. I will hear both sides impartially and vote strictly according to the merits of the case. Thus do I invoke Zeus, Poseidon, and Demeter to destroy me and my house if I violate any of these obligations, and to send me many blessings if I obey them well."

Xanthippus made the sacrifice. When he was done a slave brought him a basin of water and a towel to wash his bloodied hands. I noticed there was a spot that did not come out, but thought it impolitic to mention.

Xanthippus declared, "Let the prosecution begin."

Conon led the dicasts through the same logic he had developed the day before: the story of a man given to senseless violence when you least expect it. His evidence was convincing and I saw the nearest dicasts draw back as Conon's speech went on. He stopped at various times to read the evidence of Phomion, the evidence of the stallholders, and of all his other witnesses one after the other. After each reading the witness stood to confirm it had happened as Conon had said.

His manner was every bit as pedagogic as Pericles had said, and despite the sensationalism of the case I saw some dicasts beginning to drop off. Pericles leaned over to me and whispered, "He should have stopped an hour ago. Conon thinks he's making sure of his case by hammering every single point against you in minute detail, but what he's actually doing is boring the people whose minds he needs to keep active. Take heart. Most of the dicasts will never remember all his detail, and at least some of them will forget his main points too."

But the dicasts were saved from boredom by an unexpected arrival.

I knew nothing of it until a minor commotion broke out at the back of the room. That was nothing unusual in an Athenian courtroom, but when the rumble became louder I turned to see the men standing at the entrance part, revealing a figure standing silhouetted against the bright light outside.

Euterpe swayed into the center of the chamber. She was wearing what for her was conservative dress: a standard matron's robe of expensive but opaque material. Nevertheless, it was firmly fitted. She had tied a broad belt around her waist so that her hips and breasts were well outlined.

Even the judges were too stunned to protest. No one was sleeping now.

"I am a modest woman," she began quietly. I stifled my laughter. "I know full well it is not the place of a modest woman such as myself to soil this august chamber with the presence of a mere woman. Imagine for yourselves then the pressure I must bear, the agony in my heart that forces me to plead with the wise men of the jury. My husband is dead, gentlemen, foully murdered. Yes, I know only too well we were never husband and wife in law, and you wise men know only too well the social demands that require a man to stay with convention. But husband and wife we were in every important sense of the words. And that is why today I must do what the Gods call upon me to do, to avenge the murder of my man."

Euterpe suddenly tore away her dress, exposing her bare breasts to the jury. The jurors were overjoyed. They stamped their feet, cheered, and whistled. Xanthippus and the Council were aghast but shifted position for a closer look. I myself studied her attractions with great appreciation. So that's what she'd been rubbing up and down my chest. I wondered if Diotima was similarly endowed.

Euterpe raised her arms in supplication and gave everyone a

better view. "Look upon me, men of Athens!" As one, the jury obliged. It's a good thing they were seated, or their chitons would all have been poking out at the front.

"Look upon me, men of Athens! I am but a poor woman deprived of her man by the hand of a perfidious murderer. I am destitute, distraught! Yes, I know what is said about me, those cruel rumors. Forget them! Think only of Ephialtes. Who can deny he loved me? He stayed with me for more than two decades in the face of malignant gossip. Ours was a true, abiding love, but we were torn asunder by foul murder. And I know that you loved Ephialtes, the man who led your democracy and was never anything but forthright and honest. Yes, you loved him too, though not, perhaps, in quite the same way as I." Laughter filled the chamber.

"Who was the man who did this? What creature of evil dared to take the life of the one we loved above all others? The deed was done by *that man*!"

Euterpe kept her body facing the jury and pointed dramatically with her left arm. Her face turned to the man she accused, emphasizing her lovely neck; her eyes flashed with malice and beauty.

Every head in the room turned to Conon, the Eponymous Archon. He turned bright red and spluttered. If there'd been somewhere to hide I'm sure he would have dived for cover.

Someone in the jury shouted, "Death!" Other men took it up and the chant of "Death! Death! Death!" carried to Conon.

Pericles leaned toward me and asked, "Did you arrange this?"

"No! I thought you must have."

"Not I." He studied her and murmured, "She's really quite good. It's a pity we can't recruit her for the democratic movement. Can you imagine that performance before the Ecclesia?"

"Order! Order I say!" Xanthippus roared across the chamber. "Guards, throw that woman out."

"Wait!" Lysanias turned to Xanthippus and said in a voice loud enough to reach the far wall, "The accusation has been made. We must hear the reason for it."

Xanthippus retorted, "We are here for the trial of Nicolaos, son of Sophroniscus, not to hear random slurs against our highest executive and, I might add, the prosecutor of this case. This is obviously a charade put up by the defense to distract our attention."

"Yet if she speaks true, then the young man is certainly innocent."

The jurors were chanting, "More! More! More!"

Xanthippus saw that he had no choice. "Very well, woman. What is your ridiculous reason for this baseless accusation? And be quick about it, we don't have all day. And put on your dress."

Euterpe held the torn material across her breast with one slender arm in such a way that a nipple poked above. She arched her back. Now she appeared as a statue of Aphrodite. Sophroniscus, who'd been enjoying the view as much as any man, pulled out charcoal and parchment and began a fast sketch.

"Ephialtes had evidence Conon has been stealing from the state. He planned to prosecute him and the Polemarch as soon as their year in office completed. Conon murdered Ephialtes to save himself."

"You have no evidence for this, I presume?"

"Indeed I do, Xanthippus." Euterpe gestured to a slave who brought forward the parchments Diotima and I had discovered.

Xanthippus leaned forward to take them but Lysanias was too fast; he snatched them from the slave. "I will keep these safe." He scanned the documents quickly. "Hmm." Lysanias looked up at Conon. "It seems we will have something to discuss at a later date."

Euterpe said, "Conon continued to persecute our family past the murder of my dear Ephialtes. He even ordered our beloved daughter to marry a vile, disgusting man whom Ephialtes would never have countenanced. Then he promised he would rescind his order if I slept with him. I love my daughter so much I made that sacrifice. At least, I assume I did. I don't remember feeling much."

Laughter rocked the room. Conon shook his head and shouted, "You lying bitch! You moaned and groaned like a—" He stopped suddenly when he realized what he was admitting. "That is, the whole thing is a fabrication. Honorable dicasts, this woman is known to be a hetaera."

"I am the true widow of Ephialtes!" Euterpe shouted back.

"Whore!"

"Liar! And your prick is tiny."

Xanthippus roared, "Throw her out! This is a court of Athens, not a bawdy house!"

Euterpe left the room amid huge cheers, clapping, and at least seven offers of marriage from lascivious jurors and one judge.

Conon's speech was destroyed. He tried to bring it back on track but there was little he could do in the face of heckling from the dicasts and demands to bring back Euterpe.

In the end, he sat. He had brought out his entire case against me, and few of the dicasts would remember it.

Xanthippus declared a break for lunch.

Pericles said, "That was one of the more remarkable cases I've ever observed. Some will believe Xanthippus' accusation that we arranged it to cast doubt on the case against you by spraying suspicion elsewhere. They will certainly vote against you. Some will forget every word Conon said and remember only those truly remarkable breasts." We sat silent in fond remembrance ourselves.

If the chamber had been full in the morning, it was positively packed in the afternoon. Word of Euterpe's performance had flown across Athens and most of the male population had arrived in hopes of more.

Xanthippus declared, "The prosecution has rested. The defense may begin."

I rose unsteadily to my feet. My heart was thumping and my mouth was suddenly dry. I felt one thousand and one sets of eyes upon me.

In that instant I forgot everything Pericles had told me about how to address a crowd. Should I face the dicasts or the judges? I'd forgotten, and it seemed terribly important to get it right. I compromised by turning to the gap between them, thus facing no one. Dear Gods, Pericles did this every day. The man must have astounding nerves and the courage of a lion.

I have never stuttered in my life, but I stuttered now, "I-I . . . er, men of Ath-Athens, hon-honorable dic-dic-dicasts." Conon was smirking. I knew the bastard thought he had this case in the bag. That made me angry. I stopped and took a deep breath. The words of my set speech came back to me, and I repeated them. "Honorable dicasts. I am Nicolaos, son of Sophroniscus, and an innocent man. I did not commit this crime.

"I had the bad luck to be standing underneath when the body of Ephialtes fell from the very rock upon which we now sit. The shock of this terrible crime happening before my eyes led me to investigate the circumstances." Now my throat caught, for the lies would begin, but Pericles had pounded into me that only the simplest story would wash with the dicasts. Seeing them before me now, I realized he was right. These were not men to delight in a subtle argument. They wanted their proof simple and obvious.

"But these other deaths are all coincidence, fellow citizens, or at least nothing to do with me. I went to see Brasidas about a bow, it is true, but it was next day he was killed, when I was far away. As for these other deaths . . ."

I proceeded by denying everything. Sophroniscus told me later that I sounded like a schoolboy reciting his homework, quickly and with intonations in all the wrong places. No matter, I got the words out when a moment before I had dried completely, and that was enough of a relief to me.

"My friend Pericles will continue my argument." This is the ritual statement that allows one man to speak for another in the courts.

The dicasts were surprised at my announcement, and not pleasantly. A man in the jury stood and shook his fist. "You promised you would prosecute the man who killed Ephialtes, Pericles. Now I see you defending the bastard!"

Pericles stood and walked to the section of benches that held his heckler. He remained silent for a moment, and the jury went quiet in anticipation. Pericles, without anger but with a touch of remorse, looked the heckler in the eye and said, "So I did, sir, and so I shall. I am sad to say Conon has charged the wrong man. If I am to bring the real murderer of Ephialtes to justice I must first help clear this young man, whose only crime has been to expend his utmost energies to assist the state.

"Gentlemen of the jury, I speak to you not only as a friend of the accused, the young man Nicolaos, I speak also as the dear friend of my mentor Ephialtes, a man I admired above all others." Pericles cast a significant glance at his father. "And I will be honest with you, it is Ephialtes I admire and esteem more than Nicolaos. Is it likely I would be defending Nicolaos if I thought he had any hand in the death of my greater friend?

"I came upon the scene shortly after Ephialtes fell. Nicolaos was already there and I say to you, gentlemen, that there is no possible way Nicolaos could have shot Ephialtes upon the Rock, then rushed down in time for me to find him where I did. It follows as night the day that Nicolaos is the only man in Athens who certainly could not have killed Ephialtes. Keep this important point in mind, for it is the beginning and the end of our perfectly simple defense. Any man could have been upon the Rock . . . any man except Nicolaos. Why, I myself had more opportunity to do the deed than he."

Pericles paused for effect, allowing the thousand and one men of the jury to contemplate such a ridiculous notion.

"We will now hear the testimony of Pythax, Chief of the Scythians."

Pythax stood and stepped forward for all the jury to see him. In accordance with judicial process he would not speak himself. He seemed nervous to me, looking about, twitching and shuffling his feet. I smiled in sympathy. Pythax didn't like public speaking any more than I.

Pericles read the witness statement of Pythax. When he finished Xanthippus completed with the formal words, "Pythax, Chief of the Scythians, are these your true words?"

The formal response is, "This is my testimony on the case." Instead, Pythax said, loud enough for everyone in the chamber to hear, "No, I lied."

Pericles dropped the parchment of testimony in shock. The jury erupted in excitement. Xanthippus shouted, "Silence! Silence in the dicasts! I remind you this is a court of homicide, not a day out at the theater." Xanthippus stared at Pythax in dismay. "Very well, Pythax, I suppose you had better have your say."

"It was no accident I happened along as Nicolaos fought Aristodicus. I was ordered to follow him. I was ordered to make sure he didn't find out too much."

Pericles was visibly distraught, his face white. He swallowed, and forced himself to ask the next question. "Who gave you those orders?" A hush fell upon the chamber.

"Xanthippus." The name rang across the court.

The dicasts leaped from their seats, shouted, screamed, and hit one another in excitement. I had seen similar behavior at the chariot races, but nowhere else.

I'm sure Apollo must have been with me, because divine inspiration struck in that instant. Suddenly I was sure I understood everything, and if I was right, I could confirm it all with one question that was burning in my mind. I shouted, "Pythax, was your job to stop me finding out about Themistocles and the Council?" The jury didn't hear me in their furor, and nor did

Pythax, but the judges did. Xanthippus gave me a long stare and Demotion appeared startled. Lysanias kept a studiously blank face. Demotion turned and said something to the Council members behind. They stirred and talked among themselves.

Xanthippus himself was shouting to have the chamber silenced, but without success. There was nothing for it but to wait for the excitement to die down. When it did, Pericles stepped forward to the judicial bench and said, "So it was you, Father. I'll have to ask Archestratus to prosecute you. I can't do it myself or I might be accounted a patricide by the Gods."

Xanthippus looked down upon his son in horror. "Pericles, my son, I said it once before in private. Let me say it again before all those assembled. I am more proud of you than you can conceive. I would never allow harm to come to you."

Pericles looked away and said, "I know that, Father. That's why it grieves me so to have to do my duty to the state." I had observed before that Pericles was given to public displays of emotion, but even I was shocked to see a tear trickle down his cheek.

"If you charge your father, you'll be prosecuting the wrong man, Pericles." Every head turned. Diotima walked into the center of the chamber, wearing her priestess robes, her head high and her manner haughty. "There's only one trial we need hear for the murder of Ephialtes. That of Archestratus!"

Archestratus grinned from ear to ear and called out, "I am honored to join such august company!"

Xanthippus groaned. "Is there a queue of women outside waiting their turn? Who is she? No, on second thought, I don't care. Throw her out!" Two Scythians took her arms and commenced to pull her back.

Diotima shouted, "Nicolaos is innocent! We can prove Archestratus hired Aristodicus to kill my father! We can prove it! He used his son's bank to hold the fee. Archestratus—" The Scythians dragged Diotima out of the chamber, still shouting accusations.

Lysanias, his eyebrow raised but his expression otherwise neutral, turned to Pericles. "As my colleague and your proud father pointed out a while ago, we are here for the trial of Nicolaos. So far the prosecutor and the chief judge have been accused of the crime. They can't all have killed him, can they? No, I thought not, so I suggest we continue with the trial at hand, and then schedule other trials until we run out of dramatic accusations or the dicasts become bored and seek other entertainment." He glanced over at the excited jury. "I don't think that will happen any time soon. I've seen them pay less attention to a play by Aeschylus." The remainder of the Council sat behind the three judges with expressions that ranged the full gamut of emotion from stony unhappiness to grim hatred. They had been reduced to this court of crime. Now even that privilege had been turned into a farce.

Pericles had more to say but it was obvious after the excitement that no one was listening. He finished his oration early with the words, "Well, gentlemen of the jury, after all you have seen and heard today, we can all agree there is considerable disagreement over who killed Ephialtes. Was it the judge presiding over this case? Was it the prosecutor? Could it be the man standing in the audience? The only thing we can say with any assurance is that it was not the accused."

Pericles sat down beside me.

Xanthippus declared, "The dicasts will proceed to vote."

Officers of the court brought out two large urns. One was made of wood, the other of bronze. Both were passed along the benches of the dicasts. With a thousand and one votes to count this took considerable time.

Pericles said to me, "It's going to be all right, Nicolaos. I doubt half the dicasts even remember your name after everything that's happened today."

Pericles might have been confident but I certainly wasn't. My life hung on the outcome of this vote!

Each dicast placed a disk into the bronze urn as it passed by them. If he thought I was innocent, he would place a solid disk, if guilty, a disk with a hole in the center. The wooden urn was for the discards. I watched intently trying to see each disk as it went in, and to keep a mental tally. I was heartened whenever I identified a solid disk, but my guts knotted at the unmistakable sight of a holed disk going into the bronze. I looked at the face of the man who had voted for my death. He had a weathered skin, a bulbous nose, and a full dark beard and dark eyes, but I could see no evil in him. If I had passed him in the street, he would have been unremarkable. The man noticed my attention and smiled at me. I looked away.

The bronze urn was carried to Xanthippus, and he, Lysanias and Demotion counted the disks. Before long it was obvious what the result would be.

The judges turned to consult the Council behind them. The old men of the Areopagus, as Pericles referred to them, did not look happy. Men whispered to one another. There was general agreement about something, except Lysanias who was angry and shook his head. A few seemed undecided, but the majority were smiling.

Xanthippus turned back to the court and declared the result. "Nicolaos, son of Sophroniscus, the dicasts have voted, eight hundred and twenty-one to one hundred and eighty. You are found not guilty of the murder of Ephialtes."

The dicasts cheered and I smiled as broadly as I ever have in my life.

But Xanthippus was still speaking. He should have completed with the formula, "Release the prisoner," but instead, he continued, "The Council of the Areopagus has considered the evidence before it and concluded, though you are not guilty of murder, you have committed treason against the State with your meddlesome, unofficial, unwarranted, and damaging pursuit of state secrets. In accordance with the constitution, that is, the remainder of it after Ephialtes finished destroying it, the crime of treason can be dealt with by the Council alone, without trial by jury. Your sentence is death, to be carried out at dawn tomorrow. Guards, return the condemned man to his cell."

For a moment there was stunned silence, then the citizens of Athens erupted. The jury, even the men who had voted against me, shouted, "No! No!" They shook their fists and surged over the benches toward the Council. Some men tore planks off the benches and held them as makeshift weapons. The Scythians, the only men present allowed weapons, placed themselves between the people of Athens and the Council, who hurriedly exited through the rear of the building.

I was grabbed from behind by Scythians and dragged outside before I knew what was happening. They hurried me down the hill and along the path to my cell, where they threw me inside and slammed the door.

19

There was fighting in the city that night, I could hear the rumble of distant shouting and see the dull glow of fires through the bars of the door. That was bad. Fire in any crowded city can turn into a conflagration that leaps from house to house. Not that the rioters cared about me personally, I'm sure, it was the principle of the thing. I reflected bitterly that Pericles had hired me to help prevent a civil war, and instead I had become the cause of one.

My mother, in tears, brought me a last meal of all the foods I had ever loved as a child, ending with honeycomb. Only the Gods know how she managed to find some at such short notice. I apologized for bringing such shame upon the family. Father gripped my hand and refused to hear my apology, saying I was an innocent man being persecuted by the powerful. When the emotion became too high Sophroniscus led Phaenarete away. His last words to me were that he would create a statue of me in the finest marble, and that it would stand in a prominent place in Athens.

Sophroniscus was a good man. He might have reminded me, but didn't, of the words he'd spoken about Themistocles, before I had begun this disastrous mission. I remembered his speech clearly.

"Exiled, criminalized, condemned, and bankrupted. You don't want this to be you, do you?"

I would like to report the condemned man ate a hearty dinner, but it isn't true. I threw it all up after they left, my stomach was in such turmoil. I wiped my mouth and sat down upon the cot and wondered what it would be like to cross the Styx and come to my final home in Hades. I knew I would wait among the recent dead for Charon to bring his ferry to the side of Life. We would crowd aboard, and he would steer us to the side of Death, where we would walk to the banks of the river Lethe. We would drink the waters and lose our memories of what we had been in life. Did that mean I wouldn't remember what had brought me to my death? It seemed important to know, though I couldn't have explained why.

I stared ruefully at the mess on the floor. The guards would see it in the morning and know I had lost my nerve. Even the rats were avoiding it. I greeted them now like old friends. A condemned man can't afford to be picky about his friends. How many other men now dead had shared their last hours with these rodents? What tales they could tell of the behavior of dead men still walking, what insights into human nature!

"Nicolaos, wake up!"

"Huh? What!" I had fallen asleep. Diotima stood at the door.

"Nicolaos, something terrible is going to happen." She sounded panicky.

"For both our sakes, don't remind me. I'm having enough trouble dealing with it as it is."

"Not only you, Nico. It's Pericles. Pericles is missing, and the fighting is getting worse."

"What's happening out there?"

"Men are rioting. People are scared. Some are throwing stones. Nobody's organized a rebellion yet. They say the people demanded Pericles lead them, but he refused before he disappeared."

"Diotima, you know you shouldn't be walking about in the city tonight."

"I have this, and this." She showed me the bow which Brasidas the bowyer had custom-built for her, and held up the sacrificial knife.

"I went to see Pericles, Nicolaos, to insist he get you out."

"But he did his part of the bargain, Diotima. He got me off the charge."

"And here you are, waiting to be executed in a few hours."

"It's not his fault, Diotima. He was as astonished as the rest of us. He even threatened his own father."

"I don't care if it's his fault or not. He's the only one I can force to do something."

"What did he say?"

"Nothing. He wasn't at home."

"He's out calming the rioters, I shouldn't wonder."

Diotima shook her head. "The slaves said he'd had a summons from Xanthippus, but they don't know where he's gone."

"It's hardly a problem for me, I'll be dead in a few hours."

Diotima hid her face in her hands and began to weep. I waited patiently. The thought that someone other than my mother might cry at my death was oddly comforting. She eventually got herself under control and looked at me with red-rimmed eyes. "I promised myself I wouldn't do this. Nicolaos, can you think of any way I could get you out of here? Pericles was my last hope."

"Not unless you can get the key to this door from those guards out there."

"They don't have it. I tried bribing them before I went to Pericles."

Steps echoed on the cold stone and Pythax walked around the bend, carrying a torch and a bundle. He dropped the bundle, which clanged loudly, and said, "Hello, little boy."

"How are you, Pythax?"

"I'm angry, angry and disgusted. I don't mind a man getting himself killed fair and square, but that ain't what's happened to you. I'm here to let you out. You're leaving Athens, little boy.

I've been to see Xanthippus, to demand he release you, but he was out, on a bad night like this too! So I'm taking it on myself to let you out. You've been crushed by men too powerful to fight, and they didn't fight fair, and you were only trying to do your best for your home. Reminds me of a man I once knew: he tried to defend his village from a whole army, and it didn't work out real well for him either."

Free. Free to leave Athens and run to safety. Free to take Diotima with me.

Diotima said, "Pythax, when they told you Xanthippus was out, did they say where he was going?"

"Yeah. The Areopagus, for some meeting or other. The slave said he had a message from Pericles."

Diotima and I shared a look. "He swore he'd avoid dubious summonses to dark alleys," I said.

"Who did?" Pythax demanded.

"Pericles. But he's gone to meet his father at the Rock of the Areopagus. It's the only place they could go tonight where they wouldn't be observed. And they both received a summons from the other."

"That's impossible."

"Pythax, let me out."

He pulled back the bars and opened the door. "You going to run now? I brought your things." On the floor were clean clothing, my sword and dagger. Pythax's idea of essential personal items.

I tore off my dirty, smelly clothes and, chattering with the cold, pulled on the clean. I placed the dagger in my belt, buckled on the sword and said, "No, I'm not running, at least not yet. First we have to stop a murder, and I hope we're not too late."

As we set off, Diotima said, "What I don't understand is why he would act now, when he already had you to take the blame."

I said, "No, he didn't, that's the point. The jury said I wasn't guilty. The Council condemned me for treason, not murder."

We ran the through the dark, overcast night. There was barely moon-glow through the clouds to show our way, we stumbled frequently, and I silently cursed every rock that slowed us down.

"Halt! Stop right where you are!" It was Antigonos and Euphrestes, the Scythians I had trained with. They were on patrol.

Pythax merely had to growl, and they recognized him at once. "Have you seen Xanthippus or Pericles?" he demanded.

Euphrestes said, "Both of them, sir! First Xanthippus, then Pericles, back along the Panathenaic Way. They were both walking south." He pointed behind him. "Is there a problem, sir?"

Pythax ordered them to close on us and they kept pace to our left and right flanks. Diotima fell to the rear but managed to stay with the group. I could hear her panting but didn't dare stop or even slow.

We came around the Rock at the base of its north face to where it joined the Panathenaic Way. To my left in the distance I could see the Agora, where many men had congregated though it was dark. They had lit bonfires. I didn't have time to worry about them.

Ahead I could see torches and hear shouts of anger, but the smoke from the torches, the distance, and the bright pin lights of flame obscured my vision. The background was sheer darkness. All we had to work with was the moving hot pinpricks of the torches, the contrast of the light they cast and the shadows they created. It was enough to tell me two men stood in the center of the Panathenaic Way where it squeezes between the Acropolis and the Rock, and some number of men surrounded them.

We came close enough to recognize Pericles and Xanthippus in the center. They were standing back to back, and they hadn't been expecting trouble. They both carried their daggers and nothing else: no shield, no sword, no spear. Both their blades seemed to be bloodied, but perhaps it was reflection of the fire-light. Their attackers were far better prepared. I tried to count them but couldn't be sure I had the numbers right: there was no telling how many might be lurking in the shadows. As far as I could see there were seven. All had swords or spears. At least one had a bow, because I could see him aiming.

At that distance he couldn't miss. The man was aiming at Pericles, who immediately dodged out of the way. The bowman shifted his aim to the now uncovered back of Xanthippus. Pericles shouted, "No!" and jumped into the path.

The arrow took him in the shoulder and spun him backward into Xanthippus, who stumbled forward, saw that his son had been shot, and shouted in rage. He stood over Pericles to protect him. Xanthippus had been a General in his day, and I saw immediately the difference in quality between a regular fighting man and a street thug. Xanthippus centered his action around his fallen son, ready to step forward if an attacker presented an opening, but returning always to his post. He was not trying to kill his attackers, but hurt them enough to keep them at bay. He didn't allow himself to become committed to any one opponent.

Despite the artful defense, he was severely outnumbered. The attackers realized their advantage and came at him from opposite directions, two on each side. Xanthippus could have jumped out of their path, but to do so would have abandoned Pericles to his death. Xanthippus stood his ground to the last moment, then feinted at one pair and whirled to the other. They managed to engage him, so that his back was now exposed. Pericles had broken off the arrow in his shoulder and now rose, blocking the blades of the pair about to plunge their daggers into the back of his father. Xanthippus risked a glance behind him and smiled. But Pericles was too weak to defend himself and he couldn't last much longer.

They saw us at last. A man shouted and I looked up to see a figure in shadow standing atop the Areopagus. He pointed straight at us.

The men who had formed a ring around the action, cordoning off any hope of escape for Xanthippus and Pericles, moved toward us. Antigonos and Euphrestes went forward to engage them, wielding their unstrung bows like short staves in their left hands and holding their daggers in their right. Pythax circled around to the left, obviously intending to flank them. I didn't see where Diotima went, but fervently hoped she'd had the good sense to back away. I decided to try and break through to the embattled pair at the center of the fighting. It seemed to me if I edged along the face of the Areopagus I would be able to squeeze past the Scythians and their opponents. It was dark enough that I might pass for a shadow.

I failed. Their leftmost man saw me, disengaged from Antigonos, who had two others to deal with as well, and came at me. I held my sword forward and that gave the man pause. I didn't recognize him. In fact, I hadn't recognized any of the men in the attack, they all had the look to me of hired thugs or unemployed mercenaries.

One of his two friends landed a nasty, cracking kick to the knee of Antigonos, and the other plunged his blade into the Scythian's throat. Antigonos went down in a spray of blood. The three turned against me.

One of them shouted, "You! This is going to be a pleasure. Kill him!" It was Rizon, and it was his blade that dripped blood. I didn't hesitate. I hefted my dagger in my left hand and threw it straight at Rizon. I didn't care if the other two got me as long as I sent Rizon to Hades before me.

My throw was terrible. The dagger turned in the air and the pommel struck Rizon on the chin. But he thought it was the blade about to strike him and flinched. It was all I needed to lunge forward on a huge extension and take him in the belly. The distance was such that only the tip and a hand's width of length entered, but I twisted and ripped as I pulled back and it was enough to cause his intestines to poke out. The pressure ripped the wound further, and a blue-red mess spilled into the dust. Rizon screamed and fell to the ground.

My lunge had gone so far it was impossible to pull back in time. I was easy meat for the two thugs. I looked at them and wondered which of them would end me, and hoped it would be quick.

My twisted position meant that I was looking upward, and I saw now that it was the elder Archestratus standing on the outcrop directly above me. He screamed, "I am the rightful leader of Athens!" He took a spear and aimed it down where Pericles and Xanthippus stood, I don't know which one he was aiming at, but it didn't matter because there wasn't a thing I could do about it. One of them would die, and Athens would collapse in civil war.

In the darkness I heard a voice shout, "Mine!" and another shout "Mine!" Two arrows were loosed. Both took Archestratus in the gut.

He dropped the spear and clutched his stomach, leaning far over. He toppled forward.

The body fell from the sky, landing at my feet with a thud. His eyes looked up at me in surprise.

My attackers had just seen their employer eliminated, and they backed away. But it didn't matter because Pythax was upon them, come unseen.

Pythax with his bare hands grabbed the heads of the men and whacked them together with such force that it sounded like stone being hammered. The heads disappeared in a mist of blood and brain.

I stood up, wincing. It felt like I'd ripped a groin muscle when I'd made that suicidal lunge against Rizon.

The place looked like the aftermath of a major battle. Euphrestes had taken a dagger in the chest and crawled away from the fight, leaving a trail of blood for Pythax and me to follow. We found him under a bush, and Pythax held him in his last moments while I went to find the others. The remainder of the hired thugs had run when Archestratus fell. I inspected the two who would have killed me. They were both thoroughly dead. One had a beard and dark hair; I recognized him as one of the men who had ambushed me in the street and beaten me.

Xanthippus was panting and exhausted. Experienced strategos he may be, but he was also an old man. I held Pericles while Xanthippus probed the wound with his dagger. Xanthippus declared, "An honorable wound but not a dangerous one. The arrowhead penetrated but there are no arteries cut. You have the luck of the Gods, son. And thank you for saving my life."

Pericles said, "It was more than my filial duty, father. Athens needs you. I need you." He paused. "I would have missed you."

I said, "Somebody else saved both your lives; in fact, two somebodies."

Pericles asked, "Who are they?"

"Me." Diotima walked in out of the darkness, carrying her bow. "Pythax and I shot at the same time. Where is he, Nicolaos? Is he all right?"

"I'm still alive," Pythax said, returning to the firelight. He was covered in blood.

Archestratus was still alive, to my amazement. He was bleeding out and would die within hours, faster if we pulled the arrows. In the meantime he was groaning and screaming in self-pity.

Diotima took out the sacrificial knife she used as a priestess, the short, curved blade that looked razor sharp, with a small handle.

I said in alarm, "Diotima, what are you doing!"

She looked at me, and at Pythax and Pericles and Xanthippus, with hard eyes.

"He killed my father, and I remind you all I am a priestess of the Huntress. This one is my rightful sacrifice."

She walked into the darkness where Archestratus lay. He

saw her coming, holding the knife. He shouted, "No! No! No!" over and over again until his voice was cut off by bubbling sounds.

Pythax said, "Well, all I can say is I'm glad I'm just a dumb guard. How are you statesmen going to explain this?"

Pericles and Xanthippus looked at each other.

I added, "Of course, it would never occur to either of you to tell the people the truth."

Pericles said, "Nicolaos, you had a taste of what happens when someone tries to tell the people a complex story. Did you notice the dicasts were perfectly happy to watch Euterpe tear her clothes off and make accusations? Did you notice when Diotima tried to explain what really happened they ignored her?"

I hate it when Pericles says something I know to be morally wrong but logically right. "For the good of the state, is it? Or for the good of Pericles and Xanthippus?"

"The first because that is necessity, the second by accident," Pericles replied. At least he had the grace to be embarrassed.

Pythax reminded us, "It'll be light soon. There better be an explanation for the corpses before then."

I replied, "Let me see if I too can be a cynical politician and tell lies for the greater good. Here's my suggestion: a quiet meeting of Xanthippus, Pericles, and Archestratus was held tonight to resolve the many problems Athens faces. A mob of drunken thugs happened along and attempted to rob them. The trio put up a strong resistance and called for help. Pythax, your two Scythians responded to the cries and saved our leaders before succumbing to their wounds. I'm sorry to report Archestratus fell while putting up a brave fight."

"Sounds reasonable. And Rizon over there?"

I shrugged. "Will anyone care? Maybe he happened upon the scene by accident."

Xanthippus said, "That sounds very believable, especially considering the fires I can still see burning. No doubt there'll be a few corpses in the streets of Athens come morning, so a small collection out here won't be too remarkable."

"I'm glad you like my story. Now, what did your meeting agree upon?"

"Did it have to agree anything? We were interrupted by the robbery."

"It most certainly did. Let me help your memory. To start with, the son of Brasidas will receive an order for new bows and equipment. I think about three hundred ought to be enough to set him up in business. An order that size will encourage the father's customers to return to the son."

Xanthippus winced but nodded. "The state coffers won't run to that sort of money. I'll donate them to the city out of my own pocket."

"How very thoughtful of you, sir. Next, the bill for citizenship for Pythax goes through."

Xanthippus and Pericles both nodded to that one. Pericles said, "The Ecclesia would have to vote on it."

"With both you and Xanthippus recommending the bill I wouldn't expect any trouble."

"True enough. Go on."

"I would prefer not to be executed in the morning."

Xanthippus said, "It's an imposition, but I suppose I'll have to forgo the pleasure this time around. No doubt, given your propensities, I'll have other opportunities. But, young man, if you expect to live to see the next noon, you must give the Council something in return for rescinding the execution order."

I sighed. I'd expected this. "I must never breathe a word to anyone that the Council made a deal with Themistocles."

"I see you can manage a firm grip on political necessity when it's your own life in jeopardy. Swear it."

"I swear. May I be visited by the Friendly Ones should I ever utter a word on the subject."

"That will do. Are we done with the demands?"

"Not quite. Diotima's intended is lying over there with his guts decorating the sand. Therefore she is now a ward of the state, not required to marry anyone."

Pericles sneered. "And the estate of Ephialtes becomes her dowry. So now we see some cynical dealing from the man who prides himself on his honesty. I suppose you're going to swear you have no plans for the lovely heiress yourself? You're no better than Rizon."

I felt my face become warm. "As long as she's a ward of the state her guardian is Conon. I don't imagine him giving her to me any time soon. My father probably wouldn't be too happy either, come to think of it."

"Conon's year will finish soon. The new Archon will most likely be happy to get her off his hands."

"That's as may be. The requirement is she not be forced to marry against her will."

Xanthippus said, "You know we can't guarantee that. The whole question lies with the Archon." He paused. "I think I can undertake to 'persuade' Conon to take no action during his term. That leaves you a clear run with his successor, and the Gods know who that will be with this ridiculous lottery system. Your father is your own problem to solve. In fact, I've noticed recently that fathers are often a problem for their sons. And, son"—Xanthippus turned to Pericles—"consider, the estate has to go to someone. This young man is probably as good as anyone. At least he has some talent to serve the State."

Pythax said, "Watch yourself, little boy. It's a bad sign when Xanthippus thinks the city might need you."

"I'm satisfied."

Diotima returned silently to the torchlight circle and nodded silently. "What happens now?" she asked.

"We go home," I said.

———

Pythax and I saw Diotima to her door as dawn exposed the disaster area that was the Agora. We skirted around smoldering bonfires made up of the building material that had been stacked waiting for use. Thick, half-burned beams poked out of the heaps, and the whole scene reminded me of the ruins on top of the Acropolis, except that this time we did it to ourselves. Building bricks and roof tiles lay scattered about the Agora and the surrounding streets; men had been using them as missiles. There were bodies, though not as many as I feared; perhaps a dozen sprawled in the Agora, and we passed three others. Many other men sat in the streets nursing wounds or sore heads; one man sat with his head in his hands, apparently unhurt but weeping.

Diotima insisted we collect Achilles and the other slaves from Ephialtes' home, and we saw them all through Euterpe's doorway. I gave Achilles firm instructions to lock all the doors, and I heard the bolt thud home the moment the door shut. Then we went our separate ways, Pythax to see what had become of his Scythians and I to return home.

I banged on our door until the sleepy house slave opened it to great astonishment. Neither Phaenarete nor Sophroniscus had slept, with the rioting in the streets and the expectation of seeing their elder son have his neck snapped in the morning.

My parents rejoiced but were intensely curious. I told them the Council had had a change of heart, which after all was true. But I had some difficulty explaining away the large amount of other men's blood splattered across the front of my clothing. I put it down to being accosted by rioters on the way home and having to defend myself. Sophroniscus knew better, but chose to say nothing, except to ask if I was quite sure I shouldn't be running for the border.

Sophroniscus brought out his best amphora of wine, but the celebration didn't last long. I'm told that I lay back upon the dining couch and fell asleep immediately. I don't even remember that.

20

I woke at midday still upon the couch. Phaenarete, normally the mildest of women, had threatened the slaves with a whipping if they woke me, so everyone was tiptoeing about.

Phaenarete gave me a mirror and asked me to take a look. It wasn't a pretty sight. The first thing I did was pick up a bucket of water and pour it over myself. A slave scrubbed me raw. Phaenarete herself bandaged my numerous cuts and applied salve to the bruises, or, as she acidly put it, the bruises upon my bruises, for I hadn't fully recovered from the beating, nor the fight to the death with Aristodicus, before going the same round with Rizon. When she was done, I looked into the bronze mirror once more. The face that stared back at me was Nicolaos, not counting the bandages and salve, but an older, harder Nicolaos. I knew I was looking at the man I would become in middle age. Partly it was because I had lost weight during the stress of the investigation and my imprisonment, to the point I had become gaunt, but more so it was the face of a Nicolaos more confident in his own abilities, and more aware of the perfidy of his fellow man.

Phaenarete tsk-tsked over my strained muscles and advised me to see a trainer at the gymnasium immediately. After all, a midwife can only do so much for a grown man.

I said, "So I shall, Mother, but first I have to see some men."

Sophroniscus overheard. "You're not still intending to pursue this ridiculous path, are you? Surely not after everything you've been through."

"Yes, Father, I am. It might be tough, and you are right that it's dangerous, but I've come through alive, and what's more, I did it, Father. I did it!"

He looked at me curiously. "What are you saying? You told us you were released because the Council took pity upon you."

"Uh, it's a little bit more complex than that, Father. I can't tell you everything, but I think you'll find the city will quiet down now. The democrats and the conservatives are going to cooperate to return Athens to calm."

"And you had something to do with this?"

"Yes, Father, I did."

Sophroniscus threw his hands up in despair.

I found Xanthippus at home, in his courtyard. He looked the worse for wear for his adventure. He was wrapped up in a blanket with a glass of watered wine beside him. A slave was massaging his shoulders.

He looked at me sourly. "You have a habit of appearing where you are least wanted."

"There is one little detail I need to clear up before I present the result of my commission to Pericles."

"And that is?"

"The man who arranged the death of Ephialtes."

"Archestratus. You said it yourself."

"There are witnesses who say Aristodicus had separate meetings with two quite different men before the assassination, and yes, the description of one of these mystery men matches Archestratus, but the second man was older. It was the older man who brought coins to their meeting. Archestratus was paying Aristodicus via his son's bank, so who was the older man and what was he doing? I can think of two possibilities."

"Who are these witnesses?"

I ignored the question and said, "Let me tell you what I think happened. Archestratus approached a few powerful and influential men—the inner circle of the Council—with a letter from Themistocles, offering to supplant Ephialtes and restore the powers of the Areopagus if they would drop the treason charge and allow Themistocles to return home. The inner Council agreed. But we know Archestratus also imported a hired assassin—Aristodicus—at the same time. Now why send a killer if the return of Themistocles was in the bag? The only possible answer is that death was part of the deal the Council agreed on. It follows immediately that the plan to supplant Ephialtes consisted of removing him permanently." I paused, wanting to see his reaction.

"Go on," Xanthippus said, picking up his cup and drinking deeply.

"Someone among the inner circle of the Council was not entirely happy with the terms, but the deal was done, so that person went straight to the assassin and altered the terms without the knowledge of the other parties. Of course, this would have required a considerable bribe to the assassin, who, having partially betrayed his employer, would probably wish to make himself scarce. Syracuse is as far away from Magnesia as you can get and still be in a civilized city.

"Now Ephialtes was shot, so I ask myself, what term of the contract had this older man altered? Pericles was due to meet Ephialtes straightaway, and Pericles was the natural heir apparent to leadership of the democrats, as in fact he proved. Aristodicus need only have waited the space of a few heartbeats to have both Ephialtes and Pericles in range, and yet he didn't."

Xanthippus toyed with his wine, smiled wryly, looked up at me. "I may not see eye to eye on most things with my son, but you can assume I objected to spending his life for political gain."

"It was a huge risk," I said.

"It was my son."

"And if I'd managed to take Aristodicus alive?"

"Pythax was there to make sure you did not."

"I see."

Xanthippus gripped his cup so tightly his knuckles went white, and said, "Themistocles has been playing us all like puppets, even from faraway Magnesia. We're going to have to do something about that."

We sat in silence for some time. It was a beautiful day in the warm sunshine.

"You said there were two possible explanations for this older man. What is your second?"

"It occurs to me that Themistocles, being the wily politician that he is, might have sent an independent observer, to ensure Archestratus acted according to his instructions. Such a man might have delivered a second payment directly to Aristodicus. That older man would be long gone, there's no point in hunting for him now." I paused for effect, then said, "I'm not sure which solution to present to Pericles, though of course, if the Areopagus made any more covert moves against the democracy that would make up my mind."

Xanthippus nodded, toyed with his wine cup, considering for a long moment. "I think perhaps the Council might be persuaded to accept the transfer of power, if there were a few concessions made their way, now that power is going to Pericles, a man they—I—admire and trust. The democratic movement is safe."

I smiled. "I think on the whole I like my second idea best. That's what I'll tell Pericles."

"Pericles will not be willing to publicly implicate Archestratus."

I nodded agreement. "There will be three levels of truth. As far as the people are concerned, Aristodicus was acting alone. For Pericles, it was Aristodicus and Archestratus. Only we will know that you, Xanthippus, could have stopped them if you'd wished. It's not in anyone's interest to talk."

"What of your lady friend with the short, sharp knife? I have no wish to spend the rest of my days wary of every young woman when I walk down the street."

"She avenged her father's death last night. She will never know."

I rose to take my leave.

Xanthippus said, "I am curious. Mere days ago, you swore you would declare the truth to the people no matter the cost."

I sighed. The same thought tormented me. "Pericles once said this to me, and I thought he was a cynical opportunist; now that I too have held the future of Athens in my hand, I have much more sympathy for him. So I say to you now what he said to me then: it's for the good of Athens."

Xanthippus smiled. "We'll make a politician of you yet, young man."

I tracked down Pythax. He was sitting upon the empty plinth in the Agora, watching the mild, pleasant, well-behaved crowd going about their business. I knew the plinth would soon be filled. Callias had commissioned a new work from Sophroniscus: a statue of Ephialtes that he would donate to the public. Sophroniscus was pleased. It would be his first major work with his new apprentice, Socrates.

Pythax eyed me. "What now?" he asked suspiciously.

"Hello, Pythax. I didn't thank you for saving my life, twice now. Three times if you count coming to open my cell door. Four times if you count telling the truth in court. If it weren't for you, I'd be a dead man."

Pythax grunted. "Like I said before, you remind me a bit of me, back when I was young and stupid, of course."

"Well, I owe you a lot."

We sat in silence for a moment.

"Xanthippus said something to me this morning. I asked him what he would have done if I'd taken Aristodicus alive and made him talk. Do you know what he said? 'Pythax was there to make sure you did not.' You said in court you'd been ordered to follow me to make sure I didn't learn too much."

I paused. "I'm glad you chose to shoot him."

Pythax looked at me sharply. He drew in a breath. "Yeah, so am I." He turned his face from me, and looked around the crowded Agora.

I hopped off the plinth. "Thanks again, Pythax."

"Little boy?"

"Yes, Pythax?"

"I didn't do it for the citizenship. I would have done what the government wanted anyway."

"Yes, I know."

I was escorting Diotima to her temple. The High Priestess had sent to say that the Polemarch had suddenly and most curiously removed his opposition to Diotima. What's more, he had recommended she be invested as a full priestess as soon as possible; her ability to make sacrifice was particularly noteworthy, he said.

Pythax passed us, looking tougher and fitter than any man has a right to be after days of murderous mayhem. He was dressed in civilian clothes, no armor, and his hair and beard had been seen to by a barber who knew his business. He was carrying a gift.

"Good morning, little boy. Good morning, young lady." He hesitated. "Is your mother in?"

We had seen Pythax face mortal combat with barely a lifted eyebrow. Here he stood before us shaking with fear.

Diotima said, "She's in. Are you sure you know what you're doing?"

"A man needs a family and a home to protect. Otherwise he's just a lonely drifter without a village, or a city. Besides, what a woman! But . . . do you think she'd have me?"

"You'll have to ask her. I do wish you luck."

He squared his shoulders and stepped forward.

The door was opened by Euterpe. "Thanks be to the Gods, a real man at last!" She dragged him inside and the door slammed behind them.

Diotima shuddered. "Do you suppose I'll have to call him Father?"

We walked in silence, taking the long way around to the temple across the Illisos. The Agora was quiet, not a rioter or malcontent to be seen. Diotima said, "Oh, look here, Nicolaos! This is where I hit you in the face with a fish."

"Yes, and over there is where you knocked over enough olive oil to grease a small army. We'd better not tell the stallholders who you are."

We laughed. The walk up the Panathenaic Way was pleasant. We stopped at the place where we had fought. It had been cleaned up by the Scythians so you'd never know men had died there.

As we looked around, Diotima asked, "Nicolaos, who do you think murdered Stratonike and those poor nurses?"

"Rizon," I said confidently.

She nodded. "I think you're right. He's one of the few who could have found the buckets of seawater in the dark, and he didn't want to live with her any more than I did. But, why didn't you suspect me?"

"I did for a few moments."

"You did?"

"Yes, but then I realized you would never have murdered the nurses too. Besides, you would have done it much more neatly. All you had to do was offer to relieve the nurses for an afternoon and then finish her in any number of ways. No one would have been in the least surprised if Stratonike had slit her own wrists, for example. No, those killings were vulgar. That describes Rizon, but never you, my dear."

Diotima hesitated, then turned to face me. "I haven't forgotten, Nicolaos, what we said when you were in the cell. But . . ."

"But that was when you thought we'd lost everything, before you had what you wanted."

"Try to understand, could I leave all this?" She cast her arm around Athens, laid out before us and glorious under Apollo's rays.

"I understand, Diotima."

"And anyway, you have your reward from Pericles," she said. Diotima was nothing if not practical.

I didn't say a word.

"Nicolaos, you do have your reward from Pericles, don't you? The house and the income?"

"Pericles is arguing about it. He says that Archestratus revealed himself before I denounced him, so it doesn't count."

"Why, that little bastard! I'll go to him and—"

"It's all right, Diotima, someone's going to put pressure on him to pay his just debts."

"Who?" Diotima demanded.

"His father, Xanthippus."

"But Xanthippus hates you!"

"Let's say he's learned to respect my negotiation skills."

"That doesn't mean Pericles will pay you."

A man approached us. It was Archestratus, son of Archestratus, backed by two tough-looking men. My hand went immediately to the dagger concealed beneath my chitoniskos. Diotima demurely placed her hands before her like a modest maiden, but I knew she had one clasped over her priestess pouch, in which lay the sacrificial knife she had used to cut the throat of this man's father.

"Ah, I find you at last, Nicolaos, son of Sophroniscus. We are mortal enemies, you and I."

"Why?" I asked.

"You killed my father."

I did not look to Diotima. "He died fighting alongside Xanthippus and Pericles."

"That is the story being put out for the ignorant people. You and I know better. Know, Nicolaos, that I will do everything in my considerable power to make your life a living misery until I send you down to Hades."

He nodded politely to Diotima and went on his way.

Diotima said, "That reminds me, Nicolaos. You don't need to worry about Pericles paying you." She reached into her pouch and pulled out a short piece of board.

"Is that . . . ?"

"I found it around the neck of Archestratus after I cut his throat. If we take along witnesses so they can't possibly argue, Antisthenes and Archestratus will have no choice but to pay us out."

I pulled out my half of the banking token and put it against hers. They fitted together perfectly.

We kissed.

AUTHOR'S NOTE

This story really happened, though not, perhaps, precisely as it appears in the book. There really was an Ephialtes. He really did create the world's first democracy. He really was murdered days later.

Democracy began in the middle of a blind spot in written history. The Persian Wars had been fought twenty years before. Herodotus recorded them. The next great war was the long and destructive fight between Athens and Sparta, which Thucydides recorded. Democracy began in the gap between, when no one was recording much of anything. The longest record is a few paragraphs in a book called *The Athenian Constitution*, which is usually attributed to Aristotle, but quite possibly was cobbled together by a couple of his students. Here's what it says (from the Penguin Classics edition):

> *Ephialtes son of Sophonides became champion of the people, a man who*
> *appeared to be uncorrupt and upright in political matters. He attacked*
> *the Council of the Areopagus. First, he eliminated many of its members,*
> *bringing them to trial for their conduct in office. Then in the archonship*
> *of Conon he took away from the Council all the accretions which gave it*
> *its guardianship of the constitution, giving some to the Council of Five*
> *Hundred and some to the People and the jury-courts. . . . Ephialtes too*

was removed by assassination not long afterwards, through the agency of
Aristodicus of Tanagra.

Later in the same book it says: "They took down from the Areopagus hill the laws of Ephialtes and Archestratus about the Council of the Areopagus . . ." From which we know a legal technician by the name of Archestratus had been assisting Ephialtes.

You can see how the characters in the story come together: Ephialtes, the reformer; Archestratus, the lawyer; Conon, the archon; and Aristodicus, the hit man, are all there to be found in the ancient sources. If you made this stuff up, people wouldn't believe it.

When Ephialtes was finished, the Ecclesia had the sole right to decide all policy, domestic and foreign. Every citizen, irrespective of who they were, had exactly the same vote, and exactly the same inalienable right to speak before the people. It was the world's first democracy.

At that moment, Western civilization began.

There are other dates you could argue for, but it's hard to go past this one: a sovereign state with one man one vote, free speech for every citizen, written laws and equality before the law, with open courts and trial by jury. Modern drama was being invented at the same time as democracy. Aeschylus was writing his plays; two young men called Sophocles and Euripides were beginning to write their own. Anaxagoras was developing a theory of matter in which everything was made of infinitesimal particles; it was the beginning of atomic theory. Herodotus was traveling the world, writing his book, and in the process founding both history and anthropology. A young kid called Socrates was outside somewhere, playing in the street, and on the island of Kos, a baby called Hippocrates was born to a doctor and his wife.

Within days of pushing through his reforms, Ephialtes was murdered. The   world's   first   political   assassination   in a democracy had happened within days of the world's first democracy, and the victim was the man who created it. The assassin was caught, but Aristodicus was a hired killer. The men behind the plot were never discovered.

It's difficult to comprehend from our distance what Athens must have gone through. The United States was traumatized when JFK was assassinated, imagine the same thing happening when your newly minted democracy is less than a month old. Anything might have happened. The old men of the Areopagus might have gathered troops and resumed control of Athens. The new government might have collapsed. Civil war might have broken out.

But if Ephialtes was killed to stifle the democracy, then the plot failed, because when they killed Ephialtes they replaced a great statesman with a political genius. Ephialtes had a lieutenant, a rising young politician by the name of Pericles.

Pericles held it together. Somehow. It must have been a challenge even for him, but Athens didn't collapse, didn't fall into civil war, and didn't lose its democracy.

Pericles was the son of two great political families. His father Xanthippus was a hero of the Persian Wars, and a member of the Council of the Areopagus. His mother was the niece of Cleisthenes, the man who had begun the drive for democracy fifty years before, and descended of an ancient lineage that had held power in Athens in ages past. Pericles was as close as you could get to aristocracy in a city that, technically, didn't have any. But he was also a political radical, and when Ephialtes went down, Pericles stepped into the breach.

Perhaps the greatest joy of writing a book like this is interweaving fiction into the fabric of truth. Nicolaos didn't exist. Socrates had no known full siblings, and yet, Nicolaos would not be impossible. The fact that Nicolaos doesn't show up in the historical record is no objection. The period is poorly documented and even some quite prominent men have only a few lines in the histories. When you throw in the fact that Nicolaos is doing discreet investigation . . . of course no one has heard of him until now.

We do know the parents of Socrates (and Nicolaos) were Sophroniscus and Phaenarete. By popular tradition Sophroniscus was a "polisher of stone," which is code for a sculptor in marble. I've accepted the tradition as true in the absence of anything better, though there's a fair chance it's apocryphal; the family trade isn't mentioned anywhere until the following century. Phaenarete was a midwife, which we know for sure because Plato says so in *Theaetetus*, one of the many books he wrote featuring Socrates.

A surprising piece of trivia is the family of Socrates and the family of Pericles had friends in common. In *Laches*, Plato names Lysimachus, the son of a famous statesman, as a close friend of Sophroniscus, in which regard he dines with the family in *The Pericles Commission*. The connection is surprising because Pericles and Xanthippus were wealthy landholders and Sophroniscus was, at best, a middle-class artisan.

The trial of Nicolaos descends into farce, but there is very little that happens at his trial that did not happen at one time or another. Athenian juries were huge: the minimum size was 101 jurors, and numbers as high as 501 were perfectly normal. The 1,001 jurors who hear Nico's trial is high, but not surprising considering the importance of the case. For comparison, the number of jurors who heard the infamous trial of Socrates sixty years later is usually given as 501, but that's because 501 was the *average* jury size for a case of heresy.

When Euterpe rips off her dress before the jurors, she is anticipating by more than a hundred years the trial of Phryne the hetaera. Phryne was the most sought-after courtesan of her day and a stunning beauty. Praxiteles, the greatest sculptor of ancient times, used Phryne as the model for his most famous work, the *Aphrodite of Knidos*. This got Phryne into trouble. By posing as Aphrodite she was claiming to be as beautiful as the

Goddess of Love. Phryne was charged with impiety, the same charge that had got Socrates killed.

Needless to say, the best lawyer of the day was among her lovers. Hyperides struggled to save her, but he was failing because the complainants had her dead to rights; for a mortal to pretend to divine attributes was a crime. It looked like Phryne would be sent to her death. With nothing to lose, Hyperides walked over to Phryne, standing in the court, and in one movement ripped down her dress.

The entire (all male) court took a close look at Exhibit A.

The charges were dismissed.

Phryne thus became the only woman in history to be declared divinely beautiful, by order of court.

I stole this famous incident wholesale for Euterpe. Or an alternative explanation is Hyperides, who as a lawyer had a fine appreciation for precedent, recalled Euterpe's dramatic gesture of a hundred years before and was inspired to try the same for his own client.

Pythax is my invention, but the Scythian Guard was very real. The Scythians were a barbarian people far to the north. The Scythian Guard of Athens was created after the Persian Wars when three hundred slaves, supposedly Scythians, were bought for the purposes of crowd control within the city. We know this from the works of two orators called Andocides and Aeschines. The trick of using a painted rope to quell the rioting mob outside the house of Xanthippus was standard operating procedure and apparently worked very well. The Scythians frequently used the same method to herd reluctant citizens to vote at the Ecclesia and is described in the comic play *The Acharnians* by Aristophanes.

The bow was the favored weapon of the Scythians and they carried it unstrung when on patrol, as a baton with which to beat, which they would happily do if faced with a disorderly drunk. By the time of Nicolaos it's unlikely the Scythian Guard

were in fact all Scythian. Their numbers would have been
replenished with whatever suitable slaves came to hand. It may
seem odd that the Athenians allowed slaves to push them around,
but the reason Nicolaos gives in the book is correct: it was illegal
for one citizen to lay hands on another, but it was legal for a
slave under approved circumstances.

There was no police force as we know it. If a crime was committed, it was up to a private citizen to charge the criminal and
prosecute him in court. It's not even certain there was a jail at
the time, because there was no such thing as a prison sentence.
Criminals were killed, fined, or exiled. There were no other
options. I created the holding cell because it makes sense there
was one to hold the condemned.

Diotima was a real person, but what little we know of her
comes from only one source: a famous book by Plato called *Symposium*. In it, Socrates credits "Diotima, a priestess of Mantinea,"
as one of his early teachers of philosophy. The only other woman
listed among Socrates' teachers is Aspasia, the future wife of
Pericles and a genius of rhetoric (which we know from Plato's
Menexenus). This was a world where women received no educa-
tion. It took enormous natural talent for any woman to rise
above such repression.

Diotima must have had a towering intellect for Socrates to
speak proudly of being her pupil, and for Plato to have passed it
on as simple fact. One wonders how a priestess from another city
could have been teaching the young Socrates anything, but
obviously it happened, and my answer to the question is as
likely as any other.

The inheritance law that forces Diotima to marry Rizon was
quite real. It was an absolute imperative of Athenian inheritance
that property remain within the family. This, and the rule for-
bidding women to own property, combined on rare occasions to
cause chaos. If there was a son to inherit then there was no
problem, but if the only possible heirs were all female, then a

search was made for the closest male relation of any sort. The heiress was then *required* to marry the distant relative, even if she had to divorce to do so, and the man was required to marry the heiress, even if he had to divorce.

Pericles himself was trapped by this rule. He was forced to marry a woman he disliked when an obscure relative, presumably the woman's father, died, leaving her an heiress. She had to divorce her existing husband to marry Pericles. They suffered an unhappy marriage until Pericles met Aspasia and fell madly in love with her. At this point things got a bit complex, but he was able to divorce his wife with her agreement because she'd borne him an heir, and Pericles took up with Aspasia. They became one of the world's first power couples, and the ex-wife married the son of Callias.

Callias, the richest man in Athens, made his money from a rent-a-slave business, supplying slaves (short-lived ones) to the state-run silver mines. He was a fervent democrat who fought in the line at Marathon, and also a diplomat par excellence. The most surprising thing about Callias, to me, is that despite his qualities and unlike most of his peers, he did *not* try to become leader of Athens. Callias was a friend and supporter of Pericles, and yet also the brother-in-law of the arch-conservative Cimon, Pericles' greatest enemy. He probably exerted a stabilizing influence.

Conspicuously offstage in *The Pericles Commission* are two men of vast importance: Cimon and Themistocles. Both had been ostracized—which means exiled for a period of ten years—before the book opens. Themistocles was the deep strategist whose battle plan saved the Greeks during the Persian invasion, but who later was accused of treason. He departed about nine years before the book opens. Cimon was ostracized mere months before the rise of the democracy. It was his departure that made it possible for Ephialtes to make his move.

So Nicolaos has survived his first taste of investigation, and he's foiled one plot, but Athens' position in the world is very far from safe. The city is caught in a cold war with the vast super-state of the Persian Empire. The Persians may have been beaten twenty years ago, but they haven't given up.

Athens has perhaps thirty thousand men to serve in the army. Their enemy is the largest empire the world has yet seen, covering all of what today we would call the Middle East, plus Iraq, Syria, Iran, and Turkey, plus the Arabic Peninsula and Egypt. It's not exactly even odds.

At the same time the league of Greek city-states that united against the Persians is collapsing. The cities bordering the Persian Empire desperately need Athens to remain strong; they know they'll be swallowed up if Athens weakens. But on the other side of Greece the powerful city-states fear the astonishing and ever-growing influence of the democracy. Corinth is in a vicious trade war with Athens, which will lead to open fighting at any moment. Sparta, an insular, ruthlessly militaristic state in which every citizen is required to be a professional soldier, distrusts the clever Athenians and fears the democracy will spread across Hellas and incite rebellion.

In the coming years Athens will be on the knife edge of disaster, and if they fail now, our future goes with them. They need a breathing space. Fifty years will do. In that time they can invent almost everything that's important to our civilization. But it can only happen if Athens doesn't fall, and with the Persians to the east, and Sparta and Corinth to the west, the world's first democracy is like a deer caught between two wolves.

Nico has his work cut out for him.

In the next book Nico will step inside the Persian Empire to meet Themistocles, who has defected to the enemy. A secret awaits him there, and he'd better be ready to deal with it, because he'll be inside enemy territory with no one to help him. No one, that is, except a priestess from Mantinea.

GLOSSARY

Agora. The marketplace. It's located immediately to the northwest of the Acropolis. The Agora and the Acropolis are connected by a path called the Panathenaic Way. The Agora is where everyone goes to hang out.

Amphora. The standard container of the ancient world. Amphorae come in many sizes. An amphora mildly resembles a worm caught in the act of eating far too big a mouthful: wide at the top, tapering to a pointy bottom. Amphorae are used to hold wine, oil, water, olives, you name it. Tens of thousands of ancient amphorae have survived to this day.

Andron. A room at the front of the house reserved for the men and their male visitors.

Archons. The city executives. There are nine archons: the **Eponymous Archon,** the **Polemarch,** the **Basileus,** and six others who serve as magistrates. The archons are elected for a year.

Areopagus. A low hill of rock alongside the Acropolis. Home to the **Council of the Areopagus**.

Attica. The area of southern Greece controlled by Athens. Most of Attica is rural, very hilly farmland. People often say Athens when, strictly speaking, they mean Attica. For example the right to vote and hold office belongs to all the citizens of Attica, not merely Athens.

Aulus pipes. A recorder-like instrument but with two pipes which form a V at the mouthpiece.

Basileus. The archon in charge of religious festivals.

Boule. A committee of five hundred citizens, fifty from each **tribe**, elected annually to manage the running of the **Ecclesia**. The Ecclesia has thousands of members, so without the Boule it would be too unwieldy.

Chiton. The chiton is the usual garment of a wealthy citizen. The chiton is a large rectangular sheet, or two sheets pinned together, wrapped around the body from the right, wide enough to cover the arms when outstretched and fall to the ankles. The sheet is pinned over both shoulders and down the left side. Greek clothing is neither cut nor shaped, so there's a lot of spare material below the arms. The chiton is belted at the waist so the extra material doesn't flop around. The chiton is worn with a **himation,** a bit like a stole, across the shoulders. The chiton is for men with no need to labor. A middle-class artisan might wear an **exomis.**

Chitoniskos. A little **chiton**, as the name implies. *-iskos* is a diminutive. A boy or young man might wear his wealthy father's cast-off chiton, cut down to size, thus becoming a chitoniskos. A chitoniskos is cut to end at the knees, but it is still pinned over both shoulders and fully covers the torso.

Choregos. The producer of a choral festival show. The choregos funds the chorus.

Council of the Areopagus. Prior to the democracy, the ultimate decision-making body of Athens. Often referred to as simply the Areopagus, or the Council. The Areopagus had the sole power to decide foreign policy, and could nullify laws made by the **Ecclesia.** After the democracy, the Areopagus became a court for murder and heresy. Membership of the Areopagus consists of **archons** who have completed their term of office.

Deme. A deme is like a combination of suburb and sub-**tribe**. All of **Attica** is broken up into demes.

Drachma. The standard coin of Greece. The average workman earns about a drachma a day. One drachma is worth six **obols**. All coins are stamped with the famous owl of Athens.

Ecclesia. The assembly of all the citizens of Athens, managed by the **Boule**. After the reforms of Ephialtes, the Ecclesia became the world's first democratic parliament.

Eponymous Archon. The archon in charge of the affairs of citizens. He is something like a city mayor. Often referred to as simply the Archon. The Eponymous Archon is the one after whom the year is named. This story takes place in the Year of Conon.

Exomis. The exomis is the standard wear of middle-class artisans. The exomis is a sheet of linen wrapping around from the right, slightly wider than the shoulders of the wearer, and falling to knee-length. The corners are tied over the left shoulder, which is all that prevents the exomis from falling off. This leaves both arms and legs free to move without hindrance.

Herm. A bust of Hermes, Messenger of the Gods. Hermes is the protector of travelers and his bust is placed at every street corner.

Hetaera. A combination of salon hostess and high-class call girl. The hetaerae are free women of great beauty. Hetaera parties are very popular with the men, but you have to be wealthy to get an invite.

Himation. A stole or cloak worn with a **chiton.** The himation is made of wool and worn across the shoulders and down an arm.

Hydria. A ceramic jar used to store water. All ceramics are made by potters in the *deme* called Ceramicus, hence the modern word.

Krater. A large bowl that sits on the ground and is used to mix wine and water.

Metic. A resident alien in Athens. Metics can run businesses and they pay taxes, but have no say in public affairs. A modern equivalent would be residents of the United States with green cards. Metics are the economic backbone of Athens.

Obol. A small coin. Six obols make a **drachma.**

Polemarch. The archon in charge of the affairs of **metics.** In ages past, the Polemarch had been the war archon, but military command has now passed to the **strategoi.**

Pornê. A common hooker. The word means *walker,* because like their modern colleagues the pornoi had to walk the streets. There is a world of difference between the pornê and the upper-class **hetaera**.

Psyche. A human spirit.

Strategos. A military General. Ten strategoi are elected each year, one from each **tribe**.

Trapezai. Bankers are called trapezai because their work tables are covered in trapezoids: straight-sided irregular shapes. The bankers do complex financial calculations by running knotted string along the sides of the shapes, whose lengths are in known ratios.

Tribe. Every citizen of **Attica** belonged to one of ten tribes. Each tribe is in turn divided into many **demes**. The tribes are handy groupings for civic administration. Almost everything is organized by tribes and demes.

Turn the page for a preview from Gary Corby's
next Athenian mystery

THE
IONIA
SANCTION

ATHENS

1

Evil deeds do not prosper;
the slow man catches up with the swift.

I ran my finger along one foot of the corpse, then the other, making the body swing with a lazy, uncaring rhythm. I stared at his feet, my nose so close I went cross-eyed as the toes swung my way.

"He was like this when you found him?" I asked.

"I touched nothing," Pericles said, "except to confirm Thorion was dead."

"Are there any sons?" I asked.

"One, of twenty-four years. He's at the family estate, according to the head slave."

Thorion had died hard. He hung from a rope tied to a crossbeam in the low ceiling. A stool lay toppled below. The fall was nowhere near enough to snap his neck; instead he'd strangled. He must have changed his mind after the air was cut off, because there were deep red scratch marks in his throat where he'd tried and failed to relieve the pressure. Yet his arms were long enough to have reached the beam to pull himself up and call for help. Why hadn't he?

There was no answer to my question, except the high-pitched wails and long, low moans that had assaulted my ears ever since I arrived. They came from the women's quarters across the inner courtyard. The wife and girl-children had begun screaming the moment they'd learned their husband and father was dead. They would screech, tear their clothes, and pull their shorn hair every waking moment until he was cremated. The caterwauling meant that by now the whole street knew Thorion was dead.

I stepped across to the narrow window facing onto the street. A small group stood below; citizens, and their slaves holding torches, the black smoke floating up to me with the distinctive bittersweet aroma of burning rag soaked in olive oil. The crowd would have entered the house by now but for the two city guards who stood at the door. The moment they were allowed, these neighbors would cut down Thorion and carry him to the courtyard, laying him out with his feet pointing toward the door to prevent the dead man's psyche from straying. Then the women would come downstairs to wash the body and dress it for eternity, with no more than three changes of clothes, as the law demands. They would place an obol in his mouth, the coin as payment for the ferryman of the dead, Charon, to carry Thorion across the Acheron, the river of woe.

The pressure would be building on the guards to let through the crowd and allow the rituals to begin. I might have only moments left to learn what I could.

"Did you know him?"

"No, not really." Pericles handed me a torn scrap of parchment. "This is the message which brought me."

THORION SAYS THIS TO PERICLES. I HAVE BETRAYED MY OFFICE AND MY CITY. NEWS OF A THREAT TO ATHENS. COME AT ONCE.

"It's not the sort of message anyone could ignore," Pericles said. "The head slave led me up here to Thorion's private office, where we found him dead. Is it reasonable for a man who intends suicide to summon someone he barely knows, purely to make him discover the body?"

"It might be if the man summoned is you." Pericles at the young age of thirty-three was recently elevated to leadership of the new democracy. Though he held no official position, already men came to him, to seek his approval before any important decision was made. I knew Pericles fairly well, might even claim to be a minor confidant, which was no easy position. The last time Pericles and I had been together in the presence of death, it had very nearly resulted in my own execution.

"The slave boy who carried the message says Thorion had a scroll with handles carved as lion heads open before him. Thorion appeared upset, shocked even. It seems obvious whatever this news is, it's written in the scroll, but there's no such scroll here. I've looked. How could it have disappeared? Something is wrong."

"You're correct, something is indeed wrong. His feet are dry." I pointed at the dry floor beneath the corpse. "Where's the urine? Everyone knows a dying man releases whatever he holds."

Pericles shrugged. "Not everyone does; not if they relieved themselves shortly before they died."

I lifted the hem of Thorion's chiton, which fell all the way to his ankles. I kept lifting until I found what I sought, at thigh level. I took a big sniff.

"He let go all right. It's on his thighs, but it didn't run down his leg."

Pericles stepped forward for a closer look, careful not to touch the body. He grunted. "You're right." He cast about the room, and so did I. Ceramics and pots and amphorae and jars stood on every possible surface, on benches and tables and even on the floor, giving the room more the look of a small warehouse than a man's private office. They must all have been imported; none had the look of the famous Athenian red figure pottery. Many appeared delicate and had small bases, yet not a single one was out of place or knocked over.

"Whatever happened, there wasn't a fight."

I lifted each pot and shook to see if the missing scroll had been dropped inside. Only one amphora rattled, and it proved to hold three old coins, not even Athenian.

I got down on all fours and crawled about, paying particular attention to the areas where a man might ordinarily stand or sit. Pericles watched from the entrance as I nosed about like a hunting dog searching for scent.

"Here, under the desk. The floor is damp, the smell is obvious."

"Let me see." Pericles, not one to fret about form when an important matter was at stake, shoved me aside and checked beneath the desk for himself. He surfaced to say, "It seems you are correct. Thorion died at his desk."

"And likely was murdered to prevent him passing on this intelligence. How could a comfortable citizen in the middle of Athens come to learn of a threat to the city?"

Pericles said, "Do you know what a proxenos is?"

"A citizen who acts for another city."

"A citizen who represents the interests of another city in its dealings with Athens. Thorion is . . . was . . . the proxenos for Ephesus."

Ephesus is a major city, across the sea on the east coast of the Aegean. The Ephesians speak Greek—they're as Hellene as we Athenians—but their city lies just within the Persian Empire.

"You think the summons had something to do with Ephesus."

"Don't you? Every proxenos receives regular news from his client city."

I nodded. "If your theory is good, then Thorion received letters today."

Pericles summoned the head slave of the household.

The man was thin, balding, and middle-aged. He shook with dread as his dead master hung before his eyes, and the most powerful man in Athens stared at him grim-faced. At twenty-one I was unimportant, and certainly less threatening to a slave, so I said, "Did your master receive any letters or packages today?"

The slave turned to me and said, "Oh, yes sir. The regular courier from Ephesus arrived at dusk, straight from the boat. He still smelled of the sea."

"You've seen this man before?"

"The same man always brings the mailbag, sir."

I glanced at Pericles. He glanced at me. This was progress.

"Was that when you last saw your master alive?"

"No sir, he was alive when I announced the second courier."

"The *second* courier?"

"The first left, taking the mailbag with him back to Ephesus. The master stayed in his office. I was summoned again later to bring a boy, and the master gave him a note for Pericles."

Pericles nodded.

"Then a second courier walked in as the boy went out the door, I hadn't even time to shut it. The second courier said he had an urgent message, sir, from Ephesus."

"What did Thorion say to that?"

"It's never happened before, sir. The master was startled when I told him."

"This second man must have given a name."

"Araxes, sir. He said his name was Araxes."

"Did he too smell of the sea?"

The slave thought for a moment. "Yes sir, now that you mention it, he did. He stayed longer than the first—I suppose he had more to say—and when he walked down the stairs he told me the master didn't wish to be disturbed until supper. I opened the door for him and he left."

"You didn't think to speak to your master after that, to check with him?"

"No sir, I always obey orders."

I sighed.

"Describe the second courier," I ordered.

"He had white hair," the slave said without hesitation.

"You mean he was old?" Pericles asked.

"No sir, I'd guess his age to be thirty, maybe thirty-five. The hair wasn't gray, it was white."

"Was he Hellene?" I asked.

"He spoke like us."

"What did he wear?"

"A chitoniskos. 'Twasn't worn either. It looked new."

The chitoniskos is cut short at the shoulders and thighs for easy movement. I wore one myself. Since the material is never cut to fit the body, there are always extra folds of material in which you could hide anything, such as a scroll for example.

"So the murderer tricked his way into Thorion's office. He slipped a loop around Thorion's neck, strangled him, and strung him up to make it look like suicide. Then he tucked the missing scroll inside his clothing and walked out."

"Oh, sir!" said the slave. "Did you say murderer? You're not suggesting the courier had something to do with the master's death are you? No, it's impossible."

His tone intrigued me. "What makes you so sure?"

"Because he spoke so nicely. I've never known a man who minded his pleases and thank-yous so well."

"You liked him?"

"Yes sir, who wouldn't?"

Pericles said, "Nicolaos, the murder of Thorion is important, but not as important as recovering the contents of the scroll. The safety of Athens depends upon it."

I nodded and rubbed my hands. "Any chance of sending a slave to Piraeus for a jar of seawater?" I had touched a dead man, and so would be considered ritually unclean and not permitted to eat until I'd washed my hands in seawater. The call from Pericles had made me miss dinner, and I was hungry.

Pericles shook his head. "The city gates closed long ago."

Why couldn't Thorion have died at a more convenient time? That was the way my luck went these days. But—"Say that again?"

Pericles wrinkled his brow. "What? The city gates closed long ago? It's true. So?"

"So Thorion was killed at night, *after the city gates closed*. The murderer is trapped inside Athens."

There was silence while Pericles absorbed that.

"The gates open at dawn," he said, his manner snappier than before, his back straighter. He glanced out the window into the dark night. "Can we catch him before then?"

"In a city as large as Athens? Not a hope in Hades, unless the murderer makes a mistake, and this man's no idiot."

Pericles' shoulders slumped.

"We could keep the gates closed in the morning," I suggested.

"Lock in Athens during the day?" Pericles shook his head. "The people wouldn't stand for it."

I nodded unhappy agreement. "Besides, that would tell the killer we're looking for him. He'd only go to ground until we were forced to reopen the gates. No, we have to let him come out into the open."

"You have a plan," Pericles deduced from my tone. "What is it?"

"The slave said the killer smelled of the sea, as did the real courier. Their boats docked at the port town of Piraeus, and they walked uphill to Athens. I'd be willing to bet our man will be lined up with the normal crowd to walk downhill back to Piraeus at first light. All we have to do is watch the traffic pass by."

"There are two roads to Piraeus," Pericles pointed out.

"So there are. I suggest that tomorrow morning, there will be a problem with the gate to the northern road."

Pericles nodded. "That can be arranged. You want everyone down the south road?"

"The south road is enclosed every step of the way within the Long Walls. If he goes that route then he can't escape; he'll be trapped in a tunnel where we control both ends."

"Brilliant," Pericles said.

"I'll be at the south gate to watch every man who passes," I said, pleased with myself. There were those who said I was too young and inexperienced for my position. This operation would prove them wrong.

I could imagine Pericles' reaction if I lost the scroll because I'd overslept. Yet dawn was far enough away that the wait would be tedious, particularly since I couldn't eat.

I solved the problem by shaking awake a slave when I returned to my father's home, and ordered the bleary-eyed man to stand over me—so he wouldn't fall asleep himself—and wake me in the predawn. I was so tired I went to sleep immediately, despite being on edge about my mission.

The slave got his revenge by kicking me in the stomach when the time came, but I didn't mind. I'd completed my two years of compulsory service in the army as an ephebe; broken sleep and rough awakenings had been the norm then.

One glance upward showed me the rosy-fingered dawn, as Homer would have called it, lighting the otherwise dark sky. I rose naked and wrapped the short material of a gray exomis about myself from the right side and tied it over my left shoulder. Such clothing is favored by artisans; I would be merely another workman, waiting at the gates to make my way to Piraeus for the day's employment.

I hurried through the dark streets, stepping in more than one pool of sewage, soaking my sandals in the stale wash water, the urine, the feces, and the rotting, rancid leftovers that neighbors had tossed out their doorways. I cursed as my feet plunged into yet another sticky, squelchy mess up past my ankles.

At the south gate, men were already lined up, shivering, yawning, and scratching themselves. Two guards stood at the head, waiting for Apollo's rays to appear in the east, when they would pull back the gates so the men could shamble through. I had visited these guards after leaving Thorion's house. They knew of my investigation and what to expect.

I walked from the end of the line in the direction of the guards, reminding myself every few steps to amble, to not appear as if I had any purpose, nodding or wishing good morning to the men I passed.

"*Kalimera.*"

"*Kalimera.* Good morning."

Most nodded back; some gave me queer or hostile looks. They probably thought I was a line jumper, something that could end with a fistfight. To them I explained I was looking for my workmate: had they seen a man with white hair? They would shake their heads and I would pass on.

Among one group were some women, haggard-looking, with unwashed hair and wearing patched linen. I couldn't imagine why they were waiting, until it occurred to me these were probably drudges whose men were too ill to work, or couldn't be bothered. One of them looked me up and down and smiled, then she blew me a kiss and said, "Gorgeous." The few teeth she retained were black. I felt myself blushing; had I been staring?

It was all too easy to pass by my suspects without even breaking step. Some wore hats, and these I had to stare at a little longer. Others held the leads of donkeys harnessed to carts, or sat atop protesting mules. A very few had horses, a luxury item.

The artisans among them had a slave or two to carry their tools and wore an exomis like mine. The common laborers wore nothing but short leather cloaks and surly expressions. The slaves stood together and told jokes. What man would rather be a slave than free? Yet the slaves did not seem hungry, and the free men whose only skill was to sell their labor looked thin and their faces were taut—I could see the ribs beneath the flesh, so perhaps slavery was to be preferred over being useless.

These men, as I say, were easily dismissed, and if a man owned slaves it was all the more easy to ignore him, because no one arriving in an afternoon can both murder someone and acquire slaves before the next dawn. The front of the line came ever closer, and still no Araxes. Had I made a mistake?

There were only two in the line before me now, a man leading a donkey, and a flattop cart pulled by a horse. Apollo peaked over the hills, and on cue in the weak light the guards lifted the heavy bar and carried it to the side.

Where had I gone wrong? The only thing I could think was that Araxes had arrived late, or perhaps wanted to hide himself in the crowd. I would stand by the gates and watch as the men passed through. Despite the chill I felt the irritating trickle of sweat in my armpits and down my back.

The man with the donkey had dark hair and beard. He grinned as I passed.

The distinct aroma of dead fish surrounded the horse cart. It was probably on its way to collect the morning's catch. Two men sat at the front, the one on the left held the reins. He was slumped forward and wore a full-length cloak to keep out the chill. The man on the right was fast asleep, leaning back in the seat with his hat over his face.

Behind the driver and his companion was a rack holding amphorae: clay pots with narrow lids, wide middles, and long tails that taper to a point; they looked like a row of pregnant worms standing upright. The amphorae exuded the strong, pungent, salty fish sauce called garos, which the fishwives make from gutted intestines fermented in large vats with seawater. No doubt the cart carried empties to be refilled. Anyone buying fresh fish would want the popular sauce to go with it. The smell made me ravenous.

The man under the hat was suspect. I leaned over and said to the driver, "*Kalimera*. I wanted to ask you—" I knocked the sleep-ing man's hat, which fell onto the seat and I jumped back.

His hair was disappointingly dark. But he didn't wake. His eyes stared, and his jaw hung slack, his tongue limp in his mouth. Across his throat was a dull red band, almost like a tight necklace, and there were claw marks in the flesh about it.

I stared for one shocked moment, then looked to the driver. His cloak had a hood. With the sun rising at his back he was a faceless silhouette.

I said, "*Kalimera,* Araxes."

He replied, "And a good morning to you, dear fellow." Araxes shoved. The dead man fell on me. I hit the ground with a corpse on top; the lifeless eyes stared into mine.

"Gah!" I pushed him off.

One of the guards grabbed Araxes' left arm. In a blink, Araxes had pulled a knife with his right and driven it into the guard's shoulder. The guard staggered back.

The other guard tried to snatch the harness but failed when Araxes lashed out with his whip.

The horse surged through the gateway, onto the road to Piraeus; the road that, according to my plan, Araxes would never reach.

I had no backup plan. None at all.

The unwounded guard grabbed his spear and ran into the middle of the road. It was a soldier's spear, not a javelin, not weighted for throwing, but the cart had not gone far. Araxes' back was crouched over, shrouded in his light leather cloak. The guard stood, legs apart. He considered his target for a heartbeat, hefted the spear, left arm pointing where he wanted to hit and eyes locked on the target, took three rapid steps forward and threw in a controlled arc, elbow firm. His right arm followed through. He kept his head up and his eyes never left the target.

It was a beautiful throw. I saw at once it would make the dis-tance.

The spear arced across space, wobbling as it did, and passed over the shoulder of Araxes, so close I thought for a moment it would take him in the skull. But it passed him by, only the Gods know how, and landed, *thwack,* into the horse's rump.

The horse screamed. It half-reared, held by the harness, stumbled then recovered. The shaft flailed wildly. The wound opened to inflict even more pain.

The spear fell from the fleshy hole and the cartwheels clattered over it. The horse whinnied and accelerated away.

The guard beside me cursed. "I aimed for the man; all I did was scare the shit out of the animal!"

Other Titles in the Soho Crime Series